SPECIAL EXCERPT

Six machetes broke through the roof, withdrew, and reappeared, the sound of their blades grinding against the plastic roofing almost unbearable.

Andre aimed his machine gun at the roof.

"Don't do it," Stephane said. "You'll do more damage than they are."

Andre held still.

"How're you guys doing?" Jake said to Louider's men at the door.

"Fine," one of the men said.

Then a loud crack echoed through the building, and the first zonbie dropped through the ceiling.

Jake shoved his flashlight in his belt, drew his Glock, pressed it against the zonbie's left temple, and fired. He heard the spewing of liquefied brain, then the zonbie collapsed and his soul rose.

Two more zonbies fell to the floor around him. Stephane's laser sight cut the room in half. Two muzzle flashes later, Jake stood alone again.

"Thanks," Jake said, spots flashing in his eye.

"Don't mention it," Stephane said.

The door crashed open, and Louider's men screamed in stereo.

REVIEWS FOR
COSMIC FORCES

"The writing is top-notch, the story compelling, bringing comparisons to F. Paul Wilson's *New York Times* best-selling Repairman Jack novels."

—K. L. Young, *Strange Aeons Magazine*

"Cosmic Forces is a fast moving, intriguing, action-and-horror-packed read that is a creative tour de force, one that will leave readers equally thrilled and breathless."

—Norm Rubenstein, *Horror World*

"The Third Helman hard-boiled urban fantasy horror tale (see *Personal Demons* and *Desperate Souls*) is an exciting entry as the tough sleuth with a heart fights monsters from the otherworld and from his plane. Readers will enjoy his three investigative cases as all roads lead to those who abuse power, whether they are from hell, earth, or otherwise."

—Harriet Klausner, *Midwest Book Review*

"Heaven and hell. A private eye who's had enough with supernatural phenomena. This is the third volume in Gregory Lamberson's Jake Helman Files, and boy was this one hell of a read! . . . The nod to H. P. Lovecraft is a good one. . . . I'm eager to find out what else is in store for Jake in the next novel."

—John Rizo

THE JAKE HELMAN FILES
TORTURED SPIRITS

Gregory Lamberson

MEDALLION
P R E S S

Medallion Press, Inc.

Printed in USA

In memory of Michael Louis Calvillo

Published 2012 by Medallion Press, Inc.

The MEDALLION PRESS LOGO
is a registered trademark of Medallion Press, Inc.

Copyright © 2012 by Gregory Lamberson
Cover design by Arturo Delgado
Edited by Lorie Popp Jones

Names, characters, places, and incidents are the products of the author's imagination or are used fictionally. Any resemblance to actual events, locales, or persons, living or dead, is entirely coincidental.

Typeset in Adobe Garamond Pro
Printed in the United States of America

ISBN# 9781605424064

10 9 8 7 6 5 4 3 2 1
First Edition

ACKNOWLEDGMENTS

I wish to thank my wife, Tamar, for the English into Spanish translations used in this novel and Helen A Rosburg and David Tocher for English into French translations. I also wish to acknowledge the creators and writers of the TV show *Wiseguy*, which ran on CBS from 1987 to 1990; their fictional Caribbean Isle Pavot is the inspiration for my Pavot Island featured in this book.

As always, I thank the crew at Medallion Press for their continued support: Helen A Rosburg, Ali DeGray, Adam Mock, Heather Musick, Paul Ohlson, James Tampa, Emily Steele, Lorie Jones, Arturo Delgado, and many others.

ONE

Busker Boy stood just outside the alley in the shadow of the French Lily Hotel as the sun, as hot as some long forgotten circle of hell, descended over the French Quarter. Not that standing in shade did much good: on this, the first day of July, New Orleans boiled like crawfish over an open fire. The temperature had reached 100 degrees that afternoon, with humidity making the thick air feel fifteen degrees hotter.

The heat continued to radiate from the sidewalks into the evening, clinging to Busker Boy's short-sleeved shirt and flesh like napalm. What he put himself through to make a little pocket money . . .

Despite his moniker, Busker Boy was neither a busker nor a boy. At thirty-six, his boyish good looks had grown flaccid, his face weighed down by the bags and crow's-feet around his eyes. His longish blond hair showed no signs of gray yet, and he still resembled a surfer from California. Born Charles Alcotto, he considered himself a man of many talents: con artist, pickpocket, burglar, occasional stickup man. He'd earned his name and reputation rolling the various street musicians who crowded the sidewalks of New Orleans, and once he'd become known among the populace, he moved into other areas of low-end crime.

Busker Boy breathed in the humid air. God, this heat was killing him. He just wanted to make his move and go home to his ratty one-room apartment not far from the French Market for a cool shower.

As the sounds of live jazz wafted out of the green brick hotel behind him, he spotted his mark. Every night for two weeks the man returned to the French Lily around this same time. Every night his driver dropped him off on the one-way street facing the hotel's rear, where a handful of gray-haired black men played brass instruments. And every night he took the shortcut through this narrow alley to reach the hotel's front entrance.

The man, who appeared slightly younger than Busker Boy, favored jeans and a polo shirt and wore his strawberry blond hair parted at one side. Four scars divided the left side of his face; Busker Boy felt certain some hellion had left her mark on the sucker. But the parallel scars did not cause the man to stand out in a crowd. The blackbird did. At all times the man carried the large raven in a cage so tall its base scraped the sidewalk.

When the man had reached the middle of the alley, Busker Boy turned, revealing himself. The approaching man narrowed one eye at him and stiffened. Busker Boy, who had real muscles from years of weight lifting and amateur boxing, saw no flab on him. The bird appeared even larger up close, two feet long from beak to tail feathers.

Ricky and Sheldon stepped into the opposite end of the alley behind the bird man. The Pascel brothers were Creole, their faces bronze, with wide noses, thick lips, and eyes almost the color of their skin. They stood over six feet tall, with gangly arms, and Ricky's shoulders stooped as though he carried a bucket of water in each hand. Busker Boy used the Pascel brothers for backup because they were easy to order around and had no problem doing wet work.

Jake Helman stopped in the alley outside the French Lily Hotel, where he had been staying for the last three weeks. The hair on the back of his neck prickled: *perp fever*, a holdover from his NYPD days.

The muscular Caucasian man ahead of him stood a little over five and a half feet tall, even with platform shoes. A golf hat with a little green feather in its band topped his all-white outfit. The man's thick chest pushed his arms back, and a predatory smile sliced his face. Jake hadn't seen him before.

Jake knew even before he glanced over his shoulder that the two men he had passed on his way into the alley, who had stood with their hands deep in their pockets, now followed him. A pair of light-skinned black men with matching eyes and hair: brothers, probably twins. One exhibited the nervous tics and twitches of a crackhead; both projected danger.

Jake turned back to the man in white, who moved forward. He cursed himself for letting his guard down just because he was close to his home away from home. A mélange of laughter, loud talking, horns, and the aroma of New Orleans cooking overloaded his senses. Without glancing at Edgar, he tightened his hold on the cage's handle.

The man in white tapped the brim of his hat. "Happy evening, stranger. That's some interesting cargo ya got there." His voice dripped like honey mixed with gravel.

"It's just a pet," Jake said in an even tone.

"A pet, you say? What kind of pet is that?"

"A raven."

"Oh, like Mr. Edgar Allan Poe. You sure that bird isn't gris-gris?" The words came out as *gree-gree*.

"I'm sure."

"You know what gris-gris is?"

Jake nodded. A gris-gris was a voodoo charm. *Interesting deduction.*

"What you doing in N'awlins, captain?"

Jake turned his back to the hotel's brick wall, with the man in white on his right and the bronze-skinned thugs an equal distance on his left. "None of your business. Tell your men to stay away."

"You lookin' for someone?"

Jake raised his left foot and drew his .38 from its ankle holster. He aimed the revolver at the bronze men, who stopped but did not raise their hands.

The man in white smiled. "Oh, looks like you got the drop on us. But I think you're bluffing."

Keeping his revolver leveled at the bronze men, Jake faced the man in white. "Try me."

"You stayin' at the French Lily. You shoot one of us, you have to shoot all three of us. You have to kill us dead, like bugs. I don't think you want to draw that kind of attention to yourself. It's unproductive."

He's right. Jake had just committed a serious mistake. He had always believed a man should never draw a gun unless he intended to use it. "What do you want?"

"I think we'll take your blackbird. I think you'll pay to get it back."

"Why don't you just rob me now?"

"I bet you'll pay a lot more for your *pet* than you've got in your leather."

"What makes you think so?"

"You take that bird everywhere you go, fella. I seen you in restaurants and on the banquette. You take it wherever you spend your days. That blackbird is worth a lot to you, and that makes it valuable to *me*." He held out one hand and snapped his fingers.

Jake felt sweat on his brow. He couldn't gun down the men, and he couldn't take all three of them by hand while protecting Edgar. Even a warning shot could land him in jail for the night, and jail time meant being separated from Edgar. "Not gonna happen."

"You want to play tough? We can play tough." The man

nodded to his companions, who advanced on Jake. "We won't kill you because then we won't get paid. But we'll beat you bad."

Jake dropped to one knee and jammed his .38 into its holster. When he hopped up, Edgar's cage remained on the dirty ground.

The bronze men produced identical switchblades that snapped open in the heat.

Sizing up his opponents, Jake aimed a kick at the one who didn't seem to be a drug addict. His heel slammed into the man's sternum and drove him backwards into garbage that reeked of seafood. As soon as Jake's foot settled on the ground, he struck the crackhead's chest dead center with the palm of his hand, hoping to stutter the man's heart.

The addict's eyes bulged and he dropped his switchblade, which Jake retrieved from the ground. The crackhead remained standing, as immobile as a scarecrow.

Edgar cawed behind Jake, and when Jake turned around he expected to see the man in white reaching for the cage. Instead, the man dove into Jake, wrapping his powerful arms around his waist and tackling him to the ground. Jake dropped the switchblade.

The man squeezed Jake's arms, pinning them to his sides. "Get the bird!"

The man Jake had kicked to the ground got to his feet and staggered forward. Jake snared the man's ankles with his legs and brought him back to the ground. The man in white worked his head up, bringing his face within inches of Jake's, gritting his teeth, his eyes firing with sadistic glee.

Jake rocked his head forward, smashing the man's nose and enjoying the angry bellow that followed. The man's face turned bright red, his trembling grimace twisting, and he retaliated by pounding his forehead into Jake's scarred cheek. Jake's arms turned to rubber, and his head rolled back. Blinking, he saw the first bronze man back on his feet and reaching for the cage.

Seeing no alternative, Jake cocked his leg and drew his .38 again. As the bronze man set his hands on the cage, Jake aimed his gun at the man's feet. He hesitated, unwilling to risk shooting Edgar by accident. Then the bronze man raised the cage off the ground. Jake angled the .38 at the cement and squeezed the trigger.

The gunshot echoed off the alley walls, and the round struck the ground, flattened on impact, and traveled along the cement until it struck the bronze man's left foot. The bronze man's leg flew out from under him, and he yelped before he came crashing down. The birdcage rolled rattling across the ground to the opposite wall, with Edgar cawing and flapping around inside.

The man in white looked over one shoulder at the bronze man, who clawed at his injured foot with both hands.

"I'm shot! I'm shot!" the bronze man shouted.

The man in white lunged for the cage, and Jake hammered the side of his head with the .38's grip. On his hands and knees, the man in white shook his head.

Jake scrambled to his feet, seized the crackhead by his shoulders, and hurled him into his twin, who sobbed like a baby.

A crowd had already formed at the rear of the alley, and now one started to form ahead: tourists holding digital cameras, homeless people drinking from brown paper bags, and locals wearing black and gold jerseys.

"Get out of here," Jake said to his attackers.

The man in white spat on the ground and stared at Jake. The bronze men hauled him to his feet and dragged him to the alley's opening, where the spectators parted, allowing them to pass.

Jake holstered his .38 and retrieved the birdcage. "You all right?"

Edgar croaked.

Jake heard a hissing sound behind him.

"Hon!" Jasmine, the French Lily's evening maid, stood behind a screen door. The young black woman's long, curly black hair framed her high cheekbones, and she wore a classic French maid's uniform. Jake had greeted her several times and had bordered on flirting with her more than once. She beckoned him forward. "In here!"

Jake knew she wanted him to open the door himself, so none of the gawkers would see her. Glancing at the curious faces at each end of the alley, he strode forward, made a show of jerking the door open, and hurried inside.

Jasmine slammed the inside door shut and locked it. "Take these back stairs to your room."

Jake glanced at the narrow stairway. "I won't be hard to find with my partner here."

"Don't worry. No one will finger you. Now hurry!"

"Thanks." Jake climbed the squeaking steps two at a time.

On the third level, he rushed along the sagging floor to his door, which he unlocked, then carried Edgar inside the room. After locking the door, he set the birdcage down on the thick bed and exhaled. He peeled off his soaking wet polo and dropped it on the floor, then entered the bathroom and splashed cold water on his face.

Returning to the main room, he switched on the air conditioner, which rumbled to life. He needed a shower but didn't feel comfortable taking one now. Moving to the curtained front windows, he gazed over the iron terrace at the street below, where a small crowd remained outside the alley. Scanning the sidewalks, he saw no sign of the man in white or his henchmen, but they could be hiding anywhere.

Who would hold a raven hostage?

Just some low-rent grifters. But that was exactly why he never let Edgar out of his sight and why he slept with his revolver under his pillow.

His gaze settled on a woman in the crowd. Wearing cargo shorts and a tank top, a navy-blue baseball cap atop her curly hair, she appeared in Olympian shape compared to the large shapes around her. Dark sunglasses and gold earrings framed her face, and her skin was the color of copper. Something about her seemed familiar, and he worried he had been in New Orleans long enough to recognize the locals, which meant they could recognize him. Maybe it was time to switch hotels.

A siren screamed down the street. When the white NOPD mini-police car stopped, the crowd dispersed, including the woman. A single officer climbed out of the bubbled vehicle and addressed the departing spectators, who shook their heads as they ambled away.

Jake closed the curtain, picked up the phone, and called the front desk. "Walter, can you ask Jasmine to come up here, please? I have a chore for her."

"Of course, Mr. Helman." Walter spoke in a friendly voice.

A few minutes later, Jake heard tapping on his front door. With his shirt still off and his chest glistening, he answered it. Jasmine stood there, appraising him.

"Thanks for your help." He held out a fifty-dollar bill.

Jasmine accepted it. "You're welcome."

"I wonder if I can ask you for another favor."

"Depends on what you want."

"I need a shower, but I'm worried those guys from the alley might come up here. Would you mind watching my bird for a few minutes?"

Jasmine shifted her gaze to Edgar, who blinked at her from inside his cage. "They won't come into the hotel."

"Just the same, it would mean a lot to me."

Jasmine entered the room. "All right. Let me tell Walter."

"You must all think I'm crazy."

"Eccentric, maybe. Like the Duck Lady, a local street person who walked the streets with ducks following her." She picked up the phone. "Walter, I'm going to babysit the bird in 307. I'll come down when I'm done."

"I won't be long," Jake said. He went into the bathroom and stripped away the rest of his clothes, which he left on the toilet seat with easy access to his .38. He twisted the gold shower handles and stepped into the claw-foot tub without waiting for the water to heat up. The gentle spray hosed the day's grime off his body.

Three weeks in New Orleans. How much longer could he stay?

As long as it takes.

A shadow passed over the clear plastic shower curtain. Jake lowered the soap. Jasmine stood nude on the other side of the curtain. Feeling himself growing hard, Jake swallowed.

She parted the curtain and joined him in the shower's spray. "I told you those men won't come up here."

Admiring her dark brown skin and full breasts, he took her word for it.

TWO

Jake ate breakfast at the same window seat in the French Lily's dining room every morning. He enjoyed gazing at the colorful people on the sidewalks, who outdid even those in Lower Manhattan. He identified the newer hotel guests because they nodded or pointed at Edgar in his cage, which Jake set upon the sill.

He had gotten a good night's sleep after spending a few hours online, rested after the workout Jasmine had given him. She was a lovely girl, and although he hadn't exactly reentered the dating scene, he appreciated her attention, fleeting though it may have been. He could get used to New Orleans.

Vincent's blue Dodge Challenger pulled over to the curb. Jake had hired the young man to serve as his guide on Walter's recommendation three weeks earlier, only to discover Vincent was Walter's nephew.

After finishing his second cup of coffee, Jake left a twenty-dollar bill on the table and returned the hostess's smile as he carried Edgar's cage out of the dining room, through the lobby, and onto the sidewalk, where the humidity blasted him.

Vincent opened the passenger door for Jake.

"I keep telling you that isn't necessary." Jake set the cage down in the middle of the backseat and secured the seat belt and shoulder strap around it.

Edgar cawed at the calypso music rising from the speakers.

"A lot of things in life aren't necessary," Vincent said. "But it's the little things that make a difference."

Jake sat up front and closed the door.

Vincent slid behind the wheel beside him. "What you got planned for us today?"

Jake held up a sheaf of printouts. "Take me to the Ninth Ward."

Vincent took the printouts from Jake and read the addresses. "Easy enough to get to, not so easy to look at, especially for a tourist like you."

"I'll manage," Jake said.

Vincent pulled out.

The Ninth Ward proved harder for Jake to see than he had expected, with its ruined houses and piles of rubble left like gravestones in the wake of Hurricane Katrina. He glimpsed the tattered remnants of disintegrating blue roofs, rusted-out trailers, and shattered tree trunks. His body turned numb at the sight of the devastation, even when he saw signs of recovery: repaired houses sitting atop new raised foundations on the same block as collapsed houses in weed-choked lots. Deep down, he knew it wouldn't recover. The grim faces of residents who refused to leave their homes depressed him even more; they resembled the shell-shocked survivors of third world countries existing in a constant state of war.

Vincent turned down a street with cracked asphalt and tall weeds. "It's a little hard to find my way around without street signs."

Staring at the ruins, Jake was sickened to think of the wealth hoarded and squandered by Karlin Reichard and the other members of the Order of Avademe, whom Jake had helped take down just three months earlier. The cabal members had been billionaires, and Reichard had flown a chocolate cake in from Germany for one of their dinners. Seeing misery around him, Jake found it impossible to rationalize the existence of Avademe, the mutant octopus creature the cabal had worshipped.

Vincent pulled alongside a trailer parked before the ruins of a house. Two black children, a boy and a girl, played in an inflatable swimming pool.

Jake got out, leaving Edgar in the car with Vincent.

A woman emerged from the trailer before he reached the swimming pool. She wore sandals, shorts, and a blue muscle shirt, her dark hair pulled back. "Can I help you?" Annoyance and suspicion tinged her voice.

"You can if your name is Elaine Roberts."

"It's rude to ask who I am before you introduce

yourself." She glanced at Vincent sitting in the car. "I know it isn't much, but this is my house."

Jake took out his wallet and handed her a business card. "My name is Jake Helman. I'm a private investigator, and I'm trying to locate Miriam Du Pre."

The woman looked up from the card. "That name doesn't mean anything to me."

"Her mother was Louise Du Pre. Her sister was Havana Du Pre until she became Havana Evans, and her niece was Ramera Evans."

The woman's brown eyes flickered. "My family lived next door to them. I was friends with Ramera when we were in school. She moved to NOLA from New York City after drug dealers killed her parents. I got my own place"—she gestured at the house—"after high school. Some place, right? Ramera attended Tulane U, then wrote some big book about vodou that riled a lot of the locals. Secret ways are supposed to stay secret, you know? After Katrina, her grandma Louise's body floated right down the streets. I never knew Ramera's aunt Miriam, but Louise mentioned her. Why are you looking for her?"

"Ramera's dead. I need to find Miriam to tell her."

"Someone kill her?"

"No." A lie: Edgar had killed the bokor, who had adopted the name of Katrina. "She fell at a construction site in New York City. Why would you think someone had killed her?"

"Because Ramera changed after Louise drowned. Who wouldn't? Last time I saw her was at Louise's funeral.

She was all fancy and educated, but she also seemed . . . dangerous. Dangerous and vodou don't mix well. I heard she went back to New York. Heard she got into trouble, did bad things." She glanced at the children in the pool. "I guess things didn't turn out so bad for me after all. Who hired you to find Ramera's aunt?"

"Nobody. I'm doing this on my own. My best friend dated Ramera. Something happened to him. I'm told Ramera's aunt is the only person who can help him."

The spirit of Jake's dead wife, Sheryl, had appeared in Jake's office and told him only a blood relative of Katrina's could reverse the transmogrification spell that had turned Edgar into a raven. Jake had since discovered Katrina's aunt was her sole remaining relative.

Elaine narrowed her eyes. "I heard Ramera was dating some big-time drug dealer out there. If he was your friend, that doesn't say much about you. If something happened to your drug dealer friend, I can just imagine what it was."

"Ramera was trouble; I'll give you that. And she did get involved with some bad men. But my friend is a cop—a good, clean cop. He didn't know what kind of woman she was, and he didn't deserve what happened to him."

"And you came all the way here to help him?"

Jake nodded.

"Louise migrated here from Pavot Island. Miriam was born there, too, but Havana was born here. Miriam went back to Pavot Island and got married. When she returned to the States, she settled in Miami. That's where she lived the last time I spoke to Louise."

Miami! "Do you know her married name?"

"Santiago. Now you know what I know."

Elaine handed the card back to Jake, and when he returned it to his wallet he removed two twenties. "Thanks for your help."

She took the money and folded it in one hand.

Jake returned to the car and got into the front seat.

"Well?" Vincent said.

"I need to get to Miami."

Standing in his hotel room, Jake called Carrie in New York City. He had left his assistant in charge of Helman Investigations and Security while he was away.

"Hi, boss," Carrie said, no doubt recognizing his cell phone number on the display on her desk.

Jake tossed his clothes into his rolling suitcase. "I'm checking out. Book me a room in Miami for tonight, even though I probably won't be checking in until morning. I'll need a car when I get there, too."

"Should I get you a motel room, so Edgar isn't a problem?"

"You read my mind."

"How long are you staying in Miami?"

"Tell them three nights for now. Find me everything you can on Miriam Santiago, daughter of Louise Du Pre, sister of Havana Evans, aunt of Ramera Evans. Miriam was born on Pavot Island. Havana was murdered in the Bronx.

Louise died in New Orleans during Katrina. Ramera died in Manhattan nine months ago."

"You hope to find Miriam in Miami?"

"That's the idea. E-mail me whatever you find but call me, too."

"It was nice having you, Mr. Helman," Walter said as Jake signed the credit card charge slip. The middle-aged black man glanced at Edgar. "And your raven. I hope you enjoyed your stay."

"Thanks, Walter. This is for you." Jake handed him a fifty-dollar bill.

"Thank you, sir."

Jake also handed Walter an envelope. "Would you see that Jasmine gets this?" He had left her a note and his business card.

"Certainly."

With a bag slung over one shoulder, Jake rolled his suitcase outside, where Vincent popped his Dodge's trunk and loaded the luggage.

"You know exactly where we're going?" Vincent closed the trunk.

Jake secured Edgar's cage in the backseat. "Not yet. Just Miami."

"Play it by ear, free as a bird. I like that." Vincent opened the passenger door for Jake, who got in.

Jake waited until Vincent sat beside him before saying, "Drive for two hours, then we'll get lunch. After that, I'll spell you for an hour."

"You're too good to me," Vincent said, shifting the car into gear.

Jake reclined his seat and closed his eyes. He heard Edgar croaking close to his ear.

His cell phone's ringtone awoke him from a half sleep seventy minutes later, and he returned the seat to its upright position.

"I've got your room and your car, five minutes apart," Carrie said. She read the addresses to Jake, who programmed them into Vincent's GPS. "There's only one Miriam Santiago in Miami. Her husband is in jail on Pavot Island. He's some kind of political prisoner." She read Miriam's address, which Jake jotted down on the back of a business card.

"Good work, kid."

Vincent drove along the Gulf Coast into Mississippi. Jake stared out his window at the gray water. First Katrina, then Rita, then the British Petroleum disaster had devastated the area. While most of the world had recovered from the economic collapse Jake had partially brought about by causing the death of Nicholas Tower, his former employer, the deep southeast continued to languish. Although microbes had eradicated much of the spilled oil, the question of how much damage these man-made dispersants would have on the ecosystem lingered like a ticking time bomb.

In Biloxi, they ate lunch in a large boat that had been carried several hundred feet inland by Hurricane Camille and then converted into a restaurant at the very spot where it had come to rest.

Jake took his turn at the wheel, and they crossed into Florida. The sudden appearance of palm trees made him feel as if they had entered a foreign country, and in Tampa, sitting in the passenger seat as the sun turned orange, he pointed out an alligator on the side of the highway. They pulled over to a McDonald's for dinner, so he wouldn't have to worry about leaving Edgar in the car, then got out and stretched their legs. Mosquitoes as thick as houseflies swarmed around them as the pink sky darkened.

"It's growing season year-round down here," Vincent said.

"I don't think I could ever get used to it."

"I know other New Yorkers. You're all the same: you think that little island you live on is the center of the universe."

Jake knew better, but he didn't say so. He fed Edgar some birdseed, then took his turn behind the wheel again.

"Let me know when you get tired," Vincent said.

"I'm tired."

"Damn."

Forty minutes after they changed places once more, the sky turned black, clouds outlined in red.

"You want me to stop at a motel?" Vincent said.

Jake yawned. "No. We've made good time so far. Let's keep going."

"In that case, are you going to tell me why you're going through so much trouble to find this woman and what it has to do with Edgar?"

"No." Jake found it highly unlikely Vincent would believe Edgar had been a cop before becoming a raven, that

Miriam Santiago's niece had caused his transformation, or that Sheryl's spirit had told Jake only a blood relative of Ramera Evans could reverse the spell.

Vincent fiddled with the radio, then turned it off.

At 2:05 a.m., they pulled into a motel parking lot and got out. The streetlamp made the bushes glow bright green, and frogs croaked in the darkness behind the trees. Jake left Vincent holding Edgar outside while he checked in, then they took the luggage to the second level.

Inside the room, Vincent looked at the double beds. "You aren't going to make me drive back now, are you?"

Jake opened the cage door, allowing Edgar to hop out onto the desk. "You can stay here tonight. I need you to take me to the car rental agency in the morning anyway. But if you snore, you sleep in your car."

"I don't snore," Vincent said. "Does Edgar?"

Edgar turned and blinked at Vincent.

Jake changed the newspaper liner in the cage. "No, but he has other more annoying habits."

Vincent switched on the air-conditioning. "I'm beat. I don't care what he does."

They took turns washing up, then climbed into the separate beds.

"You live one interesting life," Vincent said in the darkness.

Jake felt Edgar waddling across the bed. "You have no idea."

THREE

Jake steered his rented Ford Fusion through the financial district of downtown Miami, an amalgam of glass, steel, and mirrored buildings, with Edgar's cage nestled in the passenger seat beside him. Vincent had left after breakfast, their parting unsentimental.

Finding himself surrounded by international banks, Jake wondered how many of them the Order of Avademe had sunk its tentacles into and how the banks fared now without Avademe and the cabal of powerful old men manipulating world affairs to enhance their profit margins.

Jake wore sunglasses, a polo shirt, and knee-length shorts for comfort, and he had tucked his .38 into the side compartment of the door for security. He had learned the hard way not to travel without protection.

The black Fusion's GPS guided him west to Little

Havana. Green trees and plants encircled pastel stucco houses, and Latin music filled the air. Jake navigated several turns and stopped before a mauve-colored house.

Removing his shades, he gathered the large envelope in which he carried his documents and Edgar's cage and got out of the car. He passed flamingo lawn statues, then knocked on the wooden door and waited. A lawn mower hummed in the distance. A red Nissan Versa drove by, its driver a Hispanic woman in her late twenties or early thirties wearing shades, who didn't glance in Jake's direction.

The front door opened, and a woman who appeared fifty stood there, her brown skin smooth and youthful looking. She had wide greenish eyes like Katrina.

Jake's heart beat faster. "Miriam Santiago?"

The woman looked Jake up and down. She wore a shiny sky-blue dress, and her short hair had been straightened. "Yes?"

Jake handed her his card. "My name's Jake Helman. I'm a private investigator from New York City."

Miriam glanced at the card, then at Edgar, then at Jake's good eye. He wondered if she sensed his left eye was made of glass or if she was merely avoiding the scars on that side of his face, a common reaction.

"What's this about?"

Jake hesitated. After months of searching for Miriam, he didn't know how to present his request. "I knew your niece Ramera in New York City."

"Then you know she's dead."

"Yes."

"The police told me she died with a drug dealer she was

seeing. Either they jumped to their deaths at a construction site, or someone pushed them."

"She called herself Katrina."

One of Miriam's eyebrows twitched. "That figures."

"She and Prince Malachai—the dealer—were manufacturing and selling a drug called Black Magic. Are you familiar with it?"

"I was born on Pavot Island."

"Do you know what the drug is, what it does to those who use it?"

"I know what it's *supposed* to be and what it's supposed to do."

Jake felt disappointment creeping in. "You're not a believer?"

"My mother was a bokor. She taught Ramera vodou after my sister and her husband were killed. I disagreed with her decision, but I'd already moved back to Pavot Island, so I didn't have any say in the matter. It's nonsense."

Jake's heart sank. A nonbeliever would do him no good. "Mrs. Santiago, did you ever study vodou?"

"I grew up with it. I couldn't avoid it. But I never took it seriously, and I only laughed at my mother when she tried to force it on me."

The energy drained from Jake's body. "I have a problem involving a vodou spell Ramera cast. I'm told only a blood relative of hers can reverse it. I hoped that meant you."

Glancing at Edgar again, Miriam clucked her tongue. "I'm sorry. If you're looking for a witch doctor, I can't help you."

"Is there anyone else?"

"I'm the last living member of my family."

A queasy feeling developed in Jake's stomach. "Thank you for your time. If you think of anyone who can help me or any way you can help me, please call the number on my card."

"There's no such thing as magic," Miriam said as Jake carried Edgar back to the car.

That's what you think, Jake thought. He had encountered the supernatural too many times to doubt its existence. Sliding behind the wheel, Jake bowed his head.

Edgar croaked beside him.

"I'm sorry, Edgar. We both knew it was a long shot."

Sitting up, he turned the ignition for the car's air-conditioning and called Carrie.

"How's the Florida sunshine?"

"Hot," Jake said. "Miami's a bust; this case is closed. Miriam Santiago was the right person, but all she managed to do was put the kibosh on my plans."

"Sorry to hear that."

"It'll take me twenty hours to drive home. I'll spend one more night here and leave at the crack of dawn."

"You want me to find you lodging along the way?"

"No, I'll play it by ear and see as much of the coast as possible."

"Bring me some fresh oranges, will you?"

"Sure." Jake set the phone in the cup compartment for easy access. Without warning, his left hand clamped onto the steering wheel with unexpected force, like a magnet drawn to metal. He blinked at his hand.

I didn't do that.

His right hand shifted the car into gear, then seized the steering wheel as well.

I didn't do that, either . . .

His foot stomped on the gas pedal, and the car surged forward with such speed it threw his head back.

"Shit!"

He tried to reposition his hands, but they wouldn't budge. Both hands gripped the wheel as if his fingers had been welded to it. He tried to ease up on the gas, but his foot continued to press it. The Fusion whipped around an SUV; Jake's hands and foot executed the maneuver in perfect synchronization with no guidance from him. He tried to stomp on the brake, but his other foot did not respond. He had no control over his body, couldn't even turn his head.

"Edgar, we've got trouble!"

Edgar cawed beside him.

No such thing as magic, my ass!

The Fusion screeched to a stop at a red light, throwing Jake forward.

A police car cruised by, its uniformed driver casting a disapproving look in his direction.

The light turned green, and Jake's hands steered the car left onto a street lined with low commercial buildings. He spotted a couple of Hispanic men chatting in front of a cigar store and a woman unloading her baby from a car.

In his head, he heard a rhythmic sound: *thrum . . . thrum . . . THRUM!*

Almost a year earlier, he had heard similar drumbeats when Katrina had forced him to endure violent, horrific hallucinations. He had given Katrina his business card under innocent circumstances when he knew her as Ramera Evans, a publicist dating Edgar. She had used the oil from his fingertips on the card—his DNA—to cast spells on him, including tying his back into knots. And he had just given his card to Miriam.

"Damn it!" He wanted to pound the steering wheel but couldn't.

A pair of teenage girls in revealing clothing crossed the street ahead.

Moisture formed on Jake's brow. If the car sped up, he would strike both girls, killing them. He could just see it: he would mow down the innocent girls, wind up in a high-speed police chase against his will, and ultimately be charged with vehicular manslaughter and serve time in a Florida prison, where big men with tattoos would beat him for his crimes . . .

Jake wanted to honk the horn but couldn't even manage that. The car slowed down, just missing the girls, and accelerated again.

She's inside my head, he thought. *Seeing through my eyes!* He pictured Miriam sitting on a plastic-covered sofa in her house, with a video game controller gripped in her hands. Maybe a candle burned beside her . . .

"Slow down, esse!" a man called.

A big green sanitation truck appeared in the distance, blocking his lane.

Oh no.

A sanitation worker grabbed a garbage can on the sidewalk

and dumped its contents into the bowels of the truck.

The Fusion increased speed. In the passenger seat, Edgar cawed. Jake heard the drums beating, the Fusion's engine, and the sanitation truck's compacter all at the same time.

The sanitation worker climbed onto the side of the truck, where at least he would be safe from the impact. The truck's rear filled Jake's vision, and he squeezed his eyelids shut, bracing himself for impact.

His hands jerked the steering wheel left, and the car veered in that direction. Jake opened his eye and saw they had cleared the garbage truck, but now he was driving in the wrong lane. Relief washed over him, mixed with anger.

"You bitch!"

His jaws snapped shut, rattling his teeth, and he could not open them again. Protests issued from his throat and through his nostrils.

A red pickup appeared ahead, driving straight toward him.

Maybe I shouldn't have said that . . .

The truck grew closer, larger. Jake glimpsed a man wearing mirrored sunglasses and a straw hat. The man honked the truck's horn.

Jake waited for the Fusion to switch back into its lane. That didn't happen. Instead, Jake's foot stomped on the brake, and the Fusion screeched to a sudden stop.

The man jerked his steering wheel to one side, steering the truck into the opposite lane and passing Jake.

Jake exhaled. At least the pickup's driver didn't stop, get out, and beat him to a pulp.

Jake's left foot slid off the brake, and the Fusion lurched

forward. The car switched into the correct lane and navigated a left-hand turn. The sidewalks appeared deserted, though Jake saw plenty of vehicles parked in the lots of commercial buildings.

Where the hell is she taking us?

The Fusion decelerated and turned into the lot of a yellow sandstone building with Cuban architecture.

A nightclub, Jake thought as the Fusion circled the lot. The car pulled into a parking space, and Jake stepped on the brake. His right hand left the steering wheel, shifted the car into Park, and killed the ignition. Then he grasped the steering wheel again.

Jake studied the stairs leading up to the nightclub entrance and the stone balcony there.

A black metal door on the building's side burst open, and three men charged out: one black, one Hispanic, and another who looked like a mixture of the two. They ran straight for the Fusion, and against his will, Jake unlocked the doors, which the men jerked open. One of the men pried Jake's fingers loose from the steering wheel, and another seized Edgar's cage, causing the raven to caw.

Now Jake *wanted* to hang on to the steering wheel, but two men pulled him from the car. The Hispanic man snatched the keys from the ignition, and he and the black man jerked Jake forward. Jake's feet moved of their own volition, with no assistance from him. Not a single part of his body responded to his commands, and he saw no one on the street to help him.

Abducted in broad daylight.

The men guided him through the open side door and down a flight of cool, dark cement stairs to a storage cellar where cases of liquor had been stacked to the ceiling. The Hispanic man moved a metal chair into the middle of the room and pushed Jake onto it. The black man looped a dirty rope around Jake's torso several times, pinning his arms to his sides and his back to the chair. Jake had done the same thing to Simon Taggert, the head of White River Security, just three months earlier. Taggert ended up dead, though not by Jake's hands.

The man who looked mixed race set Edgar's cage on a desk piled high with papers. Jake stared down a short, narrow hall leading to a bathroom. Salsa music drifted downstairs.

The Hispanic man nodded to his comrades, who went upstairs, and stood before Jake. "Don't worry. I'm not going to hurt you. I'm not going to do anything to you."

Jake heard the metal door above swing open, and sunlight spilled down the stairs like water. The door closed, and footsteps scraped the stairs: heels clacking on cement.

Miriam Santiago.

He heard her speak another language and raised his eyebrows upon realizing it was French rather than Spanish.

The Hispanic man nodded in response to her commands, then headed upstairs.

A moment later, she stood where he had, holding a burning white candle in one hand and Jake's business card in the other. "Now let's try this again. Only this time, *I'll* ask the questions."

FOUR

Turning to the desk, Miriam looked at Edgar. She blew out the candle and set it down.

Jake regained feeling in his arms and legs, and his jaw loosened. He opened his mouth and moved his lower jaw in a circle, then opened and closed his fingers.

Miriam nodded at Edgar. "Who is he?"

"I call him Edgar."

"I didn't ask you what you call him. I asked who he is. What's his real name?"

"His real name is Edgar."

"Do you still want to play games with me after you saw what I can do?"

"Why did you do that?"

"Do you expect me to trust some gringo who comes knocking on my door, asking personal questions about my family and my relationship to vodou? I brought you here so Fernando and his men could guarantee my safety."

"Why do you need help from them? If it was really you who took me for that spin, I should think you wouldn't need hired muscle."

"Fernando isn't muscle, and I don't pay him. We're partners in this club. He's loyal to me and my husband." She gestured at the candle. "I practice white vodou. It can't be used to harm anyone, even in self-defense."

"It came damn close."

"You should be happy; you hoped I possessed a working knowledge of vodou, and it turns out I do."

Jake had to admit he *was* relieved. If Miriam could control his body from several blocks away, she just might be powerful enough to restore Edgar.

The upstairs door opened and closed, and Fernando trotted downstairs. Jake recognized his .38 in one of Fernando's hands and the envelope with Miriam's information in the other.

"This is all that was in the car," Fernando said. He handed the envelope to Miriam, who took out its contents, and set the gun on the desk.

Miriam scanned the documents, then returned them to the envelope, which she tossed onto the desk. "For a private eye, you didn't get much on me."

"My assistant did that research. I haven't had much free time."

"Who is Edgar to you?"

"He's a raven."

Without taking her eyes off Jake, Miriam said, "Fernando, use Helman's gun to shoot his friend the raven."

Fernando picked up the .38 without hesitation, clicked off the safety, and aimed the gun at Edgar, who flapped his wings in a frantic burst of motion.

With my own gun! Jake thought. "Hold it! Okay, relax. I'll tell you what you want to know."

Fernando looked to Miriam, who nodded. He clicked the safety back on and set the gun on the counter.

Edgar calmed down.

Jake faced Miriam. "His full name is Edgar Hopkins."

Miriam held his gaze. "Wait for me upstairs, Fernando."

Fernando went upstairs without complaint.

"That's a long name for a raven," Miriam said.

"It comes with a title: Detective, as in NYPD. We used to be partners until I resigned from the force, which is how I wound up as a PI. Edgar got involved with your niece, not knowing she was a wrong number. Ramera was dating Prince Malachai at the same time."

"I knew about this Prince Malachai. I had a number of conversations with my niece, and when I became convinced she had embraced black vodou, I used my contacts to see what she was up to. I couldn't believe it when I heard she was distributing Black Magic."

"So why didn't you do something to stop it? Do you have any idea how many people died because of that shit?"

"I was prepared to intervene when I learned she had created an army of zonbies. Then she and this Malachai turned up dead in the foundation for a new high-rise.

Problem solved."

"I figured out she was playing both Edgar and Malachai for fools and told Edgar. He raced off to confront her in her apartment. I got there just as she was leaving and found him like"—he pointed at Edgar—"this."

"And then you killed my niece?"

"No. She killed Malachai and turned him into some sort of superzombie, different from the others. I did kill him. I stole her drugs, and she agreed to restore Edgar to normal in exchange for her supply." Katrina had really wanted Nicholas Tower's Afterlife program, a research project on the supernatural and the afterlife that had cost millions of dollars, which Katrina had labored on. "I agreed to her terms, but Edgar had other plans. She slipped from a girder at the construction site. I tried to save her, but Edgar literally got in her face, and she fell to her death."

"Why are you coming to me now for help?"

"I believed only Katrina—Ramera—could restore Edgar. Two and a half months ago, I learned otherwise. It took me some time to track you down. I spent three weeks in New Orleans before I found a lead. That was yesterday."

"This Edgar Hopkins must mean a lot to you for you to expend so much effort on his behalf."

"He's my friend."

"He's lucky to have a friend like you."

"Edgar has a son who needs him. I promised the boy I'd bring his father back home. Can you help me?"

Leaning close to the birdcage, Miriam looked Edgar in the eye. "I can help you." She turned to Jake. "But I'm no philanthropist. I don't work miracles for free."

Of course not. "What do you want?"

Miriam set a chair before Jake and sat facing him. "You were honest with me. I'll extend the same courtesy to you."

"I'm a captive audience."

"You know where I was born?"

"Someplace called Pavot Island."

"Pavot Island is on the opposite side of Cuba and close enough for us to spit on. It's the same size as Jamaica. Pavot Island has always promoted itself as a democracy, but because we trade goods and services with Cuba over America's objections, the US government pretends Pavot Island doesn't even exist. Pavot Island doesn't belong to the United Nations; there's no US ambassador there. Check ten maps available in this country, and you'll be lucky to find Pavot identified on three of them."

Jake had never heard of Pavot Island until his search for Miriam.

"My mother, Louise, was born on Pavot. So was my father and so was I. But my father died when I was very young, and my mother brought me here for a better life. She remarried to a man named Mincey, who worked in a factory in New Orleans and owned his own house. He was my sister Havana's father, but my mother was unlucky in love, and he too died young. My mother raised Havana and me in the ways of white vodou, though she jokingly called it 'that old black magic.'

"Years later, back on Pavot, the political climate took a turn for the worse. An ambitious man named Ernesto

Malvado made dangerous noises about changing the country's direction. Pavot was a democracy, albeit a corrupt one, and Malvado preached fascism.

"I'd always felt closer to my birth island than to my adopted country, so when I was old enough to legally make my own decisions, I returned to Pavot Island and joined the Democratic Party, which opposed Malvado's corporatist party. It was in my role as an activist that I met Andre Santiago. Andre was an idealist like me, but he had something I did not: the ear of the people. He became Malvado's political opponent. Malvado had the backing of the corporations on the island, but Andre had the support of the people. Wherever Malvado went, Andre showed up with protestors, including me. It must have driven Malvado mad, but he tolerated us while he sowed the seeds of his power. Andre and I married and had two sons.

"Havana moved to New York City, where she married a man named Evans and gave birth to Ramera. Ramera was eight when Malvado finally ascended to the power he craved on Pavot. That was a terrible year for my family. Havana and her husband were murdered by drug dealers. Ramera was traumatized, and my mother brought her to New Orleans. There was nothing I could do; Ramera was a US citizen, and Andre and I had problems of our own. Malvado had his soldiers arrest Andre as a dissident. He was sentenced to prison without a trial. I was not allowed to visit my husband and pursued every legal means to do so. The stress was unbearable, and I had two sons to raise alone.

"For four years, I fought to have my husband freed,

while all around me darkness ruled the island. Pavot was always a center for vodou, but with Malvado in charge, black vodou dominated. Through a letter smuggled to me, Andre instructed me to return to the US with our sons and fight for Pavot from here. Fearing for our lives, I obeyed.

"Fernando and some of our other friends were aboard the boat that brought us here. I spent one month in New Orleans with my mother, and that's when I met Ramera. She was twelve, and her eyes chilled my soul. I know she needed me, but so did my husband and our sons. I set up shop here in Miami, where most of the people from Pavot in the US live, and established the Andre Santiago Freedom Foundation.

"For ten years that followed, I lobbied Congress and the White House to pressure Malvado to free my husband. I sent one son to college. Today Carlos is a lawyer and works for the foundation. The other, Roberto, returned to Pavot, where he joined a resistance movement and was killed.

"Ramera graduated from Tulane University and started writing a book about vodou. She visited me here to interview me about the book, which I tried to discourage her from writing. She was a beautiful woman, sophisticated, and she wanted to expose too much about our religion. The secrets of vodou are not meant to be shared with the common public. She wrote the book over my objections, and it caused controversy among practioners and believers. Ramera then accepted a high-paying research position; she told me nothing about it, told my mother it was directly related to her book.

"Then Katrina struck, and my mother drowned in her home, and her body floated through the streets. I saw Ramera for the final time at my mother's funeral. Her eyes were as traumatized as the first time I saw them, but the pain was replaced by fury. I did my best to keep tabs on her and didn't like what I learned. Vengeance and vodou are a potent and deadly combination, and now she's dead.

"My husband has been a political prisoner now for thirty years. Malvado hasn't executed him, because to do so would make him a martyr. He remains a symbol of the fight for freedom in our land."

Jake measured the woman before him. "What do you want from me in exchange for restoring Edgar to his human form?"

"Isn't it obvious? I want you to go to Pavot Island, break my husband out of prison, and bring him home to me."

Jake studied the intensity in Miriam's eyes. "Is that all?"

"I'm your only chance."

"Aren't you better suited to freeing him with your vodou hoodoo than I am?"

"White vodou isn't a very practical weapon, and if I set foot on Pavot I'll be killed on sight. I'm Malvado's political opposition. He's not worried about making a martyr out of me; he's tried to have me killed here. That's why I'm surrounded by bodyguards, all of them refugees from Pavot."

"It sounds like you need an army."

"You're selling yourself short. I told you I followed my niece's activities. There's only one reason to distribute Black Magic: to create an army of undead soldiers. Once Ramera died, any zonbies she created ceased to function. But in the

40

days leading up to her death, someone took it upon himself to exterminate her soldiers, half of them in a warehouse Ramera and Malachai used to manufacture their Magic, the rest at drug spots throughout the city. The police believe one man was responsible. I'd say whoever did that kind of damage without being caught knows what he's doing."

Jake chose not to confirm her suspicion. "How will I get to Pavot Island?"

"Take a plane. It's a short flight. Or take a boat. Pavot is a dictatorship, but Americans are allowed to travel there, even though there's no tourism trade. Once you arrive, I'll set up a meeting with a contact from the resistance."

"How will I get back here? Even if I manage to break your husband out, this Malvado isn't going to let me board a plane with him."

"Regardless of how you travel to Pavot, you'll have to take a boat back, just like all the people who come here illegally. I can arrange that."

"Are there zonbies there?"

"I never saw one while I lived there, but I heard stories. Everyone has. The tales spread fear over the island. One more reason for decent people to flee here."

"No wonder Malvado doesn't want Pavot to join the UN." Jake hated zonbies. "Ramera told me she'd summoned a demon. She called it a Loa. According to her, she fornicated with it and had its baby, which she killed as a sacrifice. That's how she learned about Magic."

"She told you that?"

"We had a chat before she died."

"Kalfu, a Petro Loa—one of the aggressive beings. One has to be willing to endure much pain to obtain that level of vodou power."

"The same power exists on Pavot?"

"Yes. Malvado has surrounded himself with bokors who do his bidding. Sugar and rum are Pavot's primary legal exports, but Malvado makes much more exporting heroin and cocaine. He must harvest Black Magic, too."

"You're not exactly selling me on this whole plan."

"Pavot is an island of great beauty and terrible secrets. The chances of you rescuing my husband are slim, and the chances of you getting off that island alive are even slimmer."

"What will happen to Edgar? I can't take him with me obviously."

"You'll leave him with me. I need to make extensive preparations for his transmogrification. It's one thing to reduce a human being into a lower life-form like a bird but another to turn a bird into a higher life-form, like a man, even if restoring a former man."

"Have you done either before?"

"No."

Jake snorted. "So you want me to risk my life on some crazy-assed mission and you can't even guarantee you can make the payment?"

"There are no guarantees in life, but I believe I can restore your friend. And if I can't, no one can. Me, my husband, and my surviving son are the only blood relatives of Ramera's, and only I practice vodou. I'm you're only hope."

Jake drew in his breath and exhaled. "All right, I'll do it.

I'll go to Pavot Island and bust your husband out of prison."

"I'm glad to hear that." Miriam opened a desk drawer, withdrew a gleaming knife, and crossed the floor.

Edgar croaked.

Jake held Miriam's gaze, ignoring the blade as it descended and cut the rope binding him to the chair. When the rope fell away, Miriam stepped back and Jake rose.

"You've got one seriously cursed family," he said. "I'll take my card back."

Smiling, Miriam drew Jake's card from the base of the candle and handed it to him.

Jake felt like a fool as he slid the card into his wallet. "How soon—?"

Rising shouts outside cut him off.

He and Miriam turned to the open vent in a glass block window ten feet away and heard a woman curse in Spanish. Jake and Miriam glanced at each other, and Miriam ran to the stairway. Jake seized Edgar's cage, then ran after her. They stood at the bottom of the stairs as the upstairs door opened, spilling sunlight into the gloom.

Shadows stretched over the wall as Fernando and his men entered with their hands raised. Fernando turned in the opposite direction, with his back to Jake and Miriam.

But the voice of the woman who had cursed outside stopped them. "Vayan abajo!" *Get downstairs.*

Jake and Miriam backed up as the three men descended the stairs with resigned expressions.

A woman entered the stairwell behind them, bathed in hot sunlight, and slammed the door. "Quedate donde yo te pueda ver." *Stay where I can see you.*

Fernando offered Miriam a regretful smile.

From his new vantage point, Jake watched the woman's copper-colored legs as she descended the stairs. She wore Timberland boots and denim shorts. Then he saw the rest of her: a pink tank top that clung to her breasts, a gold necklace that matched her earrings, and a navy-blue New York Yankees baseball cap that held her curly hair in place. She gripped a Beretta in both hands like a pro. A compact video camera dangled from her hip.

Jake had seen this woman before. Even with her eyes masked by her dark sunglasses, he knew her.

They stood in a half circle around the woman, who held her gun ready to fire. She glanced in Jake's direction.

"*Hola*, Jake," Maria Vasquez said.

FIVE

"You two know each other?" Miriam said.

"Oh yeah," Maria said. "We go way back."

Jake looked at Maria's gun. "A Beretta?"

"It's not mine."

Fernando blushed.

Maria turned to Miriam. "Next time you hire three punks to watch your back, give them *all* guns."

Miriam spoke in an even tone. "What's this all about?"

"That part of this equation is between me and Jake."

"Fernando and I own this club. If you're here to settle a score with Mr. Helman, take it somewhere else."

Maria shook her head. "Lady, I'm not going anywhere until I get some answers."

"She was videotaping you through the window," Fernando said to Miriam.

Jake frowned. What the hell did Maria want with him here in Miami?

"What did you hear?" Miriam said.

"Every crazy word you two said to each other," Maria said.

Miriam glanced at Jake, who shrugged.

"These men are freedom fighters from Pavot Island. Who are you?"

"Maria Vasquez, detective third grade, NYPD."

"That name sounds familiar."

"We spoke on the phone nine months ago."

"You called to tell me my niece was dead," Miriam said. "You asked me about Prince Malachai."

Jake couldn't believe it. Maria had spoken to Miriam before he even knew she existed.

"Good memory." The toughness never left Maria's voice.

"You sounded nicer then. Of course, you weren't pointing a gun at me."

"I didn't know you were a witch doctor."

"You're out of your jurisdiction, dear. You trespassed on our property and violated our civil rights. This is kidnapping. Or is it an execution?"

Maria lowered the gun. "It's neither. Your boys tried to manhandle me. Once I disarmed *goyo* here, I was in a bind: take off or face off. After everything I just heard, I decided to take the direct approach." She tossed the gun to Fernando, who caught it and tucked it beneath his shirt. Then her gaze settled on Edgar in the cage.

"Fernando," Miriam said, gesturing to the stairs.

Fernando and the other two men went upstairs.

Miriam looked from Maria to Jake. "I'll give you some time alone. Try not to kill each other." She ascended the stairs, muttering beneath her breath, "New Yorkers."

Maria moved close to Jake. "I saw that bird in your office—"

"Just days after Edgar disappeared."

"Fuck you! This is *not* Edgar. Don't give me that shit!"

"I don't care if you believe me or not. I don't need to convince you of anything. What the hell are you doing here?"

"The same thing I was doing in New Orleans."

Jake blinked as if he'd been struck. "You were in the crowd outside my hotel . . ."

"And outside Mrs. Santiago's house today."

"How long have you been tailing me?"

Maria took a deep breath. "It feels like years, but it's been less than one. Since this all started."

"Since *what* all started?"

"The Black Magic and the fucking zombies. I have sixty DOAs under my name on the board in Homicide. And that's just the ones who were already dead when you put bullets in their brains. It doesn't include the vics in the Machete Massacres, the people those zombies killed."

"How can you believe in zombies but not that this is Edgar?"

"I saw those things walking around the streets. Scarecrows. Zombies. Skeletons. And I saw their corpses after you did them. Teeth pulled out, fingers and toes cut off, all to make identification next to impossible. Stuffed with sawdust. *Sixty* of them. I'll give you credit: you didn't use the same gun on all of them. We counted six."

"Sixty people? Six guns? Sounds like six killers to me."

"But they weren't killed, because they were already dead. They were all autopsied. Despite all that sawdust packing, the ME determined they'd ingested Black Magic. Some snorted it, some smoked it, and some shot it up. The chemists learned that Magic contains traces of human ashes among other things. It was a never ending cycle, wasn't it? Junkies OD on Black Magic, turn into zombies. When they can't function anymore, they get cooked into Black Magic. But where did the first powder come from?"

Good question, Jake thought. "How did you figure all this out?"

"I'm a detective, remember? Bernie thinks I'm crazy, and L.T. doesn't know what to do with me. But no cover-up is going to change the truth. Yeah, cover-up: tourists might avoid the Apple if they knew real zombies walked the streets. It tends to make civilians nervous, you know?"

Jake saw she was getting worked up. "Maybe it's best never to discuss it."

"Easy for you to say. You're not on the job anymore, and you don't have sixty zombie corpses assigned to your name."

"Do you actually say 'zombie' at work?"

"You think I'm crazy? With Bernie and L.T., sure, and not even with L.T. anymore. But *other* people talk about it. Detectives familiar with the case call me the zombie lady. One prick called me Sister Voodoo. He won't make that mistake again."

"You didn't track me down because the kids are making fun of you at school."

"Edgar was kicking it to Dawn Du Pre. The last time he was seen was entering her apartment building. A man fitting your description went into the building that night, too, and was later seen leaving. Dawn left shortly before that. Edgar never left. Then Dawn turned up dead with Prince Malachai in the foundation of a construction site across the street. A little legwork by yours truly revealed she was shtuping Malachai and Edgar at the same time. Only Malachai's hoppers knew her as Katrina. Guess what? Dawn Du Pre never existed, and Katrina was just an alias. The bitch's real name was Ramera Evans. But you already know that. You knew it the night you and Edgar went to her building and only you came out."

"The night she turned Edgar into this raven."

"Stop saying that!"

"I had something Katrina wanted. She agreed to restore Edgar if I gave it to her. We met at that construction site. Things spiraled out of control. Edgar got in her face and down she went."

"Malachai was a lot deader than she was when we found them."

"She turned him into something else, some kind of superzombie."

"His face was missing."

"That was me." Jake shuddered at the memory of the back of his head caving in Malachai's face when the undead drug dealer had attempted to crush him. "Now you know my story, whether you believe all of it or not. What's yours?"

"I told you all along I was watching you. I knew you

were in this up to your eyeball. I tailed you more than once. Got to know your routine pretty well: early morning run, lunch in that little park area next to the Tower, an occasional basketball game with Martin. Between my job and your cases, I never managed to devote as much time to you as I wanted. One night I saw you hop a cab with your luggage, so I followed you to a car rental agency, then across the state before I gave up and went back. I also ran a check on your credit card activity—"

"That's illegal."

"You're a person of interest in the disappearance of a police detective. I learned you drove to New Orleans and checked into the French Lily. When you didn't return after a week, I used my vacation time to go there. I stayed right across the street, with a nice view of your room. And I got your routine down there, too: early morning pickup by your guide, Vincent Wilkins; nine hours of door-to-door legwork; back to your hotel; dinner at a different restaurant every night; online research at the hotel; early to bed. I actually felt sorry for you when I learned you were searching for Miriam Santiago. I was tempted to leave an anonymous note under your door telling you where to find her."

Jake's ears stung. "So why didn't you?"

"It became like a game. One vacation week turned into another. I dug into my sick days. Now I'm on leave. When you drove here, I didn't have to worry about following you, thanks to your plastic. I just did a little stakeout on Miriam's house. You spent a lot less time talking to her than I expected, which was disappointing. When you left her house, I was sure you finally made my tail because you drove like a madman. Then you pulled into this parking lot, and Miriam's boys yanked you out of the car, and it looked like you were paralyzed. I snuck out and found that window. It was dumb luck they brought you down here."

"Thanks for coming to my rescue, by the way."

"I'd have gotten around to it. But I was too interested in your conversation with Miriam. The two of you confirmed everything I suspected about Dawn's dead soldiers."

"It also confirmed what I've been telling you about Edgar."

"Or it proves Miriam is jerking your chain. She's playing into your delusion about Edgar to get you to Pavot Island and spring her husband."

"You're risking your career just being here."

"I promised myself I'd find Edgar or find out what happened to him. I promised that to Martin, too."

"We have that in common, except I know what happened to him."

"Too bad I can't believe anything you say. You're too dodgy, always covering your tracks. Only a guilty man does that. Your wife is murdered by the Cipher, and he gets eighty-sixed the next day, just hours after Edgar and I interviewed you. No one gets collared. No one gets interviewed about the murder. It was just some vigilante, and the city's happy anyway, right?"

Jake felt his jaw setting. "I'll say this only once, okay? Don't talk about my wife."

"I used to ask Edgar about it, and his manner would change; he'd get all quiet and evasive. I think he knew you killed the Cipher and covered for you. Maybe you made Edgar disappear because he knew the truth."

"Made him disappear where, in Katrina's apartment?"

"I don't know."

"Believe what you want, but you can't have it both ways."

"That woman who worked for Tower—Kira Thorn. She provided your alibi when the Cipher got aced, then she disappeared. Convenient."

"Tower was involved in shady business. Kira was, too. She must have had her reasons for vanishing."

Maria sized him up. "You've told so many lies to cover your own ass you can't stop. Three months ago, when Martin got sucked into that cult, Teddy Geoghegan from Major Crimes interviewed you about Mayor Madigan's wife. That was right before Madigan and a bunch of power brokers turned up dead in that warehouse in Karlin Reichard's Brooklyn shipyard."

Jake resisted the urge to clench his fists. Maria was closing in on him, throwing one piece of the pie after another at him. It was easy enough to dodge certain incidents and accusations but not one after another. "Marla Madigan hired me—"

"I know why she hired you. I know what you told Geoghegan and the FBI. I also know that one of those power brokers was Benjamin Bradley, the founder of the Dreamers. Quite a coincidence: Martin joins a cult, then the leader of that cult winds up dead, along with the husband of your client."

"The media said those guys died of asphyxiation.

Something about a gas leak."

"Another cover-up. The feds shut that crime scene down so fast it would make your glass eye spin. I spoke to one of the uniforms who first arrived on the scene. He was afraid to talk to me, so I got him drunk. He said one vic's head was crushed. Another's had been shot apart. The rest of them were floating facedown in water with great big holes in the back of their skulls. Does that sound like asphyxiation to you?"

Jake felt no remorse that Cain had crushed Myron Madigan's head with his bare hands or that he had machine gunned Weiskopf's skull into nothingness. The men had deserved worse. Hopefully they got it. "I don't know anything about that. Sounds like the ravings of a drunk."

"Geoghegan and the feds don't know anything about you and me pulling Martin out of the Dreamers' clutches. If they did, they might see a connection between you and Madigan and Reinhardt."

She's good, Jake thought, careful not to convey his discomfort through body language.

"They also might want to know how you got those gashes on your face the same night those men were killed."

"Some guys knifed me on my way home."

"Just like some guy stabbed you in the eye on your way home? You need to hire a ghostwriter for new material."

"Listen to me. Maybe you can't avoid dealing with the zombies because you were in the Black Magic Task Force and have all those bodies under your name. The two people responsible for the Magic, the Machete Massacres, and the zonbies are dead, and there's no one above them looking for revenge.

"But leave this thing with Madigan and the old guys from the Reichard Foundation alone. They may be dead, but every one of them had underlings. Some of them prospered because of what went down; some suffered. A lot of money was spent covering up those deaths. I'm talking about a daisy chain of men that links global finance, intelligence agencies, the FBI, and NYPD. You send signals that you're snooping around for the truth, and you'll wind up in a coffin—make no mistake about it. Just leave it alone. It doesn't concern you."

Maria stared at him and swallowed. She appeared angry and ready to cry at the same time. "No shit. You think I'm stupid? But how does it concern *you*?"

"You don't need to know that. It's got nothing to do with Edgar, and he's why we're both here."

She gazed at Edgar. "How the hell can you tell me that's my partner?"

Jake raised the cage and opened the door.

Edgar flew straight for Maria, who dodged to one side with a yelp.

"Don't be afraid," Jake said.

Edgar landed on Maria's shoulder, which dipped from his weight. She lifted her face to him, eyes fearful. Perched on her shoulder, he stood taller than her head.

"Edgar, is that you?"

Edgar cawed and nestled his head against Maria's cheek.

Tears rolled out of her eyes, and she caressed the raven's feathers with trembling hands. "How did you let this happen to you?"

"Love is blind," Jake said.

"You really came all the way down here to change him back?"

"Yes."

"And you're going to Pavot Island to free Andre Santiago from Malvado's prison?"

"Like the woman said, it's Edgar's only chance."

"Then I'm going with you."

Jake did a double take. "That's what you think."

"Edgar was my partner, too. Malvado's a dictator. His prison is supposed to be a house of horrors. You'll need backup."

"Miriam said she'd arrange for me to make contact with someone who can help me."

"You'll need more help than that."

"Uh-uh. No way. It's too dangerous."

"What, you think I can't handle myself? Look how I dealt with Miriam's so-called freedom fighters."

"Yeah? They're human. Malvado's surrounded himself with bokors, vodou witch doctors. That means zonbies, astral projection, pain curses—things you can't even imagine."

She glanced at Edgar. "My imagination's gotten pretty active."

"You'll do more good here. Miriam needs to run tests on Edgar before she can restore him. I'd feel better if you were here to watch over him, especially if I don't come back."

"But if I go with you, the odds of you coming home double. We have the same objective. You're not the only one willing to risk his life to bring Edgar home to Joyce and

Martin. Believe me, I'm just as stubborn as you are. You go to Pavot without me, and I'll just follow you anyway."

Jake sighed. "All right. We'll go together. But I don't like it."

Maria stroked Edgar's feathers. "Who says you have to?"

SIX

"This is Pavot Island." Miriam gestured to the map spread out across the table she, Fernando, Jake, and Maria stood around in the otherwise empty nightclub. "It's approximately three thousand square miles. Malvado is a capitalist, not a communist like Castro, but he's a dictator. When a man oppresses his people, they don't care about his political philosophies. Malvado uses Pavot Island's treasury as his personal bank, the population as his workforce. Pavotians sneak out on boats, rafts, inner tubes—anything that will transport them. Many don't survive the trip. But the promise of a better life is worth the risk."

Fernando pointed at the center of the map. "Pavot City is the nation's capital. Malvado's palace is on the outskirts. There are three smaller cities"—he moved his finger along the map's terrain—"here, here, and here. Each city has at least one suburb. There are eleven villages surrounding the cities and their provinces and isolated farms and plantations beyond them. The blank spots you see are the fields where Malvado grows the poppy for his heroin and cocaine."

Miriam lit a cigarette. "The palace forms a triangle with these two complexes that face the national rain forest: El Miedo prison and the central military headquarters. Andre is in El Miedo."

"El Miedo means 'fear,'" Maria said to Jake.

"Two million people live on Pavot," Fernando said. "They're primarily black, Hispanic, and a mixture of the two. It was originally populated by the Tainos who inhabited the Caribbean prior to the arrival of Europeans. First the Spaniards mined it for gold; the Tainos had no immunity against the diseases brought from Spain, and they died out. Then the French came with their African slaves. In 1804, the slaves on Haiti rebelled against their oppressors, which inspired a similar revolution on Pavot. The French and Dutch rulers fled for their lives."

"Three languages are spoken on Pavot," Miriam said. "English, French, and Spanish." She glanced at Jake. "You'll get by." She turned to Maria. "You'll get by better."

"I speak French, too. What little I remember from high school anyway."

"You couldn't ask for a better shotgun," Miriam told Jake.

Maria cocked one eyebrow. "See? I just got here, and I'm already proving my value."

Miriam looked at Jake. "Yours won't be the only white face on the island. The US government may not approve of

Malvado, but plenty of US companies have factories there. Cheap labor trumps other concerns, even when the workers are tortured."

"What happens when we land?" Jake said.

Fernando pointed at an airstrip near the coast. "There's only one airport for civilian and military personnel."

"You'll stay at the island's only resort," Miriam said. "Malvado developed the beach for tourists, but they never came. Only one resort hotel remains. One is a number you'll find significant: one television station, one news radio network, one newspaper, one monthly magazine, one voice: Malvado's. But books, magazines, and DVDs from abroad are permitted, and pirate radio stations have begun to pop up. The island residents have limited Internet access; it's an intranet, like some companies have. Forget about cell phone service.

"On day one, you relax on the grounds. On day two, you play tourists, which will give you a chance to see parts of the island. You'll visit Pavot City for dinner. Go to a restaurant called Coucher du Soleil. Whoever your contact is will reach out to you there."

"You don't know who that is?" Jake said.

"As a precautionary measure, no. Tell him what you need, and he'll arrange it. We've dug a tunnel that leads beneath the prison. Most likely you'll use that to get in and out. Once you've met your contact, you have five days to carry out your plan. Since the resort will know you're booked for seven days, Malvado's secret police will know that, too. The sooner you move, the better."

"Once we have your husband—"

"You'll travel to the northeast tip of the island. French pirates smuggled rum there once. We'll have a boat waiting to bring you back to the US, but it can leave only at night."

"And if we're caught?"

"You'll be tortured and killed in El Miedo. No one but us will ever know you were there."

"Just how helpful will our support be?"

"Any of the men or women who join you will lay down their lives for my husband. They're fighting for Pavot's freedom."

"Then why haven't any of them tried this on their own?"

"There have been previous attempts. Twenty years ago . . . ten . . . five. Each incident resulted in new security procedures, with Andre relocated to a different cell. If you fail, it will upset our intelligence again."

"If we fail, we'll be killed."

"If you fail, you'll pray for death."

Jake followed Maria to the same car rental agency where he'd gotten his Ford Fusion. He couldn't believe she had tailed him to New Orleans and then Florida and that she had figured out so much about Katrina and her zonbies. He had underestimated her threats to watch him. He laughed at the thought of her disarming Fernando and his men. She was a tough cookie. Good NYPD. He had to keep his eye on her.

Maria exited the rental agency office and opened

the passenger door, then eyed Edgar in his cage. "Am I supposed to ride in back so he has a good view of the glove compartment?"

"Put him back there. He's used to it."

Maria unbuckled the seat belt around the cage, which she lifted in two hands. "Sorry, partner."

Edgar croaked as Maria positioned the cage in the middle of the backseat and secured it with a seat belt and shoulder strap. Then she sat up front and closed the door. "Now I really feel naked. First no gun, now no car."

Jake pulled into the street. "I know what you mean. I hate to travel without a piece."

She turned in his direction. He could not see her eyes behind the dark sunglasses. "You're not traveling naked. You fired off that shot in the alley next to your hotel in New Orleans."

"I drove from New York. I had no trouble transporting my gun."

"Is that why you drove from New York?"

"No. I drove because I won't let Edgar out of my sight."

Maria shook her head. "I'm still not sold that's him."

"Yes, you are, or you wouldn't be going with me."

"Maybe I just don't want to let you out of my sight. Maybe I'm afraid that if anything happens to you, I'll never get to the bottom of this."

"I'm risking my life to save my friend. You're risking yours for the same reason, not to solve a mystery."

"*Mysteries*, plural. I've got more than one file on you."

"I don't know if I should be flattered or worried."

"What happened in that alley?"

"Three clowns jumped me. They thought they could hold Edgar for ransom."

"You needed to fire your weapon at birdnappers?"

"It was a warning shot. There were three of them."

"So? I turned the tables on Miriam's boys, and there were three of them."

"Your guys were shorter."

"*I'm* shorter."

"What can I say? I have a bad habit of getting jammed up."

"How'd you get out of there without being seen?"

Jake didn't feel like telling Maria about Jasmine. "Sometimes I'm as lucky as I am unlucky."

"I've read transcripts of your interviews with Geoghegan. You're good at being evasive."

"I have a strong sense of self-preservation." He pulled into the motel parking lot. "I assume you're staying within view of my room?"

"You know it."

"It's not smart to stay at the same location as your stakeout subject, you know."

"It's not like I have backup. It isn't easy watching someone 24/7."

"I could have seen you."

"You saw me plenty of times. I guess I never made much of an impression on you before."

"I never saw your legs or that tan before, and eyes are a person's most identifiable feature." He parked, switched off the ignition, and faced her. "Do you want to have dinner?"

"Sure, why not? We've still got plenty to discuss. As long as it's on you. I'm tapped out, and I've already charged more than I can afford."

Jake didn't want to answer any more questions, but he saw no point in avoiding Maria since they were going to be traveling together anyway. "Just don't expect anything fancy. We have to go somewhere with a patio, so I can bring Edgar."

"I approve of your chaperone."

They got out at the same time, and Jake took Edgar out of the backseat. "How about we meet down here in an hour?"

"Make it an hour and a half. I want to shower."

Jake showered too and shaved. Then he picked up his phone and struck a number in his contacts. The phone on the other end rang two and a half times.

"Hello?" The boy's voice was so much deeper than it had been the last time they had seen each other.

"Hey, Martin."

At the mention of Martin's name, Edgar hopped around in his cage.

That's a good sign, Jake thought. Sheryl had told him Edgar was losing a little more of his humanity each day.

"Jake! Do you have any news?"

Jake felt a weight on his shoulders whenever Martin asked him that question. "I don't want to get your hopes up, but I think I'm onto something."

"You serious?"

Jake heard the restrained excitement in the boy's voice. "I'm serious that it may be nothing. I won't know for another week or so. I wouldn't even tell you this, except I'm going to be incommunicado at least that long, and I don't want you to worry."

"Okay."

"You listening to your mother?"

"Yes."

"Tell her I said hello, and keep your fingers crossed."

Maria stepped out of the shower and toweled herself dry. She blow-dried her hair, put on a bra and panties, then picked up her phone and touched a number.

"Speak of the *diabla*," Bernie Reinhardt said in his customary monotone. "I was just thinking of you. How goes the Sunshine State? Do you look like Malibu Barbie yet?"

"I could star in a Coppertone commercial," Maria said.

"When are you coming home? I get lonely poking at these stiffs without you. I keep catching myself talking to them."

Maria lathered cream on her legs. "Maybe another week."

"That's a long time. What gives?"

She drew a disposable razor along one leg. "I followed Jake to a meeting in a nightclub. One thing led to another, and I ended up walking three hombres into the meeting at gunpoint."

"Apparently you lived to tell the tale."

"Jake and I are flying to Pavot Island. Before you ask,

that's in the Caribbean."

"Please tell me you aren't eloping. It will break your mother's heart."

"I'm almost thirty. My mother wants grandkids."

"Your mother's already got a dozen grandkids."

"Four."

"What's on Pavot Island?"

"A dictator, a prison, and hopefully some answers."

"And Helman."

"Don't worry about Jake. I can handle him."

"That's what I'm worried about: keep your hands off him. I don't care if he's Genghis Khan or just misunderstood. He's trouble from the first bite to the last."

"We've had this conversation before. I don't care about Jake. I want to find out what happened to Edgar."

"And you expect to find the key to that particular mystery on Pavot Island?"

Maria considered the question as she shaved her other leg. "I expect to find the answer or accept there is no answer and move on."

"You always know the right thing to say to me. When do you leave?"

"In the morning. I'll be out of reach. Cell phones are contraband over there."

"Good luck, partner."

"Thanks. I really hope to see you again soon." Maria shut her phone down.

SEVEN

Jake leaned against the car door, dressed in jeans and a black V-neck T-shirt, with Edgar parked in the backseat and the engine running for air-conditioning.

He heard a door open and close on the upper level and almost failed to recognize Maria when she approached. She wore a green summer dress that left her arms and legs exposed and matching strap-on sandals with heels. Her curly hair hung loose around her shoulders, lighter than he remembered it thanks to the sun, and she wore makeup. The last time he had seen her looking so attractive was on the night he had dinner with Edgar and Katrina, and Edgar had surprised him by inviting Maria as his date.

Maria stood before him with an expectant look on her face, the dry breeze blowing her hair. "Is something wrong?"

"Hm? No, I was just thinking about tomorrow." He

opened the passenger door for her and studied her legs as she sat down and hissed at the hot upholstery. Closing the door, he walked around the car and got in beside her. "The front desk clerk recommended a place not far from here."

"Thank God," she said as he pulled into the street. "I was sick of eating fast food while you checked out every Cajun joint in New Orleans."

"Stakeout's a bitch."

"I didn't see you jogging every morning like you do in NYC."

She's almost as bad as Laurel, Jake thought. Laurel Doniger, a psychic healer, occupied the storefront in Jake's building. Every time she touched Jake—sometimes intimately—she learned everything there was to know about him. "I was on a tight schedule. My budget for this operation is far from unlimited."

Maria fiddled with the radio until salsa music replaced Jake's rock. "You do all right for yourself as a PI, though, right?"

"Yeah, I do okay." *When my clients live to pay me.*

Ten minutes later, they sat on the patio of a restaurant facing the Atlantic. Seagulls hovered in the breeze, rising and falling like kites as the sunlight faded, and sailboats traveled the waves. Jake held birdseed out to Edgar, who pecked at the food from within the cage on the tabletop.

"Do you always dote on him like that?"

"When I can. When I can't, my assistant does. When she can't, a neighbor does."

"That psychic lady downstairs from your office?"

Damn. Jake would never grow accustomed to people

knowing so much information about him. "Sometimes."

"You doing her?"

Sometimes, Jake felt like answering again, though the truth was, *not anymore.* Other than a couple of interludes with Laurel and the one with Jasmine, he had been celibate since Sheryl's murder. "No."

A young woman with tanned skin and long dark hair stopped at their table. She wore a belly shirt and denim shorts. "I'm Maribel. Can I get you anything to drink?"

"I'll have a margarita with salt," Maria said.

"Just water," Jake said.

"He'll have a beer."

The waitress looked at Jake with raised eyebrows.

"Make it a Corona Light," he said.

"I'll be right back."

When Maribel had left, Jake said, "Are you trying to corrupt me? You know I don't drink."

"Edgar told me you're no alcoholic."

"No, I'm not. But drinking can lead me to worse habits."

"Coke, right?"

He nodded.

"How'd you fall into that trap?"

"I didn't realize an interrogation was on the menu tonight."

"Like it or not, we're going to be partners for the next week. I want to know more about your character."

Jake drummed his fingers on the tabletop. "Homicide was more complicated than I realized. A few cases gave me nightmares, so I started drinking more. Then I found that wasn't stopping the nightmares, so I tried something stronger."

"How long?"

"Six or seven months. Then I killed those skells in the bar." Kevin Creed and Oscar Soot: *Dread and Baldy*.

"And you resigned so you wouldn't have to take the drug test?"

"It seems to be pretty common knowledge in the department."

"You miss getting high?"

Pursing his lips, Jake shook his head. "I've been through so much since then. I know booze and drugs could never dull the pain." He did miss Sheryl; too bad she had run off with an angel.

Maribel returned with their drinks and set them down. "Are you ready to order?"

"I'll have the scampi," Maria said.

"Same here," Jake said.

Maribel collected their menus and disappeared inside.

Jake studied the sweating bottle of beer and squeezed it. Since defeating Old Nick in the Tower and defying Cain, he'd hardly thought of alcohol, let alone cocaine. But he'd carried a small part of Sheryl's soul inside him, and he never knew if her energy kept his demons at bay or cleansed him. She had reclaimed that part of herself, and now he was on his own.

"Don't drink it if you don't want to. I just thought, who knows what's going to happen over there? Enjoy a cold one. But if you're worried you can't stop after one . . ."

"I can stop." He raised the bottle to his lips and allowed the cold beer to wash over his tongue, which curled with pleasure, and down his throat. He put the bottle down with a satisfied sigh.

"I know how you felt. I thought Homicide would be glamorous by NYPD standards." Maria sipped her margarita.

"Do you have nightmares?"

She looked him in the eye. "Only since you dropped sixty zombies on my doorstep."

"*Zonbies,* with an *n.* I dropped a lot more than sixty. Edgar and I wiped out a factory full of them in the Bronx, probably a hundred in all. That puts my total at over a hundred." He resumed drinking.

"Why didn't Edgar tell me?"

"He wanted to protect you. Not just from the danger but from the knowledge."

"I might have been able to help."

"Or you might have been killed. Or Edgar could have been killed and you'd be in that cage right now. It doesn't do any good to look back and wonder."

"You really took those sixty *zonbies* out by yourself?"

"All by my lonesome." The beer tasted so good going down he wanted to moan.

"How'd you manage it?"

"Katrina and Malachai had my back against the wall, and Katrina had already transformed Edgar. Desperate times, desperate measures."

"You shot them all in the head."

"It's the only way to stop them, other than blowing them to pieces. Their brains act as receivers so they can receive telepathic commands from their bokor. Drain their liquefied brains, break off that communication, and free their souls."

"Souls?"

Staring at the golden cross around Maria's neck, Jake hesitated. He had let his guard down and said too much. "Figuratively speaking."

"You're an atheist, right?"

"Not anymore." He finished his beer.

"You ever killed a living person besides those two skells?"

The Cipher. An assassin named Ashby Morton who worked for White River Security. Weiskopf from the Order of Avademe. And in collaboration with a genetically engineered monster, Old Nick himself. He never counted Kira Thorn, who had been one of Tower's Biogens.

Jake picked up the bottle. "It will take a lot more than one beer to get me to confess my deepest, darkest secrets. I've offered coffee to suspects to give them oral diarrhea, but this is a new one."

Maria held his gaze. "I'm sorry. Really, I am. I shouldn't have done that."

"It's okay. I knew what you were up to."

"I just feel so desperate. My life's been turned upside down since I met you."

Jake smiled. "That makes me feel better."

"Are we being straight with each other?"

"As much as we can under the circumstances."

"Do you trust Miriam?"

"I see no reason to *dis*trust her. Her motives are pretty clear."

"We're going into a country where the US doesn't even have an embassy. One wrong move and we could disappear forever."

"That's why I tried to talk you out of going, remember?"

"But you're still going, right?"

He didn't have to answer her.

The sun had set by the time Jake parked at the motel, the night sky still bright with orange-hued clouds. Maria bopped her head to the Latin beat on the radio until Jake killed the engine.

Maria stared straight ahead. "Do you have a will?"

"Yeah. I don't have much money, but it goes to Martin if anything happens to me."

She looked at him. "That's sweet."

"How about you?"

"I had one drawn up when I joined the academy. Everything I have will go to my sister's kids. Funny, a couple of legal guns like us leaving what we have to other people's kids. Do you remember Papa Joe?"

"Sure." Joe had been the narcotics kingpin of Manhattan until Katrina's zonbies hacked him to pieces with machetes. "He had a longer run than most in his business."

"He left a fortune to his little girl. Guy was a major league wrong number: killed people, had people killed, poisoned lives. But somehow, with all that blood and ugliness, he created something beautiful, someone of his own to remember him. You and I don't have that."

"Neither one of us is exactly over the hill. It's not too late."

"I know Joe's little girl. Her name is Shana. She just turned seven. I handed her over to BCW after Joe was murdered. She saw him hacked to pieces. Zonbies, right? Poor thing was traumatized. Who can blame her? Now she lives with Joe's sister in Queens—Prince Malachai's mother. The woman's a monster, no surprise. She only took Shana in to get her hands on Joe's money. I tried to mentor Shana. Be a big sister and shit. But the aunt's her guardian and won't let me near her. She's too worried she might lose that money with a cop around."

Jake had no trouble imagining Alice Morton's greed. He had met her while impersonating a police detective in an effort to locate Malachai. "At least the girl's alive."

"But what kind of life does she have? Joe's woman led a somewhat normal life. She knew what Joe was and took his money, but she lived in a humble house and stayed out of trouble. This woman is a dragon. Her whole life is the business. Shana's doomed."

"We can't save everyone. We can only try and you tried."

Maria dabbed at one eye. "It's getting late. I want a good night's sleep before we storm the beaches. Starting tomorrow, we're both going to have to sleep with one eye open."

"Bad news for me."

Maria snorted. "I'll see you in the morning."

They got out, and as Jake retrieved Edgar's cage he watched Maria mount the stairs to the second level.

Inside his room, Jake set Edgar's cage on the bed. He opened the cage door, and Edgar fluttered out and onto the covers. "Fly. Be free."

He peeled off his shirt and tossed his watch onto the dresser. Picking up the remote control, he turned on the television. "Let's see what's on the news." He flipped through the channels until he landed on his least favorite station, then tossed the remote onto the bed. "Maybe we can learn what the weather's going to be on Pavot Island tomorrow."

Edgar squawked at a knock on the door.

"Sorry, bud. Back in the cage."

Edgar croaked in protest.

"I'm not kidding. Get in there."

Edgar hopped inside the cage, and Jake latched its door. He pulled on his shirt again and crossed the room. When he opened the door, Maria stood looking at him.

"What's up?" he said.

Maria stepped inside, reached around his neck, and kissed him.

Jake felt heat rising through his body and closed the door.

EIGHT

Jake returned Maria's kiss, pressing his tongue against hers. She slid her fingers through the hair on the back of his head, and he felt her breathing through her nostrils.

When she ended the kiss, she looked up at him. "I guess we're finally having that date you welshed on last year."

"Life got in the way: bokors, zonbies, transmogrification—"

"Shut up."

She kissed him again, and he felt her breasts and pelvis against him. Growing hard, he pulled her tighter to him.

Maria pushed him back, a playful smile on her lips and excitement in her eyes. "Are we going to make out in your doorway like kids all night?"

Jake gestured at the bed. Maria shook her head and pressed her back against the corner. Jake moved forward, his tight smile matching hers. He scooped her up in his arms, carried her across the room, and tossed her onto the bed, causing Edgar to squawk. They both burst into laughter.

"Please put him somewhere safe," Maria said.

Jake grabbed the cage. "Come on. You're staying in the porcelain suite tonight."

As he carried Edgar into the bathroom and set the cage on the tiled floor, Maria said, "Good night, partner."

Jake returned to the room in time to see Maria's green dress slip from her body and fall to her feet. As he peeled off his shirt for the second time, he admired her taut stomach muscles. Then she unhooked her bra, and he gazed at her firm, round breasts. She hooked her thumbs into the waistband of her panties and slid them off one hip at a time, then stepped out of the small pile of clothing on the floor. She had trimmed the triangle of dark hair between her legs.

"What are you waiting for?" she said.

Jake unbuckled his belt and unsnapped his jeans, which he shed with awkward motion. He freed his erection from his underwear, and Maria looked down, smiling. Jake kissed her, the head of his penis probing her moist vagina. A low moan escaped her throat, and he inhaled the scent of her perfume. He gripped her buttocks, his fingers pressing her hard muscles.

Pulling herself on top of him with her knees squeezing his sides, she lowered herself onto his erection, and her moan grew louder. Jake felt hot membrane engulfing him, and he set one knee on the bed and lowered her onto her back. Then he penetrated her heat, and she arched her back and welcomed him.

He looked into her eyes, and she continued to smile, though his thrusts caused her to open her mouth wider and emit soft whimpers.

"I've wanted you inside me for so long," Maria said. "You better not turn out to be a prick."

Laughing, he thrust harder.

"I swear to God I'll kick your ass if you turn out to be a shit."

Jake covered her mouth and she bit his flesh. When he jerked his hand back, it was her turn to laugh.

Her breath came out in rasps faster and louder, and he felt himself building to a climax.

"I don't have anything," he said. No need to tell her he had used his only condoms on Jasmine.

Craning her neck, she glanced at her purse, which she had left on the bedside stand. With sweat forming on her features, she reached for it and retrieved three condoms adjoined to each other. The purse fell on the floor.

Jake grabbed the condoms from her, tore one foil pack open, and prepared to withdraw himself.

"Don't stop," she said, almost squealing. "Please don't stop!"

Biting his lower lip, he pounded into her. Tears formed in her eyes, which widened with ecstasy. Jake clawed at the sheets, fighting the urge to come, and Maria rocked her hips against him and cried out. Feeling her hot fluid cascading over him, Jake grimaced with effort, pulled out, and fumbled with the condom. Maria continued to come, which only excited him more.

Pushing himself inside her again, he leaned close to her

face and grabbed her hair. She threw her head from side to side, small gasps escaping her lips as he rode her. When he could hold back no longer he groaned, and she pressed herself against him harder in a grinding motion. They came at the same time, and he collapsed panting beside her.

Maria drew one hand across Jake's sweaty chest. "That was great. It was also just a warm-up. If we die in an attempted prison break, I want to go to my grave knowing we gave it our all. Unrequited lust is for the birds."

They took turns washing up in the bathroom, and Jake heard Maria speaking softly to Edgar. He lowered the lights, and she turned on the radio, found a Latin beat, and raised the volume. She climbed on top of him and they kissed, and then she worked her way down the length of his body, taking him inside her mouth.

Staring at the ceiling for the first time, Jake stifled a laugh: the room had come equipped with a ceiling mirror. Maria licked him to full mast, and he found himself thinking of Laurel but not out of lust. He remembered how she had used her psychic ability to meet his every physical need, a power so fulfilling he doubted its existence. The next morning, Laurel told him he had feelings for another woman: Maria.

Now Maria stroked him with one hand and worked him over with her tongue, not fulfilling his desires but challenging them. She crawled back up and straddled him, pulling his erect penis inside her. As she ground against him, Jake slid his hands over her stomach and cupped her breasts, and Maria seized his wrists.

She looked over her shoulder from time to time to where Jake knew she saw her reflection in the dresser mirror, and when she returned her attention to him he noticed a thrill in her eyes. Arching her back, she gazed at their reflections in the ceiling mirror and let loose the laughter Jake had suppressed.

Then she pinned his wrists to the bed and leaned forward, her hair whispering over his face. "You're under arrest."

Jake didn't know if she was giving into a sexual fantasy or if she just fantasized about arresting him, but he managed to thrust deeper into her. Maria grunted in time with the music on the radio with a slight snarl on her lips. He tried to free his arms, but she forced them back down. Her hips slammed against him, and he feared she would do him damage. He saw an amused look in her eyes, as if belittling him.

Almost two years earlier, Kira Thorn had transformed into a spider creature and had straddled him in a bed this same size, and he had overpowered her even though she had eight limbs. He wasn't about to let Maria get the best of him now. With his heel planted on the mattress, he rolled her onto her back, reversing their positions, and held her wrists down as she had his. He maintained a steady rhythm, gradually moving faster, harder, and she wrapped her legs around his back. By the time she came, he experienced a tremor of pleasure followed by an explosive finish that left him gasping.

They lay side by side, regaining their breath, their bodies glistening with sweat despite the steady flow of air-conditioning. They took separate showers and crawled back into bed.

Maria traced the scars on Jake's face. "Are you going to tell me how you got these?"

"Another time." Maria may have accepted the existence of zonbies due to overwhelming evidence and had come around to accepting Edgar had been transformed into a raven, but he doubted she was ready to learn about the mutant octopus god Avademe and its amphibious children.

"That's assuming we have more time."

"Don't be so fatalistic. We'll be fine."

"You really think so? We're breaking a political prisoner out of a jail called El Miedo on some Caribbean rock. We don't even know the people we're depending on for backup, and we could be facing an army."

"We'll know when we get there if this thing is doable or not. If it isn't, we come home."

"And then what about Edgar? And Joyce and Martin?"

Jake sighed. "Then we'll try to convince Miriam to help us."

Maria rested her head on Jake's shoulder, and they slept.

Around 2:00 a.m., Jake opened his eye. Moonlight shone through the slats of the blinds. Maria stroked his penis and slid his hand between her legs, where he rubbed her wet spot. She spread her legs wide, and he knelt on his knees, then rolled her on her stomach. Looking over her shoulder at him, Maria raised her buttocks into the air, and he slid inside her once more. With one hand, she spread her cheeks apart, and Jake slammed into her. This time he felt in total control, and he waited until she had come twice before releasing himself. When he dropped beside her, a deep sleep took him.

Jake awoke with sunlight on his face. The space beside him on the bed was empty. "Maria?"

He got up and walked to the bathroom, where Edgar remained in his cage.

Shit. "I guess it's just you and me, pal."

Edgar squawked.

Jake showered and dressed, then washed his glass eye with cleaning solution. At least Maria had spared herself from witnessing that morning ritual. Standing at the bathroom sink, he inserted the eye into his empty socket and appeared whole again.

With his bag on one shoulder, Edgar's cage in one hand and the suitcase in the other, he exited the room. The bright sunlight made him wince, and morning heat beat down on him as he crossed the lot to the motel office.

Maria sat on the curb, two bags beside her. Smoke curled from the end of a cigarette between her fingers.

"I didn't know you smoked," Jake said.

"I quit a long time ago. Some bad habits keep coming back." She took a drag and exhaled. "Like you, I can have one without getting into trouble."

"You didn't say good-bye this morning."

"You were asleep. Did I hurt your feelings?"

Okay . . . "No."

"I had to go to the post office. I mailed the memory card from my camera with the footage of you and Miriam talking along with a note to my partner."

Bernie Reinhardt, Jake thought. A bit of a sad sack.

"If neither one of us comes home, I want my people to know what happened to me."

He couldn't blame her. "I'll be right back."

Leaving his suitcase at the curb, Jake carried Edgar into the office and checked out. When he returned, a white SUV idled in the lot, and Fernando loaded Maria's bags into its hatchback. A second SUV, this one silver, idled behind the first one. Jake threw his suitcase into the white SUV and carried Edgar over to the silver one. The tinted backseat window lowered, revealing Miriam. Maria joined Jake at the vehicle.

"Here are your itineraries." Miriam handed a packet to each of them. "Fernando will take you to the airport."

Jake rested the birdcage atop the SUV door. "What will you do with Edgar if neither one of us makes it back?"

"If my husband reaches Miami because of your efforts and you don't, I'll honor our deal. If Andre remains in El Miedo or worse, then your friend will remain as he is."

"In that case, I have a request." Jake handed her a business card. "If we fail, I want you to arrange for Edgar to be transported to this address."

Miriam read the handwritten address on the back of the card. "His family?"

Jake nodded. "They don't have a clue. The son has seen him before. Tell them his name is Buddy."

Miriam deposited the card in her purse.

Jake passed the shoulder bag through the window. "These are his clothes. There's birdseed in there, too. I give him cooked meat once a day. Send my laptop and my gun to my office if necessary." He stuck his fingers inside the cage and stared at the raven. "I guess this is it, partner." He felt himself choking up. "Hopefully we'll see each other again soon."

Edgar croaked.

Maria pressed her palm against the cage, and Edgar pecked at it. "Adios, amigo."

Jake slid the cage sideways through the window, and Miriam set it beside her.

"Bring my husband to me," Miriam said as the window slid up.

Jake and Maria got into the back of the white SUV.

Fernando drove forward. "Your flight departs in two and a half hours. Two and a half hours after that, you'll be on Pavot Island. We've rented a car for you. It's unlikely Malvado's police would bug the car just because you're foreigners, but don't rule out that possibility. The same applies to your resort, which is about half an hour from the airport. We got you a suite with separate bedrooms."

During the drive to Miami International Airport, Maria sat in silence while Jake questioned Fernando about their destination.

Outside the airport, Fernando unloaded their bags and shook their hands. "Senor. Senorita. Good luck."

"*Gracias*," Maria said.

Maria remained silent as they checked in and went through security.

"I'm starving," Jake said. "How about some overpriced

coffee and breakfast before we take off?"

"Whatever you say."

They located a restaurant and ordered bagels and coffee, which they both took black. Maria said nothing as they ate.

"Did I do something wrong?" Jake said between mouthfuls.

"No."

"Because I thought we had a pretty good night. Isn't that what you wanted?"

"It's what I wanted last night. Today we're serving together overseas. I don't want any emotions getting in the way."

"That's fine, but we can still talk to each other. We're not just fellow soldiers. We're partners and partners need to communicate. It's an essential survival mechanism."

"You're right. I'm sorry. I'll try not to be such a bitch."

Jake smiled. "Thank you."

They boarded a narrow jet, and Jake noted stained seat cushions and old-fashioned seat belts. The aircraft took off only half full, and fifteen minutes later, he noticed Maria reading a dog-eared paperback. *Erika Long* appeared above the title *Stormy Sands*, and a man with long brown hair and a cocky expression stood behind a woman whose apparent fear masked her repressed desires, a pirate vessel floating in a cove behind them.

Maria turned to him. "What?"

"I never figured you for a romance reader."

"Because I'm a cop? I read anything that's in print. The *Times*, the *Post*, the *Enquirer,* best sellers, cheap paperbacks. This one happens to be a classic of its genre."

"You don't say?" Jake held one hand out. "May I?"

With a look of irritation, Maria handed the paperback to Jake, who flipped through the pages, which featured standard-sized text and denser paragraphs than he expected. When he reached the inside back cover he almost dropped the book.

About the Author

New York Times and *USA Today* best-selling author Erika Long is the creator of over 20 romance novels, including the High Seas trilogy and the award-winning *Love Runs Deep*. Erika is the winner of multiple literary awards, including eight from the Romance Writers of America, for which she served two terms as president, and two from *Romantic Times*. Erika grew up on Long Island, New York, graduated with honors from Vassar, and worked as an assistant editor at Random House before selling her first novel to Lilian Kane's Eternity Books. She enjoys sailing, skydiving, and horseback riding.

The book shook in Jake's trembling fingers. It wasn't the author's name or biography that upset him but her photo. Short black hair, bright eyes framed by thick-rimmed glasses, and sensual lips. She resembled a repressed librarian and a sexual creature at the same time. Jake recognized her features despite the radical change in her appearance. He knew Erika Long by an entirely different name: *Laurel Doniger.*

"What's wrong?" Maria said.

Jake's fingers turned numb. *This has to be more than a coincidence.* "Oh, nothing. I just thought I recognized this author."

"She was pretty famous before she disappeared three years ago. The tabloids said she couldn't handle success, so she pulled a vanishing act. With the money she made off these books, she never has to work again."

Jake skimmed the biography again. "Lilian Kane I've heard of."

"Well, duh. She's the queen of romance writers. Everyone's heard of her, even if they haven't read her. They make TV movies out of her stuff all the time."

Jake handed the book back to Maria. He had always been curious about Laurel's mysterious past and knew she used an alias. She had told him on several occasions she used her psychic abilities to help people atone for past misdeeds, but she refused to divulge any more information to Jake even though he had expressed his desire to help her.

Sailing, skydiving, and horseback riding. The woman he knew had skin as pale as moonlight because she was afraid to leave her storefront, where she also lived. Laurel had used healing spells on Jake when he had suffered supernatural injuries and inflictions, and he knew she had created a blind spot around her dwelling that rendered herself and any memory Jake had of her invisible to the angels and demons Jake had encountered. This meant she feared a powerful enemy.

Now Jake knew her true identity, but he was bound for Pavot Island on an impossible mission with Maria. Laurel's predicament would have to wait until his return to New York City . . . *if* he returned.

NINE

Through the aircraft's window, Jake observed the plane's shadow on the surface of the Atlantic Ocean below. It could just as easily have belonged to a bird. The plane flew at a low altitude, and the water reflected dazzling sunlight at him. He made a mental note to research Erika Long when he had the chance, taking precaution not to arouse Maria's interest.

The captain's voice came over the loudspeakers. "Ladies and gentlemen, we're nearing our destination. Please fasten your seat belts. The temperature on Pavot Island is 105 degrees."

Within minutes, land appeared directly below them: cliffs surrounded by a seaport, then dense green trees, and finally a landing strip. The plane touched down on the bumpy runway, pitching everyone forward, and Maria gripped Jake's hand. When the shaking stopped and the plane slowed, Maria released her grip on Jake and acted as if she hadn't just sought his comfort. Jake decided it was best to roll with her needs for the rest of the trip.

The passengers deplaned down a covered mobile stairway and crossed the tarmac in blazing heat. Jake was grateful for his cargo shorts and couldn't help admiring Maria in hers. They entered a crowded terminal with high ceilings and no air-conditioning, which felt just as hot as outside. Maria grabbed several brochures from a travel agency kiosk and used them to fan herself. Most of the people Jake saw had brown or black skin.

He and Maria retrieved their luggage from a beaten old conveyor belt in the baggage claim and joined the line for customs inspection, where three men and a woman dressed in khaki military uniforms examined passports.

"Why do you come to Pavot Island, Mr. Helman?" a man with heavy eyelids and a thick accent said. Jake couldn't place the accent, though he recognized traces of French and Haitian.

"We're on vacation," Jake said.

"Why do you come *here*?"

Just looking at the man's sweaty features caused Jake to perspire. "It's more affordable than other island resorts, and we were curious."

The man gave Jake an insincere smile. "What do you do for a living?"

"Security."

"Overseas security?"

"No, domestic. I mean, in the US. New York City."

The man turned his attention to Maria. "And you, Miss Vasquez?"

"I'm a cop," Maria said.

"Oh, really? What is your specialty?"

"Homicide."

"No," the man said in disbelief. "You're so young and pretty."

"Thank you," Maria said with no trace of emotion.

The man turned to his right. "A'idah!"

The female officer came over, and the man nodded at Maria.

"This way, please," the woman said to Maria, who glanced at Jake with alarm in her eyes.

"What's going on?" Jake said.

"Just a routine inspection," the man said. "It won't take long."

With her hand on Maria's bicep, A'idah guided her toward a metal door painted yellow to match the cinder-block wall.

Jake felt his face turning hot. "Hey, wait a minute. Where are you taking her?"

"It's okay," Maria said without conviction.

The man gestured to a row of chairs bolted to the floor. "Have a seat."

Frowning, Jake waited until A'idah closed the door behind herself and Maria before sitting.

Maria stood facing a wooden examination table. A cloth partition separated her from the door.

"Take off your clothes," A'idah said.

Maria stared at the woman. "You're joking, right?"

"This isn't America. Take off your clothes now."

Glaring at the woman, Maria stripped down to her bra and panties.

"All of them," A'idah said.

Without protest, Maria removed her bra and panties and stood naked before the woman.

A moment later, she heard the door open and close behind her. The man who had summoned A'idah stepped around the curtain and appraised her. He held Maria's passport.

Maria turned to face him, giving him a full view.

"What is your ethnicity?" the man said.

"I'm Puerto Rican," Maria said.

"Were you born in Puerto Rico?"

"No, I was born in St. Vincent's Hospital in New York City. I'm a true-blue US citizen."

"You say that as if it should impress me." He looked over her body. "I'm not impressed."

"May I go now? I'm not used to being treated this way when I'm on vacation."

The man stared at her for a moment, then nodded. He slapped her passport in his open palm, then turned and walked out.

"What happened in there?" Jake said to Maria as they searched for the car rental agency.

"Just a little show-and-tell."

"Are you all right?"

"Sure. I wouldn't give them the satisfaction of

humiliating me. But if I ever see that pig in Manhattan, he's all mine."

"You've got to be kidding me," Jake said, looking at a dented pea-green Ford Fiesta. The small car appeared to have been in several accidents while receiving only the most necessary repairs.

"It's not that bad," Maria said, sliding on sunglasses.

"You're used to driving a Toyota." Jake slid behind the wheel, and Maria got in beside him. The low ceiling caused him to breathe faster. He started the engine. "You got the directions?"

"And the map."

They drove away from the airport and followed a road that wound its way up a steep hill covered with palm trees. The bright sunlight made everything seem greener.

"It's just like PR and Jamaica." Maria pressed her hand against the air-conditioning vents, then fiddled with the control. "There's hot air coming out of these vents."

"Great." Jake lowered the windows, allowing outside air in.

The Fiesta descended the other side of the hill, and they saw a sign ahead: Une station de vacance, Mt. Pleasant. Maria read the phrase aloud in French, then translated it. "Pleasant Mountain Resort or Mount Pleasant Resort."

Jake followed the side road onto the resort grounds, and they found themselves dipping and climbing several small hills along a mountain facing the ocean. They reached a single-story building with a sign that read Enregistrement.

"That's what we want," Maria said.

Jake parked the car in the building's shadow, and they got out.

"It's nice to see a blue ocean again after the Gulf," Maria said, raising her shades to gaze between the palm trees.

As they went up an incline to the entrance, dozens of geckos darted across the walk. Cool air greeted them in the registration lobby.

"Our first air-conditioning on Pavot Island," Jake said.

They presented their IDs to a man behind the desk, who smiled and bowed to them. He swiped Jake's credit card, and Jake signed the paperwork.

"Did you come on the shuttle?" the man said. "I'll call the bellman to take you to your suite."

"No, we drove," Jake said.

"Just follow the road out front up the hill. Yours is the second complex you'll pass."

"Thanks."

They located the C complex and parked in the gravel driveway, then circled the building until they located the door marked C-6, which Jake unlocked with a standard key. "None of that unnecessary electronic security for this island," he said.

They entered a wide living room with a kitchen that overlooked it. Jake pulled the chain on the ceiling fan, and Maria went straight for the air conditioner, which made a clanging sound but delivered cool air.

"Which room do you want?" Jake said.

"Let me see." Maria entered one room and drew the

curtains, admitting sunlight. "You take this one. It leads to the patio."

Jake joined her at the sliding glass door. "You don't want to be near the patio?"

Maria opened the door and stepped outside onto the wooden plank patio. "*Hell*, no. This is the first break in defensive security."

Jake followed her to the railing. The complex had been built into the side of the mountain, facing the ocean. Looking down, he saw a swimming pool and a deck thirty feet below. A dozen men and women tanned on reclining pool furniture on the deck, and another dozen frolicked in the water as live calypso music rose from beneath a covered bar. Perhaps sixty feet below to their left a white-sand beach beckoned. An iguana blinked at them from the limb of a nearby tree.

Jake fetched his bag from the living room and brought it into the bedroom, then carried Maria's into hers. "I bet there's food at that bar. What do you say we grab lunch, then go for a swim while we wait for the AC to do its job in here?"

"Sounds like a plan."

They wore T-shirts with their swimming suits and ate burgers and chips at the bar. A lone musician facing the pool played his guitar and sang into a microphone.

"It's like a vacation," Maria said.

Or a honeymoon, Jake thought. "A day of heaven before we visit hell."

Maria munched on a chip. "I'll take the day."

Sitting on a poolside cot, Jake slathered on sunscreen.

"You're glowing like the sand." Maria peeled off her T-shirt and tossed it onto the cot, revealing her blue bikini top.

Jake averted his eye to avoid getting excited.

They dove into the pool. The cool water relaxed Jake and cleansed the grime from his body. He treaded water near Maria, who moved backwards into a man-made waterfall. Jake followed her, closing the distance between them. When his face came close to hers, she swam out of the shade and into the sunlight.

Forty minutes later, they returned to their suite. The air conditioner chilled their wet bodies, and Jake watched goosebumps form on Maria's arms and legs as she braved the frigid temperature and shut the unit off.

They went into their separate bedrooms, and Jake peeled his trunks from his wrinkled, shrunken penis, toweled off, and pulled on his briefs. He didn't get any farther than that when Maria screamed.

Jake bolted out of his room, his wet feet slipping on the floor, and crashed on his left hip. Crying out in anger as much as pain, he got back to his feet and limped into Maria's room, where she stood frozen in one corner, her eyes bulging. A large white snake lay coiled in a perfect circle on the bed, the blanket disheveled where Maria had drawn it back. The snake's head turned from Maria to Jake, blinking. Jake had never seen an albino snake before.

"Stay right there." He gestured with both hands.

"I'm not moving!"

Jake ran into the living room, snatched the phone, and carried it to where Maria could see him. He called the front desk and waited.

"How can I help you?" a woman said.

"There's a giant white snake in my bed! Send somebody over here to kill it now!"

"I'll send a bellman directly, sir."

"Thank you." He slammed the phone down and sprinted into the bedroom just in time to see the end of the snake's tail disappear over the edge of the bed.

Maria stood paralyzed.

"Jump on the bed!" Jake said.

Maria leapt onto the bed and then leapt off, throwing her arms and legs around Jake, who cried out a second time as her momentum drove him through the doorway and onto the floor.

Maria sprang to her feet and helped him up, then she shoved him toward her room. "Close that door!"

After following her instructions, Jake heard a knock on the front door. "Just a minute!" He put on his shorts and answered the door. A short Hispanic man in a white linen uniform stood there holding a long pole with a claw on one end and a squeeze handle on the other. His nametag identified him as Cabey.

"Where's the snake?" Cabey said.

"In the bedroom on the right."

"How big?"

"Maybe two inches in diameter. I don't know how long."

Cabey marched into the living room and nodded to Maria, who clutched a long-handled mop like a baseball bat. Jake eased the mop handle away from the ceiling fan.

Cabey opened the bedroom door, his movements slow and tense.

"It's under the bed," Maria said in a high-pitched voice.

Cabey got down on his hands and knees and pulled back the cover hiding the space between the bed and the floor. Then he peered under the bed. His scream caused Jake to flinch and Maria to scream, too.

Cabey backpedaled out of the bedroom. "Un serpent de fantôme! Un serpent de fantôme!"

"What's he saying?" Jake said.

"A ghost snake," Maria said.

"Oh, for Christ's sake." Jake took the mop handle from Maria and strode past Cabey.

"Serpent fantôme! Serpent fantôme!"

Jake got down on his hands and knees as Cabey had done, only he held the mop handle like a lance, its tip poised before his face. With his free hand, he flung back the draped sheet.

The snake appeared even whiter in the darkness, almost glowing. It hissed at Jake, its forked tongue flicking out, then launched its fanged jaws at his face.

Jake recoiled, and the snake's jaws clamped down on

the mop handle. He seized it just behind its head, his fingers sinking into the scaly flesh. Then he dragged the pallid head forward, forcing the mop handle down the snake's throat. The serpent focused on Jake with reptilian malevolence.

Rising to his knees, Jake pulled the snake's head along the mop handle, forcing the wood deep inside its body. The snake gurgled, syrupy saliva drooling from its immobilized jaws. Jake continued to thread the creature's body along the handle. The front of the snake's body appeared rod straight, while the rest of it curled in the air. Each pull of Jake's hand brought the hate-filled eyes closer to his until the snake had been force-fed the entire mop handle and only eight inches of tail remained twitching.

Jake offered the snake shish kebab to Cabey.

He waved his hands. "No, senor! Serpiente dcl fantasma!"

"I thought you might say that." Jake noticed that Maria now held Cabey's grabber.

Stepping into his shoes, Jake carried the snake on a stick outside, threw it on the ground, and stomped its head into pulp. Its blood was red but its skull was white.

"All you have to do now is clean it up," Jake told Cabey when he went back inside.

TEN

They ate dinner at the resort's restaurant on the beach. Maria drank two margaritas, but Jake stuck with Diet Coke.

Walking up the steep driveway to their suite in the settling darkness, Jake pointed at the mop handle on the ground. "Someone took the snake."

"Why didn't they take the mop handle, too? Isn't it covered with guts or whatever snakes have inside them?"

Jake leaned forward. "I can't tell in the dark." But the handle appeared clean to him.

Maria looked around. Tree frogs chirped in the woods around them. She rubbed her arms. "Come on. Let's go inside."

Jake unlocked the door and turned on the lights. They had left the air-conditioning on and he lowered its output. Then he went into Maria's room and peeked under her bed and inside her closet.

"No ghost snakes," he said when he reentered the living room, but Maria had disappeared. Feeling a breeze coming from his room, he realized she had opened the glass door and stood smoking a cigarette on the patio, the full moon reflecting silver blades on the ocean's surface. He couldn't see her face, just her bare back above the black dress she wore.

"You look beautiful," he said when he joined her.

"You've now seen just about my entire wardrobe for this trip. I didn't pack to entertain."

Looking into her eyes, Jake saw the moon in them. "I thought you were cold."

"I didn't say that. I said I wanted to come inside."

Maria kissed him, and he tried not to show too much excitement when he responded. He knew she was riding a roller coaster.

She took a drag on her cigarette and exhaled smoke. "Who would have thought that we'd be together like this on some crazy island?"

"Not me." Although he had been attracted to her while mourning Sheryl, Jake thought he'd lost his opportunity with Maria after everything that had happened with Edgar and Katrina.

This time he kissed her. When they finished, she stepped back, pulled the straps of her dress over her shoulders, and wiggled out of the garment. She wore no bra or panties, and the gold cross between her breasts gleamed in the moonlight.

Jake took her in his arms and kissed her again, then spun her around so she faced the ocean. He unzipped his pants and dropped them around his ankles, then slid inside her. She pressed her palms against the railing and pushed against him. His hands settled on her hips, and he thrust into her wetness, her moans rising on the sea breeze. Somewhere in the darkness a seagull cawed, reminding Jake of Edgar.

Maria raised herself high in the air, removing him from her, and his penis stood naked and alone.

"Inside," she said, draping her arms around his neck. "You're not having this without a condom."

Jake swept her off her feet and carried her into his bedroom, where he set her on the bed. A pack of condoms lay on the bedside table.

"Why do you think I let you have the room with the patio?" Maria said. "I knew I'd end up in here."

He leaned close to her. "What happened to ignoring our feelings for the good of the mission?"

"Fuck it," she said, kissing him. "Fuck *me*."

He was happy to oblige.

In the morning, they ate fresh fruit from room service in their underwear.

"I'm not used to seeing you for breakfast," Jake said.

"Where am I going to go?"

"There is another bedroom."

"What, with the snakes?"

"You're a cop. You deal with vermin every day. You

mean to tell me you're afraid of a little snake?"

"Little?" She stood. "*Papi*, I've collared suspects smaller than that." She stepped out of her panties. "But what you did to that snake? I gotta say, you impressed me."

"Oh yeah?"

She straddled him in his chair. "Oh yeah."

They stood on a bluff overlooking immense green trees, the rain forest stretching before them.

With the Fiesta behind them, Maria raised the binoculars to her eyes. "According to the map, that hazy building in the distance must be Malvado's palace. El Miedo is too far away to see."

Jake took the binoculars from her and studied a three-story yellow structure gleaming in the afternoon sunlight. Terraces overlooked a fountain and a topiary garden. "You could get lost in that forest and wander around for days." He shifted his view to a dark gray building topped by spires. "That looks like a church."

"Someone's coming."

Lowering the binoculars, Jake saw a car approaching on the road below them. He tossed the binoculars through the open driver's side window onto the backseat. A moment later, he discerned a tan vehicle with strobes mounted on its roof.

"I didn't call 911, did you?" Maria said.

Jake slid his camera out of his pocket. "Go stand across

the street."

Maria crossed the street and faced him with one hip sticking out and a hand upon it. "How's this?"

Jake waved her to the left. "I can't see the palace."

She moved over.

He snapped a photo. "Perfect."

Maria returned to the Fiesta as the police car stopped next to them.

A short, dark-skinned Hispanic man with a thick mustache got out of the car and set a hat over his balding head. His short-sleeved shirt revealed slender arms, which he spread wide apart. "Bonjour. Buenas tardes."

"Good afternoon," Jake said.

"Ah. *Americanos.*" He tipped his hat to Maria.

"Si," Maria said. "Bon après-midi."

"A lovely day, is it not?"

Jake nodded. "Very."

"You are tourists?"

"Yes. We're staying at Mount Pleasant Resort."

"I have a cousin who works there. I see you are admiring our national rain forest."

"It's beautiful," Maria said. "It reminds me of El Yunque in Puerto Rico."

"Oh? I've never been there."

You've never left Pavot Island, Jake thought.

"But why do you observe our beauty from here on the roadside? We have very nice tours for our visitors."

Maria held up the brochures in her hand. "We were just on our way to see the Church of St. Anthony, but we had to

GREGORY LAMBERSON

pull over when we saw this view."

The policeman's gaze flitted to Maria's cross. "You are Catholic?"

"Si."

"St. Anthony's is the oldest church on Pavot Isle. The architecture is magnificent. May I?" He held out one hand, and Maria gave him the brochures, which he looked through. "I have a cousin who works at the Rabaud Rum Plantation. The tour is very nice, but I don't recommend driving there. They are too generous with their samples." He winked at Jake, then handed the brochures back to Maria. "And you will find much fine shopping in Pavot City, mademoiselle."

"Gracias."

The man turned to Jake. "I would like to offer you some advice, monsieur. Enjoy the resort. Enjoy our wonderful city and our attractions. But for your own safety, avoid isolated areas like this. I like to believe we have a good police force, but we have plenty of *voleurs*, and tourists are targets."

"Thank you. We'll be careful."

"Also, I recommend that you do your sightseeing during the day. Stay on the resort at night. I would regret it if anything happened to you."

"We will."

"Bonne journée."

"Au revoir," Maria said.

The man offered Maria a slight bow, then returned to his car and drove off.

"He was Hispanic," Maria said. "He understood

108

Spanish. But every time I spoke to him in Spanish, he answered in French."

"Did you see the tattoo on his arm?" Jake said.

"Yes. A black snake."

"Now we have to visit that church in case he checks up on us."

They visited St. Anthony's, then the rum factory. On a narrow highway flanked by palm trees, en route to Pavot City, Maria sampled the radio stations while Jake drove. Salsa music. Reggae. Calypso. French news. All of it sounded generic, as if produced and programmed by the same person.

"Jacek Maban is Malvado's Minister of Cultural Affairs," Miriam had told them. "No movie is shown, no program is broadcast, no concert is held, and no guitar is strung without his say-so. Nothing suggesting freedom of religion or democracy is ever absorbed by Pavot residents through legitimate means."

A city skyline appeared in the distance. Jake counted a dozen buildings at least ten stories tall and twice as many half that size. "It's bigger than I expected."

"But there's so little traffic going into the city. We've passed only three cars in the last twenty minutes, and according to the map, this is a major highway."

As they drew nearer, Jake noticed the buildings appeared gray. "They're mostly old buildings. I see just one that isn't made of concrete."

A single black tower reflected sunlight off its tinted windows.

"How much do you want to bet that's the capital?" Maria said.

"Or at least police headquarters."

Raindrops spattered the windshield, and Jake switched on the wipers. The rain came down harder, then stopped two minutes later and the sun shone again.

"Welcome to the Caribbean," Maria said. She rolled down her window and lit a cigarette.

Nerves, Jake thought.

"I wish I had my gun."

So did Jake.

Jake and Maria entered the city just after 6:00 p.m. Golden sunlight gleamed on an enormous billboard that showed a muscular black man dressed like a general in a royal-blue uniform. He was saluting, and a wide smile split his face. Three officers in khaki uniforms, rendered much smaller, saluted him from the lower left-hand corner. The style of the painting reminded Jake of US propaganda art during World War II. Behind the general, palm trees waved before a blue sky and a yellow sun. Bright red letters declared, *Bienvenue! Bienvenida! Welcome! Pavot Ville, Capitol d'Ile de Pavot.*

"Something tells me our friendly dictator doesn't smile like that in person," Jake said.

"Something tells me he isn't built like that, either."

Jake noted mostly small cars parked on the street and very little traffic. A police car passed them, then a jeep, then a taxi.

"There are a lot of bicyclists," Maria said.

"And pedestrians."

The buildings were spaced farther apart than Jake had thought at first glance, with small, single-story shops between them. He drove the length of the city in twenty minutes, then crossed over to a parallel avenue and drove back. Men of all ages drank beer outside the shops, children with serious expressions played on the sidewalks, and women in pairs pushed strollers and half-full shopping carts.

"Look at their faces," Maria said. "It's like the hood, only worse. Utter hopelessness." Chain-link fences topped by coils of razor wire surrounded buildings with curtained windows and balconies. "Most of these residential buildings are projects."

Jake didn't ask why she was so certain. On every street corner they passed the Pavot flag: a vertical red stripe over a black background. "What street are we looking for?"

"Rue de Verger."

He slowed down. "Ask for directions."

Maria called out to two black women carrying groceries, "Excuse me? *Por favor.*"

The women turned and Jake stopped the car.

"Do you speak English?"

The women shook their heads.

"How about Spanish?"

They shook their heads again.

"Nous cherchons le restaurant Coucher du Soleil dans la Rue de Verger."

Jake sighed. "What is that, *Frenglish*?"

"Let's see you do better. It's no stranger than what people around here speak. The Hispanics speak French, and the blacks speak Spanish."

The women conferred with each other, then one pointed ahead, held up two fingers, waved her hand like a swimming fish, then held up three fingers.

"Merci."

The women bowed their heads and resumed walking.

"What did they say?" Jake said.

"We're close. Two blocks up and three over on the left."

Jake followed the directions. Palm trees obscured many of the shops, and a police car passed a trio of emaciated men who looked like dead men walking.

"Scarecrows," Maria said.

Jake nodded. "They've almost turned. Where there's Magic, there's zonbies."

She looked at him. "How does it happen?"

"They OD on the shit. Literally, they die. When they revive, they're walking dead, with no minds of their own, completely controlled by their vodou master, like puppets."

"And the sawdust inside them?"

"Filler, like packing material. Each zonbie is essentially embalmed to preserve it as a working stiff for as long as possible and to cut down on the stench. Katrina had their toes, fingertips, and teeth removed to slow the identification process if any of her slaves were captured. I don't think that will be the case here, which means the Pavot Island zombies will move faster. If we encounter any, run for your life. Just remember, they won't get tired."

Maria shook her head. "I can't believe we're having this conversation."

"Considering our location, it's a good thing we are."

"There it is." Maria pointed at a restaurant with a dozen tables and chairs set up on the patio, with a low black metal railing around them. On the overhead sign, Coucher du Soleil was written in red letters over a simple yellow background.

Jake parked behind a red taxi, and they got out.

They hadn't even closed the doors when a scrawny little boy appeared from out of nowhere and ran over to Maria with his hands cupped together. "Money, please, missus?"

Maria regarded the boy with suspicion, then reached inside her purse.

Jake surveyed the street. Kids peered around trees, corners, and parked cars. "You do that and we'll be swarmed."

Maria looked around as well. The boy lunged for her purse, which she snapped out of his reach. "Hey!"

The boy ran away, laughing.

"This is almost a third world country." Jake opened the metal gate.

When they reached the restaurant's front door, a black woman wearing a red smock stepped outside. "Can I help you?"

"Dinner for two," Jake said.

"Si, senor. Would you like to eat inside or outside?"

Jake glanced at the patio. Several potted trees separated the tables, and a young couple sat nursing beers. "Is there air-conditioning inside?"

"We have fans."

"Inside then but right next to the patio."

"Very good. Please follow me."

Inside the dark restaurant, middle-aged men with mustaches sat at a long wooden bar, and Latin music played from a boom box.

A black man with graying hair and a red smock stood behind the bar and watched the woman seat Jake and Maria at a table with a view of the patio. "Can I get you something to drink?"

"Water's fine," Maria said.

"This is a lovely city," Jake said.

The woman smiled and left.

No dice, he thought. "No margarita today?"

"Like you said, we need to stay clearheaded."

"I guess I'm not getting any tonight."

"We'll see what happens when we get home."

Jake studied the menu on the place mat. *Home.* It felt strange to hear a woman use that term with him in a collective sense. "You order for me."

The server returned with two mugs and a pitcher of ice water. "Two orders of *riz, haricots, et poulet.*"

"Très bien."

When the woman left, Maria said, "Rice, beans, and chicken."

A chunky man with a bulky camera approached the table. "May I take your photograph?"

Jake looked at the man. "How much?"

"Five dollars, US."

"We've been taking photos all day."

"Together?"

"Yeah," Maria said. "Let's take one together."

Chuckling, Jake scooted closer to Maria and put his arm around her. They smiled for the camera.

The man lined up the shot. "Uno . . . dos . . . tres."

The flash caused Jake to blink. A moment later, the camera whirred, and a Polaroid photo slid out of a slot. The man set the photo on the table.

Jake took a five-dollar bill out of his wallet. "This is a lovely city."

The man pocketed the money. "It stinks like sewage."

Maria giggled as the man walked away. "Maybe you're saying it wrong."

"I'm ready for a beer."

The photo developed, and Maria picked it up and showed it to him. "We make a nice couple."

Jake thought so, too. "Si. Tu eres una mujer bella." *You are beautiful.*

"Since when do you speak Spanish?"

"I get around."

"Y tu eres muy machote."

"If you just said I'm beautiful with this face, you've lost all credibility with me."

She smiled. "I said you're very macho." She put the

photo in her leather bag. "Me salvaste de la gran serpiente blanca. You saved me from the great white snake."

Before Jake could respond, a skinny Hispanic man wearing jeans and a button-down plaid shirt stopped at their table. He had short, wavy black hair and a mustache and a beard, and he held up a large sketching pad. "Excuse me. May I draw the beautiful lady's portrait?"

"How much?" Jake said.

"Only ten American dollars."

"Let me see your work."

The man flipped a page in his pad. "Okay . . ."

"This is a lovely city," Maria said.

"I prefer living in the country," the man said.

Maria looked at Jake, who gestured at an empty seat.

"Ten dollars sounds like a bargain."

ELEVEN

The artist set a tackle box on the table and sat. "I'm Humphrey."

"I'm Jake and this is Maria."

"*Hola*," Maria said.

Humphrey smiled. "I don't get the chance to draw many Americans, especially not as beautiful as you."

"Gracias."

Humphrey opened the tackle box, removed a pencil, and with his gaze on Maria proceeded to sketch. "Will you use the tunnel?"

"To get in, yes," Jake said. "I don't know if we can get out that way. There's no telling what condition our friend is in."

"The tunnel's only three and a half feet high. We've laid dolly tracks. As long as you get our revered symbol onto a dolly, you can get out."

"How long is the tunnel?"

"A quarter of a mile—after you walk almost half a mile through another tunnel that's seven feet high."

Jake raised his eyebrows.

"We've been working on it a long time. The shorter tunnel leads to a shaft with an access panel in a cleaning supplies closet at the bottom of the cell block. Our dear friend now occupies a cell on the top level. We'll provide you both with uniforms that approximate what the guards wear. From a distance, you'll pass. Up close neither of you would pass anyway."

"How many men can accompany us?"

"None."

Jake felt his forehead crease. "*None?*"

"Keep your voice down," Maria said, holding her smile.

"That wasn't the plan."

Humphrey kept his gaze on Maria. "Let me explain to you what Miriam didn't. If you're caught, you'll be tortured to death. If anyone helping you is caught, their families will be tortured to death. Men, women, children. On Pavot Island, we work very hard for slave wages. We have nothing but our families."

"We can't do this alone. We won't even try."

"I didn't say you had to do it alone. I just said you have to enter El Miedo alone. We'll arm you, transport you, feed you. There are two towers manned by guards with big machine guns that can tear you to pieces. We can handle them. Most important, we'll get you the hell away from there to rendezvous with your escape transport."

Jake glanced at Maria, whose eyes revealed disbelief. "How many guards will be inside?"

Humphrey exchanged his pencil for a brown one. "At night with no visitors? No more than twelve, and three of them will be in the main office, watching the security monitors."

"That leaves nine."

"Two of them in the guard towers. Two more patrol the grounds with guard dogs."

"Five."

"Properly armed, with surprise on your side, they should not pose a problem. The real danger lies with the military barracks. From gate to gate, it's only a fifteen-minute drive in the daytime. You'll have at most twenty minutes from the time the first shot is fired. A diversion could throw the guards into disarray but will summon the soldiers that much sooner."

"What if he set all the other prisoners free to run wild? Will that be enough of a distraction?"

Humphrey nodded, his expression suggesting he was impressed. "That would probably work. Unfortunately, there *are* no other prisoners."

Jake raised his eyebrows, and Maria did the same. "What?"

"Andre Santiago is El Miedo's sole resident. Our minor criminals pass through our jails. Those who commit greater offenses—like murder or demonstrating against Malvado—simply disappear, never to be seen again. Andre Santiago inhabits El Miedo as a symbol of Malvado's power."

Jake and Maria traded looks. Then Jake said, "How do we know your people at the other end of the tunnel won't turn tail at the first sign of trouble and leave us stranded?"

"Don't underestimate the significance of our objective. If you succeed—if *we* succeed—it will be a turning point for Pavot. The United Nations cannot ignore Andre if he sets foot on American soil. Malvado will have no choice but to step down or flee the island. We're willing to die for Pavot's freedom. We're not willing for our families to be killed for an outside chance of freedom."

The server returned with two plates of food, which she set before Jake and Maria. Looking over Humphrey's shoulder at the portrait he was sketching, she nodded and left.

"How many men will be at that tunnel?" Jake said.

"How many do you want?"

"Twenty, fully armed."

"Then you'll have twenty-five, including me."

"How well armed will they be?"

"Guns are easy to come by. We'll be fully equipped."

"If we accept—and I'm not saying we will—when do we go?"

"We need two full days to prepare. The plan's existed in a conceptual form for some time. The longer we wait, the greater the chance of human fallibility interfering."

"Meaning, the greater the chance that someone gets cold feet and rats us all out."

"Correct. The guards change shift at midnight. We want to strike at 11:00 p.m. when the guards on duty are likely to be tired, anxious to go home, and careless."

"Eleven o'clock the night after tomorrow. What's the plan once we get out of there?"

"A camouflage truck will take you across the island to a cove where a boat will be waiting for you in the dark."

"I want to see that boat before we agree to anything."

"Impossible. It's hidden, and taking you to it will only endanger the possibility of escape."

"Then bring us detailed photos. I hear they cost five bucks, US."

"That I may be able to do."

"Make it happen or there's no deal."

"I can't make that call myself. I can only deliver your ultimatum to the people who make these decisions."

"Here's another demand: deliver the photos by noon tomorrow if you expect us to meet your deadline. Otherwise, we're leaving this island alone."

Humphrey smiled at Maria. "I urge you to be careful. A man this stubborn must always be this stubborn."

"I like him that way."

Humphrey made the sign of the cross, then turned his sketchbook around, showing them a perfect portrait of Maria. He kissed two of his fingers.

Maria's eyes brightened. "You made me look beautiful."

Humphrey cast an expectant look at Jake, who said, "He only captured what I see."

Maria laughed. "If only you always lied as well as you do when you're covering your tracks."

Humphrey tore the portrait from the pad, rolled it up,

and rubber banded it. "Forgive me for not signing it. I've lived this long by keeping a low profile, which isn't easy for a man possessing my amazing talent."

"Tell us about your organization," Jake said.

"Our problem is that we have many organizations, with many conflicting ideas about what's best for Pavot Island, while our enemies remain strong because they're unified by Malvado. We call him Le Monstre."

"The Monster," Maria said.

"I figured," Jake said in a monotone.

Humphrey lit a cigarette. "There are three main opposition groups to the rulers of Pavot. The first is the Church of St. Anthony, which funnels funds to other groups. Father Alejandro makes few political stands and publicly addresses only social issues, which keeps him busy enough.

"The second group is the People for Pavot. Some would say they are extremists; others would call them courageous freedom fighters. Malvado calls them terrorists. They have conducted several suicide missions, but Malvado is too well protected for them to reach. The People for Pavot don't have the full support of the people *on* Pavot, because they've deemed civilian fatalities as acceptable collateral damage.

"I belong to the third group, Pavot for the People. We're a network of journalists, artists, and civilians whose mission is to spread the truth about Malvado. We're the underground press, the pirate radio stations. We support the use of violence but only when used properly. To us, civilian deaths are unacceptable."

"And Miriam Santiago supports your cause?"

"La Mère supports the Church of St. Anthony and Pavot for the People, but the funds she sends also reach the People for Pavot through the church."

"La Mère?"

"Miriam is our spiritual mother. Andre is our spiritual father. We believe Le Père's release will unite the three principal groups and those who are afraid to stand against Malvado. It's our one chance for liberation. That's why my people will die for you if you free Andre from El Miedo."

Jake chewed his food. "What about your criminal elements?"

Humphrey shrugged. "They're criminals, as you say. They're only interested in illicit gains, with no political convictions."

"Malvado's a drug dealer first and foremost. That limits the amount of money your crooks can make. If Malvado's taken down, their opportunities multiply."

"The People for Pavot and Pavot for the People buy guns from La Main Noire—the Black Hand. Arms dealing is one of the Hand's principal means of income. The other is smuggling people off Pavot."

"Sounds like they're already as opposed to Malvado as you are."

"For the wrong reasons. They can't be trusted."

Jake did not pursue the matter. He had a hard enough time understanding American politics and divisions, let alone those on an island where English, French, and Spanish were interchangeable languages. "Today a policeman warned us away from the rain forest when we were alone on the mountain overlooking it. He had a tattoo of a black snake on his arm."

Humphrey blew a stream of smoke over their heads. "L'église du Serpent Noir."

Maria narrowed her eyes. "The Church of the Black Snake."

"All of Malvado's police, soldiers, and civil servants belong to his church. It's a prerequisite for government positions and advancement."

With unease growing in his stomach, Jake set his fork down. "Black magic?"

"Yes, but not quite in the way you think. The leaders of the church serve on Malvado's council of bokors, the Mambos and the Houngans. The congregation swears fealty to the church, but its members don't practice vodou."

"There's that word."

"White vodou and black vodou are common on Pavot. Get used to it."

"What about you?"

"I'm Catholic, like the beautiful lady here."

"Vodou is an offshoot of Catholicism."

"True."

"But you don't believe in vodou?"

"I don't belong to a church that practices vodou. I don't belong to any church. If I did, I would belong to St. Anthony's. But to belong to that church is to place yourself under suspicion, and I'm a coward."

"You're no coward," Maria said. "Or you wouldn't be helping us."

"Merci, mademoiselle. But my motives are selfish. I'm helping you because it will help myself."

Jake stared at Humphrey. "You're not a coward but you're evasive. You never answered my question."

Humphrey stabbed out his cigarette in the ashtray. "I've lived on this island all my life. I'll die here. I'm steeped in its culture and its rituals. I've seen people cured of diseases and healed of fatal injuries by spiritual leaders. I grew up hearing tales of the walking dead. I've spoken to people who believe with all their might that they've seen zonbies. We're a superstitious people, and I'm a man of the people."

"Have you ever seen a zonbie?" Maria said.

"I think so. Once. A special friend and I sought privacy during a community outing. We went farther into the black woods than we should have, because we knew no one would follow us. We saw a man . . . or what once had been a man." Humphrey waved a hand over his face. "His features were expressionless. His skin was gray. His eyes were white."

"What did you do?"

"I told you, I'm a coward. We ran like hell."

Dusk settled and the restaurant's patio lights came on. Maria took out a cigarette, and Humphrey lit it with his lighter.

"We saw some scarecrows down the block," Jake said.

Humphrey kneaded his eyebrows. "Scarecrows?"

"Junkies addicted to Black Magic," Maria said.

Humphrey nodded. "It's a deadly drug. Two, three weeks is all it takes to kill users."

"And then they walk again," Jake said.

"So they say."

"What else do they say about zonbies?"

"They say Malvado uses them as slaves in his fields at night, harvesting his heroin and cocaine when no one will see them."

"*White Zombie*," Maria said.

Jake glanced at her. She had been doing her research.

"I watched every frigging zombie movie you can think of in the last year."

Humphrey raised his eyebrows. "I take it you've both seen zonbies?"

"I've just seen their shells," Maria said. "Jake is the professional zonbie killer."

Humphrey bowed to Jake. "Monsieur."

"Last night we found a white snake in Maria's bed," Jake said. "Is there such a thing as the Church of the White Snake?"

"*Oui*. L'église du Serpent Blanc is as widespread as L'église du Serpent Noir, but in recent years it's been practiced in secret. Malvado had the worship halls burned down to advance his own religion. You won't see any tattoos of the white snake on Pavot."

"I've never heard of an all white snake."

"The longer you stay here, the more strangeness you will see."

Maria leaned forward. "Did someone *put* that snake in my bed?"

"Don't be alarmed," Humphrey said. "The white snake represents white vodou, which is a force for good. If someone did put it there, it was not with the intention of harming you."

Jake heard the squeaking of brakes down the street. A moment later, Maria looked past him, her eyes widening, and the couple eating behind them on the patio leapt to their feet.

"Humphrey!" the woman said, pointing.

Jake turned around as four men dressed in camouflage military uniforms ran onto the sidewalk two stores down. They wore red berets and carried machine guns.

When Jake turned back, he saw the woman and the man draw black handguns from the folds of their clothing. A burst of machine gun fire ripped the air before they had a chance to shoot, and they danced like puppets, crimson wounds appearing in their torsos.

"Run!" Humphrey reached into his tackle box and brought out a Walther PPK.

Jake and Maria bolted from their seats and onto the patio. Jake jumped over the metal railing and turned to help Maria, but she sailed past him, her handbag trailing her shoulder.

Humphrey fired two rounds, and the four soldiers ducked behind cars for cover. Maria took off down the sidewalk in the opposite direction, and Jake ran after her. He heard Humphrey's footsteps behind them.

"Cross the street!" Humphrey said.

But Maria continued sprinting toward the nearest corner, and Jake followed.

Automatic gunfire tore into the trees around them and punched holes in the parked cars.

Humphrey screamed, and Jake turned around as Maria reached the corner. Humphrey lay facedown in the street, a puddle of blood spreading across his back. He raised his head, making eye contact with Jake, then hurled his gun forward.

The Walther struck the pavement, and Jake ran for it. He grabbed the weapon, but when he turned to follow Maria, gunfire sparked a line in the street between them, so he headed for the opposite corner across the street. As he rounded that corner, gunfire blew chips off the bricks.

Flattening his back against the wall, Jake saw Maria standing across the street, face white and mouth open. She stepped forward, and gunfire sparked against the pole of a street sign on the corner. She flinched.

"Stay back!" Jake said. Crouching low, he peeked around the corner.

The four soldiers were jogging in their direction in the middle of the street. When they saw him, they kneeled and fired their weapons.

He ducked as rounds hammered at the bricks. There was no way he could take them out with the little handgun.

"Jake!"

Stretching his legs, he leaned sideways and cocked his arm like a discus thrower. Then he hurled the gun across the street. It hit the sidewalk and spun past Maria. She retrieved the semiautomatic and stood facing him.

"Run!" Jake said, standing.

"No!"

"Maybe one of us will make it!"

"I won't leave you!" Her face turned bright red.

"Do it!"

With tears streaking her face, Maria turned and ran. She glanced over her shoulder at him, then looked ahead and ran faster.

TWELVE

With machine guns cracking behind him, Jake took off in the opposite direction as Maria. Whatever street he was on had fewer shops and buildings than Rue de Verger did.

A group of men drank bottled beer outside a hardware store. One wore a straw hat; all wore stunned expressions. Jake didn't know if the eruption of gunfire or the sight of a Caucasian man running for his life had startled them. They crowded into the doorway as he ran past them.

"Run, senor!"

Jake heard three pops in the distance behind him. The Walther. He prayed Maria would make it.

As he reached the next corner, a jeep occupied by four soldiers careened around it, cutting through the intersection and passing him.

"Le voilà!" a soldier said over the engine's roar.

Jake turned the corner onto a wide street with buildings spaced far apart. A garbage truck idled up the block, and he pumped his arms as a sanitation worker dumped the contents of a receptacle into the compacter. Hearing the jeep rev its engine behind him, he sprinted around the truck. The engine's roar grew louder, closer.

Jake veered to his right, putting the truck between him and the military vehicle as the soldiers unleashed a volley of gunfire. Without slowing down, he ran up the concrete steps of a deserted building with a boarded-up doorway. He ripped the plywood free as the jeep screeched to a stop and backed up.

With no idea what to expect, he went inside.

Maria ran down the street, tears streaming from her eyes.

Goddamn it!

She didn't want to abandon Jake without a weapon, but he had ordered her to do so, and she knew he was right. There had been no way for them to reach each other without being torn to pieces by the machine guns.

Poor Humphrey! She had never seen a man killed before, let alone someone gunned down trying to help her.

Grateful she had worn sneakers, Maria ran as fast as she could. Thank God she had only resumed smoking two days earlier and still had her wind. Machine guns roared behind her, and bullets ricocheted off a metal mailbox to her left. Ducking into the doorway of a rug store, she turned and fired the Walther three times, driving the soldiers back around the corner. She had never killed anyone, much less soldiers on foreign soil, and she had no intention of starting now.

Sprinting to the next corner, she turned left, heading in the direction of Coucher du Soleil on a street parallel to Rue de Verger. Maybe she could somehow reach the Fiesta.

No car keys . . .

A woman getting out of a dark green Dodge froze when she saw Maria running straight toward her.

Raising the gun, Maria angled her body sideways, sandwiching the woman against the open door. "Donne moi tes clefs!" she said in her best French.

With her face contorting, the woman held out her car keys, which Maria snatched as she threw herself behind the wheel. Tossing the Walther onto the seat beside her, she jammed the key into the ignition, cranked the engine, and stomped on the gas pedal. The Dodge jumped forward, the open door crashing against a parked car and slamming shut.

Maria sped down the narrow street, machine gun fire shattering the windshields of the parked cars around her. A man with a terrified expression jumped off his bike and hid behind a pickup. Maria knew if she continued down the street another block or two and turned left, passing the area where the soldiers had attacked, she could find her way onto the highway.

Fuck that.

Instead, she turned right. By circling that block, she could head toward Rue de Verger.

Back toward Jake.

Jake stopped inside the abandoned factory just long enough to get his bearings. Fading sunlight seeped through the tall window spaces, illuminating broken shards of glass on the floor. He had entered an enormous former plant with one gargantuan room opening into another. Fallen bricks and cinder blocks surrounded the columns supporting the high ceiling, and gaping holes in the walls permitted views of other rooms.

At the far end, easily two hundred feet away, he spotted a stairway and ran toward it. His feet crushed glass, kicked gravel, and scraped cement. Green stalactites hung from the ceiling like daggers ready to fall. Hearing footsteps behind him, he angled right so a cracked wall hid him from view. He ducked through a hole in another wall, stepped over the skeleton of a cat, and hurried past a rusted industrial oil tank.

Men shouted behind him, and he flattened his back against the right wall of the stairway as he charged up the stairs, which were covered with clumps of dirt and debris.

Reaching the second floor, Jake was surprised to see trees growing in the middle of the floor and through a wide hole in the ceiling. He passed piles of knocked over filing cabinets and found himself in a long corridor with a dirt floor lined with doorways lacking doors. Scavengers had salvaged everything they could. Sunlight glared through an opening in the wall at the end of the corridor. He ran toward the light.

Excited voices rose from below.

Entering a room to his right, he ran past an open safe to an empty window space and glanced down at the sidewalk. His stomach tightened.

Three jeeps and two canvas-covered military transport trucks occupied the street, and dozens of armed soldiers charged into the building.

For a moment he wondered what would happen if he leapt out into space, aiming for the canvas, like they did in the movies. He decided he would break his neck.

A cacophony of raised voices and thunderous footsteps filled the stairway behind him. Then he heard the deafening sound of a fire horn.

Maria raced toward the intersection where she and Jake had parted ways. She had no intention of abandoning him in the heart of Pavot City. Passing Rue de Verger, she glanced down the street and saw Humphrey's corpse fifty yards ahead of the jeep the soldiers had arrived in. All four soldiers stood in the street, brandishing their guns.

That isn't right, she thought. *What the hell is going on?*

A car heading toward her stopped at the next intersection, and a pair of Humvees passed her. She stomped on the brake, her pulse racing. When the street cleared, she drove slowly forward and stopped at the corner, where she spied half a dozen military vehicles and a score of soldiers armed with machine guns in front of an abandoned factory.

The approaching car passed her, followed by another.

"Son of a fucking bitch, Jake!"

She grabbed the Walther and laid it between her legs for easier access. How could she reach Jake?

Another Humvee drove by and tears obscured her vision.

Then a fire horn wailed, and in the rearview mirror she saw both of the cars that had passed her come to a sudden stop. An oncoming car across the street stopped as well. The vehicles settled as their drivers killed the engines.

She winced, torn with indecision. Then she turned the car around and floored it.

Jake ran through one doorway after another, passing overturned desks, typewriters, and rusted electrical equipment. Seeing no reason to make it easier for them to identify Maria, he took his camera out of his pocket and dropped it down a hole in the wall. He told himself there had to be a stairway at the end of the corridor, where the sunlight flooded through the window space.

Then he hit a concrete wall. He looked around, but there was only one way out of the deep room, and that was through the corridor, where the soldiers would see him.

"Sheryl?" he said. "Abel?"

He didn't think so.

"Cain?"

No shimmering gold light, no lingering stench of sulfur.

"If anyone cares to intervene, I'd sure appreciate it."

No way out. No one to help. He felt like a trapped rat.

Moving to the doorway, Jake took a deep breath. He estimated he had traveled half the distance to his destination. Hopefully the number of soldiers in the building meant Maria had escaped. He took comfort in that. Good woman.

Exhaling, he entered the corridor and turned right. He didn't know how many soldiers had come upstairs or what they were doing. He just ran.

To his enormous relief, he was much closer to the corridor's end than he had guessed, and he saw a sun-bleached building across the street.

Twenty more steps . . .

Then he heard a high-pitched whizzing sound, like a bottle rocket being launched in a backyard, and a trail of greenish-brown smoke spiraled over his shoulder. What resembled a compact flashlight struck the dirt floor ahead of him and spun, spewing smoke out of both ends. With no other choice, he charged into the noxious cloud, shielding his eye with one arm and holding his breath.

Smoke penetrated his eyelid and nostrils, and fire scorched his lungs and brain. Staggering forward, he slammed into the cinder-block wall framing the missing window. He sucked in fresh air, which did no good. The window space sucked the smoke outside, enveloping him. His eye and throat burned and he coughed, which only forced him to breathe in more gas. Bracing his hands on the concrete sill, he considered jumping, but instead he turned to face his attackers.

Through the gas he discerned a dozen camouflage men standing forty feet away. Wearing black gas masks and clutching automatic weapons, they stood motionless, as if waiting for Jake to drop. But he lurched forward, still coughing, hot tears streaming down his face.

One soldier stepped forward with his machine gun raised. As he neared Jake, he lowered his weapon, gripping it in both gloved hands.

Jake raised his hands. Maybe they would take him prisoner if he submitted.

The soldier stopped, planted his boots apart like a batter over home plate, and held his black weapon ready to fire.

Jake realized he was doomed. He thought of Edgar, whom he had failed, trapped forever in the body of a raven; of Martin, waiting for him to bring his father home; and he pictured Maria's face.

The soldier squeezed the trigger, and the ensuing muzzle flashes lit up the smoke.

Jake took the charges full in the chest. It felt like a dozen men punching him. Falling back, he felt still more impacts as he slammed onto the dirt floor and gasped for breath, his chest on fire.

As Maria rocketed past Rue de Verger, she heard machine gun fire coming from the four soldiers who had killed Humphrey. She wove between cars that had stopped in the street, as commanded by the fire horn. She pushed the

Dodge as fast as it would go, slowing only to make a left turn, then another. Glimpsing the tall black tower, she vowed that if she survived and Jake did not, there would be hell to pay.

Civilians turned their heads as she passed them. Their stunned expressions told her no one disobeyed the fire horn. Then she heard the police siren behind her. Looking in the rearview mirror, she saw a single brown car pursuing her. Tilting her head forward, she flexed her fingers on the steering wheel, then tightened them.

Let's dance.

Maria shifted into the oncoming lane, then into the proper lane, a police car following her lead. She repeated the move, and the car remained on her tail. Waiting until she saw a motionless car facing her, she switched back into the oncoming lane. The police car did the same, and she remained in the lane until the last possible second, then returned to the correct lane. Guessing the policeman must have registered the vehicle dead ahead, Maria eased up on the gas and dropped back, riding side by side with the police car.

With no time to brake to avoid colliding with the stopped car, the policeman jerked his steering wheel to the left, driving into the curb between two parked cars, the impact lifting the police car's back end into the air. The police car slammed down onto the street and rocked back and forth.

Gritting her teeth, Maria raced out of the city and boarded the highway ramp.

THIRTEEN

Lying on his back, Jake focused on the ceiling. Peeling paint gave way to corroded steel and electrical wires dangling from holes. Tear gas swirled above him and he convulsed.

Only when the soldier who had killed him looked down at him through his gas mask did Jake realize he felt more pain from the gas than from the wounds in his chest. He knew bullet wounds caused victims to go into shock, and the pain would be unbearable in a few minutes. Was this how Dread and Baldy had felt, bleeding to death on the floor of Kearny's Tavern after Jake had plugged them in self-defense?

The soldier beckoned to his comrades, and two came over. They seized Jake's arms and hauled him up, then dragged him toward the stairway with his feet trailing him.

Jake looked down at his chest and saw no blood or bullet holes.

Impossible!

The soldiers at the top of the stairs jerked their heads forward and back, their gas masks emitting strange, muffled sounds.

Laughter.

His confusion amused them. Then it occurred to him: the lead soldier had fired rubber bullets designed for riot control. As they supported him on the way down the stairs, his cloudy mind raced. It was so hard to think with the tear gas burning the passages in his skull.

The man and woman who had sat behind him and Maria at Coucher du Soleil had been planted there by Humphrey to let him know when they had arrived. The soldiers had killed them and Humphrey with live ammunition and used it to intimidate Maria and him. But they had used rubber bullets to take him down, which meant their orders were to capture him alive. Maria might still be alive as well! Unless she had issued her own death sentence by firing the Walther at them, in which case he was indirectly responsible for her death.

At the bottom of the stairs, the soldiers threw him to the floor. Glass and gravel bit into his palms. Away from the gas, his lungs and mind cleared. The soldiers peeled off their gas masks.

"Get on your feet!" The soldier who had shot him drew a .45 from his holster.

Jake got up. "There was a woman with me—"

The lead soldier nodded to another, who swung the butt of his machine gun at Jake's head, knocking him to the floor.

Seeing red flashes, Jake checked to make sure his glass

eye had not fallen out of its socket.

"Get up!"

Jake rose again, his head aching. This time he kept his mouth shut.

The soldiers led him outside, where a police officer handcuffed his hands behind his back and two soldiers pushed him into the back of a Humvee and sat on either side of him.

He counted at least two dozen soldiers, all wearing red berets. His scattered thoughts returned to Maria.

With the sun setting behind her, Maria raced forward in the Dodge, checking her rearview mirror for pursuers and seeing none. She had to assume Jake was dead; no unarmed man stood a chance against an army, not even one who had dispatched a hundred zonbies.

No more tears, she thought. *Later, not now.*

There was no way she could break Andre Santiago out of El Miedo alone, which meant Edgar was doomed to remain a raven. All she could do was try to get off Pavot Island alive.

Damn it!

Why had Humphrey contacted them in public? Malvado's forces must have had him under surveillance despite his efforts to maintain a low profile. Now he and his friends were dead, and Jake probably was, too. A simple check into Jake's itinerary would reveal she had arrived on

Pavot with him. She could not return to the resort, could not fly home, and had no other emergency contact. She was on her own.

Jake . . .

Her chest quivered. Maria had been intrigued by him since she and Edgar had interviewed him regarding Sheryl's murder at the hands of the Cipher. At Sheryl's funeral, after an unknown vigilante had killed the Cipher—a man named Marc Gorman—she had felt sorry for Jake. After that, she had suspected Jake of executing Gorman, but Edgar had always deflected her queries. In time, she grew to admire Jake for cleaning up his life; he stopped drinking, smoking, and using cocaine. Before she knew it, she felt an attraction to him, one she resisted while he mourned Sheryl.

Almost a year after the murder, Edgar and Dawn Du Pre had invited her to dinner as Jake's date. The evening had gone well until she and Edgar were called to a crime scene. Then everything had gone to hell. Dawn. Katrina. Prince Malachai. Edgar's disappearance. And sixty fucking corpses stuffed with sawdust under her name in Special Homicide.

Jake.

Her life would never be the same if she survived, a prospect she very much doubted. The last rays of sunlight glinted off metal in the distance ahead, and she tensed. Two police cars were parked front bumper to front bumper across the highway, leaving no room to pass them. Four cops stood before the vehicles with shotguns resting on their arms.

"You've got to be joking."

She turned on the radio and cranked the Latin beat up

to a deafening volume, then stepped on the gas and aimed the car straight for the point where the two police cars met. The officers scattered mere moments before she plowed into their cars.

Bracing for impact, Maria closed her eyes. The car rocked from side to side, and she heard the sounds of metal twisting and glass shattering. But the Dodge kept moving. Opening her eyes, she glanced in the rearview mirror and watched the cops scurrying around their misshapen, useless vehicles.

Maybe I'll make it out of here alive after all.

In the backseat of the Humvee, Jake looked out the windows at the civilians on the street, who watched the procession of vehicles with dread in their eyes. Through the windshield, he saw the black tower that had drawn his attention upon their arrival in Pavot City, and a sick feeling developed as he realized that was his destination.

The soldiers spoke to each other in low, mundane tones in French and Spanish. They were just doing their jobs, which happened to entail murdering civilians, gassing Jake, and blasting his chest with rubber bullets.

The Humvee followed two jeeps down a parking ramp alongside the black building and descended into a basement garage with ceilings high enough to accommodate the personnel transport truck. Only military and police vehicles occupied the garage.

The driver parked, and the two soldiers beside Jake took him out of the vehicle. His throat still ached, and the smell of gas lingered in his nostrils, but at least his eye was okay.

The soldiers' footsteps echoed in the garage as they led him to double metal doors in the gray cement wall. One soldier punched a code into the keypad on the wall, and the doors unlocked. They guided Jake inside, where they nodded to a soldier behind a counter. The man looked at Jake with curiosity but said nothing. They walked Jake down a corridor, passing a desk where two female soldiers entered data into computers. One of the soldiers flirted with the younger of the two women, who offered him a demure smile in return.

Just forget about me, Jake thought.

They took him into a bare room with cinder-block walls. No windows. Two chairs and a desk. Jake had been in rooms similar to this one more times than he could remember, interviewing suspects and being interviewed by cops. Edgar. Maria. Teddy Geoghegan from Major Crimes. Homeland Security. The FBI. He had promised himself he would do everything in his power to avoid any more official interviews, but here he stood. Familiarity truly bred contempt.

One of the soldiers pointed at a chair. "Sit down."

"How about removing these bracelets?"

The soldier smiled. "I'm sure the handcuffs will be taken off when the time comes."

What the hell does that mean? Jake sat behind the desk, his cuffed hands pressing against the small of his back, every movement causing the pain in his chest to flare.

The soldiers left without saying another word, the door closing with a sharp sound and a click that told him he had been locked in.

Taking a deep breath, he searched the room for a camera and located one in the far upper corner. At least he didn't see a rubber hose or electrodes.

What the hell do they want with me? I haven't done anything yet, except kill a white snake. These guys should be happy about that.

The door opened, and a tall, muscular man in a tailored black suit entered carrying a file folder. He was the first Caucasian Jake had seen since landing on the island, and it took him a moment to recognize the man's bald head and bushy mustache. Then his body turned numb.

"It's a small world, isn't it, Helman?"

Bill Russel.

Maria switched on the headlights as she raced down the highway in the battered Dodge. A mountain loomed ahead, and she decided the highway was different than the one they had taken into Pavot City. The car had only a quarter of a tank of gas left, and she didn't see any exits for refueling.

Where the hell am I?

She didn't envision stopping to read the map in her bag, and she couldn't turn around and go back. That left continuing on until she ran out of gas and had to abandon the vehicle. She passed a meadow occupied by cows, the trees in the dark woods behind them clawing at the dark sky. The Dodge's headlights illuminated stark-looking barbed wire fences.

As she accelerated up an incline, the engine coughed and whirred—or so she thought. The noise grew louder, and she noticed lights floating in her side mirror. An enormous circle of light appeared on the asphalt ahead of her, and she realized a helicopter trailed her at close range. The light grew more intense, the whirring louder, and looking over her shoulder, she saw the aircraft pursuing her.

Maria weaved from one side of the road to the other. Machine guns mounted on the helicopter's sides lit up the night, and the heavy ammunition tore holes in the highway and the car's trunk. The sound of the rounds ripping through the metal caused her to flinch, but when the chopper failed to fire again and finish the job, she suspected it was herding her to a specific destination.

Then she heard a high-pitched whine, and two rockets soared over the car, the exhaust flames illuminating the parallel trails of smoke. The missiles traveled side by side and impacted the highway ahead at the same time. The double explosion hurled twin fireballs into the sky, and the concussion forced Maria to grapple with the Dodge's steering wheel to regain control of the swerving vehicle.

As a sheet of orange flame sliced through the air toward the vehicle, she jerked the wheel to the left. For an instant, she glimpsed the woods in the distance and the field below her. Then the flames clung to the back window, and the continuing concussion drove the car over the embankment with greater force. All she saw was the grass at the bottom of the hill as the vehicle raced toward it.

Maria stomped on the brake, and the stilled wheels dug into the ground, but the vehicle continued its trajectory. The embankment was so steep the front of the car was going to crash into the level ground before the wheels touched it. Releasing the steering wheel, she threw the door open and jumped out of the car. She rolled down the hill, the wind force from the hovering helicopter chilling her. She heard the car crash as she struck the level ground, continued to roll, and finally stopped.

Still gripping the Walther, she sat up. Flames continued to burn on the highway above her, flooding the scene with orange light, and the Dodge rested at the bottom of the hill, its front end crushed and smoke billowing out from under its ruptured hood.

The sound of the helicopter grew louder, the wind greater, and the spotlight illuminated the ruined car, its door open.

Maria leapt up and ran toward the woods. Her handbag slid off her shoulder, and she managed to pull it over her head so she wouldn't lose it. She heard the helicopter's engine speed up, and she didn't have to look over her shoulder to know it was chasing her.

The spotlight traveled along the ground, searching for her, and as it drew closer she reversed direction and circled it.

Can they still see me?

Her sneakers pounded the thick grass, and the helicopter's roar became deafening. The spotlight swung back, and she found herself running in the center of a wide circle of bright white light. She dropped to her knees and bowed her head, and the spotlight moved on. Raising her head, she saw it heading in her direction again as the helicopter turned around.

She sprinted away from the light's trajectory, straight toward the helicopter. If the soldiers in the copter spotted her, they could cut her in half with the machine guns, but it was the only way to escape the spotlight. She almost ran in place beneath the helicopter, which dropped closer to the ground, and feared the wind would knock her over. Then she was free of the force, with the copter behind her, and charged toward the woods.

The copter turned around, the spotlight moving in a wide circle, then flew in her direction. Its nose dipped closer to the ground as it increased speed.

They see me!

The spotlight swung in her direction, bathing her and the woods with light. She ran into a thicket of bushes, swinging her arms before her face so her forearms smashed the branches. Dozens of thorns tore her flesh. Pain flared in her thighs, and her ankle caught in an unearthed root, bringing her down to earth. She pulled her foot free and crawled beneath the branches, avoiding more thorns.

The light became brighter, the sound of the copter louder, and the trees around her shook, debris and dust swirling around her. She scrambled out of the bushes and drove herself forward, escaping the light. The machine guns roared behind her, decimating the foliage in the illuminated zone. Thanks to the light, she was able to sprint forward, avoiding collision with the tall trees.

The light followed her, and the shadows of the trees ahead of her got smaller. Maria hurdled over a fallen tree trunk, then skidded in the dirt to a noisy stop. She dove backwards, rolling behind the downed tree for cover.

The copter's machine guns unleashed their full power, assaulting the woods with a ferocity Maria had never witnessed. Chips of bark flew from the trees, which seemed to cry out and claw at the air with their limbs. Branches snapped, dirt kicked up, and dust swirled. And still the light grew brighter, the helicopter closer.

Maria pressed her fists against her ears to dull the noise. As bullets tore into her shelter, she screamed in defiance.

Then the shadows of the trees shifted, the light receded, and the chopper altered course. Though dust lingered in the air and broken branches dangled around her, the trees stopped shaking.

They're leaving.

With her breath escaping in tortured rasps, Maria sat up and peeked over the tree, its surface hacked apart as if by an ax. She held the Walther close to her face, a feeble gesture she knew. The gunfire had reduced much of the wooded area to rubble, and through the trees she saw the chopper beyond them.

It turned around once more, facing the woods, and she squinted as the spotlight shone on her. The aircraft hovered in place for a moment. Then it settled on the ground, and three soldiers clutching machine guns jumped out.

FOURTEEN

Realizing his mouth hung open, Jake snapped it shut.

"You look like you've seen a ghost," Russel said, crossing the room. He dropped the folder on the table beside Jake.

"More like a spook. Or an *ex*-spook."

Russel was an ex-CIA operative who now worked as a freelancer with an international client base. Jake had met him at the Tower, where Russel had been brokering a deal for Old Nick and Kira Thorn to sell genetically engineered monsters to a Filipino dictator. The deal went south when Jake killed Tower, who was about to seal another monstrous deal, this one with the demon Cain. After Jake also killed Kira, Russel disappeared.

Jake had always suspected they would run into each other again one day. He had equipped the New York City building—where he rented office space and served as security consultant in exchange for reduced rent—with sophisticated surveillance equipment in part to protect himself from any surprise visits by the man who now stood before him.

"What the hell are you doing here?" Jake said.

Russel sat on the edge of the table, with one foot above the floor. "That was going to be my line."

"I asked you first."

Russel smiled without showing any teeth. "I'm not handcuffed."

"I'm on vacation."

Russel snapped his fingers. "That's right. You're a private eye now, aren't you? How . . . classical."

"From the look of things, you've gone from carrying the bag for one dictator to another."

Russel's smile faded. "Do you really think it's smart to antagonize me, given the gravity of your situation?"

"Somehow I don't think it matters one way or the other. You're going to do whatever you want no matter what I say."

"You're partly right. I'm going to inflict an extraordinary amount of pain on you, but the information I extract could have a definite bearing on the condition of your corpse when I'm finished."

"You're just saying that."

Russel's eyes twinkled. "And you're determined to make me enjoy myself."

Jake glanced around the room. "This is some building. Did Malvado give you a title, or are you just his errand boy?"

Russel got off the table without wrinkling his suit. "Oh,

I have a position with the government of Pavot Island. I'm Malvado's Advisor of International Affairs. But really, I run his secret police."

Jake pursed his lips as if impressed. "Fancy. The last time I saw you, you were trying to sell genetic hybrids to President Seguera."

"And the last I saw of you, you were of no consequence at all. But my perception of you was wrong. You proved quite consequential to Nicholas, Kira, and me. You killed him, her, and my deal."

"Who says I killed Nick and Kira?"

"I found them in the Tower that night. Nick was already dead: a bullet through the palm of his hand, one of those creatures inside his body, and the creature and his body sliced and diced by glass from a broken skylight window. Kira was in a state of shock until I tended to her. She told me what happened."

"I suspect she left out some very important details." *Like Cain, Abel, and Tower's clone.*

"I'm sure you're right. She was quite a number. I'm sorry you killed her."

"Again, who says I did?"

"I helped her clean up the mess in the penthouse and arranged for Nick's personal physicians to sign his death certificate. Since they swore they were present when he died, there was no need for an autopsy."

"A smooth cover-up."

"As the top-ranking surviving member of Tower International, Kira sent me to Manila to assure Seguera that production of his little monsters would go forward as scheduled. Unfortunately, that never happened. Kira disappeared the day she told me she planned to take care of you. Obviously, you took care of her instead."

"If you say so."

"That left me in Manila, literally holding the bag when Seguera's Biogens never arrived. The country was already in political turmoil. Since I'd given him certain assurances, I had no choice but to stay in the Philippines and try to quell the revolution by conventional methods. With the overthrow of his government imminent, Seguera paid me to get him out of the country, which I was more than happy to do."

"So you brought him here . . ."

"Malvado demanded a fortune, but Seguera escaped with his country's treasury, enough to keep me on his payroll as his trusted right hand."

"And yet now you work for Malvado."

"My new employer demanded more and more money from my former employer. The handwriting was on the wall. Eventually, Malvado offered me Seguera's mansion and an attractive position to put the man out of his misery. It's a beautiful mansion."

Maria dashed between trees, trying to get as far away from the soldiers as possible.

The helicopter's spotlight seeped deep into the woods, casting ominous shadows. Once inside the forest, the three men fanned out, the laser sights on their machine guns scanning the woods.

Perhaps three hundred yards ahead of them, Maria hid behind a tree. Only when she reached inside her bag did she see how badly the thorns had scratched her arms and legs; a spiderweb of blood crisscrossed each of her limbs.

Training her binoculars on the soldiers, she grimaced. The glare from the spotlight reflected off the lenses, creating distortion. But she discerned enough to know the men wore night vision goggles. If she put too much distance between herself and them, they would be able to see her, but she would be blind. She had to stay within the illuminated forest.

Crouching low to the ground, Maria moved away from the men at a forty-five-degree angle. Her chest hurt. She had never been pursued by bad guys before. But were they bad? They were soldiers following orders, she reasoned. Soldiers who just happened to have mowed her stolen car with machine gun fire. Soldiers who had launched incendiary bombs at the highway ahead of her. Soldiers like those who had gunned down Humphrey and who had—

Don't think it!

—murdered Jake.

Fuck, yeah, they're bad.

The trees cleared and she stopped, her feet sinking in the soft embankment of a narrow river or deep creek. The current looked strong enough to carry her away if she gave it a chance, but she was a lousy swimmer. Still, if she could find something to hang on to . . .

She searched for a fallen tree limb, something that

would float and support her. Spotting what appeared to be driftwood, she lifted a small log into the light and inspected it. It would float all right, but she doubted it would enable her to do the same. The log broke in half in her hands even as she heard the machine gun fire, pulp assaulting her eyes. She dropped the log's halves and flopped to the ground. Fifty yards ahead, a soldier sighted in on her with his laser scope, which she didn't need her binoculars to see. With her elbows digging into vegetation, she gripped the Walther in both hands and took aim.

Intense red light filled her vision.

Fearing blindness, Maria shut her eyes and squeezed the trigger three times. The shots rang out one after another, and she smelled gunpowder. But she heard no scream. Opening her eyes, she saw a glowing red line arcing from the ground where the soldier had stood into the trees above. The beam did not move.

Leaping to her feet, she ran as fast as she could along the river in the opposite direction of the current and away from the remaining two soldiers. She didn't get very far before the sound of machine gun fire forced her to dive face-first into moist earth. Scores of rounds ripped into the trees around her. Wiggling like a snake toward a wide trunk for cover, she wished she had headed toward the man she had killed instead so she could have claimed his weapon.

The man she had killed.

Thinking about it, she felt no remorse. Maneuvering around the tree, she got to her feet and pressed her back against the trunk.

Silence.

A glowing red dot moved along the trees like a firefly. Then it appeared a hundred yards away: a footbridge spanning the river to the other side. If she could only reach it . . .

They'll cut me in half before I can cross it.

A twig snapped and a footstep fell. One of the soldiers had closed in on her. The red dot on the tree ahead told her he was approaching on her right side.

Holding her breath, Maria prepared to expose herself in order to shoot the predator. Then she saw another red dot on her left.

Damn it!

With no other choice, she broke into a run, zigzagging in a manner that allowed her to keep trees between her and the soldiers. Machine gun fire ripped the night, and she heard shots splintering bark. The footbridge drew closer: eighty yards . . . fifty . . . twenty . . . Maria ran out of trees for cover and hid behind the last one.

The soldiers stopped firing. The helicopter's spotlight barely reached where she stood, but moonlight gleamed on the river. She had gotten so close.

Sweat trickled down her face and stung her eyes. Her lungs felt on fire. Two laser beams sliced the darkness on either side of her, but one of them moved farther upstream, which meant she had a chance to take out the closer soldier. If she could get his weapon, she'd stand a chance of taking out the third soldier as well.

Maria waited, listening for the man's footsteps, but heard none. And then he stood right beside her in profile, facing the footbridge, unable to see her because the night vision goggles limited his periphery vision. She could shoot him at point-blank range and steal his gun, but the shot would alert the remaining soldier, reducing the odds of her making it to the footbridge. Instead, she swung the butt of the Walther's grip into the soldier's nose, shattering it.

He uttered a startled cry, which she doubted could be heard over the distant drone of the chopper, and he dropped his weapon to reach for his nose.

Maria stepped before him and pistol-whipped his head. He sank to his knees, and she hit him again; this time he went down.

She scooped up the machine gun and ducked behind a different part of the tree to hide from the other soldier, whose laser beam continued to move away from her. She pulled the goggles off the man at her feet and wore them around one wrist like a bracelet. Then she ran.

"I guess you owe me something, all things considered," Jake said.

Russel's face darkened a shade. "Don't kid yourself. In the course of defending Seguera in Manila, I was forced to take certain measures that became more public than I wished. As a consequence, I am something of a man without a country, which makes this country look not so bad in comparison. I have reason to believe my former colleagues in the CIA have been sanctioned to kill me on sight should I show my face in countries where I previously conducted business. They really don't care what I do in this shit hole. I've always been a free bird, a wandering spirit. Now I'm as much a prisoner here as you are."

"Let's trade places."

"I don't think so. You've cost me in other ways, too. I had stock in Tower International. It's worthless now. And I held seats on the board of directors for White River Security and the Reichard Foundation, with which you became intimately acquainted. White River is in disarray; the FBI's going after them with everything they've got. The Reichard Foundation simply ceased to exist. All because those caesars met with a suspicious case of asphyxiation."

The Order of Avademe. Old Nick had belonged to their organization at one time. "The world is better off without them. The economy certainly is."

"Don't tell yourself that you've changed anything. Their lackeys have splintered off into smaller groups and are quietly plotting to pick up the slack. The free market was never designed to be truly free. Guys like you are meant to sweat income taxes, and guys like me are meant to retire in mansions."

Jake believed him. "Reichard and Taggert trusted you even though you worked for Old Nick?"

"They hired me to spy on him, which is why he put Kira in charge of the company. They were smart old codgers, but for my money, Nick was always one step ahead of them."

"He made fucking monsters and you sold them."

Russel snorted. "Nick's Biogens were no different than munitions or anything else I sold to countries like the

Philippines and Pavot Island."

"Those things ate people!"

Russel choked back laughter. "You should see the things Malvado has harvesting his drugs."

"And you work for him."

"He's no worse than Nick was, and you worked for Nick. He's no worse than Reichard and his boys were, and you wanted to *join* their club. Spare me your high-and-mighty-white-knight routine."

"Malvado uses black magic to rule this island. The population lives in fear. Aren't you afraid?"

"Uh-uh." Russel reached in between the buttons of his shirt and took out a bronze medallion. "Recognize this?"

Jake stared at the amulet, with its carved figure of a hero wielding a sword against a monstrous demon. "The Anting-Anting." According to legend, the Anting-Anting protected its wearer from demons.

"Seguera gave it to Nick. I took it off Nick's corpse and wore it when I killed Seguera."

"How poetic of you."

"What are you doing here?"

"I needed a cheap vacation."

"And somehow you wound up eating dinner with a man suspected of belonging to a terrorist organization?"

"He was an artist. I paid him to draw a portrait."

"Of whom?"

Jake held his tongue.

Opening the folder on the table, Russel took out a piece of paper. He turned it over, revealing the portrait

Humphrey had drawn of Maria. "I think this vacation has cost you a lot."

Maria stormed onto the wooden bridge, her footsteps echoing through the night. Almost immediately, she heard a man shouting at her. Turning, she saw a red laser beam moving along the wooden railing in her direction. She ran. Halfway across the bridge, gunshots rang out behind her. Spinning on one heel, she saw the silhouette of the man she had taken the gun from aiming a handgun at her.

The red dot of the machine gun she now held found the man's sternum, and she squeezed the trigger, igniting the darkness with muzzle flashes. The recoil knocked her off her feet, which saved her life: machine gun fire coming from the direction of the other soldier decimated the wooden railing where she had just stood. Over the gunfire, she heard the man she had shot scream, followed by a splash.

Rolling over, Maria crawled across the rest of the bridge. Behind her, the man continued to scream and splash, thrashing around in the river. As soon as her raw palms slapped grass and dirt, Maria launched herself into the woods. Ducking behind the first tree wide enough to accommodate her, she peeked around it.

The soldier she had shot staggered around in water up to his hips. Half a dozen shapes as silver as the moonlight clung to him, and blood flowed from open wounds. He sank below the surface, which turned turbulent, and did not rise.

Maria's eyes widened. *Piranhas!*

The remaining soldier ran to the embankment and stared at the water where his comrade had fallen. Then he looked straight at Maria and aimed his machine gun at her. She aimed hers as well. The man lowered his weapon, and his body convulsed. At first Maria thought the sound she heard over the river's rushing was sobbing. Then she raised the night vision goggles to her eyes and activated them. The world blossomed with bright green light, and she saw the man had doubled over with laughter. Lowering the goggles, she watched him shake his head and walk away.

What the hell?

Turning from the river, she entered the woods.

Jake tried not to react to the sight of Maria's portrait.

"You entered the country with Maria Vasquez." Russel took a printout from the folder and held the photocopy of Maria's passport photo beside the drawing. "Quite a resemblance, don't you think? That terrorist had talent."

Jake knew Russel was baiting him, trying to get him to comment on Humphrey.

"Miss Vasquez is a homicide detective with NYPD. You were a homicide detective with NYPD. She used to be partners with a man named Edgar Hopkins. *You* used to be partners with Edgar Hopkins. Mr. Hopkins vanished nine months ago. It stands to reason the two of you came here in search of this common denominator." He laid the printout and the drawing on the table. "What's Hopkins got to do with Pavot Island?"

Jake said nothing.

"Where's Vasquez?"

His heart beat faster. Maria was alive!

"Did the two of you come here to assassinate President Malvado?"

Jake clenched his teeth.

"So, we're back where we started?"

Jake blinked.

"Don't say I didn't warn you." Crossing the room, Russel opened the door and waved.

Two soldiers with red berets entered. Jake noticed the soldiers wore machetes on their belts.

"Take off his handcuffs," Russel said, closing the door as the soldiers marched toward Jake.

The soldiers jerked Jake to his feet, throwing him off balance. He heard a clicking sound, and the handcuffs came away, freeing his wrists.

Russel folded the drawing of Maria and put it and the printout inside the folder, which he set on a chair. He looked at Jake, then at the soldiers, and nodded at the table. The soldiers wrapped Jake's arms in theirs and dragged him toward the table.

Jake planted his feet on the floor and struggled. "No . . ."

Standing before him, Russel delivered a powerful blow to Jake's solar plexus.

Jake cried out and doubled over.

Russel sank his hands in Jake's hair and jerked his head

back, then leaned close to his face. "Where's the woman?"

Jake spat in his face.

Wiping his face on his jacket sleeve, Russel looked at the soldiers. "Left arm."

The soldier on Jake's right pinned Jake's arm behind his back, threatening to break it. The other soldier forced his left wrist down to the table and pulled his arm taut.

Jake saw peeling paint on the tabletop. Dents. Scratches. Blood.

Oh, God, no.

Standing beside the soldier on Jake's right, Russel drew the machete from his belt.

"Don't do it," Jake said. "I'm an American."

Russel positioned the machete's blade against Jake's forearm, three inches above his wrist. "This isn't America." He raised the machete above his head with both hands.

"No, don't!"

The machete left a trail of reflected light as Russel swung it into Jake's arm. Jake screamed as the blade bit into his bone. Pressing his left hand against Jake's arm, Russel pried the machete free. Jake continued to scream as blood gushed out of the gaping wound in his arm. Then Russel raised the machete and brought it down again, separating Jake's left hand and wrist from his arm.

Jake's agonized screams made his throat raw, the room spun around him, and he spiraled into darkness.

FIFTEEN

Maria didn't know if any other soldiers had gotten off the helicopter, so she moved deeper into the woods away from the river.

Moonlight slatted through the trees, causing rocks and moss to sparkle. Occasionally she raised the night vision goggles to her eyes, and the forest lit up around her. Stepping over another fallen tree, she swatted at mosquitoes swarming around her. She lowered the goggles, opened her bag, and found a packet of insect repellent towelettes and ran one over her arms. It burned her scratches and she hissed. Then she rubbed the towelette over her legs.

When she stood erect, she no longer saw the moonlight cutting through the trees ahead. A tall figure stood silhouetted before her, blocking the silvery light.

Maria recoiled. Taking a step back, she raised the

goggles. The blossoming green light revealed African features, but the man's white eyes appeared pure green, with no irises or pupils, and did not blink. She had seen that same flaccid expression scores of times on homicide victims in general and on the faces of sixty DOAs in particular: the faces of dead men and women. Jake's zonbies.

No, no, no.

Maria felt her blood rushing from her head. She had seen many corpses before but none standing upright. The man slapped a cold, leathery hand around her wrist, and she knew there was no way this was some junkie who had overdosed on a Caribbean toxin.

I will not scream.

Sucking in her breath, she drew the Walther, pressed its barrel against the man's forehead, and pulled the trigger. Despite the intensity of the muzzle flash, the goggles protected her eyes.

Fluid spurted out of the bullet hole in the man's head. He rolled his eyes and collapsed.

Maria stared down at the corpse, which did not rise. Jesus Christ, she had seen a zombie with her own eyes, and she had put it down! Was this an act of murder or self-defense? Was it even killing?

She couldn't remember how many rounds a Walther's clip held, but since it had been used in Hitler's army, she guessed six, plus one in the chamber. She had fired four shots, which left maybe three.

Branches snapped all around her. Shadows moved. Silhouettes revealed themselves.

Tucking the Walther in the waistband of her shorts, Maria leveled the machine gun. Jake had warned her to shoot the zonbies in their foreheads, as she had. Firing at their torsos would do no good. She needed to see the whites of their eyes.

Six men and women in tattered clothing emerged from the trees. Maria had to assume they saw her with their ghastly, unblinking orbs as they staggered moaning in her direction. They brandished machetes.

The Machete Massacres, she thought.

This was no crazy theory. It was really happening. The damned things were coming after *her*.

She raised her weapon to her shoulder and pressed one goggle against the sight. A glowing red sun flared over a man's pallid green flesh. She located a crease above his eyebrows and squeezed the trigger. A third eye appeared in the man's head, and he seemed to spit out of it. Then he collapsed and stopped moving.

The other zonbies had drawn closer. She turned in a circle, facing others, her heart racing. A female with an afro lifted her machete. Maria fired and missed, striking a tree instead. The woman brought the machete down, but before she could complete her arc Maria had fired again, striking her forehead. The woman's head snapped back, liquid spewing out of the crater in her forehead like tobacco juice.

In the time it had taken Maria to exterminate the woman, the other creatures had moved even closer to her. She had no choice but to fire a short, concentrated burst at them, driving them back. As expected, the torso shots had little impact, and the dead things resumed walking in her direction. Bracing the machine gun against her shoulder, she let it rip. She struck two of the remaining zonbies in their heads, dropping them, but did far more damage to the surrounding trees.

Turning sideways, she aimed the weapon at another approaching female. She waited until she could see the whites of her eyes—

And then a machete struck the barrel, ruining her aim as she triggered a burst of gunfire. Instead of destroying the female zonbie's head, she tore her torso open from between her breasts down to her crotch. Jerking her head to the left, Maria saw a Hispanic man pulling his machete back for another swing. She aimed her machine gun at his head at point-blank range and fired. The head exploded skull fragments and brain juice in all directions, and she glimpsed an airborne eyeball soaring past her.

When she heard the zonbie strike the ground, she turned to the woman whose torso she had ruptured. Sawdust and unrecognizable organs poured out of the giant fissure in the woman's chest, where fabric and flesh hung as indistinguishable rags. Maria aimed and fired. The woman's head shook from the impact, and she dropped as Maria's gun clicked.

Goddamn it!

Maria slung the weapon over her shoulder in case she stumbled across an ammo clip. Drawing the Walther, she bent over and seized a fallen machete. Traces of rotten flesh on the handle caused her to shudder. She heard footsteps behind her. Turning, she sprinted in the direction of the footbridge. Her chest and throat ached. As she drew closer to the edge of the woods, she heard the chopper and saw dirt kicking up in the bright light shining through the trees. The chopper hovered in the clearing above the river, creating turbulence on the water's surface.

They're waiting for me.

The men in the helicopter knew she would try to flee the woods as soon as she encountered the zonbies. If she set foot on the bridge, the chopper's machine guns would rip her to shreds. If she dove into the river, the piranhas would tear her to pieces, especially with her arms and legs all scratched up. She had no choice but to remain in the woods. Taking a deep breath, she took off, following the river once more. Holding the machete in one hand and the Walther in the other made for awkward running.

A heavyset Hispanic woman with bright orange hair came out from behind a tree, her eyes glazed with a sheen of milky blue death. Maria feared she would waste a bullet if she fired while running, and she gripped the machete in her weaker left hand, so she slammed the Walther's grip down on the woman's crown. A dull moan escaped the woman's parched lips, and she sagged onto her haunches. Slowing to a stop, Maria aimed the Walther at the forehead of the woman, who looked up at her with unblinking eyes. Wishing to preserve her limited ammunition, Maria shifted her machete into her right hand and resumed running.

A lanky man with mixed race features lumbered ahead of her. Maria thought she might run around him, but he extended his arms at his sides like a defensive basketball player, grasping at the air with one hand while his other hand waved a machete.

Maria cocked her right arm over her left shoulder as she ran straight at him and brought the machete down at an angle. The blade cleaved the man's skull above his right eye just below his brain. The eye looked up at the blade. Maria tried to yank the blade out, but it was wedged in her target. She shifted the Walther into her right hand, grasped the machete's handle with her left, then pressed the gun against the man's skull and squeezed the trigger. The shot blew the man's head back, painting the foliage behind him with brain fluid, the velocity of the impact freeing the machete.

Two shots left. Maria scooped up the zonbie's machete, slid it under her belt, and ran.

She didn't get far before almost running into the arms of a squat male zonbie with a bald head. Realizing that every time she fired the Walther the gunfire drew the attention of other zonbies, she jammed the gun in the waistband behind her and drew the other machete, one blade in each hand.

The zonbie swung his machete at her, and she jumped back to avoid it. He swung again, and this time she struck his blade with one of hers, producing sparks, and buried her other machete in his forearm. She applied pressure to that blade as she wrenched it free and felt the metal scraping bone. Had she been stronger, she might have cut off his sword hand.

Without acknowledging the sawdust seeping out of his wound, the zonbie swung his machete into Maria's left side.

She cried out as he pulled the blade and it sawed through her flesh. Then she stepped forward and plunged one of her machetes in the side of his neck.

To her astonishment, he opened his mouth and unleashed a hoarse cry, as if summoning his fellows. He swung the machete at her side again, and she moved closer to him so that his arm just wrapped around her back. Maria raised her left arm, waited for him to cock his arm, then buried the machete in his forearm. She had hoped to strike the same wound and hopefully chop the forearm off but missed by a good three inches. Still, the blade sank into bone, allowing her to twist his machete arm away from her.

The zonbie snapped his teeth at her face, and she flinched, then jerked the other machete out of his neck in a shower of sawdust and struck again. This time the blade struck the same gaping neck wound, a feat she repeated several times as she attempted to hack his head off. Finally, she gave up and pulled her other machete out of his forearm. He collapsed in a heap, his head flopping around on his ruined neck like a beached fish.

Maria took off, her breath coming in tortured rasps. Jake had told her a single bokor controlled an army of zonbies. Did that mean a bokor had seen her in action and knew which direction she was headed? Did all of the zonbies know? She had already lost track of the river, but using the drone of the helicopter as a marker, she headed deeper into the woods, closer to danger.

Maria ran almost a quarter of a mile into the woods before she had to stop to catch her breath, the danger being that the zonbies might hear her.

If they can hear, she thought.

She pushed the goggles on top of her head and wiped sweat from her forehead and around her eyes, then stretched the sore muscles in her arms. Coquis croaked around her, something they hadn't done around the zonbies. Did that mean she was safe?

Maria pulled the goggles down, adjusted them, and walked. Another quarter of a mile in and the woods came to an abrupt stop. She stood in high grass, facing a field. A road on her right led to a complex of six barracks illuminated by work lights. Seeing no zonbies, she crept forward.

A farm?

No, but definitely something organized. As she neared the complex, she realized the buildings were made of cinder blocks, with corrugated metal roofs. She stopped and crouched. A guard marched around the corner of the nearest building, clutching a semiautomatic rifle. She narrowed her eyes. He was dead. Hugging the earth, she waited for him to pass and move on to the next building. Then she ran to the closest window, stood on her toes, and peeked inside through a dirty pane of glass.

The building was the size of an army barracks, with mattresses scattered around the floor. She estimated as many as fifty men and women, mostly in their twenties and thirties, sat huddled in small groups. At first she thought they were zonbies, but then she realized they were scarecrows: filthy, emaciated creatures fixing before crossing over.

A man inhaled a cloud of Black Magic from a glass pipe, and his head rolled around on his neck, his eyes unblinking. A woman shoved a needle in her arm and looked heavenward. A pair of young girls took turns snorting black powder off a broken piece of glass. A man lay on his back, his chest rising and falling with effort.

They're dead and don't know it.

She looked left and right. No sign of the guard.

A shooting gallery in the middle of nowhere? Drug addicts close to death guarded by an armed zonbie?

She ran to the next building. Inside the unoccupied structure, she noticed a dozen examining tables. Near each table were metal tubs stained with blood and piles of big bags that reminded her of those she had seen for peat moss.

Sawdust, she thought.

Plastic tubes ran from the tables to the tubs, and flies swarmed the area.

This is where they drain their blood and stuff them.

Settling on her heels, Maria searched for any sign of security. Satisfied she was safe, she ran around the building to its corner and spotted the zonbie guard marching two buildings away. As soon as he was out of sight, she sprinted to the next building. Through the window, she saw mats, rugs, and mattresses on the floor.

Sleeping quarters?

The bokors needed to rest, and Humphrey had said

the zonbies supposedly harvested Malvado's drugs at night. They had to stay somewhere during the day.

She went to building four: more mats and rugs. More of the same filled building five.

There must be hundreds of them.

One building remained, and smoke billowed out of two different chimneys on its roof. The guard emerged around its corner.

Maria pressed her back against the wall, then hurried to the other end and circled that way. She ran to the last building and peered through a window. She saw another dozen tables, half of them occupied by nude male and female zonbies with rotting features. These tables had no tubes or tubs but rather wheeled carts. Two clothed zonbies stood at each table, and Maria watched in horror as they raised their machetes and hacked at the limbs of their emaciated "patients."

She realized the naked zonbies were in much worse condition than those attacking them: their tight skin had split at the seams. They did not even react to their dismemberment, and the standing workers tossed the severed limbs into the carts. Then each pair of zonbies worked in tandem to throw the trunks of the dismembered zonbies into the carts, which they pushed to the far end of the building.

Maria ran the length of the building for a better view. Through the next window, she saw the zonbies toss the limbs and trunks into an iron oven.

An incinerator. The zonbies were reducing other zonbies to ash.

Black Magic.

Jake had told her he and Edgar had "killed" as many as a hundred zonbies at an abandoned factory in the Bronx.

That must have been an operation similar to this one.

Turning from the window, she pressed her back against the wall and looked from side to side, relying on her ears as much as the goggles to locate the zonbie guard. She dislodged herself from the wall and was about to move when the zonbie marched past her from the opposite side.

No. *Another* guard!

Somehow she had managed to avoid him without even trying. He didn't notice her and disappeared behind the next building.

Maria exhaled and moved sideways along the building to the far corner, which she rounded. Facing deep fields, she saw over a hundred silhouettes in the distance. Maria pushed the goggles up on her head and blinked several times, allowing her eyes to adjust to the darkness without the aid of the night vision. A full moon cast silver light on the zonbies toiling in the acres of bloodred flowers.

Malvado's poppy crops.

She spied two figures on horseback, then two more.

Overseers. But are they alive or dead?

A roar filled her ears, and bright light caused her to wince. The helicopter soared overhead, its spotlight moving around on the ground. Bathed in light, she looked away. The copter flew over the field, its light revealing many more zonbies than she had discerned on her own. None of them reacted to the aircraft.

Recalling the map as best she could, Maria knew there

were more fields beyond this one, then a mountain and even more fields. She didn't want to head back in the direction of the first building, because both guards were in that area. That left returning through the woods to the river, which made sense now that the chopper had left. Securing her goggles once more, she turned and froze.

Both guards stood twenty feet away.

SIXTEEN

Maria jumped, even though she had sensed the guards even before she saw them. The zonbies lifted their rifles in unison. Seeing no other choice, she ran straight toward them. She zigzagged, and the zonbies followed her. Then she threw herself sideways at the closest zonbie's legs, which snapped like branches, and the dead thing collapsed over her. She rolled onto its sternum and sat up on the balls of her feet.

The other zonbie aimed its rifle in her direction. Maria swung one machete at the rifle's barrel, deflecting it, then chopped at one of the zonbie's knees with the other. The undead creature toppled over.

The first zonbie sat up behind Maria and thrashed around on his broken legs, attempting to create enough space to aim its rifle at her.

She drove her elbow into its mouth, shattering its front

teeth and knocking it down. Then she stood, leaving the one machete buried in the second zonbie's knee. She brought her remaining machete down with all her strength into the second zonbie's skull.

The dead thing's eyes rolled in their sockets, and its body convulsed. Then it turned still and fell back with the machete protruding from its head.

Maria spun on one heel, facing the first zonbie, which pointed its rifle at her as it struggled to sit up. She unslung her machine gun and swung it like a bat at the rifle, which flew out of the zonbie's hands. Moving forward, she raised the machine gun over her head and slammed the stock down on the zonbie's head. The dead thing blinked several times.

"Son of a bitch," Maria said, swinging the gun harder. This time she heard the cracking of skull, but the zonbie continued to blink. Grunting with strain, she swung the weapon a third time, splitting the zonbie's skull open and the machine gun's stock to pieces at the same time. Brain fluid spurted out of the rupture, and the zonbie fell.

Maria discarded her broken weapon and stood gasping for breath in the moonlight. What the hell had she gotten herself into?

In the distance, the chopper turned around.

Maria spied a crawl space under the barracks. She pulled her machetes out of the second zonbie and rolled the corpse under the space, then sat on her ass and kicked it out of sight. She did the same with the first corpse and threw the broken machine gun in after them. Sliding one machete under her belt, she carried the other machete and one rifle.

Firepower, baby.

She strode to the end of the building. With the chopper no longer at the river, she hoped to make it to the bridge by dawn. Stopping in her tracks, she sucked in her breath as a dozen machete-wielding zonbies emerged from the woods she had escaped. Her fingers tightened on the rifle. Then another dozen zonbies appeared behind the first group.

Ah, fuck.

The helicopter grew louder behind her.

Grunting with frustration, she ran back to the end of the building facing the fields and the chopper. The spotlight moved across the ground far away, and she sprinted to her right, passing the buildings designed to house the zonbie workforce. The field angled across the land ahead, trapping her between the undead harvesters and the security patrol. She stopped at the first building and located its screen door, which opened when she turned its handle.

No need to lock in junkies when you're providing their drug of choice.

She entered the dark building still wearing her goggles. The stench of feces, urine, vomit, and sweat assaulted her, almost causing her to pass out. Jesus, what she would have given for some vapor rub to dull the nauseating smell. Gagging, she steadied herself. Around the room, junkies fixed. In the green glow of the night vision, they appeared as dead as the zonbies.

They're just one step removed.

She crept through the crowd of sweating flesh to the rear of the building. Along the way, she opened four windows to let the stink out, allow fresh air in, and provide her with some escape routes if she got jammed up. Some of the scarecrows looked at her, but their faces showed no concern, and they returned to their drugs.

Passing two emaciated people attempting to have intercourse despite the man's lack of an erection, Maria reached a far corner, pressed her back against it, and slid to the floor. From this level, she observed a woman on her hands and knees snorting black powder off the floor and a man inserting a needle up one nostril. Moans coalesced into a wail of confused ecstasy and misery.

Jesus.

Draping the machete across her lap, she set the rifle behind her. She opened her bag, found some tissue, and wiped the cuts on her arms and legs. The tissue came away red and wet. She pressed one hand against the wound on her side and winced, then reached into her bag, took out her cigarettes, and lit one.

A few heads turned in her direction, then away.

Maria took a deep drag and exhaled. Humphrey had said the zonbies worked in the fields at night when no one would see them. If he had been right, all she needed to do was survive until dawn, and then she could waltz off the plantation.

When she finished her cigarette, she stabbed it out on the floor and rested her head against the wall. Believing the living skeletons around her posed no threat, she closed her eyes.

Maria awoke with a start and stared into pitch darkness. At first she thought she had removed the goggles in her sleep, but when she reached up with one hand she felt them where they belonged. Their electric charge had just died. She took them off and gasped at the sight of the creature on top of her. The naked scarecrow had pulled himself alongside her leg, which he proceeded to hump with his erection. With a disgusted cry, she shoved the scarecrow off her and jumped to her feet.

The man rolled over, grabbed another woman and a man with glazed eyes, and poked each of them with his organ.

Looking outside the window, Maria saw a shade of purple in the sky. In the distance, two or three hundred figures lumbered toward the complex, the overseers trotting their horses among them. They appeared human and bored.

Quitting time, she thought. She would have to wait until the zonbies were all packed away before she cut out. She turned back to the scarecrows on the floor, most of them unconscious.

The screen door opened, and she dropped facedown to the floor. A shadow filled the doorway. Maria reached out for the rifle. A zonbie entered the far end of the building, carrying a metal bucket. Swallowing, Maria pulled the rifle close to her body, hiding it. She located the machete a foot away.

Shit.

And she remembered she had tucked the Walther into the

rear waistband of her shorts, where the zonbie would see it.

Double shit.

The zonbie reached into the bucket and tossed something onto the floor near the scarecrows at his feet.

Food?

No. Handfuls of plastic dime bags.

Black Magic.

He might as well have been executing them with a gun while they slept, except then they could not serve as Malvado's slaves.

Maria watched the zonbie make his rounds, tossing quantities of the drugs at the sleeping scarecrows.

One of the skeletal junkies stirred, saw his treat, and lunged for it on all fours. He snatched a dime bag, tore it open with his remaining teeth, dumped the Magic on the floor, and snorted it up each nostril. He rolled over onto his back, rubbed his nose, and gazed at the ceiling.

Next, a naked woman looked up and followed a similar routine. By the time she had stopped snorting, the man had started masturbating. She crawled on top of him and pushed her vagina against his penis. Within seconds, they each grunted in a mockery of lovemaking.

Maria slid her hand across the floor, and her fingers curled around the handle of the machete, which she slowly drew closer to her, careful not to scrape the metal blade against the wooden floor. Holding the blade a quarter of an inch above the floor, she brought it to her hip, her shoulder aching with strain. She rolled two inches to one side, pushed the machete beneath her body, and laid flat.

When the zonbie turned his back to her, she rolled in the opposite direction, her cheek pressed against the filthy floor, and pulled the rifle beneath her. At last she had hidden both weapons, but now she experienced extreme discomfort. And she still had to worry about the Walther.

The zonbie moved closer. As the sky outside brightened, she noticed he wore leather sandals, his toenails were long, and his black skin seemed powder gray. Sweat formed on Maria's forehead, and she tried to regulate her breathing. She closed her eyes halfway and saw the zonbie step before her. She prayed the thing didn't notice the handgun. A painfully long moment passed, and she fought the urge to open her eyes.

I have to look fucked up enough to pass for one of these things.

A few packets of Magic landed near her face, and her eyelids twitched.

Damn it . . .

The zonbie walked away and she exhaled. Opening her eyes, she stared at the packets of Black Magic. Malvado was killing his people to create a workforce he did not have to pay or worry about betraying him. The zonbie returned to the front of the building, and even before he exited Maria heard scarecrows stirring and snorting Magic.

A hand came down on the packets before her, and she looked up into the bulging eyes of a woman with dark skin.

"It's all yours, sweetheart," Maria whispered as she got up onto her knees. "You need it. I don't."

She gazed out the window. Dawn had come, and none of the zonbies remained in sight. But how could she know they were inside their shelters, and even if they were, how did she know none of them looked out the windows?

A dull moan rose behind her, and when she turned around she saw other scarecrows had awakened and were consuming their drugs. All except one: a shirtless teenage boy who lay on his back. His chest did not rise or fall, and flies buzzed around him.

Maria grabbed the machete and took a step closer to the boy. *Oh, Christ, don't tell me I have to perform mouth to mouth on one of these—*

The boy opened his eyes and stared at the ceiling.

Maria froze in midstep.

The boy sat up with no visible sign of effort and turned his head in her direction like a windup doll. He rose and looked at her with unblinking eyes.

Oh, my God. He overdosed in his sleep. This is how it begins.

The boy pointed at her. His mouth opened in slow motion, and he uttered an unintelligible sound, "Ah-AH-ah . . ."

Maria's gaze darted around the room.

A few of the scarecrows glanced at the boy, then returned to the religious exultation of their addiction.

The boy continued to babble, his sounds growing louder.

Not a boy, Maria told herself. *A zombie.*

Moving around the scarecrows on the floor, she made straight for the newborn dead thing, who continued pointing and grunting. His flesh and eyes had not yet changed color, and he still appeared human, albeit a pathetic one. She buried the machete in the dead boy's skull. His eyes rolled and he sank to his knees. She wrenched the machete free, and he toppled over, chunks of brain falling out.

Maria had killed two soldiers in adrenaline-fueled self-defense and thirteen zonbies, but only this one had felt like an actual kill.

With her chest heaving, she returned to the window. No way did she intend to cross the entire building again. She picked up the rifle, tossed it out the window, then climbed through it and leapt to the ground, where she rolled across the grass and came up in a fighting crouch. She had never appreciated fresh air so much in her entire life. Retrieving her weapons, she tucked the machete into her belt, gripped the rifle in both hands, and ran. She headed toward the woods but also in the general direction of the fields.

Running with the rifle proved awkward, and Maria stumbled more than once but never fell. She didn't look behind her, fearing what she might see. Her desperate, heavy breathing filled her ears. The overseers were human, yet she saw no living quarters for them or their horses or vehicles for transportation. Did they ride the animals to work?

After a quarter of a mile without incident, Maria stopped and turned around. The buildings stood silent, with no movement around them, appearing abandoned. No more smoke rose from the rooftop of the Black Magic factory.

Dropping the rifle on the ground, she bent forward with her hands on her knees and vomited. Once finished, she stood straight and folded her hands behind her head, drawing in breath. She spat on the ground, propped the rifle against one shoulder, and walked toward the fields.

Acres of red poppies stretched before her.

Heroin. For all the misery Maria had witnessed in New York City because of drugs—addicts, robberies, murders— it felt oddly emotional to see the source of such devastation. How many souls had been harmed or destroyed because of such destructive greed?

Reaching into her bag, she took out the minibinoculars and focused them. Beyond the red poppies, acres of blue flowers matched the early morning sky.

Cocaine, she guessed. Malvado was a one-stop drug lord. *Someone's got to destroy him.*

But it wouldn't be her. She just wanted to get the hell off Pavot Island.

The temperature rose with the sun as Maria moved through the woods. Sweat streaked the grime and blood on her flesh, and she hacked at loose branches and vines with the machete. She didn't know what her first move would be once she escaped the woods.

A vine waved in the breeze before her, and she cocked her arm to knock it aside with the machete. The end of the vine opened, revealing fangs and a tongue that flicked in the air as a hiss escaped it. Maria gazed into the thick snake's malevolent eyes. Just yesterday the sight of such a serpent caused her alarm laughed and walked on.

Emerging from the foliage, Maria gazed at the riverbank. She wasn't sure how many miles upriver she had walked from the footbridge since the previous night, but she assumed the same breed of piranhas swam this water as well. Wiping sweat from her eyes with her arm, she followed the current.

Forty minutes later, Maria discovered a rowboat trapped in a crop of rocks. Peeling blue paint revealed rotting gray wood lined with cracks. Refusing to set foot even in shallow water, she crawled over the rocks and retrieved a frayed rope floating in six inches of water inside the boat.

Returning to the riverbank with the boat towed behind her, Maria coiled the rope at her feet, making sure the boat didn't break free and drift away. She pulled the boat onto the bank and stood it on one side, dumping out brown water and rotten leaves. Setting it back down, she tested the floorboards. They squeaked and groaned but didn't break.

She set the boat in the water, got into it on wobbling legs, and sat on the bench. The current immediately seized the craft, and Maria took control of the oars and steered the boat around the rocks. She had never rowed a boat before, and she found herself turning in a circle. When she rowed against the current, one oar snapped.

"Shit!"

Discarding the broken oar, she tried to stabilize the

boat but failed. Traveling backwards, the boat picked up speed, which she did not see as a positive development. She debated using the rifle as a makeshift oar but rejected the idea. It was too important to her survival. Instead, she rowed the lone oar with both arms and managed to turn the boat around.

Thunk.

Maria looked down at her feet. At first she thought the boat had struck a rock, but then she heard the sound again. And again. Beneath the water, something pounded on the bottom of the boat. The pounding grew faster, louder, and she felt the vibrations through the floorboards.

The piranhas!

She had to reach shore fast. Feeling the vibrations of the predators through the boat's bottom, she rowed faster and with great effort steered the boat closer to the opposite bank. The aft of the boat struck the rocks, and the boat rebounded away from her destination.

Glancing over her shoulder at nothing but cascading water, Maria rowed with all her strength, and this time when the aft hit rock she leapt toward land, her arms and legs flailing. She hit the ground harder than intended, then sat up and watched the river carry the boat away. She saw no sign of the piranhas.

Maria limped along a paved road flanked by bright green grass and lush trees. No traffic passed her, thank God. She could only imagine how she looked, her limbs streaked with blood and mud. Half a mile away, she saw a white house and a barn and a wooden corral-style fence that surrounded grazing cattle.

In the late morning sunlight, she found the events of last night almost impossible to accept. Emotion lumped in her throat, and she felt tears running down her cheeks. She had to learn what had happened to Jake.

Ducks in a pond flapped their wings as she crossed a dirt driveway and passed a green pickup. She stepped onto a long wooden porch with a sagging roof and knocked on the wooden frame of a screen door.

A Hispanic girl no more than twelve opened the inside door and stared at Maria through the screen. She made no effort to hide her disgust at Maria's appearance.

"Do you speak English?" Maria said.

The girl didn't answer.

"Are your mommy and daddy home?" Maria said in French.

The girl withdrew from sight, and then a woman who looked just a few years older than Maria appeared. Her eyes widened, and to her credit she did not gasp.

"Please," Maria said. "Please help me."

SEVENTEEN

When Jake opened his eye, he had no sense of his location. Ceiling tiles came into focus, where naked fluorescent bulbs hummed, and sunlight streamed through windows around him. His dry throat ached.

Where am I?

He tried to recall what had happened to him.

Pavot Island . . . Humphrey . . . Maria!

He attempted to sit up but found himself unable to move. Tipping his head forward, he saw wide leather restraints buckled across his chest, waist, and thighs, pinning his arms to the bed. Turning his head left and right, he took in a dozen empty beds around him.

A hospital ward.

An intravenous tube from an IV bag hanging on a stand beside him dispensed clear liquid into his left arm.

Russel . . .

He remembered the soldier pinning his arm to the table in the interrogation room while Russel drew back the machete.

Oh no.

He had to turn his head so his right eye could see his bandaged left arm. Tears formed as he raised the stump where Russel had cut off his hand and wrist. The restraint across his waist could not hold down an arm missing a hand. Blood seeped through the dressing.

Oh, my fucking lord.

Muscles in his cheek and neck twitched, and a sound escaped through his nostrils before he tipped his head back and screamed. Hurried footsteps echoed at the far end of the ward, but he continued screaming.

A Hispanic woman in a nurse's uniform leaned over him. "Relax, mister. Screaming will do no good."

"Fuck you! They cut off my fucking hand!" Spittle flew out of his mouth.

"If you think screaming will bring your hand back, then go ahead and scream. But you're setting yourself up for a major disappointment."

Tears burned his eye. "That shit-fucking cocksucker . . ."

The nurse glanced at his chart. "Mr. Helman, you can call me Ramona. I'll probably be your nurse for the rest of your stay here."

Jake didn't like the sound of that. "Where's here?"

"L'hôpital de la Pitié."

Jake's heavy breathing continued. "Hospital of Pity?"

"Mercy Hospital."

He snorted at the irony.

"We're just a clinic serving some of the farming communities and sometimes El Miedo."

Jake pictured the map of Pavot Island. "Those communities are sparsely populated, and El Miedo has a single prisoner."

"And we're a small staff."

He swallowed. "You have to help me. I need to get word to an American—"

"There's no US embassy here."

"But there are a bunch of US companies. You can get word to someone at—"

Ramona shook her head. "Listen to me very carefully. I'll do what I can to make you comfortable while you're here, but that's all I'll do."

"I was traveling with a woman. We were separated in Pavot City, where I was apprehended. Do you know if she survived or escaped?"

He heard more footseps.

"I don't know anything," Ramona said.

A man in a white lab coat joined them. He wore glasses and a stethoscope and appeared to be of mixed race descent, with light brown skin and frizzy black hair. Ramona handed him the clipboard, and he took Jake's pulse, then listened to his heartbeat.

"I'm Dr. Mathieu." He gestured at Jake's face. "How did you get those scars?"

Jake grunted. "An amphibious monster swiped me with its claws in Brooklyn."

Showing no expression, Mathieu removed a penlight and shined it in each of Jake's eyes, which caused him to frown. "And your eye?"

"A scarecrow strung out on Black Magic mistook it for an eight ball."

Mathieu pocketed the penlight. "Your vital signs are strong. We'll probably keep you here for a day or two, then send you on your way."

"Send me where? Home?"

The doctor's expression turned grave. "That's unlikely."

"Wherever I go, I'll end up back here, won't I?"

"Probably."

"Will I be missing my other hand? Or maybe a foot?"

Mathieu said nothing.

"You call yourself a doctor? You're a barbarian. What kind of Hippocratic oath do the doctors on Pavot Island take?"

"I realize you're upset. Nurse Faustin and I stopped your bleeding and cleaned your wound. We sutured it, disinfected it, and are providing you with painkillers. We saved your life. Pass judgment if you will, but we're doing all we can for you. We don't enjoy certain freedoms you do in the United States. Now if you need anything, tell Nurse Faustin." The doctor walked away.

"I have to piss," Jake said.

Ramona reached under the bed and brought up a plastic urine bottle, which she uncapped. Looking at Jake with dispassionate eyes, she unbuckled the belt of his shorts and unzipped his fly. Jake closed his eye as she pulled down his briefs and fumbled with his penis, inserting it into the bottle. Sighing, he emptied his bladder.

Ramona woke Jake again in the afternoon. She cranked the bed into an upright position and spoon-fed him rice and beans.

"Do you have a family?" Jake said.

"I have family all over the island."

"Do any of them oppose Malvado?"

"I'm not discussing politics with you. Stop talking and eat." She lowered her voice. "I can see you're a fighter. You'll need your strength."

"*You* need strength—all of you. My country and the United Nations obviously don't give a damn about this island, so you need to take care of yourselves."

"I've lived here my entire life. Most of us have. Foreigners don't move to Pavot Island to live, just to advance their careers by running factories. That's all we are to Americans: a cheap resource easily exploited. The corporations that run your country don't want that to change."

"That's why you have to take charge of your own destiny."

Setting down the spoon, Ramona looked at him. "That's easier said than done. It's hard to revolt when you have children, elderly parents, bills . . ."

"You have to be willing to make sacrifices to improve life *for* your children."

"Really? Is your country so perfect? Freedom there is just an illusion to keep the masses happy. At least here we *know* we're slaves to a corrupt system."

"No, my country isn't perfect." He gestured with his stump. "But we don't maim our prisoners."

"How do you know? Your government detains suspects indefinitely, with no hope of trial. They send prisoners to black sites where no one knows what happens to them. You don't even know who your real leaders are. We know Malvado."

"That's why you can overthrow him if you'd all just pull together."

She offered him a patronizing smile. "Okay, you're right. It's that simple. I'll start the revolution on my next day off."

"That's a start."

Male voices echoed at the far end of the ward.

Ramona's expression turned serious, and she carried Jake's lunch away.

"Was it something I said?"

Two soldiers wearing camouflage fatigues and red berets jogged around Ramona, who kept walking. Jake tensed up as they approached his bed, but they passed him and stood at the opposite end of the ward with their machine guns aimed at the floor.

Four more figures emerged from the hallway. Registering a large man in a royal-blue uniform and Russel's bald head, Jake swallowed the last of his food.

Ramona nodded to these men as she passed them, and Jake realized none other than Malvado himself walked beside Russel. He had to admit the dictator's shoulders were as broad as they had appeared in the billboards, and the man stood six inches taller than Russel.

Two tall and muscular dark-skinned men dressed in civilian clothes followed them. Jake's testicles crawled deep inside his scrotum for protection. As the men stopped at the bed, two more red berets took position at the ward's entrance.

"This is Helman." Russel motioned to Jake, who felt his blood simmer at the sight of the man who had maimed him.

Malvado looked Jake over.

A man that size could break me in two even if I wasn't helpless in a hospital bed, Jake thought.

Malvado leaned closer, allowing Jake to discern gray stubble on his shaved head. The man who had ruled his country with an iron fist for three decades looked into Jake's one good eye and spoke with a deep voice and a heavy accent. "You're a private investigator, eh? Like Tom Selleck." His white teeth gleamed.

Jake tried not to show fear. "Yeah, Magnum, PI, without the mustache."

Malvado made a wiping gesture over his face. "Maybe you should grow one and a beard, too."

Meaning I should try to cover up my ugly face? Jake remained impassive.

Malvado scowled and made a dismissive gesture. "William, this man is nothing. Put him to work in the fields."

"I was hoping to interrogate him some more."

Try it. Jake didn't know what he would do to Russel, but he relished the opportunity.

"How will he help harvest my drugs if you cut off his

other limbs?" Malvado's accent became more pronounced as his voice grew louder. "Do as I say."

Russel bowed his head. "Of course, Mr. President."

Malvado turned and marched away, and Russel followed like an obedient dog. The other two men in the party stood glaring at Jake. They looked almost identical, like younger versions of Malvado, with tight black hair.

Brothers, Jake thought. *His sons. The Uday and Qusay of Pavot Island.*

The two men followed their father.

Jake stared at the nearest ceiling fan. With no air-conditioning, the fans and windows provided the only relief from the blistering heat.

Ramona returned with a pan of water and some rags.

"Your fearless leader is charming," Jake said.

Ramona unbuttoned his shirt, revealing a dozen purple bruises where he had been shot with the rubber bullets. She dipped a rag into the water and washed his chest and underarms.

"You're afraid to say anything about him, aren't you?"

The look in her eyes confirmed his suspicion.

The light outside turned orange as Ramona finished feeding Jake his dinner: chicken, carrots, and rice.

"It's been a long day for you, hasn't it?" Jake said.

Ramona wiped the corners of his mouth with a napkin. "I work long days when we have patients, shorter ones when we don't. I'm sure it's been much longer for you."

"Malvado wants to put me to work in the fields. What does that mean?"

Ramona's eyes showed sympathy, but she said nothing.

"Yesterday right before he was shot dead, a man told me zonbies harvest Malvado's heroin and cocaine for him."

"Do you believe in zonbies?"

Jake nodded. "We had an epidemic of Black Magic in New York City last year. It did some crazy things to people."

"I don't know anything about that."

A door slammed, and two soldiers wearing red berets marched along the ward to Jake.

"We're converting him," one of the soldiers said.

Jake stared hard at the two men. "I don't think I like the sound of that."

Ramona looked down at him, chart in hand. She opened her mouth to speak, then closed it. Instead, she unhooked the IV tube from Jake's arm, swabbed the puncture, and applied a Band-Aid to it. Then she lowered the bed.

The soldiers stood at opposite ends of the bed and wheeled it away. As they did, Ramona made the sign of the cross, which didn't ease Jake's mind.

The soldiers wheeled him feetfirst to the red door at the opposite end of the ward. The soldier Jake was able to see opened the door, and they brought him into an empty room except for a battered wooden desk. They parked him alongside one wall and exited. Alone, Jake gazed up at a dirty light fixture. The room had no windows.

How the hell do they intend to convert me? He knew of only one way for a living person to become a zonbie, and a component of the process included a fatal overdose of Black Magic.

He hoped he had gotten through to Ramona, but he doubted it. She was right: the people on Pavot Island accepted Malvado, Black Magic, and zonbies as part of their daily existence. It was a long shot that the nurse would risk her life to save his. She had family, and Humphrey had said Malvado struck out at his enemies through their families.

Minutes passed.

Half an hour?

The door swung open and Russel stood there. Behind him, a rubber stopper struck the tiled floor again and again.

A cane, Jake concluded.

A hunched-over old woman entered the room, her gray hair pulled back beneath a scarf folded into a triangle. Despite the heat, she wore a shawl. Wrinkles like crevices crisscrossed her brown face, and she wore gold hoop earrings, like a gypsy. One of her eyes bulged in its socket, and her pupils seemed to look in different directions.

She's a witch, Jake thought. *A Mambo.*

Grasping the cane, the woman stopped at the bed and studied Jake. He had no doubt she was evil to her core.

Leaving the door open, Russel entered the room and stood near Jake. The old woman hobbled over to the desk.

"This is Mambo Catoute," Russel said. "She's the high priestess of the Church of the Black Snake and the most powerful bokor on Pavot Island. When she's through with you, you'll wish you'd spent a few more days in my company."

Jake struggled against the restraints. "You're as bad as Malvado and this old witch."

"I never said I wasn't. You're the one who pretends to be a hero."

Jake heard a match being struck, and a moment later dark smoke curled toward the ceiling from before Mambo Catoute. When she stepped away from the desk, Jake saw the wick of a thick black candle burning. His eyes widened at the sight of the smoke.

Black Magic.

The old woman cackled, and he noticed she missed several teeth.

Russel flicked off the light, leaving the candle's yellow flame glowing.

Jake sucked in his breath and looked away.

Russel chuckled. "That won't do any good. How long can you hold your breath? Not long. This Magic will *own* you. After a few hours in here, you won't be able to stop thinking about it, and we'll be only too happy to provide you with what you need." He helped Mambo Catoute out of the room and closed the door.

Sweat formed on Jake's brow. He clenched his teeth. He had given up cocaine two years ago when Sheryl had found his stash and kicked him out of their apartment. Next he gave up alcohol after Sheryl had left a piece of her soul inside him and then cigarettes. He had started exercising again, gotten himself into shape, felt healthy. Now this . . .

It isn't fair!

Rocking from side to side, he hoped to knock the bed

over. His efforts only exhausted him, forcing him at last to take a deep breath. His mouth and nostrils gulped sweet-smelling air, and in the darkness as his chest swelled, the Magic took immediate effect.

Jake exhaled a tremulous breath. His jaw slackened. His mind clouded. His heart rate sped up. His senses tingled and awakened. His eyelids fluttered. He inhaled the sweet-smelling smoke again, then smiled and moaned with pleasure. He forgot all about Sheryl and Laurel and Maria and Edgar and Malvado.

Like magic.

EIGHTEEN

Maria desired a long, hot bath but had no time for luxury and settled for a shower instead. The steaming water stung her scratches, blood and mud swirling at her feet. She soaped herself up twice and shampooed and conditioned her hair. The deep gash in her side required stitches. Although she buried her face in her hands, she did not cry again.

After drying off, she applied disinfectant to her wounds. The scratches were too long and too numerous for that. She wrapped a roll of gauze around her waist until she had used it all up, binding her deepest wound. Pulling on a terry cloth robe, she faced the mirror. Although she *looked* sane, she doubted she would ever be the same.

In the kitchen, she sat at the table. Rosa, the mother, served her a plate of scrambled eggs, which she devoured, and a mug of strong coffee. Celia, the daughter, sat watching her with a dour expression.

"Merci," Maria said.

Rosa joined her with a cup of coffee. "Your clothes are in the dryer. I got most of the blood out of them."

A tall man with a thick mustache entered the kitchen and leaned against the sink. Hector wore boots, jeans, and a long johns top with the sleeves rolled up, covered with a light layer of dirt. "Celia, go into the living room."

"I don't want to."

"Do as I say."

Pouting, the girl obeyed.

Maria sipped her coffee. "That's so good."

Hector folded his arms. "As you see, we have a daughter."

Rosa cocked her head. "Hector . . ."

"It isn't just us. We have to think of her."

"I don't want to endanger you," Maria said. "I'll be on my way as soon as my clothes are dry. I appreciate what you've done for me."

"We won't turn you away," Hector said, "but we have to put you in touch with people who will take you someplace safer."

Maria held his stare. "Someone I can trust, I hope."

"I called a friend who's an activist. He knew the man who was killed accompanying you in Pavot City yesterday. He's coming to help you."

You mean he's coming to get me out of your hair. "Thank you."

"What happened to you?" Rosa said.

"She went where she didn't belong," Hector said.

Maria wanted to challenge him, but she couldn't be rude after they had taken her in, so she just sipped her coffee.

Maria sat on the cement steps of the porch, smoking a cigarette and stroking the back of a white cat, when a dusty Subaru Outback pulled into the driveway. She had changed into her clothes.

A short, balding Hispanic man with a wide mustache got out of the Subaru. He wore a dark green plaid shirt. Crossing the lawn, he spoke in English. "Good afternoon. Are you my tourist?"

Maria smiled. "Forgive me for being an ugly American, but I think I've seen enough of your country."

Setting one foot on a step, he leaned on his knee. "Then we'll have to see about getting you home." He held out his hand. "Jorge De Jesus."

She shook his hand. "Maria Vasquez."

"Puerto Rican?"

"By way of Manhattan. Are you a member of Pavot for the People or the People for Pavot?"

"Honestly, I forget. I wish to see Le Père liberated from El Miedo and reunited with La Mère. Nothing matters more than freeing Pavot Island from Le Monstre."

Maria inhaled smoke and allowed it to seep through her nostrils. "More people on this island need to share your attitude."

Jorge glanced at the house. "They're good people. It's difficult to live under the thumb of a dictator. Please tell me what happened. I know you met Humphrey at Coucher du Soleil."

Maria recounted how Humphrey had been killed

outside the restaurant and she and Jake had been separated.

A tear ran down one side of Jorge's face. "Forgive me." He wiped his face on his shirtsleeve.

"I'm sorry. Hector said you and Humphrey were friends."

"A euphemism." Jorge groaned, then raised his gaze to the sky. "This is not the time for tears."

Maria clasped her free hand over his. "There's never a wrong time to mourn our loved ones." She stabbed out her cigarette and stood. "I jacked a car and fled the city. A chopper firebombed the highway, driving me into the woods."

"We call it La Forêt Noire."

"'The Black Forest.' How appropriate. Have you ever had the pleasure?"

Jorge shook his head. "Anyone who goes there remains there. Until now."

"A river stocked with piranhas divides the woods. It's a smoke screen to hide Malvado's drug crops. Your Black Forest is lousy with zonbies. I saw how those things are made and the Magic."

"How did you survive?"

"I put down more than a dozen of them."

"I've never heard anyone claim that before."

"I'm from New York."

Jorge smiled. "I think I like you."

"It's your turn to share. What happened to my partner?"

"I don't know."

"Is it likely they killed him?"

"Oui. If they took him prisoner, they tortured him to

death in Pavot City, or they'll repurpose him."

"You mean turn him into a zonbie?"

Jorge nodded. "I have contacts all over Pavot. I've heard nothing about Jake Helman being taken into custody. You have to assume he's dead."

Maria's eyes watered. "Humphrey joked about being a coward. He was anything but."

"I know." Jorge's voice cracked. "He was a good man. When Malvado's officers discover what you've done, they'll turn this island upside down looking for you. We need to get you someplace safe fast, and then we have to send you back to Miami."

"I was thinking the same thing."

As Jorge steered the Subaru out of the farmhouse's driveway, Maria, sitting in the backseat, stared at the woods across the road.

Zonbie land, she thought.

"Malvado thinks nothing of killing our people to create slaves," Jorge said.

"Is that the only plantation?"

"There are five that we know of."

"Which could mean as many as fifteen hundred zonbies. How long do those things last? He must need a steady supply of scarecrows."

"What the jails don't provide, he gets from the general population. Black Magic is easy to come by in our cities. It's cheap, and the drug dealers are never arrested—"

"Because they work for Malvado."

"They serve a function for him anyway."

They crested a hill.

"Get down," Jorge said, his tone serious.

Maria glimpsed one police car and one military jeep parked in the middle of the street at the bottom of the hill. Crouching behind the seat, she counted four uniformed figures standing in front of the vehicles.

"Reach below your seat. There's a lever there wrapped in fabric that matches the carpet and upholstery."

Maria felt along the bottom of the seat. "Got it."

"Pull it and take your weight off the seat."

Sliding off the seat, she pulled the lever, and the seat cushion popped up. Raising it higher, she gazed down at two rifles, one machine gun, and boxes of ammunition. Without waiting for instructions, she laid her rifle and machete over the other armaments and crawled on top of them, the Walther in her pocket. She had to bend her knees to fit inside the compartment, and the weaponry pressed against her.

"Before you close the seat, locate the lever from inside."

Maria slid her hand along the bottom of the compartment, discovered an opening, and touched the lever. "I have it."

"After you put the seat down, raise the lever and hold it inside. No one will see it, and it will be impossible to open the seat from the outside."

She lowered the cushion, cutting off the light, and

heard the seat lock into place. Pulling the lever inside, she took a deep breath. With the gap for the lever providing the only ventilation, the temperature climbed.

Maria felt the car slow and stop. She heard Jorge's muffled voice but could not make out his words over the sound of her own breathing. His tone sounded gentle, easygoing. Two more voices: a man's and a woman's. The car stopped vibrating and the front door closed.

Jorge got out.

Silence for a moment. The air grew stuffy. The compartment felt like what she imagined the inside of a coffin must be like, only less comfortable.

The voices grew louder. Weight sank into the seat above her; the upholstery squeaked and springs groaned. The woman spoke to the man, warbling as if underwater. A loud metallic sound followed.

The hatchback.

Knocking, banging, hands sliding. Metal scraping against metal. One of the inspectors prodded the vehicle with what must have been the barrel of a gun.

If they fire at the seat . . .

Sweat soaked her body. She couldn't breathe.

So fucking hot!

The hatch closed, then the rear doors, then finally the front door. The engine roared to life. Jorge spoke again and the car eased forward.

Maria counted to ten and pulled the lever. The seat popped open a crack, and she sucked in fresh air.

"Raise the seat but don't sit up yet."

With one hand, she lifted the seat higher, and air-conditioning settled over her. "Thank you."

"You're welcome."

"If they'd found me, they would have killed you."

"I don't want to overstate things, but on Pavot Island we live with that fear every day."

"I couldn't do it."

"You'd be surprised how strong the will to survive is. Look what you did last night."

He's right.

"You can get out now, but you'd better stay flat."

Maria climbed out of the compartment, set the seat down, and lay across it. "This is a lot more comfortable than lying on those guns."

Twenty minutes later, as the Subaru climbed a mountain road, she peeked out the window and recognized the rain forest stretching below. A short while later, the Church of St. Anthony came into view.

"Don't get up yet."

Maria felt the car slow down and saw the church as they circled it. After several seconds, they stopped in the shadow of a wide garage.

Jorge got out, opened one of the gray wooden doors, then got back in and drove the Subaru inside. He removed a flashlight from the glove compartment and set it on the seat beside him, then spoke without turning around. "St. Anthony's is often under surveillance by Malvado's secret police. I'm going to get out and close the garage door behind me. When I do, walk over to the wooden shelves against the wall. Pull back the mat and you'll find a trapdoor. Climb down the ladder and shut the trapdoor. Don't let it slam. Follow the tunnel until you can go no farther, and wait for me there."

Jorge left the car, closed the door, and exited the garage. The wide door swung shut, and light seeped in through the cracks in the walls.

Maria stepped out and removed her weapons from the hidden seat compartment. Light glinted off an old Mercedes, a pickup, and a riding lawn mower, and tacked crates obscured tools hanging on the walls. Standing before the wooden shelves covered with paint cans and cleaning chemicals, Maria pulled back the floor mat, exposing the square trapdoor with an iron ring secured to its surface. Setting the rifle down, she seized the ring in both hands and opened the trapdoor, her back straining with effort. She stared down at the iron rungs bolted into the concrete walls of the shaft and a cement floor.

Very professional.

Maria climbed halfway down the ladder, the rungs cool to her touch, then picked up her rifle, closed the trapdoor, and descended into murky grayness. Dull light illuminated the tunnel, and when she reached the floor she saw that three caged work lights hung from a yellow cord strung along the low ceiling. She followed the cord, passing a sofa, a cot, a table, and chairs. At the end of the tunnel she glimpsed hinges and the outline of a door, which opened away from her, revealing Jorge and a short priest.

"Maria Vasquez, meet Father Alejandro."

The priest's features were tanned. Maria guessed he was forty, though he appeared younger.

"Miss Vasquez." Alejandro held out his hand.

Shaking the priest's hand, Maria felt rough skin. Alejandro did hard work in addition to offering spiritual guidance. "Nice place you've got here, Father."

"This tunnel was part of the church's original construction. It was sealed off generations ago. My predecessor reopened it. I'm glad you like it, because you'll be staying here until we can arrange for you to leave Pavot. In the meantime, please join us." Alejandro gestured inside the room where he and Jorge stood.

Maria followed them into a red-carpeted office with two desks and a copy machine.

Alejandro arranged three chairs so they faced each other, and Maria sat. He opened a small refrigerator. "May I offer you something to drink? We have soda, juice, and beer."

"A beer would be great."

"Jorge?"

"The same."

Father Alejandro opened three bottles with pirate ships on their labels, served his guests, and sat between them. "You've stirred up some excitement; the police and military have doubled their patrols. But your picture hasn't been broadcast on TV, so the people don't know what the commotion is about, only that three members of the People for Pavot were killed in Pavot City yesterday."

Maria sipped her beer, which tasted damn good. "What about Jake?"

"Our news organization is a propaganda arm of the government, and our underground press has no access to government matters. We only know that many soldiers were dispatched to an abandoned factory in the neighborhood where our three friends were killed. Shots were fired and the soldiers left. I fear your companion is no more."

Jake. Maria's jaw tightened.

"We need to get you off this island immediately."

"Miriam said she arranged for a boat to transport us tomorrow night."

"That will be too late. You're now an enemy of the state. As long as you're free, the population will be subjected to Malvado's ruthless methods. It's imperative that you leave tonight and that Miriam announces your return to Miami. When Malvado realizes you've escaped, life here will return to normal."

"How do you propose I leave?"

"One of the US companies with a factory here bottles the very beer we're drinking. They have a cargo ship leaving tonight. You'll be on it."

NINETEEN

Gazing at the ceiling, Jake experienced ecstasy. Mambo Catoute's candle continued to spew Black Magic smoke into the air for him to breathe. He no longer remembered why he was unable to move his arms and legs, but he regretted being unable to play with himself when he felt so good.

The door opened, and two soldiers wearing gas masks entered. One walked over to the desk and pinched the candle's flame.

No! Jake feared he would never experience such a perfect high again.

The other soldier stood before Jake, aiming the machine gun at his face. Jake's heart beat faster. The first soldier joined the one closest to him. They both looked down at him through the bulbous, insect-like goggles of the masks and spoke to each other in Spanish or French. Hell, it could have even been English. It was too muffled for his stoned ears to decipher. The soldier who had extinguished the candle reached down, and Jake tilted his head to see the restraints holding him in place. The soldier unfastened them and they fell away.

That was nice of him, Jake thought.

The soldier with the machine gun motioned for Jake to exit the room, but when Jake got off the bed he folded in half and struck the floor. Feeling no pain, he rolled over. The soldiers hauled him to his feet.

"Thank you," he said.

They dragged him out of the room and into the hospital ward, where the open windows let hot air in and black smoke out. Dusk had settled over the palm trees outside the clinic. The soldiers peeled off their gas masks, revealing sweaty features. One was black, the other Hispanic.

Ramona stood near an empty bed, watching him. As they passed her, she made the sign of the cross.

Nice lady, he thought.

The soldiers took him through a door and to a flight of cement stairs. Halfway down, they dumped him on a landing. His face and palms slapped cement, but he felt no pain. One soldier said something he didn't understand, and the other laughed. They lifted him, pushed open a metal door, and guided him through an empty corridor to a set of glass doors. Two more soldiers guarded the entrance.

The doors opened, and Jake felt fresh air on his face. An olive green military truck idled in the parking lot. The men dropped the vehicle's gate, heaved Jake into the back of the truck, and secured shackles around his ankles.

"Don't try to climb out," one of the soldiers said. "The truck will drag your face off."

Why would he try to climb out of the truck? He just wanted to enjoy this feeling, which he hoped would last forever. Listening to the truck doors close and the engine rumble, he closed his eyes and felt the vibrating metal.

Russel gazed out at the night sky from the backseat of his limousine as his chauffeur drove through the security gates of Malvado's palace. Half a dozen armed soldiers stood at attention, and many others patrolled the grounds.

During his time on Pavot Island there had been a number of minor attacks on the government: a suicide bomber here, an IED there. In each instance, minor damage had been inflicted, and neither Malvado nor his sons had ever been in real danger. But Russel had developed a keen sense for trouble in nations such as this, and his gut told him trouble was brewing. Although Malvado had ruled the island for three decades, change was in the air, and Russel prided himself on sensing when the wind shifted direction.

The limo drove up the long driveway, past elaborate gardens of tropical plants, colored rocks, and glowing fountains. Work lights illuminated the grounds and the palace, a hybrid of Versailles and the White House. The central portion of the château, which served as Malvado's home, stood three stories high; the wings on the left and right, which extended from the main building at forty-five-degree angles, were two stories each. The right wing served as Malvado's military center, while the left wing served as the parliamentary headquarters.

The limo stopped at the military wing, and the chauffeur got out and opened the door for him. A staunch believer in rank, Russel did not acknowledge the driver. He crossed the walk and mounted the steps below the enormous Pavot Island flag. Two soldiers wearing red berets saluted him, and he returned the gesture as they opened the doors for him.

Inside the great hall, two more soldiers offered salutes, and Russel signed in at the admittance counter. Glancing at the other names above his, he saw he was the last to arrive, which caused a slight pang in his stomach. Punctuality was important to him, and Malvado might take his tardiness as a sign of disrespect. Like other dictators he had known, Malvado demanded respect at all times.

Nearing another pair of armed soldiers, Russel straightened his tie. When they opened the grand door for him, he did not return their salute because he was too focused on organizing the information in his mind.

Malvado sat at the head of the thick oval table in a chair that would have resembled a throne had a smaller man sat upon it.

As usual, his sons, Maxime and Najac, sat at his left hand and his right hand. The brothers made Russel nervous these days. He recognized their hunger for more power and envisioned a scenario in which they assassinated Malvado and fought for the seat of control. Russel did not wish to get caught in a death dance between them, but he would be risking his own life to warn Malvado about the danger they posed.

Malvado was no fool, and he told his sons he intended to retire one day so they might rule in his place, implying that Maxime, as the elder son, would become president and Najac vice president. Maxime seemed satisfied with this plan but impatient to see it implemented, while Najac remained silent on the matter. Russel had good reason to believe Najac had his eye on the top spot.

Either way, he trusted neither son and saw no reason to believe they trusted him. Unfortunately, most of his money was tied up in the Pavot Island National Bank, and any effort to move it would arouse Malvado's suspicion. He had been investing small sums very carefully, creating just enough of a fund to survive if he needed to flee the island but not enough to permit him the lifestyle to which he had become accustomed.

The usual suspects sat around the table: Mambo Catoute, dressed in an elegant black dress, beside Maxime; General Buteau, who headed the military, beside Najac; and Colonel Solaine, the head of the police, beside him. The alliances were clear to Russel. Did Malvado see them?

The dictator glared at Russel as he sat beside Mambo Catoute. "Thank you for joining us."

Russel felt the eyes of everyone but Mambo Catoute on him. "Forgive me, Your Excellency. I wanted to make sure our prisoner was in no condition to escape."

"Do you doubt the competence of our military and police?"

General Buteau and Colonel Solaine stiffened.

"Not at all," Russel said. "But Helman has proven himself difficult before. His actions interfered with the plans of both Nicholas Tower and Seguera."

"Mambo Catoute administered the Black Magic, did she not?"

"Yes." Russel knew to answer Malvado's questions directly without any maneuvering.

"Then he is useless, except to work on my plantations."

Russel bowed his head. "So he is, Mr. President."

"What I want to know is where this *woman* is. William, please bring everyone up to speed."

Russel faced the others one at a time. "Her name is Maria Vasquez. She's a police detective from New York City, just like Helman was before he became a private investigator. They were both partners with Edgar Hopkins, another police detective who disappeared last year. Vasquez and Hopkins investigated a series of murders by drug dealers during an epidemic of Black Magic."

Malvado shot Mambo Catoute a sharp look. "Where did that Magic come from?"

"I don't know," Mambo Catoute said in a raspy voice that reminded Russel of a snake. "Someone else discovered the secret."

"How?"

"I may be the high priestess here on Pavot, but don't forget New York City and Miami are crawling with Houngans and Mambos from here and Haiti. The Creoles in Louisiana have their own churches."

Malvado turned to General Buteau. "I want the security around my plantations doubled. Tell the guards to shoot any trespassers."

Buteau nodded. "Yes, Mr. President. But—"

"What?"

"You told me you wanted the Americans taken alive. That's why my men fired warning shots and rubber bullets until the woman reached the Black Forest."

"I do want her alive. I want to know why she and Helman are here. But I won't risk my crops to satisfy my curiosity."

"She killed thirteen of my zonbies," Mambo Catoute said.

"You mean my *father's* zonbies," Maxime said.

Mambo Catoute bowed. "Yes. Forgive my slip of the tongue."

Malvado turned to Colonel Solaine. "You're unusually quiet."

Russel watched Solaine summon the courage to speak. He and Buteau often tried to blame each other for their failures. "I've circulated the woman's photos and the drawing to my precincts. My men know what she looks like. But with the public in the dark . . ."

Malvado smiled like a shark. "Are you questioning my methods?"

"No, sir. Of course not."

"This woman is a foreigner. She's been in the country for three days, yet none of you can find her. Someone is helping her. I want to know who."

Silence hung heavy in the room.

"Mambo Catoute, why can't you use your powers to track her down?"

Catoute cast a fearful look at Russel, whose stomach tightened. "The hotel suite she shared with Helman was swept clean: carpets, floors, and furniture vacuumed, hairbrushes, clothing, and makeup taken, drains and toilet sanitized. The car they rented was clean, too."

"Who cleaned that suite?"

"The staff did a general cleanup but not the thorough job I found," Russel said. "Someone went into that room after the cleaner and before me."

"Without DNA, there's nothing I can do," Catoute said.

Malvado rose. "Every one of you in this room will share responsibility if this *putain* escapes. She's seen my crops and my slaves, and she knows we took Helman into custody. It's one thing for peasants to go to the United States on a rubber raft; they go there as illegals and tell no one but their own kind about our activities here. It's another thing entirely if an *American policewoman* tells the world what she witnessed. Until she's apprehended or killed, I want Maxime to receive hourly progress reports on what you're doing to resolve this situation."

Like children, they stared at the table while Malvado strode out of the room.

TWENTY

Mambo Catoute—born Puri Catoute seventy-one years earlier—made her way into the limo waiting outside the palace. Although she felt safe on the palace grounds, the chauffeur doubled as her bodyguard and drove her the quarter of a mile to the L'église du Serpent Noir. During the short drive, she paid little attention to the fountains and gardens that decorated the grounds.

The chauffeur parked at the church—the largest on Pavot Island—and got out and opened her door. Sensing the man's fear as he helped her out of the vehicle, she ignored him. She hobbled forward with the use of a cane, but her legs felt strong, her back firm. She couldn't complain about her health considering her age. She had made more than one deal with a devil resulting in the finest lifestyle one could hope for on Pavot Island: luxurious living quarters, fine clothes, servants, and power. Catoute had helped Malvado seize control of Pavot, and he had rewarded her with a seat at his table.

Inside the church, a tall man and a slender woman waited for her near the railing that overlooked the sunken worship hall. Catoute didn't need to see their features to recognize Issagha, the top Houngan in her court, and Sivelia, Catoute's granddaughter, whom she was training to one day succeed her. Catoute had known her servants would be waiting for her, anxious to hear any news of Malvado's inner circle.

They're becoming too curious, she thought.

Issagha wore a black African robe with white patterns, his hair in a slight afro. In his midfifties, he had served Catoute well, never overstepping his position and patiently rising in the ranks. Sivelia, twenty-two, was lithe and sexual, her wide eyes ever observant. Catoute had hoped her daughter, Pharah, would follow in her footsteps, but Pharah had refused to embrace the Church of the Black Snake, so Catoute had taken her daughter's daughter under her wing instead.

"Mambo Catoute," Issagha said with a slight bow, his voice echoing across the worship hall. An enormous chandelier hung suspended behind him, its candles casting long shadows over the stained glass that covered the windowless walls.

"Is all well?" Sivelia said as Catoute approached them. She cradled a glass jar in one arm.

Catoute narrowed one eye, an involuntary action that occurred with greater frequency. "Unexpected trouble. I need to pray for guidance."

Sivelia held out the jar, its deep red contents visible in the light. "As you ordered, *Grand-mère*."

Catoute wrapped her gnarled free hand around the jar. "I can always count on you, child." But could she? As a true child, Sivelia had been loving and obedient and as a new woman had been anxious to please Catoute. Now she seemed only anxious to learn everything Catoute knew. *Too fast, too fast.*

"May I pray with you?"

"Thank you, girl, but no. I must be alone with my thoughts if Kalfu is to help me. I'll see you both in the morning. Return to your rooms."

"As you wish."

Issagha bowed again.

Descending the knotty pine stairs that divided the rows of wooden pews forming a hexagonal pattern, Catoute listened for whispering by her underlings but heard none. They lived in the church, which served as a center for studying vodou and living quarters for the top practitioners of the dark arts on Pavot Island. Between the domed ceiling and the sunken theater, the hall resembled the inside of a sphere. Her footsteps echoed as she reached the glossy wooden floor and passed the pulpit from which she addressed her followers during prayer sessions.

At the opposite end of the floor, she opened a wide-paneled door and descended a curved stairway to a subterranean level illuminated by conventional lights. Passing her office and the restrooms, she stopped at a black door that she unlocked with a long skeleton key.

Flipping a wall switch, she turned on dimmer lights in the high ceiling and entered her summoning chamber, where she prayed and instructed her top priests and priestesses. The circular chamber, fifty feet in diameter, occupied the space directly beneath the worship hall. Catoute closed the door and lowered the heavy wooden bar across it, preventing anyone from entering uninvited. Two thousand five hundred unlit white candles surrounded the chamber, resting upon tiered shelves. The candles glowed in the soft overhead light. A smaller circle, twelve feet in diameter, marked the floor's center, drawn by Sivelia with chalk under Catoute's supervision.

Catoute set the jar down on another pulpit and unscrewed its lid. The strong odor that rose from the crimson fluid caused her to frown. Rolling up one sleeve, she drew a dagger from the folds of her dress and pressed its tip against a two-inch scar. The blade sliced into her dry flesh, and she cut open the scar. She held her arm at an angle, allowing her blood to flow into the jar.

After sixty seconds, she put the dagger down and wrapped her arm in a bandage. Sivelia would stitch her up later. Screwing the lid back on, she shook the jar several times, mixing its contents like paint. From the bottom of the pulpit, she took out a plastic container the size of a bucket and a pump with a nozzle attached to a short hose. She poured the jar's contents into the container, affixed the pump, and pressurized the device.

A silver mug joined the sprayer on the pulpit, then a bag

of gunpowder and a bottle of Pavot Island rum. Catoute filled one-third of the mug with gunpowder, the rest with rum, and stirred the contents with the dagger, cleaning her blood from its blade at the same time. After sliding the dagger back into her robe, she took a thick black candle and a box of kitchen matches from the pulpit.

With her concoctions prepared, she carried the candle and matches to the center of the circle and settled on her knees. Then she set the candle on the floor, struck a match, and lit the wick. Grimacing, she rose once more, returned the matches to the pulpit, and carried the sprayer to the circle. She aimed the nozzle at the chalk and squeezed the trigger, and a fine stream of blood sprayed out with a hiss. Walking around the circle, she traced the outline Sivelia had made, covering the white chalk with blood. When she had finished, she admired her handiwork. Despite an unavoidable sense of dread, her pulse quickened with excitement.

Catoute sat cross-legged on the floor. She cleared her throat and bowed to the candle. A moan rose from within her, followed by a chant, the words a mixture of French, Spanish, and African tongues. The chant grew louder, the rhythm of the sounds more urgent, almost sexual in nature. She had learned some of the words from her mother and others from her studies.

Please come, she thought. *I need you more than ever.*

In the center of the circle, the candle's flame flickered as if a breeze had swept through the chamber.

Catoute continued chanting.

A shadow passed over the floor but only within the circle. Tiny black threads appeared in the crack between two floor stones, like the legs of a spider. The threads expanded and multiplied until a black dome the size of a bowl rose from the floor. A ring of brown appeared beneath the dome, then a forehead, fine eyebrows, closed eyelids with long lashes, and a wide nose. The head emerged from the solid floor, supported on a taut neck. The male body levitated like someone rising from beneath the surface of a still pool. Lean arms, a six-pack abdomen, and a penis both long and thick emerged from the stone. Powerful thighs gave way to sturdy knees and strong calves. When the bottoms of his feet became level with the floor, the figure stopped rising.

Catoute blinked at the beautiful body in awe. The man, perhaps seventeen years old in appearance, opened his eyes, which glowed red. She had never forgotten those mesmerizing eyes. He stretched his body in a manner that seemed almost feminine.

Kalfu, Catoute thought, rising.

The man-boy looked at the floor, then swept up the mug in one graceful move and gulped down the gunpowder and rum mixture. Catoute watched his Adam's apple bob up and down as he tilted his head back. He discarded the mug, which made a hollow clanging on the floor, and smacked his lips. Ripples, like waves in the ocean, ran from his head to his feet. His red eyes widened, and for an instant he projected the demeanor of a very old man. Then he composed himself and moved forward, setting one foot in front of the other, like a model on a runway.

Catoute stood her ground four feet beyond the circle.

The being reached the blood on the floor and stopped, toeing the line. He stared into Catoute's eyes and exaggerated the movement of his lips as he spoke. "*Pu-ri.*"

The sound of his voice caused Catoute to tremble, both from fear and sexual arousal. "Kalfu, my lord."

The red light in Kalfu's eyes grew brighter. "It's been a long time, girl. At least by your measurement."

Catoute offered him a crooked smile. "I'm surprised you even recognize me."

"Your soul looks the same as when you were twenty-two. Better, even, because you've done such wicked deeds. I can hardly wait to drink your essence." His gaze flitted to the crimson circle. "Why have you summoned me this way?"

When Catoute had first summoned Kalfu, he had not materialized before her. Instead, she saw him walking on the street in Pavot City days later. He was the most beautiful man, the most perfect creature, she had ever seen, and she knew he was the Loa she had sacrificed a white dove to meet. Without saying a word, she invited him to her apartment, where they made hungry love. Then he showed her his true self, both physically and spiritually, and raped her for hours. By the end, she had experienced rapture.

"Because I can," Catoute said. "I've learned a great deal since the days when you shared your knowledge with me."

Kalfu extended one hand as far as the space above the circle's edge. His palm and fingers flattened as if he had pressed them against glass, and his eyes showed amusement more than anger. "I taught you well."

"You planted the seeds of my learning. I taught myself."

"I'm insulted. When I take a woman, she's mine body and soul. It's been three decades since our last encounter. I find it hard to believe you haven't fantasized about me every day since we last shared flesh."

"Oh, you still make me wet, my lord. Even in this shriveled-up old shell. But you'll not have my soul today, demon."

Kalfu spread his arms in a gesture pleading innocence. "I'm no demon, chéri."

Catoute cackled. "You would say that. You always have. Save your charms for some ingénue."

Kalfu's nostrils flared. "You didn't use your own blood."

Catoute showed him the bandage on her forearm. "Just a little of it. I haven't menstruated in twenty years, and I haven't been a virgin for a lot longer than that."

Kalfu smiled. "Your granddaughter."

"She's saving herself for you, lord."

Kalfu licked his chops. "When can I have her?"

"When I say so. That girl is dying to unlock your secrets so she can replace me as the top Mambo. I'm not ready to lie down and decompose yet."

Kalfu's chest rose and fell. "You summoned me. There's a price to be paid for that. Produce the girl, or crawl into this circle and open your legs."

Catoute made a dismissive gesture with one hand. "Don't tempt an old woman. You'd give me a heart attack for sure."

Kalfu looked down, and Catoute followed his gaze to

his throbbing erection.

"Don't even think about leaving me like this, girl." The words came out sounding like a threat.

"You want me to stroke you? Forget it!" She didn't intend to reach inside the circle.

Kalfu snarled. "Give me the girl's blood."

Catoute glanced at the sprayer, then stooped and picked it up. Pumping the handle a few times, she stepped forward. "Open up."

Kalfu smiled and opened his jaws wide. Catoute aimed the nozzle and squeezed the trigger. A crimson stream jetted out, splashing Kalfu's face before echoing inside his mouth. The sprayer had only one good pump in it, and the stream ran out of steam and dribbled on the floor. Catoute discarded the sprayer, and Kalfu tilted his head back and gargled the blood in his mouth.

When he finished, he showed her his long tongue, which appeared even longer slicked with blood. Catoute watched him sink to his knees, seize his penis in both hands, and stroke it raw with great pulls and jerks. She well remembered that enormous member tearing apart her insides decades earlier. Kalfu threw back his head and unleashed a roar that rebounded around the walls. Black semen flew from the head of his penis, and she found herself craving a taste.

Get your head on straight, you old fool.

Kalfu fell face-first to the floor, slapping the cement. His breathing grew ragged, then more relaxed, and he laughed. "What fun! To walk in human form is to serve the needs of the flesh."

"I called you here for a reason, lord."

Kalfu rose. "You keep calling me that, but you've served another for years."

Catoute grunted. "Malvado's your servant, too. By serving him, I serve you. He paid for this church and filled its congregation. And he drove the Church of the White Snake underground."

"He's had a good reign."

"I fear it's in jeopardy."

"The affairs of men aren't mine to preserve or destroy."

"His sons wear your symbol on their arms, but they're not true acolytes. Don't be surprised if your name loses some of its luster once he's gone."

Kalfu thrust a finger at her and she flinched. "Don't appeal to my vanity. You lack the faculties to crawl inside my mind."

Catoute made a broad bow. "Forgive my clumsy expression. Sometimes I'm not as articulate as I wish. I meant no impertinence."

"While you live and breathe, it's your responsibility to enlighten Maxime and Najac about the benefits of serving me."

"They're thugs, just as Malvado was before I seduced him."

Kalfu sneered. "You're too withered to seduce them."

"Unfortunately, you're right."

"But your granddaughter will make one of them happy."

She nodded. "I've planned for the future—after you've had her. But circumstances are speeding up my timetable. I wish to delay any drastic changes in the current state of

Pavot while I prepare Sivelia for her future duties."

Kalfu stared at her hard, the red in his eyes intensifying. "What is it you want?"

"Maria Vasquez is a policewoman from the United States. She's here on—"

Kalfu's eyes blazed. "Do you believe anything of significance occurs on this island without my knowledge?"

Catoute shuddered. "Of course not. But this woman has gotten under Malvado's skin. He badly wants her brought into custody. There's a political struggle within his cabinet. Whoever brings her in will curry his favor . . . and his allegiance."

"You want to be that person."

"The challenges that lie ahead for me will be easier with Malvado's full support."

Kalfu crossed one arm over his chest and rested the elbow of the other upon it, the fingers of his right hand curled around his chin and lips as he pretended to mull over the situation. Catoute always had to play the unsuspecting audience member to his theatrics.

Unfolding his arms, he stood before her in a relaxed manner. "Nothing comes without a price—not even between old lovers. You already have Vasquez's consort Jake Helman in custody. Bring him here and give him to me, and I'll see to it the woman is yours."

Catoute struggled to show neither the surprise nor the consternation she felt. She had not expected Helman to enter the equation. Kalfu's interest in him suggested that Russel had a more astute grasp of the man's potential for trouble than Malvado did, yet another reason for concern. She chose her words carefully. "Forgive me, lord, but we've dealt with Helman—"

"*You've* dealt with him. Malvado has. I haven't."

She realized Kalfu didn't intend to tell her why he wanted Helman. "We introduced Black Magic into his system. He's already begun the journey to join the walking dead."

"I don't care if he's alive or a zonbie. I only care that his soul is intact. Bring him to me in any form, so long as he can still walk. Dead, he's of no use."

He wants Helman's soul.

"Do not interpret my motives, Puri. Bring me Helman. Stand him inside this circle. When I finish with him, I'll deliver his bitch to you."

"Malvado wants to see him as a zonbie harvesting his drugs."

"I don't care what Malvado wants. Neither should you. You say I'm your master; prove it."

"Yes, lord. Of course. It shall be done."

Kalfu returned to the middle of the circle, where he picked up the burning candle. He studied its flame for a moment, then blew it out. When the candle struck the floor and broke in two, he had already vanished.

Catoute sniffed the candle's scent in the air. Whoever Jake Helman was, he had angered the demon she worshipped. Kalfu wanted him alive, which meant the demon world couldn't claim the man's soul if he died. But Kalfu had told her he could not directly interfere in the affairs of men, and that had to include punishing or killing a man with a good soul. She studied the circle of blood.

I created a temporary portal between our worlds, one that prevented Kalfu from touching me despite my soul already belonging to him.

But if she had entered that circle, the demon could have done whatever he wished to her.

In that circle, he must also be able to harm a good man.

The rules as she understood them did not apply within the summoning circle. She had stumbled upon a new secret to the universe. Regardless, she would deliver Helman to Kalfu as promised.

TWENTY-ONE

The truck stopped moving, and Jake heard doors open and close. The two soldiers appeared and lowered the gate. One uncuffed the shackles on his ankles, and then they eased him out of the truck and onto the ground. The sudden infusion of fresh air caused Jake to reel, but the two men supported him.

Jake gazed at the stars in the clear sky, then at the moon, and finally at the fields below them. Hundreds of silhouettes toiled in the distance.

Who are they?

The soldiers guided him to the closest of several single-story buildings. As they entered the structure, one soldier flipped a switch, and a ceiling light came on.

Two dozen men and women scattered on the filthy floor in pairs and small groups looked up. Most were at least half-naked, which allowed Jake to observe their skeletal bodies. The air was foul.

"Scarecrows," Jake thought. Or had he spoken out loud?

"What?" one soldier said.

Jake looked at the man. *Sorry. I was talking to myself.*

The other soldier spoke in French. They guided Jake to the rear of the building and propped him up in the corner. They did not seem to care when he slid to the floor. On their way out they flicked off the light, enshrouding Jake in darkness. A moment later, he heard a bell ringing.

Is it dinnertime?

The truck started, and its headlights passed through the windows and along the ceiling.

Jake glanced around the room. What the hell was he doing with a bunch of scarecrows?

The silhouette of a tall man filled the doorway, then lumbered forward, making its way through the crowd.

He's walking funny.

A sense of dread swept over Jake, though his limbs felt too much like rubber to react.

Heavy, thudding footsteps. The man passed a window through which a work light shone, and Jake glimpsed dead eyes and stiff features.

A zombie!

The creature stood before him, silhouetted once more, holding a metal bucket. He reached into the bucket with the other hand and came out with a fistful of something Jake couldn't see. The zonbie's hand rotated on his wrist, and the shiny objects struck the floor. Then he turned and

240

walked away, some of the scarecrows pawing at his legs until he dropped more of the packets for them.

Jake scooped up the packets: plastic dime bags like he had seen after a former drug informant named AK had stabbed him in the eye. Jake had killed the man in self-defense. He rubbed the packets between his fingers. When he had held the substance before, he had flirted ever so briefly with the idea of snorting it and had resisted the temptation. Now he tore one of the packets open and dumped the fine black powder into his palm. Among other ingredients, Black Magic consisted of the ashes of incinerated zonbies.

Jake buried his nostrils in his palm and inhaled the powder, which froze his nasal passages and burned his throat. The universe seemed clear. He wanted more Magic.

Maria sat in the front seat of the Subaru next to Jorge. Through the windshield she saw the cargo boat docked at the pier. The vessel appeared old but large, its sides scored with years' worth of scars from the elements. A jeep carrying four soldiers passed between them and the ship.

"Just a routine patrol," Jorge said.

Maria stared at the gangway leading up to the ship's deck. "Where will I be staying?"

"In the hold with several refugees."

"So I could get caught?"

"It's possible, but no one has been discovered on this ship before."

"What time is it?"

"It's 11:04. My contact expects you in half an hour. The ship is scheduled to leave at 1:00 a.m."

She took out her cigarettes. "Do you mind? I can get out."

Jorge lowered her window. "I don't mind, if you don't mind losing the air-conditioning."

"Tough call." Even at night, it felt like 90 degrees. She lit a cigarette and inhaled. "What a waste."

"I'm sorry you didn't get what you came here for."

"It almost doesn't matter." Her eyes moistened. "Jake." She swallowed. "Humphrey."

"Do you want me to cry, too?"

"Misery loves company."

Jorge managed a sad smile. "I'm glad I met you. My American friend."

"You're my second friend on Pavot Island."

"Humphrey once had a chance to go to America as part of an artist exchange program. He would have been able to escape and live a free life, but he cared about me too much, cared about this country. I wish he'd gone when he had the chance. Now I'm glad you're leaving early."

"If I thought staying would accomplish anything . . ."

"You're too hot now. You'd only be killed."

"God, I'm so tired." Leaning her head back against the seat, Maria covered her eyes with one hand.

A voice spoke Jorge's name through a burst of static, and he raised his hand radio, which was not unlike the devices used by NYPD.

"Go ahead," Jorge said.

"Your cousin called," the voice said in French.

"Which one?"

"Florence Nightingale."

A nurse, Maria thought.

"She says she treated an unusual patient today, who was escorted out a couple of hours ago."

Maria saw the news in Jorge's eyes when he turned to her.

"Jake's alive," she said.

"My cousin Ramona is a nurse at a clinic not far from our military base. Your *novio* was treated there, then taken away by soldiers."

"And I know where they took him."

"Even if he's still alive, it's too late to save him. Please just get on that ship."

Maria flicked her cigarette out the window. "I came here with Jake. He sacrificed himself so I could get away."

"Then honor his wishes. If you're caught, you'll both die for nothing. Worse than death—you'll both become zonbies in Malvado's fields."

She didn't blink. "I'm not leaving without Jake."

After taking a long, hot shower, Sivelia dried off and rubbed oils into her flesh, then blow-dried her hair and applied makeup. Crossing her spacious air-conditioned apartment in the Church of the Black Snake, she entered her bedroom and selected a sheer black nightgown from her walk-in closet. The second bedroom housed her library, where she kept her totems and herbs and practiced her rituals.

In the living room, she lit several candles and played an American jazz CD she had bought on the black market. Life was good, but she intended to make it better.

A key turning in the lock on her front door caused her to smile. Her visitor was always on time.

Najac entered the apartment and closed the door behind him. Sivelia strode forward in high heels, swaying her hips to the jazz beat. Najac glared at her, which she knew meant he approved of her attire.

She ran her painted nails up his chest and over the shirt he left unbuttoned to reveal a triangle of black skin. "Did anyone see you?"

"What difference would it make if they did?"

Even though Sivelia knew he feared their relationship being discovered as much as she did, she allowed him to play the role of the macho alpha male, which was what she wanted him to be one day.

Pressing her lips against his, she slid her tongue inside his mouth. Najac wrapped one arm around her back, crushing her against him, and she felt him growing hard even as she turned wet between her legs. Careful not to offend him, she eased him away. His playful smile contained the hint of a sneer, and she saw danger in his beady eyes, which he had inherited from his father.

"You're going to make me burst, woman."

Now Sivelia smiled. "Would you sacrifice everything we've worked so hard to achieve for one night of pleasure when we're so close to realizing our dreams?"

Najac grunted. "I might."

"And I'd make you feel like a king. But in the morning you'd still be a prince and my body would be worthless."

Najac took in a deep breath and let it out in a sigh. "How much longer?"

"The old woman's taught me everything she's willing to while she remains head Mambo. But I've learned quite a bit on my own, and this week I figured out something else. She made me draw a circle on the church floor and give her a jar of my *sang menstruel*. Both were used to summon Kalfu; I know it. All I need to do is get my hands on her book, learn the incantation, and I could summon him myself."

Najac caressed her face. "It isn't fair. I should have you before that demon does."

"We both have to make sacrifices, my lord." Sivelia rubbed his wrist. "That's what it will take for you to be king and me to be your high priestess. It's time for a new generation to rule Pavot Island."

Najac locked his hands behind the small of her back and stared down his nose at her. "When you become pregnant, Mambo Catoute will suspect Kalfu, won't she?"

Sivelia nodded. "You have to kill her immediately after Kalfu takes me—even before you kill your father."

"It's my brother who worries me. He has to suspect I want Pavot for myself."

"We'll kill him together."

Najac smiled. "I like the way you think."

"That's why I'll make the perfect queen." She had it all figured out: she and Najac would have a much closer relationship and a more equal partnership than her grandmother currently enjoyed with Malvado.

Clenching his teeth, Najac unzipped his pants and freed his erection. "Work some of that magic on me."

Sivelia reached down and grasped his shaft. Kneeling, she took him into her mouth and gazed up at him.

Najac grimaced, his snarl becoming more pronounced.

She knew he was capable of cruelty, but his crude actions paled in comparison to what Kalfu would do to her when she finally summoned him.

The metal gate powered open, and Jorge pulled into the driveway of a one-story house and parked beneath the carport. When they got out, the gate had already closed. Maria put on her baseball cap.

Jorge pointed at the backyard. "This way."

Following him around the house, she saw the wide doors of a barn standing wide open, spilling light onto the lawn. Caribbean music drifted out of the interior. As they approached the barn, she saw no other houses around. A black four-door Dodge Ram occupied the lawn.

Inside the cluttered barn, which had been converted into a garage, two men puttered around with greasy engine parts. The taller one seemed more familiar with the space and more concerned with the task before him. He wore brown leather cowboy boots and jeans. The other man had a generous beer belly. He tapped his friend, who turned.

The tall man moved forward. "Comment allez-vous?" *How are you?*

Jorge embraced him. "Je suis vide." *I am empty.*

The man patted Jorge on the back. "He was a good man."

Jorge didn't bother to wipe the tears from his eyes as he gestured to Maria. "Maria Vasquez, my brother, Armand."

"Comment allez-vous?" Maria said.

"C'est la vie." *This is life.*

Jorge motioned to the heavyset black man. "Our friend Stephane."

"Como estas?" Stephane said.

"Je suis vivant." *I'm alive.*

Stephane nodded. "Would you like a beer?"

Maria eyed the can. "When we're done."

"Can you shoot?" Armand said.

Maria raised her T-shirt, revealing the Walther. "I'm a New York City cop."

Armand raised his eyebrows. "Oui?"

"Si," Maria said. "How about we stick to English?"

"How much ammo do you have for that?"

"Not enough."

Armand opened one of the trunks, and Maria saw it was eighteen inches deep with handguns.

Moving forward, she reached past Armand and grasped a Glock. "This is more like it." She pulled back the slide. "But I'll still take ammo for the Walther."

Armand handed her a silencer and two magazines. "For the Glock." He handed her another silencer and two more magazines. "And for the Walther."

Maria screwed a silencer into the barrel of each gun.

"Take this, too." He gave her a sheathed hunting knife.

Jorge selected a Beretta. "One's enough for me."

"My brother's so conservative," Armand said as he and Stephane armed themselves.

Maria clipped the sheath to her belt. "What are you doing with all these guns, and why are we loading up with those doors open?"

"We've been preparing for revolution for years," Armand said.

"And there's no one out there to see us," Stephane said.

Maria watched Jorge attach a holster to his belt. "Guns. Tunnels. I don't know why you haven't already overthrown Malvado."

"We need a trigger," Jorge said. "It hasn't happened yet."

Armand passed out rifles. "But it will. Now let's go get your friend."

TWENTY-TWO

Maria sat next to Jorge in the backseat of the black Dodge Ram while Armand drove and Stephane rode shotgun. The truck prowled the highway and exited onto a side road with no streetlights.

"Thank you for doing this," Maria said.

Armand didn't even glance at the rearview mirror to see her. "You came to Pavot Island to free Le Père. You didn't have to do that."

I did, Maria thought. "We failed. You don't owe me anything."

"No, we don't. But any enemy of Malvado's is a friend of ours. Even if you didn't accomplish what you set out to do, you'll do more good back in the USA, where you can help La Mère spread the word about the atrocities you've seen here, than you'll do as a martyr lying dead in a ditch or working in Le Monstre's fields as a zonbie. You're too beautiful for that anyway."

She rubbed the scratches on her arms. "I don't feel very beautiful right now."

Armand turned onto a two-lane road that rose and dropped, each side flanked by tall trees. Maria shuddered. Even in the dark, with no discernible landmarks, she recognized the woods on her left.

"We're getting close," Stephane said.

Maria turned to Jorge. "I don't want anything to happen to any of you. We have to make this fast, in and out."

"I don't plan to wait around and introduce myself," Jorge said.

In the front seat, Armand and Stephane said nothing. The headlights illuminated the trees ahead, and two metal signs on the left glowed white. Armand slowed the truck, and Maria saw a side road between the signs. The truck stopped at the first sign, which repeated the same message in French, English, and Spanish.

STAY OUT. RESTRICTED FEDERAL PROPERTY.
ALL TRESPASSERS WILL BE SHOT.

Armand made the turn. "There will be two armed guards at the gate. Stephane and I will handle them."

They proceeded along the bumpy single lane, the trees around them growing denser, darker. Armand slowed to follow the twists and turns, and light appeared between the trees. A chain-link fence topped with coiled razor wire came into view, a security booth beside it. Maria saw a bridge beyond the fence and knew it spanned the piranha-populated river.

Two soldiers holding machine guns emerged from the booth and stood before the fence. The truck stopped and Armand lowered his window. One soldier hurried over to the open window, while the other ran around to the passenger side, where Stephane lowered his window.

"What the hell do you think you're doing?" the first soldier said in French. The truck was so high he had to look up at Armand. "Didn't you see the signs?"

Armand feigned innocence. "I'm sorry but we're lost. Can you help us with directions?"

Before the soldier could answer, Armand raised the Glock from between his legs, aimed it out the open window, and fired it twice. The silencer muffled the shots, but the muzzle flashes caused Maria to blink. At the same time, Stephane fired his gun twice. The soldiers' bodies jerked, their faces disintegrating into bloodshed, and they toppled to the ground. Armand and Stephane leapt out of the truck, straddled their victims, and fired one more round into the head of each man.

Two more soldiers appeared from behind the booth, their machine guns readied for action.

Realizing unsuppressed machine gun fire would alarm anyone in earshot, Maria jerked her door open and jumped out. "Look out!" Her feet slammed onto the ground, and she aimed her Glock with both hands and squeezed the trigger.

Her shots stopped both soldiers in their tracks, and

before either man could fire or fall, gunshots from Maria's right tore into their torsos. Their bodies collapsed in unison, punctured with bullets.

Maria glanced at Armand as Stephane circled the front of the truck and Jorge hopped out behind her.

"Nice work," Armand said. He pulled on a green ski mask. "A little late but follow my lead."

They each pulled on a different colored mask: Maria's was brown; Stephane's was blue; and Jorge's camouflage. Jorge seized the wrists of the soldier Armand had shot and dragged the corpse into the woods, while Stephane did the same with the man he had killed. They proceeded to strip the men.

Armand gestured to the last two men killed. "We can't save their shirts, but everything else is good." He grabbed one corpse by the wrists and dragged it in Jorge's direction.

Maria did the same with the remaining soldier, who moaned as she struggled with his weight. His eyes locked on hers, then fluttered. The dying body left a trail of blood. Maria dropped the still figure beside the one Jorge had left.

"Get his pants, boots, and weapons," Jorge said as he stripped the corpse at his feet.

Maria unlaced her corpse's boots and pulled them off, then unbuckled the military belt around the pants. Once she had removed them, she returned to where he had fallen and collected his machine gun.

Armand walked out of the security booth carrying a case of ammunition. The four of them tossed their booty into the back of the truck, then resumed their positions inside.

"Seat belts," Armand said.

Maria pulled her shoulder strap across her torso and buckled it.

Armand backed up the truck, then floored it. The Ram raced forward and smashed through the gates. The truck sped onto the bridge, and she glanced over its railing at the dark water below. They reentered the woods.

"If you come into contact with any zonbies, shoot them in the head," Maria said. "*Only* in the head."

Jorge looked puzzled. "Why?"

"Because that's the only thing that will stop them. Anywhere else will be a waste of ammo."

A second checkpoint loomed ahead: a security booth but no fence or gate. Two soldiers armed with rifles stood at attention in the middle of the road.

"What's with those guys?" Stephane said.

Maria studied the soldiers. They had waxy skin and didn't blink as the truck's headlights lit up their faces. "Those aren't soldiers. At least not *living* ones."

"What are you talking about? They're wearing uniforms. They look normal."

"They're wearing makeup. Someone wanted to make them *appear* alive."

Armand stopped the truck and rolled down his window.

One of the zombie sentries came over to his door and peered inside.

"Oh, shit," Armand said, gazing at the man's undead features.

The zonbie stared at Armand long enough to register

his presence, then raised his rifle's stock to his shoulder.

"Look out!" Jorge said.

Armand threw his door open, slamming it into the zonbie before the dead thing could fire. Then he hopped out and stepped around the door, so Maria saw only his head. Two muzzle flashes accompanied by high-pitched whistles told her he had killed the zonbie.

The second zonbie aimed his rifle at the windshield. Stephane fired two shots from his open window. Neither shot hit the zonbie in the head, but one sent him spinning to the ground. Armand ran around the front of the truck, aimed his Glock, and fired. The zonbie's brain fluid spurted out of his skull, fully illuminated by the headlights, and the reanimated soldier dropped out of view.

Armand gathered the dead soldiers' guns and climbed into the truck. "Screw *their* clothes." He passed the weapons to Maria and Jorge, who stashed them on the floor.

"Were those really . . . zonbies?" Jorge said.

"They were dead." Armand closed his door and resumed their course. "Call them what you want."

Stephane wiped his forehead. "Ay Dios mio."

"You were right," Armand said to Maria. "Only shots to the head work."

Jorge said, "Zonbies foutus." *Fucking zonbies.*

"Something other than blood came out of their wounds. Powder or—"

"Sawdust," Maria said. "Packing material. Filler."

"How do you know?"

"Jake put down scores of them in New York."

The road turned again, and within a moment the trees cleared, providing a clear view of the stars in the sky and the compound of buildings below.

"It's the first building," Maria said.

Armand killed the headlights, allowing the fog lights to provide the only illumination. He slowed as well, cutting down on the engine noise. Maria doubted that would make a difference. The work lights around the compound cast a glow on the buildings, and the door to the drug den became visible as they drew closer.

Armand stopped ten feet from the structure, and all four of them poured out. Armand and Stephane clutched two rifles with mounted laser scopes.

Stephane looked at the fields to their right. "Holy mother of God . . ."

The others turned in the same direction. Silhouetted figures worked in the distance, overseers on horseback supervising them.

"There must be hundreds of them," Armand said.

Clutching a flashlight in one hand and her Glock in the other, Maria sprinted into the shooting gallery, followed by Jorge. Inside, gagging on the stench of human sweat and waste, she thumbed on the flashlight and passed it over the faces of the scarecrows on the floor.

They blinked at her, some of them looking barely human.

"Oh, mon Dieu," Jorge said, his words obscured by his mask. He stared at the wretched addicts before him. "These are my people. Malvado's got to pay for this."

Maria strode forward, stepping around the bodies curled on the floor. "Jake?"

In the far corner, a fully clothed man stirred, though he didn't look at her.

She aimed the flashlight at him. *Oh, my God.*

Jake's mouth hung open, a lazy, stoned look on his face. Stopping before him, she saw torn plastic bags on the floor. He had ingested Black Magic. Kneeling beside him, she gasped, tears filling her eyes. Jake's left arm ended in a bandaged stump.

"You sons of *bitches*," she said, spitting the words.

Jorge kneeled beside her and took Jake's wounded arm. "At least he's alive. Let's go."

Maria reached beneath Jake's right arm. "Come on. We're getting you out of here." Pulling him to his feet, she groaned. "Why did the two smallest people come in to carry him?"

Jake blinked at Maria and a moan escaped his lips.

Maria and Jorge dragged him across the floor, and Maria didn't care when she stepped on a scarecrow by mistake. She didn't consider them human and just wanted to get Jake the hell out of here.

As they neared the door, three silencer shots fired in rapid succession outside. Then a zombie stepped inside. He held a metal bucket in one hand and drew a machete from his belt with the other.

"Take Jake," Maria said. As Jorge complied, she aimed her Glock at the zombie's forehead at point-blank range and squeezed the trigger.

A hole appeared in his forehead, and he rocked backwards like a drunkard, a stream of liquefied brain gushing into the air, and collapsed at their feet.

Exiting the building, they almost tripped over the bodies of two armed zonbie sentries.

Armand and Stephane continued to fire in the opposite direction.

"Get in the truck!" Armand said.

They hauled Jake to the truck and pushed him into the backseat. Turning, Maria saw a dozen zonbies with machetes advancing on her comrades, who had difficulty hitting their targets in the head with handguns in the darkness and couldn't shoot their rifles without alerting the slaves in the fields. The zonbies advanced in herky-jerky motions, their bodies absorbing some of the bullets.

"Stay with him," Maria told Jorge before she ran over to Armand and Stephane. "Take it to them!"

As soon as the men stopped firing, Maria charged straight at the zonbies.

"Holy shit," Stephane said.

Maria halted ten feet short of the first zonbie, leveled her Glock, and fired. The first shot missed. The second burrowed a hole through the top of the zonbie's skull. The creature's body twisted, his eyes seeking the moon in the sky before he landed on his back and stopped moving.

As the remaining horde closed in, Armand and Stephane joined Maria and opened fire. The silencers coughed flames and suppressed rounds, and dead scalps creviced, eyeballs popping and liquid brains oozing. The humid night air filled with gun smoke, and before it had cleared, the zonbies lay unmoving on the ground.

"Back to the truck," Maria said. She knew the zonbies they had just exterminated had been workers assigned to the Black Magic factory. Halfway to the truck, an alarm rang and the work lights grew brighter, pinning them in the glare. Facing the field, she saw hundreds of figures turn still, rotate toward the compound, and start running. "Oh, shit."

Armand climbed into the truck, and Stephane ran around to his side. Maria heard their doors close, but she remained riveted on the spectacle before her. The overseers on horseback galloped into the tide of running corpses, gaining speed.

Jorge opened the rear door. "Maria! Get in!"

She hopped in next to Jake, and the truck surged forward even before she had closed her door. Armand drove deeper into the compound.

"Where the hell are you going?" Maria said.

"We're not leaving without inflicting some serious damage," Armand said.

"Are you crazy? There are hundreds of those things!"

Stephane pulled two rum bottles out of the bag at his feet. Strips of cloth dangled from the neck of each bottle, and Maria smelled gasoline.

Molotov cocktails, she thought.

"Which building do they make the Magic in?" Armand said.

"The last one."

As Armand steered the vehicle forward, Maria saw

naked zonbies staggering out of their destination. Y incisions divided the torsos of the dead men and women. Their flesh had turned to leather and showed signs of decomposition. Some had only one arm and still managed to wield machetes. Others had no arms at all. One hopped around on a single leg. Maria knew they had been selected for dismemberment in the Black Magic factory, destined to become ashes, and they had been ordered into action because she and her fellows had destroyed the workers.

"I'll handle these," Jorge said as Armand braked the truck.

Stephane jumped out first and lit the cocktails' fuses with a lighter. Blue flames blossomed near each of his hands. Jorge got out beside him and started firing his Glock. He shot more zonbies in the chest than the head, but the bodies were in such bad shape the dead things seemed to be more adversely affected than the other zonbies had.

Stephane ran up to the building and hurled the first bottle through a window, which shattered. A moment later, flames burst inside the building, blue light spilling outside.

Maria leaned forward. "We have to get out of here!"

Armand ignored her. Jorge continued firing and dropped three of the maimed zonbies. Stephane threw the second cocktail through another window, producing a wall of fire inside. Then he drew his Glock and joined Jorge in shooting the remaining zonbies. As they climbed inside the truck at the same time, a man wearing robes ran screaming from the building, his clothing and hair trailing flames.

"Houngan dog," Stephane said as Armand gunned the Ram forward.

They circled the compound, and a dozen zonbies emerged from the woods, their machetes reflecting moonlight.

"That's a security patrol," Maria said.

They raced away from the security zonbies, only to see the army of slaves from the field had gained a great deal of ground and had almost reached the compound.

"How did they get here so fast?" Armand said.

"They don't run out of breath because they don't breathe," Maria said. "They don't get tired, either. They'll maintain that speed. I told you we have to get out of here."

"Stop the truck," Jorge said.

Maria looked at him.

"Stop the goddamned truck!"

"What for?" Armand said, his voice reaching a crescendo.

"So I can get into the truck bed. The only chance we stand is if one of us uses those machine guns we've got stockpiled back there."

"Damn it!" Armand stomped on the brake, and they all lurched forward.

Jorge jerked his door open, jumped out, and slammed the door. Maria watched zonbies growing steadily closer from both sides.

Jorge scrambled into the truck bed. "Go! Go!"

Armand sped forward, and Jorge picked up a machine gun and opened fire into the crowd of pursuing zonbies.

"That little *princesa* has balls," Stephane said.

"He's my brother," Armand said.

Jorge's machine gun roared in a continuing burst, and rising puffs of sawdust glowed red in the receding taillights of the pickup.

"He'd better not fall out," Maria said. "If we stop again they'll be all over us."

The road twisted into the woods and Armand decelerated. Maria saw phantom figures racing through the woods on both sides of them. Stephane rolled down his window, revealing one more Molotov cocktail.

"You blow up my truck and I'll kill you," Armand said.

"Wait until we cross the bridge," Maria said. "That way you might actually stop them."

The truck roared through the second checkpoint, where they had passed the zonbie soldiers made up to look human. In the light, Maria saw an army of zonbies running after them at an impossible speed.

Pressed against the truck's gate, Jorge stopped firing. He tossed the machine gun aside, picked up another, and resumed firing.

Several zonbies fell to the ground, their heads ruptured, and the zonbie horde trampled them without slowing.

Armand sped onto the bridge, the Ram vibrating as it passed over the boards. Stephane sparked his lighter, igniting the fuse, and leaned out his window with the bottle. He hurled the Molotov cocktail down on the bridge, and it burst into flames, causing Jorge to drop his gun and shield his face. The flames spread across the bridge, preventing passage.

A few zonbies staggered through the flames and toppled face forward. No more appeared.

"Stop the truck," Maria said as they cleared the bridge. The truck skidded to a stop.

Maria opened her door and hopped out. "Get your ass back in the truck," she said to Jorge, who joined her on the ground. "You're either a brave little fucker or very stupid."

Jorge smiled. "I could say the same thing about you."

Across the river, the zonbie army stood still along the embankment on each side of the bridge.

"They must know about the piranhas," Maria said as she and Jorge got into the truck. "Or they've been ordered not to cross the river."

The truck moved forward.

"We're not out of the woods yet," Armand said.

Ten minutes later, speeding along the road, they spotted two helicopters in the sky.

Armand killed the headlights, turned down a narrow side road, and slowed the Ram to a crawl. "The trees will hide us."

"Where are we going?" Maria said.

"We know a place on the west coast. At this speed, we'll be there in two hours."

Stephane glanced at Jake, unconscious between Maria and Jorge. "How many more like him were inside that building?"

"Twenty or thirty," Maria said. "But none of them were this healthy. In my country, we call them scarecrows. Don't beat yourself up. They were practically zonbies already. There's nothing we could have done for them."

Silence settled over the truck. Maria put her arms around Jake and pressed her head against his.

TWENTY-THREE

Sitting in the backseat of his moving limo, Russel massaged the bridge of his nose. Late night emergency calls came with the territory, but this was the first one that had ever involved Malvado's zonbies. So far, Russel had done a pretty good job avoiding Pavot Island's supernatural elements, other than dealing with Mambo Catoute and her circle of witch doctors.

As the chauffeur navigated the limo through the woods, flashing strobe lights became visible through the trees, and then the first checkpoint came into view. Police cars and military jeeps flanked the road, and officers clad in khaki and camouflage uniforms guarded the perimeter.

The limo stopped at the open gates, and Russel lowered his window for the police officer who approached. "How many?" Russel said.

"Four sentries killed and stripped of their uniforms,

their weapons missing. The woods are littered with the bodies of those other things, and we had to pull three dozen of them out of the road so our vehicles could get through. General Buteau and Colonel Solaine are in the compound."

Without acknowledging the officer, Russel turned to his chauffeur. "Drive on."

Ahead, a fire truck idled near the smoldering bridge, and half a dozen vehicles blocked the entrance. Soldiers and firemen stood around the vehicles.

Russel told his chauffeur to pull over, and he got out.

A lieutenant greeted him. "They torched the bridge. It's safe to walk across, but no vehicles are allowed. Would you like me to accompany you?"

"That won't be necessary." Russel crossed the bridge, pausing only to look at the charred area where the fire had been put out. Smoke still lingered in the air. His footsteps sounded loud in the night, and he gazed over the railing at the river below. Too bad the trespassers hadn't tried to cross it; a lot of problems would have been solved.

On the other side of the bridge, soldiers stood near flares set up on the ground. All of them wore red berets, the sign of the elite. Only the top soldiers and police were allowed in the compound. No one else was permitted to see the zonbies, although Malvado had instructed his officers to encourage talk of their existence among the rank and file. He enjoyed ruling his subjects through fear.

Russel said nothing to the soldiers as he passed them. Motionless zonbies littered the road. He didn't look forward to Malvado's reaction. At the second checkpoint, he counted four dead zonbies and an equal number of living soldiers and police. He conferred with another soldier, then proceeded.

Several work lights illuminated the compound. Police officers scrounged around in the grass for evidence, and soldiers guarded the perimeter.

Russel found Buteau and Solaine standing near the smoldering ruins of the Black Magic lab. Unlike Maxime and Najac, the army general and police colonel worked well as a unit. Neither man seemed to desire greater responsibility than the other, and they appreciated having someone with whom to share the blame when things went awry. They stopped speaking as Russel approached, something to which he had still not become accustomed. The military and police operated in the open, following established guidelines, while Russel had been given carte blanche to operate in the shadows.

"Gentlemen, I see we have a real cluster fuck on our hands."

"As long as all three of us take responsibility, he can't blame only one of us," Solaine said.

Just like a cop, Russel thought. Glancing at the fields, he saw the zonbies and their overseers had returned to work.

"The overseers directed a band of workers to hose down the building," Buteau said.

"How much damage was done?"

"At least six kilos of Black Magic," Solaine said. "We don't know how much heroin and cocaine was in there. A total loss, which is why the overseers went right back to work."

I can't blame them, Russel thought. "What's the body count?"

"Seventy zonbies and counting," Solaine said.

"And one Houngan," Buteau said. "As far as we can tell, his bodyguard didn't make it out of the building alive, either."

"Do we have any security video?"

"Just at the checkpoints," Solaine said. "A black truck with three men and one woman. They wore masks."

A woman, of course. "License plates?"

"Fakes."

"How many junkies are in building one?"

"Maybe twenty-five," Buteau said.

"Administer overdoses as soon as a new Houngan shows up. At least we can cut down the losses to the workforce."

"The American isn't among them," Solaine said.

"Of course he isn't. He's who they came for. Destroying the drugs was just a bonus."

The officers exchanged looks.

"We don't have to wait for a Houngan," Buteau said, nodding in the direction Russel had come from.

Turning, Russel saw three figures approaching in the distance: a tall man and a young woman trailing an old woman. *Issagha, Sivelia, and Mambou Catoute.* "Looks like the gang's all here."

The sun shone bright on the lush green vegetation. Jake walked through a jungle with Sheryl, who held Cain's hand. Cain appeared human, with flesh pulled over his muscular physique and long brown hair extending from his scalp.

Jake knew him as a fiery demon with translucent skin and glowing organs. The three of them were naked, and Sheryl caressed Cain's bicep as they walked.

This isn't right, Jake thought. *Sheryl belongs with Abel. I guess she changed her mind again.*

They both spoke to him, but his dream lacked audio. Another couple joined them: Abel and Laurel Doniger, also naked. Abel shook Jake's hand and clasped Cain's shoulder. It was nice to see them getting along. Abel didn't seem jealous to see Sheryl with his brother, and Sheryl didn't seem jealous to see Abel with Laurel.

Heaven is a very nice place.

Or was this hell?

Laurel isn't dead.

Or was she?

All five of them swam in a lake at the bottom of a waterfall. The two couples frolicked and splashed water at each other, leaving Jake alone. He wondered what had happened to Maria.

A bird cawed, and Edgar alighted on a rock in the water.

I guess it's just you and me, sport.

Edgar spoke and Jake heard his words clearly: "You've lost your hands."

You're wrong. I lost only one of them. To prove his point, Jake raised his arms from the lake. Edgar was right: both of them ended in stumps.

"And your eyes . . ."

Panicking, Jake reached for his eyes with the stumps, which pressed against his empty sockets.

"You're in no condition to help me."

The world went black, like a television that had just been switched off, and Jake screamed.

Jake opened his eye. At least he still had one. His head throbbed, his face and chest felt tight, and his nasal passages felt dried out and drawn in. The feeling reminded him of a cocaine hangover.

Black Magic . . .

Bill Russel and a vodou witch doctor had forced him to breathe in the smoke from that candle, and he recalled dozens of scarecrows on the floor around him while he snorted the vile black powder. He wondered if he had kept any of the plastic bags.

A pillow supported his head, and he was lying on his back. The ceiling came into focus.

Stalactites?

Flickering orange light highlighted the giant mineral daggers poised above him. Turning his head to the left, he saw cabinets, a table, and chairs positioned along a natural rock wall that supported several torches. Turning his head farther, he saw Maria sleeping on her side on a thick rug laid over a wooden floor. But where the hell were they? He tried to sit up, but the tightness in his chest increased, and he fell back onto the foldout cot with a groan.

"Jake?" In an instant, Maria stood at his side, her sleepy eyes filled with concern. It had been a long time since anyone had really given a damn about him.

"You're a sight for a sore eye," he said. His throat felt raw. Reaching up to brush her curly brown hair out of her face, he saw the stump where his left wrist and hand had once been, and the image of Russel burying the machete in his arm flashed through his brain. His head sagged into the pillow, and he felt the strength leaving his arm, which dropped onto the mattress.

Jesus Christ. Russel fucking maimed me. For almost two years he had feared the man would take revenge on him, and now it had come to pass. *I want to kill him.*

Maria's eyes turned shiny and reflected the firelight. "You're alive. Whatever else they did to you, you're alive."

This time he reached up with his right hand and caressed her face. "Where are we?"

"In a church."

Of all the answers she could have given him, that one was the furthest from his mind. "In a cave?"

She nodded. "The Church of the White Snake. When Humphrey said religion went underground, he wasn't kidding."

"What are we doing here?"

"Hiding. The whole fucking country must be looking for us."

"Water . . ."

Maria moved to the cabinets and filled a glass with water from a pitcher. Jake noticed dozens of deep scratches on her legs and arms. When she returned to his side, she held the glass while he gulped the water. Then she set the glass down.

"The last thing I remember, they doped me up with some vodou smoke and threw me into a drug den out in the middle of nowhere."

"We came and got you."

He raised his eyebrows.

"Three friends helped me. They're good men, like Humphrey. We killed a lot of zonbies getting out. I'm not a virgin anymore."

"Where are they?"

"Jorge's asleep in the next room. Armand and Stephane are guarding the mouth of the cave. This place is enormous. You'll meet them all later."

Jake swallowed and the soreness returned to his throat. "Thank you."

She brushed his hair out of his eye, her fingernails scraping his forehead. "You're welcome."

"I feel terrible."

"You look terrible."

"You look—"

Maria leaned forward and kissed him. Her lips and tongue tasted sweet. When they parted, she said, "I'm sorry. I had to do that."

He managed a smile. "You deserve it."

"So do you." So she kissed him again.

Sitting in his usual seat at the palace conference room table, Russel straightened his shoulders when the door opened and Malvado entered, followed by his sons.

Russel, Buteau, Solaine, and Mambo Catoute had been sitting in the room for almost twenty minutes, saying very little to each other. They had parted ways in the middle of the night, and Russel had grabbed only an hour's sleep before reporting for the emergency meeting Malvado had called.

Now the dictator stood before them in his royal-blue uniform. Najac stood on his left, Maxime on his right. Malvado glared at every individual in the room, then dropped into his chair. Maxime and Najac sat, too.

"I've read each of your reports," Malvado said. "I want to know only one thing: How did this happen?"

The leaders stared at the table.

"I ordered you to double the security."

"We did, Your Excellency," Buteau said. "It wasn't enough."

"Three men and a *woman* . . ."

"We've taken impressions of the vehicle's tire tracks," Solaine said. "We *will* identify who they were."

"You mean you'll identify who the *men* were. We already know who the woman was!" Malvado pounded a beefy fist on the table. "In all the years that my slaves have worked the poppy fields, no one has ever assaulted them, not the People for Pavot and not Pavot for the People."

"That's why we never thought anyone would strike the plantations." Buteau spoke in a delicate tone. "Our citizens, even the terrorist rebels, are too terrified to go near them."

"Yes. The people are frightened. But this woman is not. And she has infected others with her lack of fear. I want her found, and I want her brought to me so I can flay her alive."

Russel didn't doubt the sincerity of Malvado's words. "When I first accepted my position, I recommended a complete overhaul of the security measures at every government installation, including the plantations."

"I have an army! We're not at war, so they have nothing better to do than guard my crops. We don't need expensive sophisticated equipment."

Knowing better than to press the point, Russel said nothing.

Malvado rose and circled the table. "Whatever Helman and Vasquez came here for, the only thing they can do now is run. They have to get off Pavot. General Buteau and Colonel Solaine, I want boots on the ground and helicopters in the air. Deploy as many men as it takes to turn this island upside down. Conduct a search of every house, farm, apartment, and abandoned building on Pavot. Find these two Americans. Kill their accomplices, but bring the man and the woman to me."

Russel felt sweat forming on his bald head as Malvado stopped behind him.

"William, I want you to interrogate all suspected dissidents and their family members. Incarcerate anyone you suspect of treachery. We need to replenish the slaves I lost last night."

"Yes, sir."

Next, Malvado stepped behind Mambo Catoute. Across the table, Maxime opened his laptop and powered it on.

They worked out a cue in advance, Russel thought.

"Mambo Catoute, be ready to convert our impending prisoners to zonbies as soon as possible. Have as many priests and priestesses standing by to assist you as necessary."

Russel's unease grew. As he understood it, only Mambo Catoute had the knowledge and powers to resurrect Black Magic overdoses as zonbies. He knew she had taught her closest followers, especially Sivelia and Issagha, the basic steps so one of them could one day replace her, but she held the deepest, darkest secrets to herself.

"Yes, my lord."

Malvado stopped behind Najac, where everyone but his son could see him. "Maxime, show Najac what you've discovered."

Maxime rotated the laptop so it faced Najac. Russel had a full view of the screen, which showed a man and a woman standing near an apartment door. He sensed Mambo Catoute stiffening beside him, and Najac narrowed his eyes.

That's Najac and Sivelia!

Maxime tapped a key on the laptop and the footage played, the audio low but audible.

Sivelia: Did anyone see you?
Najac: What difference would it make if they did?
Sivelia kissed Najac.

Najac started to rise. "Father, I—"

Setting his hands on his son's shoulders, Malvado eased him back into his seat. "Shh. Watch."

On the screen, the lovers parted.

Najac: You're going to make me burst, woman.

Sivelia: Would you sacrifice everything we've worked so hard to achieve for one night of pleasure when we're so close to realizing our dreams?

Najac: I might.

Najac lunged across the table for Maxime, who jumped to his feet. "You traitor!"

Sivelia: And I'd make you feel like a king. But in the morning you'd still be a prince and my body would be worthless.

Malvado jerked Najac back. "Who's a traitor?"

Najac: How much longer?

Malvado grabbed Najac by his ears, raised his head, and slammed his forehead down on the table's edge. Najac screamed.

Around the table, the cabinet members sat rigid with fear.

Sivelia: The old woman's taught me everything she's willing to while she remains head Mambo. But I've learned quite a bit on my own, and this week I figured out something else. She made me draw a circle on the church floor and give her a jar of my sang menstruel. Both were used to summon Kalfu; I know it. All I need to do is get my hands on her book, learn the incantation, and I could summon him myself.

Leaning forward, Malvado wrapped his arms around his son's head.

Najac clawed at his father's arms. Blood poured out of the opening in his forehead, blinding him.

Najac: It isn't fair. I should have you before that demon does.

Malvado gave Najac's head a sharp twist, and the sound of his neck snapping filled the room.

Sivelia: We both have to make sacrifices, my lord. That's what it will take for you to be king and me to be your high priestess. It's time for a new generation to rule Pavot Island.

Standing straight again, Malvado continued to twist Najac's head until his son faced him over his back. "Look at me when I'm talking to you!"

Najac: When you become pregnant, Mambo Catoute will suspect Kalfu, won't she?

Clutching Najac's ears once more and staring down into his son's countenance, Malvado raised his face close to him and slammed the back of his head down on the table with such ferocity that Russel felt the vibration.

Sivelia: You have to kill her immediately after Kalfu takes me—even before you kill your father.

Malvado raised Najac's head and smashed it down again.

Najac: It's my brother who worries me. He has to suspect I want Pavot for myself.

And again.

Sivelia: We'll kill him together.

With the fifth pound, the back of Najac's skull split open, and gore splattered the table.

Najac: I like the way you think.

Malvado continued to slam Najac's head on the table, crushing it into pulp, each blow spattering those seated with blood. The dictator's features twisted into a snarl.

Sivelia: That's why I'll make the perfect queen.

Finally, Malvado hurled Najac's corpse on the floor, and with his chest heaving stared at his followers. "Make no mistake. I am in control of Pavot Island, and I demand fealty from my subjects. I will tolerate *no* conspiracies, *no* disloyalty, and *no* disrespect. Even from my own blood."

The only movement Russel made was to blink. The fear in the room had grown palpable.

"William, I rely on you for intelligence. Why did I have to learn from Maxime that Najac was plotting against me?"

Russel felt his leg trembling. "I'm sorry, Your Excellency. I failed in my responsibility. I had no idea he was this ambitious." *Because I suspected he and Maxime were teaming up to overthrow you.*

"You and Maxime will work together until this crisis has passed. I want him fully involved in every action you take. If you're my eyes, he's my ears."

Russel cleared his throat. "As you wish." Now he would be unable to discover if Maxime had designs of his own on the palace.

"Mambo Catoute, I suggest you choose your next apostle more carefully."

"Yes, lord." Mambo Catoute's voice cracked.

Malvado glanced at Maxime, who closed the laptop. "For my sake, make it a man this time."

God has spoken, Russel thought.

TWENTY-FOUR

Maria helped Jake around the corner of the makeshift room into an open cavern where several portable toilets had been set up. After he had finished, they returned to the room and sat on chairs, the foldout table between them.

"Who's Bill Russel?" she said.

Jake's stomach clenched. "An ex-CIA spook I know from my days at the Tower. He was brokering a deal between Old Nick and President Seguera from the Philippines. I sabotaged the deal. Now he's here, heading the secret police." He raised his stump. "He did this."

"You woke up delirious in the middle of the night. You mentioned him and a lot of other people."

The room suddenly felt much smaller. "Oh?"

"Weird shit."

He held her gaze, waiting for her to continue.

"Kira Thorn. Cain and Abel. Something called Avademe."

Jake blew air out of his cheeks.

"If I hadn't seen those zonbies up close and killed them the way you told me to, I'd think you were crazy. I still don't know what to think."

"There are days when *I* don't believe the things I've seen, when I doubt my own sanity."

"You talked about the Realm of Light and the Dark Realm. Heaven and hell, right?"

"In a manner of speaking."

"*Cain and Abel?*"

Jake didn't want to say more. The knowledge that human beings ascended to other dimensions when they died had provided him with sleepless nights rather than comfort. There was no telling how any one mind would cope with that information, and Maria had already been through a lot. "If we get off this island, I promise to tell you my life story."

"The boat that was supposed to transport us off the island with Andre Santiago leaves at midnight tonight. We're going to be on it."

"Midnight's a long way off. Anything can happen before then."

A short man with a wide mustache and a receding hairline entered with a coffeepot. "I'm glad to see you looking better."

"I feel like death warmed over," Jake said.

"It's this Caribbean climate."

Maria rose so Jake did the same.

"Jake, this is Jorge. He and Humphrey were close."

Jake shook Jorge's hand. "I'm sorry about Humphrey. He was a good man. Thank you for looking after Maria and for saving my life."

"You're welcome. As you can see, I brought you coffee. We have plenty of sugar but no milk or cream."

"Thanks. I take it black anyway." Jake sat back down.

"I'll take sugar," Maria said, sitting as well.

Jorge set the pot on the table and retrieved three mugs from a cupboard. "We make our coffee strong here." He filled the mugs, then pulled over a chair and sat.

"The stronger the better," Jake said. He had been unable to stop thinking about Black Magic since he had awakened and needed something to appease his craving. Jorge's coffee did not disappoint him. "This is some layout."

"There's much more here than you see. There are many secret churches here on Pavot, but this is the largest. Over time, Mambo Pharah has turned this one into a warehouse. It's more practical for her to preach to smaller groups in homes, which draws less attention."

"Mambo Pharah?"

"The high priestess of the Church of the White Snake. She's the daughter of Mambo Catoute, who holds the same position in the Church of the Black Snake. It would be too confusing to call them both Mambo Catoute, so Pharah uses her first name. It's not a sign of disrespect; she's beloved by the community she serves."

"If Mambo Catoute is an old crone, I saw her. She lit

a candle made out of Black Magic and made me inhale its smoke."

"That's her. She's Malvado's spiritual advisor. She's very powerful and feared by many."

"But her daughter pitches for the other team?"

"Yes. Pharah's here in the church now."

Maria bit her lower lip. "Um, she kind of cast a spell on you."

Jake narrowed his eye.

"Only so Mambo Catoute couldn't use your missing hand to cast a spell on you," Jorge said. "It was for your own protection."

"And yours, I bet."

Jorge nodded. "We put you in this chamber so if the soldiers followed us they wouldn't find you. This cave is a maze of caverns. I don't want either of you to wander off alone or even with each other. Unless there's trouble, you'll need a guide."

"Humphrey said he didn't belong to this church. Do you?"

"No. I'm a traditional Catholic. But my brother, Armand, and our friend Stephane are members. You'll meet them soon."

"Sooner than you think," a male voice said.

Three people entered the room: a tall Hispanic man, a chubby black man, and a dark-skinned woman who wore a scarf in her hair and a white snake around her neck. The serpent looked identical to the one Jake had killed in Maria's room at the resort.

Jake, Maria, and Jorge rose.

"This is Armand and Stephane," Jorge said.

Jake shook their hands and met their eyes. "Thank you."

Armand nodded.

"And this is Mambo Pharah."

Pharah moved closer, appraising Jake. "You and Maria have stirred up a hornet's nest of trouble."

"We're sorry," Maria said. "We meant well."

"Sometimes trouble is a good thing. It spurs men and women to action."

Jake gestured at the white snake around her neck. The serpent studied him and Maria. "I killed a snake just like that the other night."

Pharah smiled. "Do you really think so?"

Maria stepped back. "Please don't tell me that's the same snake."

"Miriam told me you were coming. She trusted you, but I wanted to know your intentions for myself. This snake is my familiar, like a witch's cat. It contains a small piece of my soul. I had it smuggled into your room to observe you, and I watched you through its eyes."

"What did you learn?" Jake said.

"That you're afraid of snakes," she said to Maria, then turned to Jake. "And you're not."

"I'm over my fear of snakes," Maria said. "Just not ghost snakes."

"You have nothing to fear." Pharah grasped the snake below its head and held it close to her face. "This is neither a snake nor a ghost. It's the symbol of this church."

"You worship that?" Jake said.

"No. We worship Bondye, the one true god. But he is too great, and we're too insignificant to pray to him directly. So we pray to the Loa, who serve as intermediaries between our world and the next."

"Like saints," Maria said.

"The Loa are lesser gods, like angels and demons. Malvado and my mother, Mambo Catoute, worship Kalfu, one of the Petro Loa, the aggressive beings."

Kalfu, Jake thought with growing realization. Katrina had worshipped Kalfu.

Pharah gestured at the table. "Please sit down. Finish your coffee. You need liquids to purge your system."

Jake and Maria sat again, but Jorge offered his seat to Pharah, who accepted it.

"We're safe for the moment," Pharah said. "My bodyguards are protecting the cave's mouth."

"Kalfu's supposed to be a badass," Jake said, which caused Maria to raise her eyebrows.

Pharah seemed pleased. "You know of him? Good. It will save us some discussion."

"We had a zonbie problem in New York City last year."

Pharah nodded. "Ramera Evans."

"Katrina," Maria said, echoing Jake's thoughts.

"She came here years ago and asked for my help with a research project she was doing on vodou."

Afterlife, Jake thought. It always came back to Old Nick.

"I turned her away. My mother did not. Ramera spent a year studying with her. I wasn't surprised to hear she started her own Black Magic operation under another name."

"She told me she sacrificed her infant to Kalfu in exchange for the secrets of Black Magic," Jake said.

"My mother did the same thing. The child would have been my older sister."

Maria set her coffee down. "You travel with bodyguards, and people know you're the leader of this White Church. If Malvado's declared war on your religion, why hasn't he killed or imprisoned you?"

"Even Malvado knows you can't force people to worship a god against their choosing. Everything is a choice always. Members of the Church of the Black Snake get the best jobs, the best interest rates with the bank, the best schools for their children. Malvado's opposed to creating martyrs, which is why Andre Santiago remains alive in El Miedo. He doesn't see me as a real threat because I'm a woman. And I suppose I've remained free because Puri Catoute is my mother and Malvado is my father, though he's never claimed me." Pharah looked around at the surprised expressions in the room and chuckled. "Malvado has his way with all the women in his court. He keeps two wives in the palace and twice as many mistresses. His sons are just as bad."

"What turned you to the White Church?" Maria said.

"Bondye turned me to it! I grew up in the palace in the Black Church with my mother, who groomed me to one day replace her. But I had a spiritual awakening and left the palace to live among the people and study with clerics. My mother was outraged and never forgave me. But she pretended to when I married and had children of my own. I thought I'd raised my eldest daughter, Sivelia, properly, but my mother seduced her with the palace lifestyle and indoctrinated her into the Black Church. Now it's me who will not forgive her. But I have other children, and they know better than to make the same mistake Sivelia has."

Jake finished his coffee.

Pharah reached over and felt his forehead. "You're in a bad state. And I don't mean Pavot Island."

"Tell me about it."

"Get back on that cot so I can treat you."

What the hell? Jake clambered onto the cot.

Pharah tapped Maria's arm. "Remove his shirt and pants."

Pulling Jake's shirt over his head, Maria whispered, "Not exactly what I had in mind."

"Me, either."

Jake's shorts joined his shirt on the floor, and he stared at the ceiling.

Pharah pulled her chair over to the bed and sat. "Give me that jar."

Stephane passed her a large pickle jar filled with murky water.

"What's *that*?" Jake said with alarm creeping into his voice.

Pharah unscrewed the jar's lid. "Nothing for you to worry about, dear." She took a pair of tongs out of her pocket and dipped them into the water. Jake recalled Kira Thorn doing the same thing once. The tongs came out holding a five-inch-long dark shape that glistened and curled in the air. "It's just a leech."

"That's damned big for a leech."

"I breed them this way. Wipe that look off your face. You've fought soldiers and zonbies. Don't be afraid of a little bloodsucker."

"I realize vodou is an ancient religion, but leeches don't do a damned bit of good. All they do is leave sores and scars."

"That's where you're wrong. These leeches will suck the Black Magic out of your body. The doctors who once used them got the idea from Houngans. They just didn't know what they were doing or why."

Pharah dropped the leech on Jake's stomach, and he shrieked at the slimy sensation.

"Don't be a baby," Maria said.

It took only one minute for Pharah to apply six leeches to Jake's body. He shuddered as he felt them adhering to his flesh and sucking on it.

Pharah raised two fingers. "In two hours, the Magic will be out of your system. Then you'll only have to worry about the psychological addiction. I brought your belongings from your resort suite, by the way. We removed them so my mother could not use them against you. Change into fresh clothes, take what you need, and burn the rest. No one here needs to be connected to you." Turning to leave, she spoke to Maria. "Keep him drinking liquids."

"I will."

Facing the men, she said, "Libération de l'île Pavot."

"Libération de l'île Pavot," they said in unison.

Mambo Catoute seethed with anger as she crossed the front courtyard of the Black Church. She had known Sivelia was ambitious and impatient, but she had not suspected the girl was foolish enough to conspire with Najac against her and

Malvado. Not only did she feel betrayed, she felt stupid and embarrassed. She would have to work hard to regain Malvado's confidence.

She had been cultivating Sivelia since the girl had turned fourteen, had wooed her with the rich lifestyle afforded by the palace, and had convinced her to preserve her virginity for Kalfu. Perhaps she had taught the bitch too well.

A soldier stationed at the entrance to the Black Church descended the concrete steps and waited at the bottom for her. Then he offered her his arm, which she took without saying anything, and helped her to the top.

Inside the lobby, Issagha stood waiting at the fountain with the little traitor. At least Issagha, sure and steady, was far enough along in his studies to replace Sivelia; Catoute wouldn't have to start over from scratch. But her dream of creating a dynasty of palace bokors had been dealt a fatal blow. Now all she could do was preserve her own standing in the cabinet. Facing her two subordinates, she showed no trace of emotion.

"Are you all right?" Sivelia said. "You look tired."

Traitor! "I'm fine, child. Thank you for your concern."

"What happened?" Issagha said.

"Lord Malvado is beside himself over the loss of his slaves. He wants me to resurrect a fresh batch—too many for me to do by myself. You're both ready to assist me more than I've allowed you to in the past."

Issagha bowed. "As you wish, Mambo."

Catoute saw glee in Sivelia's eyes.

"Anything to help you, Grand-mère."

How generous, you witch. "Issagha, you know what materials are required. Gather and prepare enough for fifty resurrections and have them transported to the compound at the plantation outside Pavot City. Sivelia, come with me."

Issagha bowed again and hurried off.

"Anything to lessen your burden." Sivelia took Catoute by her arm. They entered the church together, their footsteps echoing along the balcony, and walked down the stairs.

"You've worked hard these past years, girl. It's all about to pay off for you."

"I've only ever wanted to make you happy."

Unseen by Sevilia, Catoute scowled. They passed the podium, descended the second flight of stairs, and entered the summoning room.

"Pull the bar down," Catoute said. *I may as well get as much work out of you as I can.*

Sivelia grabbed the thick wood in both hands and lowered the bar into the locked position. They crossed the floor, passing the second podium, and stopped at the summoning circle. The blood on the chalk had dried to the color of rust but remained intact.

"The blood's a mixture of yours and mine. Yours, because this summoning spell requires *sang menstruel*. Mine, because I've already made a pact with Kalfu. Once you've formed a similar bond, only your blood will be required. Gather the pieces of that candle, and kneel facing me in the center of the circle."

Sivelia did as instructed. Catoute removed a box of kitchen matches from the podium and tossed it into the circle. The box landed before Sivelia, who snatched it up.

"Holding the candle halves together, light the wick."

Sivelia removed a long match, then stacked the candle's halves on top of each other. She struck the match on the box's side, producing a flame that flared and shrank with a gentle hiss. She looked at Catoute with anxious eyes, and the old woman nodded. Sivelia lit the wick, waited for its flame to grow, then shook the match out and tossed it aside.

"Chant with me," Catoute said, and the ancient words rose from within her in a singsong fashion. She had only taught Sivelia the basics of the old tongue, so she chanted in a clear manner.

Sivelia repeated the words, her gaze darting from Catoute to the candle to the edges of the circle.

A shadow passed over the circle alone, and a breeze caused the flame to flicker. Catoute stopped chanting, and Sivelia did the same.

Now we'll see what you're really made of.

The top of Kalfu's head materialized through the floor, and the demon rose, facing Sivelia, his back to Catoute, who moved along the circle's outer rim for a better view. Sivelia gasped as Kalfu's delicate features settled before hers. Catoute saw Kalfu's red eyes reflected in her granddaughter's. Kalfu continued to rise, and Sivelia tipped her head back to stare at his face. His penis became erect and Sivelia's eyes widened and she rose.

"You're beautiful," Sivelia said, tears of wonder in her eyes.

Kalfu raised his hands to her face, then hesitated. His fingers danced in the air inches from her cheeks, and then he jerked his head in Catoute's direction. "What's the meaning of this, old woman?"

"As I'm sure you know, Helman's escaped. Vasquez and some rebels rescued him from Malvado's plantation. But he's still on the island, and I intend to present him to you as promised. In the meantime, I honor you with this sacrifice."

Sivelia stepped back, her features contorting. "Sacrifice?"

Catoute felt her face twitching with anger. "You plotted against me, girl. The incantation you just chanted was a call for sacrifice."

Sivelia spun on one heel, attempting to flee the circle, but before she had reached the perimeter's edge Kalfu seized her hair and snatched her back. "Grand-mère, please!"

"You little ingrate," Catoute hissed.

Sivelia pushed at Kalfu. "I've waited to give myself to you half my life!"

Kalfu pulled her close to him. "And I've observed you just as long. I had other plans for you—long-range plans. This old wretch has undermined us both."

Catoute aimed her cane at Kalfu. "The bitch sought to undermine *me*, which I'm sure you knew all about. Curse your supposed noninterference. You could have warned me."

"Let me go," Sivelia said. "Her time is almost up, and I swear I'll serve you well."

Catoute cackled.

"A wise offer," Kalfu said, "but no longer possible under these circumstances."

Tears streamed down Sivelia's cheeks. "No . . ."

Catoute watched Kalfu transform into his true flesh

form and relished Sivelia's terrified screams. The Loa tore her dress to shreds, then turned his attention to her skin. Bones snapped, flesh stretched and ripped, and blood flowed. Catoute almost felt sorry for her granddaughter as Kalfu mounted the girl's reconfigured body from behind and thrust the horn between his legs into her openings. Sivelia pleaded for Kalfu to stop, for Catoute to help, and, realizing neither would happen, for death to take her.

As Kalfu feasted on the girl's tissue, Catoute didn't have to wonder what would happen to her if she failed to deliver Helman to her master.

TWENTY-FIVE

The first leech died on Jake's right thigh. He felt the sucking stop, and then the creature turned still and rolled off him, leaving a bloody sore covered in mucus-like slime.

"Thank God," Jake said as Maria picked up the dead parasite and deposited it into a waste container.

The next one died a few minutes later, and within half an hour Maria treated all six wounds with disinfectant that caused Jake to curse.

"How do you feel?" Maria said.

"Like I've been through detox but I can't stop thinking about that shit."

"How did it make you feel?"

He thought about it. "Vile. And yet there was something soothing about giving myself over to it. The repercussions didn't matter as long as I was able to desensitize myself to the world."

"Is the world such a bad place?"

"Sometimes it is. You know that. Sometimes it's beautiful. But darkness has a way of trumping beauty."

"That's pretty bleak."

"I need to find cleaning solution for my glass eye." Jake raised his stump. "And I'm worried that if this gets infected, I could lose my entire arm." He pointed to his face. "These scars will never heal unless I have plastic surgery. My wife was murdered, my best friend was turned into a raven, and I seem to have as hard a time avoiding zonbies as I do staying clean. It's a little difficult to find much sunshine."

Maria stepped close to him. "But not impossible."

"No, not impossible."

She kissed him, then put her arms around him. "I was worried about you."

"I worried about you, too."

She sniffed his shirt. "You stink."

"You stink, too."

Maria looked into his eye. "The guys are cooking breakfast. I saw one of those old claw-foot tubs in another room, rigged with a wood-burning stove. What do you say we heat some water, act social, then chase everyone off so we can take a bath together?"

"That sounds proper."

Sitting at a long table in a wide room in the cave, they ate bacon and eggs wrapped in tortillas. Walls had been erected to create a buiding-like atmosphere, and mounted torches burned.

"There's nothing like a good home-cooked meal in a cave," Maria said.

"My brother's the cook in the family," Jorge said.

"It's true," Armand said. "Jorge even manages to ruin toast."

"What do you guys do for a living?" Jake said.

"I work in the salt mine," Armand said. "Stephane owns a horse ranch."

Stephane grinned. "I bought it to be a tour guide, only the tourists never showed up."

"Won't you be missed at work?" Maria said.

Armand shook his head. "Because I don't wear the black snake on my arm, they only call me when they need me."

"Where's Pharah?" Jake said.

"She'll be back," Stephane said. "She went to the market for groceries."

"We won't be here that long," Maria said.

"Bondye willing," Armand said.

Jake looked at the faces around him. "How did you know where to find me?"

Jorge gestured to Armand. "Our cousin is a nurse at the clinic where they took you."

"Ramona?"

Jorge nodded. "I almost had Maria on a boat when we got the news. From that moment on, she was an unstoppable force."

"This is some woman," Stephane said.

With his admiration for her growing, Jake gazed at Maria. The torchlight caressed her features.

She didn't look away.

Jake winced as he settled into the bath, the hot water burning the sores left by the leeches. He dangled his left arm over the edge of the tub, keeping his bandaged stump dry.

Maria stripped before him and opened her mouth as she stepped into the steaming water. "Speaking of scars, these scratches had better heal." She eased herself into the water, and they sat facing each other with their knees raised and their heads resting on the edge of the old tub. "Christ, that feels good."

"Add taking a bath in a secret cave to the list of things I never expected to do in my life."

She stared at him with relaxed features. "This is all so crazy. I can't believe it's been less than a week since Miami."

"Time flies when you're battling the supernatural."

Maria straightened her legs so they pressed against Jake's. "How do you do it? *Why* do you do it?"

"I don't have much choice. Trouble follows me. Maybe I'm cursed."

"I hope Edgar's okay."

"I do, too."

"If we make it out and Miriam keeps her word, what do you think he'll say about all this?"

"I have no idea. I just hope he can put his life back together." Jake felt himself growing hard.

"I think you like me," Maria said, nodding at his erection.

"I think you're right."

Sliding her hands through the water, she closed her fingers around his shaft and tightened them in sequence over and over, like a flautist.

Jake moaned and grew harder.

"You feel awfully tense. Got a lot on your mind?"

Jake grabbed the side of the tub as Maria stroked him. "You sure you're a cop?"

"I've always been a multitasker."

He felt the pressure building inside him. Maria glided forward through the water and leaned closer to his face. He looked up at the stalactites and let loose a groan, then closed his eyes.

Sitting at his desk and poring over a ledger, Father Alejandro looked up when he heard vehicles approaching. After removing his reading glasses, he stood at the window and peered outside. A black limo, a jeep carrying two officers, and a troop transport truck pulled into the parking lot.

What in God's name?

He hurried out of his office to the side exit. Outside, his heart skipped a beat when he saw Bill Russel, the head of Malvado's secret police, and Maxime, one of the dictator's sons, walking toward him from the limo. The army officer climbed out of the jeep and mobilized the soldiers jumping out of the transport truck.

"What's the meaning of this?" Alejandro said as Russel and Maxime reached him.

Maxime slapped him. "Speak when spoken to."

Alejandro felt a stinging in his cheek. "I don't understand."

Russel stepped between them. "Father, may we speak inside?"

Alejandro watched the soldiers fanning out across the property, some of them heading toward the garage. "What are these men doing?"

Russel gestured to the door. "Inside, Father. Please."

Alejandro glanced at Maxime, who had always struck him as an unreasonable brute. He led the men to his office. "Kindly tell me what this is about. I've done nothing wrong."

"Haven't you?" Maxime said.

"No, I haven't."

Russel motioned to the chair at Alejandro's desk. "Sit."

Alejandro did as Russel suggested, and Russel pulled a chair over and sat, too. Maxime remained standing.

Russel took two pieces of paper from inside his jacket and unfolded them. "Have you seen either of these people?"

Alejandro studied the passport photos of Maria Vasquez and Jake Helman. "No, never. Who are they?" As a rule he accepted that to tell a lie was to break one of the Ten Commandments, but as an intermediary between La Mère and the various organizations opposing Le Monstre, he knew that protecting hundreds of people's lives justified a little creativity.

"Two Americans, like me," Russel said. "They've murdered a number of Pavotian soldiers and have sabotaged some of our national agriculture. At least three citizens are

298

helping them. It's imperative that we bring them to justice before they can escape the island. We're willing to show certain leniency toward their accomplices if they come forward."

Leniency, Alejandro thought. *You mean torture or enslavement.* He didn't believe the stories that Malvado populated his drug fields with the walking dead, but he did believe Malvado enslaved his enemies. "I'm sorry, Mr. Russel. I haven't seen these people, and I don't know who these accomplices are. I can't help you."

Russel offered him a sympathetic smile. "Father, I'm pressed for time. You're the figurehead of legitimate opposition to President Malvado. We've allowed you a certain amount of breathing space because we want the world to see that we're tolerant of dissenting views."

Alejandro felt sweat forming on his forehead. "I don't know what you're talking about. I'm no dissident. I'm just a simple priest, loyal to Pavot Island."

"But are you loyal to President Malvado?"

"Yes, of course. I—"

"Now you're lying to me. I know you've communicated with Miriam Santiago in Miami. You funnel cash from her to the rebels."

"I don't know what you're—"

Outside, a soldier called out.

Alejandro's heart beat faster. *What have they found?*

Russel's cell phone rang. Answering the call, he locked his eyes on Alejandro's. "We'll be right there." Russel hung up. "Let's go outside, Father. Our soldiers have made an interesting discovery."

Rising, Alejandro felt Maxime staring at the back of his head. He didn't trust the man behind him.

They crossed the driveway to the garage, which also served as a maintenance department. As soon as Alejandro saw the soldiers gathered there, he knew they had discovered the tunnel.

Russel smiled at the trapdoor in the garage floor, then glanced over his shoulder at the sweating priest, who turned pale. "What have we got here?"

A muscle in Alejandro's cheek twitched. "It's an old maintenance tunnel linking this garage to the church."

"What do you use it for?"

"Nothing, really. A shelter from hurricanes."

"Let's take a look."

Russel climbed down the ladder and surveyed the tunnel's contents: furniture, canned food, a radio. He knew a hiding place when he saw one.

Alejandro descended the ladder, followed by Maxime.

"Did you hide either Maria Vasquez or Jake Helman here?"

"No, I've never hidden anyone here."

"Again, you're lying to me. I know it. I'm placing you under arrest and seizing this church and its assets for Pavot Island."

Alejandro appeared as if Russel had struck him. "You can't do that. The Vatican—"

"—has no authority here. You were born on Pavot

Island, and you'll die here. Whether or not you cooperate with us will determine how soon that day will come."

Jake and Maria followed Jorge's directions through the caverns. They supported each other as they stepped over slime and moss, and Maria carried a torch. Bats clung to the stalactites, and a rock outcrop overlooked a deep, wide chasm that appeared bottomless. Streams emptied into darkness.

"This place is huge," Jake said.

"I see light ahead."

They followed the incline to the sunlight at the mouth of the cave. They heard gulls cawing and waves crashing before they saw Armand and Stephane and the sand and ocean beyond them. Jake squinted at the bright light.

"Hola," Maria said.

"Did you bring us lunch?" Stephane said, setting his machine gun down.

"No, we came to relieve you," Jake said.

Armand and Stephane exchanged doubtful looks.

"Go ahead. I can still handle one of those."

Armand passed his weapon to Jake. "Show me."

Jake slung the machine gun's strap over his shoulder, grabbed the gun's trigger handle with his right hand, and leaned his bandaged stump over the barrel.

"I'm not convinced."

Maria picked up Stephane's weapon and posed with it. "How about me?"

Armand chuckled. "All right, *you* convinced me." He turned to Jake. "Stay inside the cave, gringo. You glow like a ghost, and a patrol boat will spot you from half a mile away."

Stephane chuckled, and they left Jake and Maria at the opening. A rock nook hid the cave's mouth from the water, which crashed into the small cove.

"It's hard to believe such a beautiful place has so much evil," Maria said as she sat in the sand.

Jake removed the machine gun, set it down, and sat opposite her. "There's evil everywhere." He looked at his stump. "I still feel my fingers. Right now I'm opening and closing them."

"Phantom pain," Maria said.

Jake watched the ocean spray against the rocks.

Maria lit a cigarette. After taking a drag, she offered it to Jake, who shook his head.

"Got something on your mind, Helman?"

"A lot of things."

"Like Kalfu?"

Jake pulled a slate stone out of the sand and skipped it across the water. "Malvado's army and the zonbies pose a more immediate threat."

"In New York the Machete Massacres were committed by zonbies carrying machetes, right? But the zonbies who wiped out Papa Joe and his crew carried machine guns and Glocks, and a lot of the ones you put down carried guns. Except for a few guards at the plantation, the local breed sticks to machetes."

"It all depends on who's calling the shots. Katrina

designed the Machete Massacres to elicit fear in ethnic groups familiar with island magic, but her dealers and soldiers packed modern artillery. Here on Pavot, Malvado needs a workforce to harvest his crops. The one thing Malvado has in common with Katrina and Prince Malachai is a desire for free labor with undying loyalty." Jake narrowed his eye. Malvado owned sugarcane plantations and rum factories, not just poppy fields. He needed far more zonbie slaves than those who worked on his plantations.

"Angels and demons." Maria reached inside her shirt and took out the gold cross that hung around her neck on a chain. "I was raised in a religious household. I've always believed in God and heaven. But demons? Not so much."

"Hold on to your beliefs. Don't change them because of me. It will be easier to get through the day."

"It's not all about you, baby. There's fucking *zonbies* on this island. If that doesn't point to the devil and an army of demons, I don't know what does. But half the people on this island worship a certain demon, and you tell me that Katrina did, too. Same demon, same walking stiffs. I detect a pattern."

Resting his head against the rock wall, Jake inhaled the ocean's salty fragrance.

"So you never encountered this Kalfu?"

He shook his head.

"But you believe he exists?"

"I have no reason to doubt it and plenty to believe it."

"What about Cain and Abel?"

"I'd rather not discuss them."

Maria puffed on her cigarette. "I know it was my choice to come here, but I went through a lot to save your ass, and now I'm stuck. I think I deserve to know any information you've got about these Realms of Light and Dark."

"You'll just think I'm insane."

"I already wonder if *I'm* insane."

Jake stood. "If you think that hearing what I have to say about Cain and Abel will make you feel better, you're mistaken. But there is something I want to tell you."

"Shoot."

"I killed the Cipher. If you're still looking to bust someone for that job, I'm your man."

She exhaled smoke. "Deep inside, I always knew it. Did Edgar help you cover your tracks?"

"Not directly. But I learned later that he had his own suspicions and pulled a string or two that protected me without my knowing it."

"You're a pair of real interesting guys."

"Yeah."

She stood as well. "The Cipher killed your wife. I get that. You did what you thought you had to do. I might have done the same thing if a serial killer killed someone I loved." She tossed her cigarette in the sand and crushed it. "As a cop, I can't condone what you did. But I understand why you did it."

"So you don't want to take me in?"

She walked over to him. "It doesn't matter if I want to or not. Whatever happens when we get off this island, I feel close to you. Too close to put the job above."

He held one side of her face, the sea breeze blowing her hair. He felt close to her, too. "I've got something else to tell you."

"Shit, Jake, are you trying to bring my whole world down?"

"I don't intend to leave without Andre Santiago."

Maria's eyes flared with anger. "Are you fucking *kidding* me? We've got to get our asses out of here!"

"I came to help Edgar, but it's gotten bigger than that. Our friends inside are downplaying the danger they're in— danger we've put them in. You know there're all kinds of ways the local bulls can tie them to us, including the fact that they're here protecting us instead of being wherever they belong."

"And you think busting Santiago out of prison will change that?"

"Maybe."

"But you're willing to take the chance?"

"People here have risked their lives for us. Everyone on this island is oppressed. There are scarecrows and the zonbies. If nothing else, if we get Santiago back to the US, an investigation by the UN could put an end to Black Magic on Pavot Island."

"Jesus Christ. They've got that boat ready for us. We have a damned good chance of escaping with our lives, and you want to throw that away?"

"We already made our plans. If anything, the circumstances are even more ideal now, because Malvado's forces are preoccupied with finding us."

"That's one way of looking at it. Another is that those

forces are already marshaled and waiting."

"I've made up my mind. I have to do this. But I want you on that boat."

"Now I know you're bugging. You've only got one wing. You *need* me."

"You've done your share—more than your share."

"So have you. I'm not leaving without you."

TWENTY-SIX

Tree branches whipped at the Dodge Ram's windshield as the vehicle drove along the narrow jungle road at sunset. Armand drove with Stephane beside him, both men wearing black. Jake, Maria, and Jorge rode in the back, Jake and Maria clad in shorts and T-shirts, Jorge in black like his friends.

"I still think we should all go in with you," Jorge said.

Jake frowned. "That wasn't the plan. Besides, we only have two uniforms."

"And you only have one hand."

"But I have two," Maria said.

"It won't matter if they see our faces, since we're already public enemies number one and two," Jake said.

"Just remember who number one is," Maria said.

Jorge raised his hands. "I give up. The next time you

two get a hotel room, make sure you don't leave the USA."

Chuckling, Maria put one arm around Jorge's shoulders. "But then we'd never see you, O fierce one."

Jorge rolled his eyes.

"I appreciate your desire to go in there with us, Jorge—we both do—but we don't know these other men. We're counting on you to be our lookout in the tunnel and for Armand and Stephane to take out the guards in those towers."

"We're your guys," Stephane said.

The sun had set by the time they reached a clearing surrounded by dense trees.

"Everybody out," Armand said.

They climbed out of the truck, and Armand glanced at his watch. "Jorge, show them the view while we're waiting."

Jorge pulled out a machine gun and threw another one to Maria. "This way, *Americanos*."

Jorge led them through a thicket and up an incline, and they crouched behind a rock ridge. He handed them a pair of night vision binoculars. Maria looked through them first, then passed them to Jake.

Thirty feet below, a field stretched for half a mile. A forest had been cleared, leaving hundreds, perhaps thousands, of stumps rotting in the ground. At the end of the field, a chain-link fence topped with coils of razor-tipped wire separated the field from a stone fortress. Guard towers rose from the front left and rear right corners of the fenced in area. Pale yellow light shone out some of the barred windows, but most of them surrendered to the darkness.

El Miedo, Jake thought. "It looks smaller than I thought."

"We have a small population and a number of local jails. Remember, El Miedo has only one prisoner."

They heard another truck arrive behind them.

"Come on," Maria said. "We'll see that place up close soon enough."

They returned to the Ram, which had been joined by a silver SUV, just as a van pulled up. By the time a second SUV had arrived and discharged its passengers, Jake counted twenty-five men and women holding guns.

"There's no time to introduce you to everyone. We're one branch of the People for Pavot. There are eighteen branches across the island." Armand addressed the circle of freedom fighters. "This is Jake Helman and Maria Vasquez. They were sent by La Mère to take Andre back to Miami with them. Your job is to do everything you can to slow down the black snakes when all hell breaks loose. My job is to deliver them to their transport.

"I want the driver of each vehicle standing by to drive them just in case the rest of us don't make it. Space your vehicles out along the road, facing in the opposite direction. Park in the brush, so other vehicles can get around you if necessary. Everyone knows where to rendezvous. We've waited a long time for a spark to ignite this revolution and longer for Le Père to be freed. This is the beginning, but a price will be paid. Libération de l'île Pavot."

"Libération de l'île Pavot!"

The drivers returned to their vehicles and turned them around. As the other men and women checked their weapons, Armand gathered his party and everyone shook hands.

"Good luck," he said to Jake and Maria.

"You, too," Jake said. "All of you."

"Hopefully we'll see each other back here in an hour or so." Armand nodded to Stephane. "Let's go, *ami*."

Armand and Stephane moved off into the jungle, their sniper rifles slung over their shoulders.

Jorge led Jake and Maria into the jungle in the opposite direction. He turned on his flashlight, and they did the same. Seventy yards from the road, they stopped at a large tree trunk.

"Don't tell me," Jake said.

Smiling, Jorge bent over, felt along the sides of the trunk, then pulled back the top, which was attached by a wide hinge on the inside. Jake and Maria peered down, and Jake saw only darkness. Jorge aimed his flashlight at the wooden ladder rungs bolted to the shaft's wall.

"Under the circumstances, you should go first," Jorge said to Jake.

Jake swung one leg over the tree stump, set it on the top rung, then swung the other leg over and plunged into darkness. Jorge's flashlight beam showed the bottom, perhaps ten feet below. When Jake's sneaker touched the ground, he aimed his flashlight at the ceiling.

Seven feet, he estimated. He pointed the flashlight into the tunnel, which swallowed the light. Directing the beam, he glimpsed supports and crossbeams spaced every eight feet. The walls and ceiling were flat and straight.

Maria descended behind him, and he heard Jorge close the stump and join them. Darkness pressed in.

Jorge lit a lantern, which cast dull light over them. "We

have half a mile to travel, which will take us to the prison fence. Then another tunnel that's not so spacious. The floor here is level and clear of stones, but it's still just dirt, and you'll encounter the occasional tree root. Every crossbeam has four holes drilled into it two inches wide, with a pipe that runs to the surface for air. Some of them are clogged with dirt and leaves. If you have trouble breathing, you have a small oxygen mask and tank in one of your backpacks. Use it sparingly, in case the ceiling caves in."

"I guess smoking is out of the question," Maria said.

They set off.

Jake and Maria used their flashlights to supplement the light from Jorge's lantern.

"How long did it take to dig this?" Maria said.

"Decades," Jorge said. "The original diggers started with the final tunnel you'll use, then worked their way back to where we started. If Le Père was a younger man, we might have continued another half mile. The time for rescuing him is running out. It's good you came when you did."

"I wish Humphrey was alive to see this."

"So do I."

They reached a dead end. Jake lowered his flashlight beam to a perfect black square in the cinder-block wall. Two six-foot lengths of PVC piping extended from the hole.

"Mi Dios," Maria said.

Jake got down on his knees and shone the flashlight around the inside of the tunnel. The parallel tracks of PVC pipe running on the ground faded into darkness, and a single metal track hung from the ceiling. "It's only three feet high."

"Three and a half," Jorge said. "It just seems like less with the tracks."

Maria used her flashlight to illuminate three flat dollies similar to those used by auto mechanics. "I take it these are our wheels?"

"Oui."

Jake and Maria crouched around one dolly. Four skateboard wheels had been screwed underneath each corner of the board. One inch of padding covered the top surface, with thicker padding to support the rider's head. Jake studied a metal device, like an arm, attached to a pole set into a hole on the right side. A two-foot bar covered with a long foam rubber grip extended from the arm above where he expected the rider's chest would be, with four small wheels above it, which he spun one by one. The device reminded him of exercise equipment in a fancy gymnasium.

"I see these wheels attach to the upper track, but how does this thing work?"

"Like a pump," Jorge said. "Traveling headfirst, you push the handle toward your feet, and the tension propels you forward. Then the spring pushes the handle above your head so you can push it down again. You can go fast with minimal effort."

"A quarter of a mile is a long way," Maria said.

"We've run tests many times. A man in good condition can run a quarter-mile track in sixty-eight seconds. A man in average condition can jog the same track in two minutes. Even going slow and steady, coasting as much as possible, you can make the trip in five minutes, ten at the most."

"It looks to me like it takes two hands to push that bar down."

"It will be difficult to operate with one hand but not impossible."

"I can still use my left arm," Jake said. "Just not my hand."

"Don't you dare." Maria's voice took on an arch tone. "You could break your sutures and rupture your arm open. With your heart pumping at that rate, you'll bleed to death before you reach the end of the tunnel. Then I'll really be screwed."

"I'll go in Jake's place," Jorge said.

Jake shook his head. "Forget it. We need you here to coordinate with the teams above. I'm in good shape. I've been working out. I can do this. What's at the end of the tunnel?"

"A station of sorts. For the last eight feet, the ceiling is as high as this one. The first person to arrive will have to lean his dolly against the wall so the next dolly can enter that space. You'll find an iron ladder bolted to the wall. Fifteen feet above, you'll find the access panel."

"Is there light in there?"

"No, you'll need your flashlights when you reach the station. In the tunnel, there is a small bulb in the arm"—he pointed at the dolly—"powered by your motion. As long as you pump, you'll be able to see the ceiling."

"What if something goes wrong in the tunnel?"

Jorge motioned to a hole on the left side of the dolly. "Move the arm into this hole, and operate it the same way. It will reverse your direction—as long as your path is not obstructed by your partner. There are no real brakes; pull up on the bar to slow down. When you reach the station, the top wheels will encounter stoppers that will bring your ride to an end. Expect a jolt."

Jake looked around the floor. "There are three dollies."

"One for each of you, plus Andre. The empty dolly will have to travel between the two of you, with the person in the rear pushing it along."

Jake realized that if he had agreed to allow others to accompany them, transporting everyone would have been a laborious process, with a speedy escape impossible.

Maria looked at Jake. "Can you handle that?"

"Yes."

"Then I go first."

Jorge said, "When you've both reached the end, take a full five minutes to relax your arms before you climb the ladder. When you return with Andre, we'll have to run the half mile back to the entrance. It won't be easy."

Maria stood and removed her backpack. "Unlike the rest of this adventure. Send me in."

Jorge and Maria positioned the first dolly on the PVC tracks. The skateboard wheels fit perfectly. Maria hopped onto the dolly and grasped the bar with both hands. Jake set her backpack across her thighs, and Jorge slid her machine gun under one leg.

Jorge raised his hand radio. "We're at the access point and ready to go."

Stephane's voice squawked over the radio. "I'm in position."

"So am I," Armand said.

Jorge nodded to Maria, who glanced at Jake.

"I'll see you on the other side," she said.

Before Jake could answer, she pressed down on the bar and disappeared into the tunnel.

Jorge positioned a second dolly on the tracks, pushed it into the tunnel, then positioned the third dolly, which Jake climbed aboard, his back and buttocks resting on a blue mat nailed to the dolly's surface. His legs dangled over the edge just under his calves. The bar extended above his head, and he placed his right hand on its center.

Jorge set Jake's backpack on top of his thighs and the machine gun under one leg. He put one foot on the edge of the dolly between Jake's legs. "Let me give you a push."

The dolly surged forward, and Jorge and his flashlight disappeared. The skateboard wheels ran smoothly on the tracks, but the heat made Jake feel as if he had entered an oven. He pulled down on the bar, and the dolly increased speed, a spotlight of dull gold appearing on the ceiling. The spring-loaded mechanism popped the bar back into place, and the light moved above Jake's face, allowing him to glimpse the ceiling inches beyond his fingers. The claustrophobic sensation in the narrow tunnel reminded Jake of the MRI machine he had been in when Katrina had cast a spell on him.

He pushed the bar down again with ease and established a steady rhythm. Whoever had designed the contraption knew what he was doing.

Jake's dolly bumped into the empty dolly ahead and propelled it along. Despite the smooth ride, he felt vibrations beneath him. The golden light intensified when he pushed the bar, then faded when the bar returned to position. Each push caused his dolly to bump against the one intended for Andre. He hoped Maria was making good time, so they wouldn't get jammed up.

Maria.

Jesus, she had turned out to be a pot of gold, a fiery soldier with strong convictions. Jake admired her as a cop, a fighter, and a lover. He didn't want to let his feelings for her cloud his judgment, and he didn't want to lose her. Just thinking about the possibility made him pump the bar harder, the dolly's vibrations increasing with its speed, sweat forming on his brow. He knew she could take care of herself, but he felt compelled to ensure her safety anyway. And how could he do that with only one hand?

Russel.

He had disliked the man upon meeting him in the Tower and had feared what he might do after Jake had killed Old Nick and Kira. Jake had always expected to run into Russel again but had not expected to walk right into his clutches in another country where he had no legal protection.

Laurel.

His psychic confidante proved yet another complication. They had shared sexual experiences together but had both realized a romantic relationship was out of the question. Reading his mind, Laurel had even forced Jake to admit he had feelings for Maria. But Jake considered Laurel a friend, and he knew she had become a shut-in because she was hiding from someone or some*thing*. He wanted to help her with her problem, which she had so far refused to share with him. Maria had inadvertently provided him with a clue to Laurel's past.

A romance writer!

Now he wondered if he would ever see Laurel again.

By the time the wheels on the dolly encountered the braking system at the end of the tunnel and he lifted the bar in the opposite direction to help slow the dolly, Jake had worked himself into a full sweat. The dolly shook as it decelerated, and he heard Andre's dolly crash ahead of him. Then his dolly slammed into that one, and he felt himself hurtling off the padding. He squeezed the bar, which snapped him back into position, and felt as if his arm had been ripped off. He clenched his jaw to keep from screaming as the dolly rebounded back into the tunnel with him still on it.

TWENTY-SEVEN

Jake cursed in the darkness. He heard one of the dollies ahead turn over, then light enveloped him.

"Are you all right?" Maria said, her voice more distant than he would have liked.

Jake groaned. "I can't move my arm. I think it's broken." He reached for the bar with his stump—

"Don't!"

He stopped in midmotion. "I need one good arm to crawl, and I don't have one."

"Move your ass to the bottom of the dolly, and use your feet."

Sighing, he did as she said. His soaking wet T-shirt clung to the mat beneath his back. Unable to grab either side of the dolly for leverage, he raised one knee and kept a foot on the dolly, using his other foot to propel him toward

Maria, like skateboarding in reverse. The light around him grew brighter, and he emerged from the tunnel into darkness again.

Squeezing the flashlight under one arm, Maria caught the dolly and stopped it, then helped him sit up, which caused him to growl in pain. "Jesus, how fast did you want to get here? You were pushing me, too. I didn't even have to pump the last half of the way."

"I have a lot on my mind."

"And I don't?" Maria swung her flashlight around the concrete walls, illuminating the station Jorge had described—a very small room, like a walk-in closet. Locating the lantern Jorge had mentioned, she picked it up and lit it, then kneeled beside Jake. "Where does it hurt?"

"Shoulder . . ."

She raised his right arm straight out, and pain lanced through it, causing him to moan. He felt her probing his shoulder, and his torso spasmed.

"You've just dislocated it. Hang on. I'll pop it back in. Keep your arm straight."

"Wait. Do you—?"

Before he could stop her, she popped his arm back into its socket. He gasped as pain shot through his upper body, then receded. He rotated his arm in its shoulder cup.

"All the king's horses and all the king's men couldn't put Helman together again, but one little Latina did the trick."

Jake panted. "It's so hot down here."

Rising, Maria unfastened her hand radio from her belt and raised it to her mouth. "We got here in one piece, no thanks to my partner."

"Copy that," Jorge said.

Maria handed the flashlight to Jake. "Here. Give yourself a show." Stepping out of her sneakers, she stripped off her shirt and shorts.

Jake watched her take the combat boots and camouflage uniform out of her backpack and put them on, then fasten her gun belt.

"These boots are big even with the stuffing in the toes. You gonna sit there admiring the view, or are you going to get dressed?"

Jake unclasped his backpack and took out his uniform and boots. "Cut me some slack. Technically, I'm crippled." He stood and removed his sneakers, then peeled off his wet shirt.

Maria unbuckled his belt, opened his shorts, and pulled them down around his ankles. "I got no use for helplessness." She aimed her flashlight at him, and he got dressed. "But I love a man in uniform."

"Yeah? I haven't worn one in a long time."

She shone the flashlight at the ceiling between them, and they adjusted each other's black berets. Then she set one dolly headfirst on the tracks and the other behind it. They armed themselves with gear from their packs, which they filled with their discarded clothing.

"Okay, five minutes to recuperate and get our heads together," Maria said. "Sit down, soldier."

They sat side by side on the second dolly. Jake held his flashlight, too.

"Smoke 'em if you got 'em," he said.

"Not in this heat. Besides, I quit again."

"Glad to hear it."

Maria sighed. "We're going to have to kill these guards."

"I know."

"You okay with that?"

"Not really. I kind of promised myself I'd only kill in self-defense from now on. Human beings, that is."

"When we pull Santiago out of there, it will be self-defense."

"Maybe."

"I mean, we're doing some good, right? These berets are black, but we're really wearing white hats."

"I don't know. I hope so. I'm telling myself these guards have black snake tattoos. If they worship Kalfu, their souls are already dark."

"As in the Dark Realm?"

"Yeah."

"So, do you see these souls?"

"Only when someone dies in front of me or when a zonbie's soul escapes from his head."

"And you can tell if they're headed north or deep south?"

"That's the size of it."

"How long have you had this gift?"

"Since the Cipher killed Sheryl."

Maria paused. "You've got some serious baggage, you know that?"

"It's occurred to me."

"That's okay. I can deal. Maybe."

Jake had his doubts. "Time?"

Maria glanced at her watch. "Two-minute countdown."

"Good luck." Jake held out his hand.

Maria shook it. "You, too." She kissed him, then stood. "Hey, do me a favor?"

"What's that?"

"If I get killed and you see my soul heading in the right direction, tell my mother, okay?"

Jake stood. "We're both going home."

"I want you to promise me you'll do what I asked. It'll mean a lot to her."

"I promise."

"Okay, let's go kick some ass." Maria climbed the ladder first, her machine gun over her shoulder and her flashlight in one hand.

Jake followed her, the climb difficult because he had only one hand.

Maria stopped climbing when she could go no farther and shone her flashlight on the access panel, three feet wide and three feet high. With his feet on the rung just below her, they stood shoulder to shoulder. She twisted the simple locks, and he stashed his flashlight in his belt to help her remove the panel.

"Sorry," she said. "You're low man on the totem pole."

Squeezing one edge of the panel, Jake descended the ladder, leaned the panel against the wall, and climbed the ladder again.

Maria inspected a second panel. "This one will only pop out on the inside."

Jake pointed at a piece of glass the diameter of a penny set in the panel. "What's that?"

Maria climbed higher, even though she had to crouch

to fit in the shaft. She pressed one eye against the glass. "It's a peephole. I'm looking at a mop closet with all sorts of interesting things: paper towels, cleaning solutions, toilet paper . . ."

They twisted the locks.

"Try not to make any noise," Jake said.

"No shit, gumshoe."

They pushed on the panel, which came free. Jake clawed at the edge of the panel so only one corner struck the floor. Then he pushed it to the left, and Maria took over and slid it sideways. She climbed through the space and stepped over a slop bucket to make room for Jake, who followed. They faced the gray metal door, a naked bulb in the ceiling illuminating the closet.

Maria touched the back of Jake's hand with the back of her left hand. They looked at each other.

"Ready?" Jake said.

"Now or never."

Jake opened the door halfway. Maria exited the closet and turned to her right, disappearing from his view. He stepped out, left the door open just a crack, and went left.

Do or die, he thought.

The security station, a glass-walled office that looked out on the cellblock area, was twenty yards ahead. As Jake strode in that direction, he saw three men inside. Except for their military uniforms, they could have been three guys working at a car rental agency or in a mechanic shop. None of them noticed him.

Stopping at the door, Jake heard Maria's hollow-sounding

footsteps on the metal stairs behind him. Without turning around, he reached for the doorknob, which didn't budge. Conscious of the security camera looking down at him, he knocked on the door. The voices on the other side grew quiet. Keeping his face turned from the camera, he gave it a little wave. Then the door opened, and a thick-shouldered Hispanic man with a pencil-thin mustache stood before him. Unable to draw his Glock without alerting all three men, Jake kept his arms at his sides.

The soldier registered surprise, no doubt at seeing a Caucasian, then dropped his gaze to Jake's missing hand. Jake threw a punch at his nose, smashing it. The man gasped and staggered back inside. Jake took a canister the size of a shaving cream can from his belt. The other two soldiers rose from their seats. Jake bit down on the cap, pulling it off, and pressed the button on top. Then he tossed the canister into the middle of the room, where it spewed smoke.

Let's see how you guys like it.

One soldier ran for a console while the other reached for his gun. Jake drew his Glock, but the silencer caught in its holster. The first man reached the console; the second drew his pistol. Jake's heart beat faster as he freed his weapon.

Choices, choices.

He shot the soldier at the console in the ass, and the man fell back coughing gas. Jake stepped inside as the soldier with the gun fired a round into the doorway. He swiveled in the man's direction and fired. The recoil jerked his arm; he was accustomed to firing with two hands. The soldier's head snapped back, then forward, a hole in his forehead. His eyes rolled in their sockets, and he flopped to the floor.

A moment later, a dark soul rose through the gas. The man Jake had punched got on his hands and knees, ready to stand, and Jake kicked him in the head, knocking him unconscious.

Jake removed the gas mask from his belt, fixed it over his head, and walked to the center of the room. Through the gas, he saw the soldier he'd shot in the ass continue to cough. Jake kicked him in the head, too, and the man slumped over. He scooped up the canister and pressed its button, killing the gas.

At the console, he scanned nine monitors. On one, an armed soldier rounded the cellblock corner on the third floor. On another, Maria climbed the metal stairs to the fourth level. And on another, a man was reading with his back to the camera in the only cell with a light on.

Andre Santiago.

Jake searched the buttons and toggle switches, but they were labeled in French, so he tried them all. With each movement, he glanced at the windows looking out on the cellblock. Lights went on and off. Fans started and stopped. The cellblock doors unlocked.

Bingo.

Gunfire erupted outside, creating a patch of spiderweb cracks in the bulletproof glass. Glancing at a monitor, Jake saw a soldier unleashing his machine gun at the control station.

Cat's out of the bag.

On the monitors, Jake watched Andre dive to the floor of his cell with his hands over his head; on the fourth level, Maria raised her machine gun to her shoulder and blasted away.

Bullets strafed the cement floor outside the station, and the soldier firing at Jake screamed and dropped his gun as he fell.

Good girl.

On the monitors, he saw the soldier on the fourth floor run around the corner.

Maria!

Jake bolted across the room and out the door, ripping off his gas mask just in time to witness the dark soul of the soldier Maria had shot rise from his corpse and fade. The cellblock's architecture prevented him from seeing Maria or the soldier advancing on her. He called Maria's name but doubted she could hear him over the machine gun fire. Backing up against the far wall with tall windows, he saw Maria stop firing. He didn't see the soldier she had just shot, but he glimpsed the flickering dark light of the man's soul.

Maria headed for Santiago's cell, but fresh machine gun fire pressed her back, bullets ricocheting off the bars around her. She opened the door to an empty cell. Jake spotted the soldier who was firing on a catwalk perpendicular to the cell block, level with Maria. He aimed his Glock but knew the man was too far away to hit with accuracy.

Then Jake heard footsteps behind him, coming from around the corner of the closet they had used to enter the prison. Turning, he saw two soldiers running in his direction twenty yards away. Without giving them the chance to get any closer, he dropped to one knee and opened fire. It took four shots to bring them down and two more to finish them off. Their souls rose in tandem.

The soldier on the catwalk continued to fire at Maria, who dropped to the floor for safety.

Jake ran to the corpse of the man Maria had shot outside the control room and seized his machine gun. Holding the gun over his stump, he fired a blast at the guard on the catwalk, strafing the wall below. The man spun in his direction. Jake fired again, covering a wide area in a haphazard manner. The man screamed and slumped against the wall.

Jake didn't wait to see the soldier's soul rise. *There's got to be one more around here somewhere*, he thought as he charged up the stairs, his boots clanging on metal. When he reached the third level, he saw the missing soldier duck around the far corner. Faced with going after the man or joining Maria, he continued upstairs.

On the fourth level, he made eye contact with Maria, who had trained her machine gun on him. He pointed at the far end of the platform, and she joined him. They stood still, listening. Footsteps echoed on the ground floor, and the last soldier bolted for the control station.

"I can't aim this thing!" Jake said. "Take him out before he sounds the alarm."

Without hesitation, Maria raised the machine gun's stock to her shoulder and took aim. Jake stepped away and she fired. The gunfire cut across the soldier's back, toppling him.

She lowered the gun, a shocked look on her face. "I shot him in the back . . ."

"This isn't the street; it's a war. Come on."

They ran across the platform to the illuminated cell.

Its occupant backed up against the wall beside his toilet. He appeared to be sixty, tall and slender, with tight gray hair and reading glasses.

Jake raised his machine gun in a nonthreatening manner. "Come with us, Mr. Santiago."

The man's eyes widened. "Who *are* you?"

"Your wife sent us," Maria said. "We're taking you to Miami."

Andre rushed over to a small table and hefted a boxful of hardcover books.

"You can't bring those," Jake said.

"These are my journals. Thirty years' worth of writings. I'm not going anywhere without them."

"Whatever you say. Let's just get the hell out of here."

"There's another prisoner below us."

"Sorry. He's on his own."

They hurried along the platform to the stairs.

"Are you mercenaries?" Andre said.

"No, just Americans who want to police the world," Jake said.

"Thank you!"

They descended the stairs, and on the third level heard a voice call out, "Maria!"

Oh no, Jake thought as all three of them turned their heads.

A man in priest's robes stood outside a cell, clinging to its door for support.

"Father Alejandro!" Maria ran over to the man.

"No, no, no, no," Jake said.

Andre leaned close to him. "It looks like your partner

has broader concerns than you."

Jake grunted. "Let's hope her compassion doesn't get us all killed. We've gone through a lot to get you out of here."

"No doubt for great reward."

Jake pressed his machine gun into Andre's hands. "Stay here." He hurried along the platform as Maria draped one of the priest's arms around her shoulders.

What the hell?

Then he saw the bandaged stump where the man's right foot should have been, and his stomach twisted.

"This is Father Alejandro from St. Anthony's," Maria said. "He helped save my life." Her tone made it clear she did not intend to leave him behind.

"Let me take him. We need your hands free." Jake wrapped his right arm around Alejandro's back. "Father."

Alejandro put an arm over Jake's shoulders, and Jake grasped his wrist.

"I've heard about you. I thought we'd never meet."

They made their way to the stairs.

This isn't good, Jake thought.

Andre held out his hand to Alejandro. "It's good to see you face-to-face."

"Same here."

Jake sighed. "Can we just get the hell out of here? Hopefully our men took out the guard towers, but according to our intel, there are still two soldiers left."

A deafening alarm rang out, and Jake and Maria glanced at each other.

TWENTY-EIGHT

Maria touched down on the dimly lit station's floor first. Shining her flashlight up the shaft, she watched Andre descend with his box of books clutched under one arm, then Father Alejandro, who hopped down one rung to the other awkwardly, and finally Jake, with only one hand.

What a motley bunch, she thought.

"Problem number one," Jake said. "There are four of us and only three dollies."

"That's not a problem. Father Alejandro and I are both small. We can share my dolly."

Jake glanced at the dollies with a skeptical expression. "That will mean twice as much weight."

"That's okay. We'll have four hands instead of two to push the bar."

"Fine. You two go first."

"Uh-uh. We'll go last. If anyone tries to follow us, I'll be able to use this." Maria tapped her machine gun. "*You* go first. If there's any trouble at Jorge's end, you'll be able to deal with it a hell of a lot easier than Mr. Santiago." She glanced up the shaft. "Hurry!"

Jake climbed on top of the first dolly.

Maria set her foot on the dolly's edge and shoved it forward, sending Jake into the dark tunnel. She gestured at the dolly. "Get the picture?" she said to Andre.

"Vividly." Andre clambered onto the second dolly and grasped its bar.

Maria set the box containing Andre's journals on his thighs. "It's a quarter of a mile to the other end. You'll be there in no time." She sent him on his way, then reached for the dolly leaning against the wall.

Up above, fists pounded on the supply closet door.

Maria set the last dolly on the tracks. "You first, Father." She helped him onto the dolly. "Go on. Grab the bar."

"What about you?"

Machine gun fire blasted the door above.

Jake arrived at the other end of the tunnel, and Jorge helped him to his feet.

"That was a hell of a smoother landing than the first one," Jake said, grateful to be out of the narrower tunnel.

Jorge raised the lantern, which cast gloomy light around them. "Armand and Stephane took care of the guard tower sentries."

"Yeah? Too bad they didn't get the patrol in the yard."

"I'm sorry."

"Don't be. For all we know, extra men were posted out there. There's no accounting for the unexpected."

"Did you get Le Père?"

As if on cue, Andre emerged from the tunnel. Sitting up, he grabbed his box of books, and Jake and Jorge helped him out.

"Mr. Santiago, I'm Jorge De Jesus. I've looked forward to this day for a long time."

"Not as long as I have." Andre clasped Jorge's shoulder. "But thank you for everything."

"Step away from that opening," Jake said as he cleared the second dolly from the tracks.

They stared into the tunnel.

"What's taking them so long?" Jorge said.

Jake bit his lip. "Maria had to set the last dolly on the tracks, and we had an unanticipated complication."

"Father Alejandro," Andre said.

Jake didn't see Jorge's reaction because he was staring into the tunnel's darkness. A faint light appeared, like a firefly. "Here they come!"

Jorge held the lantern above the opening, and Jake waited for the last dolly to arrive. He heard the wheels on the tracks and the steady sound of pumping. The dolly rocketed out of the tunnel and ground to a halt in the dirt. Alejandro released his grip on the bar and sat up, shaking his head.

Jake felt numbness spreading through him. "Where the hell's Maria?"

Using the dolly's arm for leverage, Alejandro stood. "We didn't both fit. She told me to take the dolly and said she'd crawl behind me."

"And you *listened* to her?"

"She's a very persuasive woman with a machine gun, and I'm a priest with one foot."

"Help me get this dolly back on the tracks," Jake said.

Andre set down his books, and he and Jorge lifted the dolly.

"Turn it around. I need to see where I'm going in case she really is crawling in there. If I crash into her I'll kill her."

They positioned the dolly as Jake ordered, and Jorge switched the arm from one side to the other.

Jake climbed aboard. "Give me that machine gun. I can't pump and shoot at the same time, but maybe Maria will need it."

Andre fit the machine gun under Jake's leg.

"You'll never both fit," Alejandro said.

"We'll manage. Give me a headlight."

Jorge wedged Jake's flashlight into the side of the arm. "I don't think this will help . . ."

"You guys get going. We'll catch up. Send me to El Miedo!"

Jorge set his foot behind the dolly and gave it a sharp kick, sending Jake back into danger. Jake pumped the bar with all his strength.

Stubborn. Fucking. Woman!

He promised never to allow Maria to use logic to sway him against his gut instincts again. Raising his head, he saw little but darkness. The flashlight made the tunnel on Jake's left-hand side gleam but provided no more illumination than the spotlight on the arm.

I'll go as fast as I can, then slow way down when I reach the halfway point.

He saw something ahead: faint orange light, growing brighter.

Oh, shit!

He pulled the bar in reverse as hard as he could, braking the dolly, then grabbed the arm, jerked it out, and shoved it into the opposite hole. Throwing his head back, he pumped the bar. The orange light grew brighter, closer. He pumped faster and harder, but the fireball gained on him. In seconds, he felt the light and heat on his face. Then he shot through the tunnel's opening and slammed into the dirt.

"Get down!" Jake rolled off the dolly and over to the side wall, where he lay facedown in the dirt. A sheet of orange flames escaped the tunnel, followed by another and another. When the fire seemed to have abated, he jumped up and sprinted over to the cinder-block wall beside the tunnel's opening, where he felt safe. "Is everyone okay?"

"Oui!" Jorge called out. "Our feathers are just a little singed."

Bending over, Jake stared into the tunnel. If Maria had been in there, the fire would have burned her to death. If she hadn't, there was no way he could safely travel the tunnel if the soldiers on the other end discharged another fireball.

Damn it!

Pounding the cinder-block wall, he wanted to call out for Maria, but under either of the scenarios he had envisioned, it was best that the soldiers considered the rest of them dead for as long as possible. With tears in his eyes, he joined his companions.

"What the hell was that?" Alejandro said.

"A flamethrower." Jake saw that Jorge and Andre supported the priest between them. "What about your precious books?"

"Fuck 'em," Andre said.

"I'm sorry about this, Mr. Helman," Alejandro said. "So very, very sorry."

"Maria's Catholic. I should have figured she'd take a chance like this. You boys run ahead. I'll catch up in a minute."

As the three men hobbled off, Jake retraced his steps until the beam of his flashlight revealed Andre's box of journals. Jamming the flashlight under his left arm, he scooped up the box.

I really hope you're the real deal, Andre.

Making his way through the oppressive darkness, he rejoined the others.

"Thank you," Andre said. "You didn't have to do that. I'm sorry about your friend."

Jake didn't care if they noticed his tears in the glare of his flashlight. "You can thank me and honor Maria's wishes by moving faster."

The sounds of their scuffling grew more urgent.

"Why are you doing this if you're not a mercenary, Mr. Helman?"

Jake pointed his flashlight at the ground ahead. "Your wife had a niece."

"Ramera."

"Among other names. She flooded New York City with

Black Magic and turned my best friend into a raven. My friend managed to kill her anyway. I'm told that because of their shared bloodline, Miriam is the only Mambo who can reverse the spell. Your freedom is the cost of her services."

Silence hung in the air. Jake realized he had not discussed Edgar's condition with anyone on Pavot Island. Now he didn't care if they believed him or not.

"I'm sorry about your friend," Andre said. "And I'm sorry my wife probably got Miss Vasquez killed on what amounted to a suicide mission. I'm afraid her devotion to the concept of my freedom has become an obsession."

"Edgar was—*is*—Maria's friend, too. She wanted to come here. No one forced her. She knew what chances she was taking, and when she sent Alejandro into the tunnel alone she knew what sacrifice she was making."

Jake needed to shut down his emotions. It was the only way he could survive this ordeal. He intended to send Andre to Miami without him. At least Edgar would be saved. He didn't care about Malvado, Andre, Father Alejandro, Mambo Catoute, Jorge, Armand, or Stephane. He didn't care about Russel or avenging Maria's death.

You can't get revenge against an entire army.

He didn't give a damn about Pavot Island or anywhere else for that matter. With Maria dead, he wanted only one thing: enough Black Magic to make his pain go away, regardless of the consequences. He felt dead already. And Pavot Island was the perfect place to find Magic.

"Jorge! Jorge!" Armand's voice came over Jorge's hand radio.

"I couldn't break radio silence to call him," Jorge said as he unfastened the radio from his belt and raised it to his mouth. "Go ahead."

"They're closing in on us. What the hell's going on down there?"

"We have Le Père. We're halfway through the main tunnel."

"Hurry. We have to get out of here!"

"We're moving as fast as we can. We have an injured member of our party."

"They have Maria."

Jake jerked his head up. "What?"

"They're loading her into a helicopter in the prison right now."

Jake's heart beat faster.

"Go ahead," Andre said. "You're not doing anything now except hold that flashlight anyway."

Jake glanced at the box of books in his hands, then at Andre.

"Like I said before: fuck 'em."

Jake looked at each man, then dumped the box and ran ahead.

It was like running blind. Jake pumped his arms for speed,

and the beam of the flashlight in his hand bounced around the tunnel walls, floor, and ceiling, disorienting him more than lighting the way.

She's alive! Maria's alive!

He tripped, flew through the air, and crashed to the ground, tasting dirt. With one hand missing, just getting up required extra effort. His feet projected him forward, he regained his balance, and he plunged ahead.

Jorge had said a man in decent shape could run a quarter mile in sixty-eight seconds. Jake doubled that figure to account for the darkness. Then his shoulder slammed into a support beam, and he plowed into dirt once more. He reached up to massage his right shoulder, praying he hadn't dislocated it again, only to flail at empty space with fingers he no longer possessed.

On his feet again, running, spanning the walls with the flashlight, detecting the support beams, avoiding them, crushing dirt with his combat boots. He thought he glimpsed a bat up ahead, then realized it was one of the wooden rungs beneath the secret trapdoor. He slowed and used his right hand to break his trajectory into the wall. Gasping for breath, he doubled over, then folded his hands behind his head, filling his lungs with oxygen.

An explosion roared somewhere above him.

Grimacing, Jake scrambled up the rungs. At the top, he searched for the locking mechanism. Instead, he found a wooden handle in the middle of the fake stump's top and shoved the hinged stump open. As he climbed out, the sky lit up.

Flares, he thought. Malvado's forces were searching for

them. *Searching for me.*

He turned in a circle, searching for the way back to the minicaravan. Another flare lit up the sky, and he glimpsed a reflective metal surface in the distance. Charging forward, he weaved between trees and emerged from the foliage onto the road in front of the camouflage van. The vehicles formed a straight line to Armand's Dodge Ram, all of them hidden by palm fronds. Far in the distance, lights rose high into the sky.

A helicopter!

He sprinted down the road. Figures crouching in the woods swung their guns in his direction.

Maria!

A flare went off, and he saw the helicopter in detail: red with white markings. It turned and receded even farther into the distance.

"No!"

Armand and Stephane whipped in his direction even before he crashed into the Ram. They came over to him, keeping the truck between themselves and the prison.

"Is that the chopper?" Jake said between ragged gasps.

"Yes," Stephane said. "I saw it land when I was making my way back from the guard tower. Soldiers marched Maria out in handcuffs. I'm sorry. There was nothing I could do."

"Where's it going?"

"It's heading toward Pavot City," Armand said. "That means the Ministry of Defense."

In his mind, Jake saw Russel chopping off his hand. "You have to take me there."

"No. We're here to transport Le Père. Everyone is risking his life, just as Maria did."

"Then give me one of these vehicles so I can go after her myself."

"Even if that was possible, it would be *im*possible. The city will be under lockdown. There's no way you can get in or reach the ministry."

A single blinking light, all that remained of the helicopter, winked out.

Jake looked at Armand. "If they do to her what they did to me, she'll wind up in that clinic or on the plantation. If we get Santiago on the boat, will you help me rescue Maria?"

"You're boarding that boat, too."

"Not a chance. Not while Maria's here."

"She's a special woman. I can see why you'd risk your life for her. But the chances of her surviving the night are slim, especially if we're successful."

"Will you help me?"

Armand gave Jake a long, contemplative look. "Oui."

Jake spun on one heel and charged back up the road. At the van, he veered right. The sky lit up, but this time he heard a loud whistling sound. A deafening roar followed, and a fireball rose from the trees between him and the road.

They were just waiting for the chopper to get clear.

Locating the stump, he climbed through its hatch and down the ladder. "Jorge!" He ran again. Two hundred yards in, he found his party. "They're bombing the jungle. We have to hurry!"

"What about Maria?" Alejandro said.

"They took her away on a chopper." Jake turned to Andre. "I won't be accompanying you to Miami."

"I understand," Andre said.

"Leave me," Alejandro said. "But leave me a machine gun."

"If we leave you and Maria's killed, then she'll have sacrificed herself for nothing," Jake said. "I won't allow that to happen. We're all getting out."

An explosion above them shook the ground. Dirt poured from the ceiling.

"Come on!"

All four men moved as fast as they could. Another explosion sounded from farther away.

"They're blanketing the area," Jorge said.

Another explosion. This time the tunnel ceiling caved in behind them, and the concussion knocked them down. Through the dust and the wide hole in the ceiling, light from a burning tree illuminated the rubble around them.

"Up there!" Jake said.

He ran over to the rubble and climbed to the top. Grabbing a tree root, he hauled himself onto the ground. Andre and Jorge helped Alejandro to the top of the pile. Jake planted his heels in the dirt and extended his hand, which Alejandro grasped, and he pulled the priest up with him. Jorge went next and helped Andre to the surface.

A flare lit up the sky, followed by three sequential explosions that scorched the jungle. Machine gun fire erupted around them.

"This way!" Jorge said.

Jake put Alejandro's arm around his shoulders and

helped Andre support the man. They followed Jorge through the jungle.

Another explosion blew chunks of earth at them, and the ensuing fireball engulfed the treetops. The machine gun fire grew louder and more plentiful, and a woman screamed.

When they emerged onto the road near the van, Jake gasped. Flames consumed the next three vehicles, including the Ram, and smoldering bodies lay scattered along the road. In the jungle on both sides of the road, rebels fired their machine guns at advancing ground troops.

"Armand!" Jorge bolted toward the farthest inferno.

The back doors to the van opened, and Stephane called out, "This way! Hurry!"

"Go on," Jake said.

Andre helped Alejandro to the van, and Jake sprinted after Jorge, the heat from the various fires making his skin hot. He caught up with Jorge, who kneeled beside Armand's blackened corpse, recognizable only because of his cowboy boots. Setting his hand on Jorge's shoulder, Jake kneeled beside him. Jorge wept.

"We can't stay here," Jake said.

"First Humphrey. Now my brother."

"They'd both want you to live."

A burning tree limb crashed ten feet away from them. Jorge made the sign of the cross, then kissed two fingers and touched them to the charred head.

Jake pulled him away, and they ran down the road. Around them, the freedom fighters retreated, blasting their machine guns.

The cargo van took off, then stopped, its doors swinging

open. Jorge scrambled into the van first, and Stephane helped Jake in, then slammed the doors. The van sped away.

"We just might make it," Andre said.

Stephane went to the front of the van and sat in the passenger seat. Jake didn't recognize the driver.

Jorge wiped tears from his eyes.

Alejandro set his hand on the man's back. "I'm sorry for your loss."

"He didn't receive last rites."

"God will look after him."

The van rocked from side to side, and branches scraped it.

"We're getting off the road," Stephane said. "It will be too easy for them to follow us once they break through our defenses. Shandre is taking a narrow side road used by horse-drawn carts."

An explosion shook the van.

Alejandro bowed his head and prayed. Jake felt helpless to do anything. For the moment, his fate was out of his hands.

The machine gun fire stopped.

"What's happening?" Jake said.

Jorge looked at him with no emotion. "Air support."

A plane soared overhead, so close its engine drowned out everything else. Jake saw a fighter plane streak through the black sky ahead. A series of explosions lit up the jungle behind them, casting orange flames on the back windows. Napalm burned across the jungle, incinerating anyone in its way.

The van cut across the island to a coastal road that it followed north.

"We're far from the action now," Stephane said. "In half an hour, we'll reenter the jungle."

Like Jake, Andre kneeled at the back windows.

"This is some country you've got," Jake said.

"It was once. It will be again."

"You really think you can make a difference over in the US?"

"There's no doubt in my mind."

"Good. I need you to do me a favor."

"Anything."

"The odds are pretty good I won't get home. I need to know your wife will keep her promise: she has to make my friend human again."

"The woman I married would never break her word." Andre paused. "Assuming this raven really is your friend and assuming Miriam has the power she says she has."

Thanks, Jake thought.

They drove through the jungle again, and Jake closed his eye. The occasional sound of a helicopter would wake him, and Shandre would stop the van.

The van stopped and Stephane turned around. "Boucanier Cove, folks."

Jorge opened the side door, and Alejandro remained in the van with Shandre. Andre, Stephane, and Jake joined Jorge outside.

Andre inhaled the fresh air. "Wonderful. I'll miss this land."

"You'll be back soon," Jorge said.

"I hope so."

Stephane led them through the foliage to the edge of a cliff overlooking the cove. Nestled near the rocks, a schooner bobbed on the water.

Jake spotted another boat in the distance. "What's that?"

"A patrol boat," Stephane said.

The distant whine of a helicopter grew louder.

"Take cover!" Jorge said.

They scrambled into the jungle. The sound of the helicopter intensified, and the trees around them swayed. The helicopter flew over them to the cove.

"That's not good," Jake said.

The helicopter hovered above the water near the schooner. Exhaust flames shot from its sides, and two rockets burst forward. The air-to-surface missiles spiraled toward the schooner, which exploded into twin infernos. The helicopter turned and soared away.

"What now?" Andre said.

Jake looked him in the eye. "I guess we'll just have to take back your country."

TWENTY-NINE

Handcuffed in the helicopter and surrounded by armed soldiers, Maria saw Pavot City below. Military vehicles patrolled the outskirts of the urban area and traveled its streets. She had never witnessed such a mobilization before. A glance at her watch showed the time as 11:45. Fifteen more minutes and, God willing, Jake and Andre would be safely aboard the boat bound for Miami.

Leaning her head against the padded wall of the chopper, she exhaled. After sending Father Alejandro into the tunnel beneath El Miedo alone, she had held the encroaching soldiers back with her machine gun until they had dispersed gas into the station. When it came down to it, they had taken her with relative ease. If she'd had her own gas mask, like Jake, it might have been a different story. But there had been just one mask, and they had agreed he would take on the soldiers in the control room.

A beacon flashed in the distance, providing a signal to the pilot. A dark shape became discernible in the darkness: Pavot Island's Ministry of Defense, where Bill Russel had interrogated Jake and hacked off his left hand with a machete. Maria suspected she was about to meet Mr. Russel.

Leaning to one side for a better look out the window, she saw flames below: dozens of bonfires in the street. Smoke billowed out the windows of a factory as well. Fire trucks had been dispatched in a wide radius to combat the fires, and scores of figures ran down a street.

They're rioting. They know Andre is free!

The helicopter circled the dark tower, and she glimpsed a helipad below. The aircraft descended and touched down on the roof.

The soldier on Maria's left threw a lever bolt into the unlocked position and opened the hatch. He hopped out and faced her, beckoning her forward. Unable to use her hands for support, she scooted across the seat, and the man gripped her bicep and helped her down without too much force. The spinning blades above whipped air around her, blowing her hair in her face, even as they whined to a stop. From this angle, she saw glowing hazes all across the city.

The soldier who had sat on her other side jumped down and grabbed her other arm, and the two men led her across the roof to two glass doors in a square structure that slid open, admitting them. Crossing the carpeted floor to a pair of elevators, she saw a door marked Aircraft Control. The first soldier palmed a button between the two elevators, and a door slid open. They boarded the elevator, which serviced thirty floors. The lead soldier pressed a button numbered 20, and the door closed and the elevator descended.

On the twentieth floor, they followed a hallway to a room protected by a security scanner and two wall-mounted cameras. The first soldier swiped his ID card, the door unlocked, and he pushed it open. The second soldier guided Maria inside, where half a dozen khaki-clad police officers spoke on telephones and pecked at computer terminals, hurrying from one station to another with the frenetic energy of drone bees.

The soldiers stood Maria at a counter and spoke to a middle-aged attendant in French. "Be careful. She's supposed to be dangerous, believe it or not."

You bet your ass I am.

The middle-aged attendant called to a uniformed black woman who came over. Maria appraised the woman. Late twenties, straight, shoulder-length hair.

I might be her if I grew up here.

"Empty your pockets," the female soldier said.

Maria removed her cigarettes from her pants pocket.

"The cross," the woman said.

Maria took off the gold cross from around her neck and added it to her belongings.

"You're not a soldier. Take that uniform off."

Maria looked around the room at the men. Few of them paid any attention to her. She unlaced her combat boots and removed them. At least her toes felt better. Then she unbuttoned her camouflage shirt and dropped it on the floor and stepped out of the cargo pants. She stood before the soldiers in a gray muscle shirt and black panties.

"This way," the woman said.

Maria and the two soldiers who had brought her in followed the female soldier into an anteroom. Through the glass in another door, she glimpsed a dozen female prisoners in civilian clothing standing, sitting, and lying in a number of jail cells. But the woman took her through a different door, which led to a row of empty cells.

"What's wrong?" Maria said. "You don't want me to spread the word to the other ladies that Andre Santiago is free?"

The woman opened a cell door and nodded for Maria to enter. "We're protecting you for your own good."

Maria entered the cell and sat on the lower bunk. "I don't need protection, girlfriend. *You* do."

The woman studied her, then left with the other two soldiers.

Maria glanced around the cell: a sink, an exposed toilet, and a dirty towel were the amenities. A security camera looked down on her. She stretched out on the bunk, folded her arms behind her head, and willed herself to remain calm.

Mambo Catoute watched Malvado storm into the war room, Maxime trailing him. Using her cane, she rose a moment later than the other people around the table, including Buteau and Solaine, who had been frantically juggling laptops and cell phones to coordinate their troops just moments before. Only Russel seemed calm to her. The man had participated in conflicts all over the world and had evacuated President Seguera from Manila, only to kill him at Malvado's request.

"*What* is going on?" Malavado said. "I want reports from everyone, starting with General Buteau! How did Santiago escape from El Miedo?"

Buteau folded his hands on the table as Malvado sat and glared at him. "The rebels constructed a narrow tunnel beneath the prison. Security tapes show two of them dressed in military uniforms entering the cellblock through a storage closet. They killed all but two of the guards on duty and liberated Santiago and the priest. They escaped through the same tunnel, but my two surviving men apprehended one of them at the tunnel: Maria Vasquez."

A cold look of satisfaction swept over Malvado's features.

"We have her in custody at the Ministry of Defense," Russel said.

Score those points, Catoute thought.

"How is it you never discovered this tunnel?" Malvado said.

Buteau made a face. "I don't know. The tunnel was three-quarters of a mile long, with tracks that carried rather unusual transportation dollies. They must have spent ten years digging it."

Malvado shifted his gaze to Russel. "I expect El Miedo to be full very soon. I want you to do whatever's necessary to make it secure."

"I'd be happy to, Mr. President."

"I don't care if it makes you happy or not. I just want

it done. General, kindly explain the fires burning in the jungle outside the prison."

"As soon as I received word the prison had been compromised, I ordered troops there from our central base and engaged rebel forces. We destroyed three of their vehicles and killed twelve of them. We don't know how many escaped."

"How many casualties did we suffer?"

"Eight, in addition to the seven in the prison."

"Then I would say they won this battle, wouldn't you? Especially since Andre Santiago is free."

"Our coastal patrol located the boat Miriam Santiago sent to transport Santiago off the island, and we destroyed it with one of our helicopters. There's no telling how many men were on board."

"Or if they were even from Pavot."

Buteau didn't respond.

"At least your men apprehended the woman. I want them rewarded for that."

Buteau nodded.

"I'll interrogate her as soon as I leave here," Russel said.

He never misses an opportunity to prove he's essential, Catoute thought.

But Malvado ignored Russel. "Shut down the airport and the shipyards. No one leaves Pavot Island and no one arrives. All business stops until my enemies have been punished. Colonel, what is the situation in Pavot City?"

Solaine sat straight. "We have riots in our cities. Buildings are burning. I've ordered all units to bring the situation under control."

"Use rubber bullets and gas."

"Some of them are firing at us."

"Dead civilians do me no good. Living civilians can become undead slaves. I don't care how many casualties you suffer, I want every Pavotian who's rioting to be taken alive to El Miedo." He glanced at Catoute. "Begin administering Black Magic to them. I want them converted as soon as possible."

Catoute bowed. "Yes, my lord."

"William, inform Pavot News I intend to address the people immediately."

"Of course, Mr. President."

"I'm going to declare martial law. Any citizen who does not wear the black snake will remain in their homes until further notice. I want Jake Helman's face on-screen until he's captured. Offer a reward of one million dollars to anyone who provides information leading to his arrest and two million dollars for information resulting in Santiago's arrest. I want them both brought to me."

Russel held up his cell phone. "I've already received dozens of calls from representatives of the US companies doing business here. They're alarmed, to put it mildly. A public crackdown right now could cause them to pull up stakes. If you publicly acknowledge Santiago's escape and subsequent capture or execution, the world will turn against you."

The balls! Catoute thought. Buteau and Solaine held their breath.

Malvado narrowed his eyes at Russel, who offered no reaction. "Anything else?"

"Now that we have Vasquez, there's no reason to search for Helman. He'll come to us. I guarantee it."

Malvado stood. "I *am* declaring martial law. Our retaliation will be swift. By dawn, these riots will be squashed. Within twenty-four hours, all other matters will be settled. None of these companies will fold shop. As for your public relations recommendations, I concur. We'll continue to run cooking shows throughout the night. Bring Vasquez here when you've finished with her. But I warn you: if Helman *doesn't* come for her, you'll suffer in his place. I would hate for that to happen."

Russel bowed his head. "Yes, Your Excellency."

Malvado looked around the table. "Return to your command posts. We'll meet again in the morning."

The men in the room filed out, Maxime and Russel together.

Malvado turned to Catoute. "What is it?"

"Forgive me, lord, but I wonder if I might ask what you intend to do with Helman."

Malvado frowned. "I *will* see him harvesting my drugs as a zonbie. What business is it of yours?"

"I've promised him to Kalfu."

Malvado's lips twisted into an angry smile. "Who are you to promise anyone on Pavot to Kalfu? Wasn't he satisfied with your granddaughter?"

"It was no act of generosity on my part. Kalfu demanded I give this man to him."

"What kind of man incurs the wrath of a Loa?"

"I don't know. Kalfu doesn't share information with me."

"What will happen to you if I refuse?"

"Kalfu will be most displeased."

"What do I care what he does to your wretched old soul once you've died? You'll be of no more use to me then anyway."

"Quite right. But he'll also be displeased with *you*."

Malvado grunted. "Do you ever feel you've made a deal with the devil?"

Catoute suppressed her desire to laugh. "Every day."

"When we have Helman, give him to Kalfu with my blessings. It's the woman I want."

"Yes, lord. That brings me to my second point. If Russel's right and Helman comes for Vasquez, it would be easier for me if he came for her in the Black Church."

"You would deny me my vengeance?"

"Not intentionally. I'd do my best to preserve Vasquez for you, but Kalfu is wily. It's possible he might claim her as well without warning me."

Malvado pouted. "Bring the bitch to me first. I'll make my decision after I've seen her."

"Thank you, lord." Seeing the fear of Kalfu creep into Malvado's features, Catoute believed she had succeeded in her entreaty.

The van stopped at the edge of the jungle near the cliffs leading to the beach.

"This is as far as we go," Shandre said.

They got out of the van, and Shandre and Stephane stretched a net covered with foliage over it.

"Thank you for your help, gentlemen," Andre said. "I'm sorry for the loss of those brave souls outside El Miedo."

"Thank us by leading us," Stephane said. "Tonight was just the opening salvo. Malvado will unleash his dogs in full force."

"That's why we have to stop him," Jake said.

Shandre aimed his flashlight at the jungle. "There are other vehicles here. A *lot* of them."

Peering in the darkness, Jake saw pickups, SUVs, vans, and simple automobiles hidden in the foliage. "At least they're not olive green."

Emerging from the jungle, they gazed behind them. Above the trees, flares lit up the sky like fireworks, and helicopters became visible in the distance.

"The army's out in force," Shandre said.

They descended the cliffs to the beach, Jake and Andre assisting Alejandro, and made their way toward a dark rock face. The night tide slapped waves against the sand.

"This isn't the cave Maria and I guarded earlier," Jake said.

"It's a different entrance," Stephane said. "There are several."

"Stop!" The voice seemed to come out of nowhere.

Stephane and Shandre raised their hands, Jake and Andre raising only one as they supported Alejandro.

Four figures appeared in the moonlight, machine guns raised to their shoulders. A flashlight beam caused Jake to squint.

"Identify yourself," one of the approaching men said.

"I'm Andre Santiago and these are my friends."

"It's true, then," another man said, lowering his weapon.

"We're seeking sanctuary in the Church of the White Snake. I believe Mambo Pharah is expecting us."

All four men stopped before Andre and gazed at him.

"Father Alejandro," one of the men said, "are you all right?"

"No. But I will be."

"Do any of you know your way through the caverns?" the first man said.

"I do." Stephane strode past them, and the rest of the party followed, leaving the sentries behind.

Inside the cave, illuminated by torches, Shandre said, "Those guys weren't Pavot for the People."

Stephane shook his head. "No, they were People for Pavot."

"You guys need to get your *p*'s in order," Jake said.

They descended an incline lined with stalagmites. Stephane and Shandre relieved Jake and Andre of supporting Alejandro. After making a few turns, Jake and Andre stopped before two wooden doors. Each man gripped one of the round metal knockers and pulled the doors open.

"Holy shit," Jake said.

An aisle separated two blocks of wooden pews. Each block consisted of ten pews, occupied by a hundred men and women, two hundred people in all, beneath a high rock ceiling. Dozens of lanterns and torches lit the space. Mambo Pharah stood at the end of the aisle with two men.

Jake allowed Andre to walk ahead of him, and the people on the pews rose. Hands reached out and Andre shook them. Deafening applause filled the cathedral. Jake felt self-conscious as the reverent people regarded him. When they reached the end, Jake saw tears streaking Pharah's cheeks.

Andre embraced her and shook hands with the two men, who appeared to be in their mid- to late forties.

Andre turned and faced his supporters, who chanted: "Le Père! Le Père! *Le Père!*"

Stephane and Shandre sat Alejandro down on the dais as Andre raised his fists in the air.

"The man on the left is Janvier, leader of the People for Pavot," Stephane said. "The one on the right is Renaud from the People for Pavot."

Pharah raised her hands, silencing the freedom fighters. "Tonight we celebrate the freedom of Andre Santiago, Le Père! We mourn the lives lost in that endeavor! And we plan for the liberation of Pavot Island!"

The chant started low and grew louder: "Libération de l'île Pavot! Libération de l'île Pavot! Libération de l'île Pavot!"

THIRTY

Maria heard the door outside the cell area open, followed by footsteps. The female soldier had returned, accompanied by the two men who had brought Maria in. Maria sat up on the edge of her bunk.

"Come with us," the woman said.

Maria walked barefoot out of the cell. "Some shoes would be nice."

The woman handcuffed Maria's wrists behind her back and guided her forward. They entered the anteroom and turned right into a corridor that extended from the occupied cells. Maria sketched a layout of the floor in her mind in case she had the opportunity to escape, not that she expected to get very far barefoot and wearing only underwear. The woman unlocked an office door, and her male counterparts led Maria into a sparse room with a table, two chairs, and no windows in its cinder-block walls.

Interview room, Maria thought. She had been in dozens of them at police precincts throughout Manhattan and the other boroughs of New York City.

The woman unlocked Maria's handcuffs and gestured for her to sit in the far chair, which she did. Then the woman stood against the wall, with the men standing on either side of the door.

Minutes passed, then the door opened and two more men entered: a broad-shouldered Caucasian with a bald head and a bushy mustache, who wore a suit, and a muscular black man, who wore slacks and a tight pink polo. The black man looked like a younger version of Malvado, so Maria guessed he was either Najac or Maxime. She had heard of only one white man tied to Malvado.

Her gaze dropped to the metal table, its surface nicked and scratched. Was it her imagination or did she see blood?

Jake.

She hoped he and Andre had escaped.

The white man closed the door. "Miss Vasquez, it's so nice to finally make your acquaintance. I'm Bill Russel and this is Maxime Malvado."

"I know who you are."

"That's good. It will save me the time of regurgitating my resume."

"I bet you leave a lot of jobs off it anyway, don't you?"

With a thin smile, Russel sat. Maxime stood near him with his arms folded across his chest. Russel reached into his jacket pocket and took out Maria's cigarettes and lighter, which he set before her. "Go ahead. Smoke. We allow such things on Pavot Island."

Maria drew a cigarette from the pack and lit it. "The benefits of living in a free society, I suppose." She turned sideways on the chair and felt Maxime watching her.

"You're not at all what I expected. So much trouble caused by such a petite young lady."

Maria puffed on her cigarette. "I'd like to speak to someone from the United States."

"I'm the closest there is to a representative from the US."

"Then I want a lawyer."

"I'm sorry. Did somebody read you your rights? If so, they shouldn't have because you don't have any."

"Some free society."

"I won't ask your reason for coming here, like I did Helman. That much is obvious now. The question is: What possible connection do you and Helman have to Andre Santiago?"

"We came for a cheap vacation. We had dinner with a nice man your thugs shot dead in the street. We got separated and shit happened. We just did what was necessary to survive. We're innocent victims of this island's fucked-up politics."

Russel smiled. "No, this all has something to do with a man named Edgar Hopkins. I just don't know what. We destroyed the boat, by the way."

Maria's body tightened and her heart beat faster.

"Don't be alarmed. We don't think Santiago and Helman had boarded it yet. They're still on the island somewhere. We'll get them."

Maria sat facing Russel and blew smoke over his head. "I doubt it."

"Two men can't hide from an army for very long. Trust me on this point."

"I don't trust easy, and something tells me I'd *never* trust you."

Russel set his right hand palm up on the table. "Give me your hand."

Maria stared at the open hand, which looked powerful. "I'm not the marrying type."

Russel's smile broadened. "Please. Your hand."

Trying to hide her fear, Maria slid her hand inside Russel's, which closed around it with a viselike grip.

"I'd like to know the names of the people who helped you."

"Do I look like a rat?"

"No, you look like trouble." He squeezed her hand and she squirmed. "I could break your hand, you know."

Maria tapped her cigarette in the ashtray. "Not if I break yours first."

"Let me show you something." With his free hand, Russel reached into his pants pocket.

Now.

Balling her right hand into a fist, Maria drove her cigarette straight into Russel's eye.

Russel screamed, his face contorted with pain, and fell back in his chair, landing on the floor, where he clawed at his injured eye.

Maria bolted upright. The soldiers raised their machine guns, but with Maxime stepping between them and their target, they couldn't fire. Maria seized the back of her chair and swung it at Maxime, striking him so hard with a metal leg that his face wobbled around his skull before he fell next to Russel, who continued to scream.

The female soldier moved forward, drawing something from her belt. Maria recognized it as a Taser.

Ah, shit . . .

The woman squeezed the trigger, and Maria felt needles burying in her chest. An instant later, her head flew back, her limbs turned limp, and she crashed to the floor.

Andre sat at one end of the dining table, with Janvier on his left and Renaud on his right. Pharah sat at the other end, with Alejandro on one side of her and Jake on the other. As simple soldiers in the coming battle, Jorge and Stephane had not been invited to attend this strategy session.

"There are riots in all three cities," Pharah said, her white snake curling around her neck. "Cars are overturned in the streets, and empty buildings are burning. Word of your escape is sweeping the island."

"Who are these people?" Andre said.

"Students. Activists. Frustrated civilians. Some who have waited decades or their whole lives for you to lead them against Malvado."

"We need armed fighters, not martyrs."

"The soldiers are dispersing the crowds with gas and rubber bullets. They don't want civilian casualties. They want a fresh supply of meat to become zonbies. Beginning at dawn, Malvado's forces will round up all our brothers and sisters who don't wear his tattoo and move them into El Miedo and other jails. We have no choice but to attack before then. At least these riots are preoccupying the army and police."

The fierce urgency of now, Jake thought.

"How do you know these things?" Renaud said.

"I have a person deep undercover in the government."

"Is he in Malvado's inner circle?"

"No, but he—or she—is close to someone who is."

"Name this person. If we're to base our actions on his intelligence, I want to know who he is."

Pharah shook her head. "For now, he remains my operative."

"I don't like it."

"We have to work together," Andre said. "It's our only chance for survival. How many troops do we have?"

"Each man in the cathedral represents a larger group from Pavot for the People or the People for Pavot," Janvier said.

"We have a thousand men and women waiting for a signal," Renaud said.

"And we have three thousand," Janvier said.

"Yes, but are they willing to die for our cause?"

"Twelve of them did just an hour ago. Now their families are in jeopardy."

"Throw in armed civilians who aren't aligned with either of our organizations, and we have maybe six thousand total," Pharah said.

Andre shook his head, a grim look on his face. "Against

twenty thousand soldiers and who knows how many police officers? Plus, they have helicopters and tanks and Humvees. The odds against us are too great."

"The trick is to concentrate our firepower on the right targets," Renaud said. "The palace, the central military base, the Ministry of Defense. If we can take them, Pavot is ours."

"We've drawn up dozens of attack plans," Janvier said.

"As have we."

Jorge entered the room. "Forgive me for interrupting. You have a visitor, Andre."

A Hispanic man with straight white hair swept back from his forehead passed Jorge. He wore cargo shorts and a matching shirt, and he carried a footlocker.

With raised eyebrows, Andre rose and circled the table.

"That's Louider Sanchez," Alejandro said to Jake under his breath. "The head of La Main Noire—The Black Hand. He and Andre were best friends until Malvado incarcerated Andre. Then Louider turned to a life of crime."

Louider set the footlocker on top of a counter and faced Andre, who stopped before him. The two men sized each other up.

"So it's true," Louider said.

Nodding, Andre spread his arms wide. "I'm a free man."

Louider and Andre embraced.

When they parted, Louider grasped Andre's shoulders. "You look fit, *mon ami*."

"And you look like a successful businessman."

Louider nodded. "Do not begrudge me that achievement."

Andre clasped Louider's arm. "We do what we have to in order to survive. You'd have done no good occupying a cell beside me in El Miedo or a grave."

"Or walking the earth as one of Malvado's undead."

Renaud stood. "He's a parasite with no loyalty to anyone but himself."

Louider gestured at Renaud. "Don't forget who sold you your weapons." He glanced at Janvier. "All of you. Or who transported our refugees to Florida. And who provided the boat and crew that Malvado destroyed tonight."

"For a price," Renaud said.

"Oui, for a price. I'm a businessman, as Andre says. But now I've come to join your fight, to stand by my friend Le Père."

"He's right," Alejandro said. "Louider's provided services that have kept the movement alive."

"How many men do you bring to the table?" Janvier said.

Louider shrugged. "Five hundred, maybe a thousand. But I bring a lot more than that: trucks with registration numbers clearing them for travel during crises like the one rocking our cities. Trucks. Equipment. *Guns*."

Throwing back the latches on the footlocker, Louider removed a compact machine gun with a thick clip, a laser-mounted scope, and a grenade launcher.

Jake's eye widened. He had seen the gun model before; he had helped slay Avademe with just such a weapon, courtesy of the Order of Avademe. Karlin Reichard's Brooklyn shipyard had housed hundreds of crates containing such weapons.

"What is that?" Renaud said.

"The ATAC 3000," Louider said. "The cutting edge of modern warfare. One provides the equivalent firepower of ten men with conventional weapons. And I have a thousand of them."

"That makes the equivalent of fifteen thousand men between us, conservatively speaking," Alejandro said.

"We still need more men," Andre said.

"I have an idea," Jake said.

Everyone turned to him.

"What are you even doing here?" Renaud said. "You're not a Pavotian."

"He's here at my request," Pharah said.

"And mine," Andre said. "*I* wouldn't be here if it wasn't for him."

"It's okay," Jake said. "He's right. I don't have the same patriotic investment that the rest of you do. But I am fighting for my life and for Maria's. Neither she nor I can hope to get off this island with Malvado in charge, and the clock is running on her meter."

"What's your idea?" Andre said.

"It won't be easy." Jake looked at Pharah. "And you'll have to take a big risk."

"Wake up."

Maria opened her eyes. Her head hung forward, and she felt her hands cuffed behind her back. The surface of the metal table, with its telltale signs of torture, came into focus. She tried to move her legs, but her ankles were tied to the chair. She raised her head. Russel sat before her once more, a gauze bandage taped over his eye. Maxime stood beside him, his arms folded across his chest. His nose had been taped, and greenish bruises circled his eyes.

"You look like a pirate," she said to Russel.

"And you look like a woman tied to a chair," Russel said. "Why did you put that cigarette out in my eye?"

"I decided to go cold turkey."

"The doctor says my cornea is burned. Odds are I won't see out of this eye again."

"Good. It serves you right for what you did to Jake, you son of a bitch."

"Do you think it's smart to abuse people who have the power and means to torture you?"

"You're going to do what you're going to do: kill me or turn me into one of those zonbies. I figured I'd give you something to remember me by."

Russel stood. "Jake. A little retribution meted out for your wounded lover."

"Who says we're fucking?"

"You went through an awful lot of trouble to rescue him. You killed living soldiers in addition to zonbie slaves."

"I'd do the same for any partner."

"Like Edgar Hopkins?"

Maria stayed quiet.

"Well, I can understand the desire for retribution. I'm feeling it myself right now."

Russel gestured to the female soldier, and she and Maxime moved to Maria. The woman stood behind her and braced her arm under Maria's chin, grasping one side of her head, holding her still. Maxime set his hands on Maria's shoulders, squeezing them so she couldn't tip her chair back. Russel held his hand out to one of the remaining soldiers, who drew his machete from its sheath and set its handle in Russel's palm.

Russel closed his fingers around the handle and stepped beside Maxime, facing Maria, whose heart pounded in her chest. Russel waved the long blade before her eyes.

Oh, Jesus, no.

"Tell me the names of the men who helped you rescue Helman and free Santiago."

Tears filled Maria's eyes. "Fuck you."

Russel nodded to the woman behind Maria, who jerked Maria's head back so she stared straight at her interrogator.

"This is a cold business poorly served by childish emotions. You'll tell me what I want to know eventually, and then you'll wish you'd saved yourself a great deal of pain and your beauty. If you and Helman are reunited, he'll be *your* better-looking half."

Maria spat at Russel, but her saliva only wrapped around her own chin. Russel touched the tip of the machete against her jawline, then drew it over her cheek. She felt the blade dimpling her flesh. It stopped just beneath her right eye. Sweat formed on her brow, and she smelled the odor under her arms.

"Retribution can be a pleasant experience for some and agonizing for others." Russel raised his elbow so Maria saw the entire blade except for its tip. He rotated his wrist, wiggling the tip so it pressed against Maria's lower eyelid.

Her tears caused him to go out of focus, and she closed her eyes. The machete's tip pressed against her nerves, and she felt it breaking through her skin.

The door opened and a hoarse voice cried out, "Stop!"

Maria opened her eyes. Tears trickled down her cheeks, and Russel came into focus, his head turned toward the withered-looking old woman who had just entered the room.

"What is it, Catoute?" Russel sounded surprised to see the old witch doctor.

"President Malvado wants us to deliver this woman to him at the palace immediately. In *one* piece."

Lowering his machete, Russel glanced at Maxime, who shrugged with obvious disappointment.

Maria felt a blood drop trickling down her cheek from beneath her eye.

"It looks like you've been granted a temporary reprieve," Russel said.

Catoute moved forward, her black cane tapping the floor. The old woman's appearance caused Maria to shudder.

"I wouldn't count on it," Catoute said.

THIRTY-ONE

The helicopter soared over the rain forest, the jungle terrain outlined in light from the ongoing barrage of flares in the night sky. Still handcuffed, Maria sat between two soldiers once more. Russel and Mambo Catoute sat opposite her, Maxime in the cockpit. Maria still felt nervous in the old woman's presence. If Jake's theories were correct, she was responsible for the zonbies.

Clearing the rain forest, the helicopter headed in the direction of two buildings: the château palace Maria had seen from afar with Jake and a darker, more foreboding structure, with a domed roof surrounded by spires.

L'église du Serpent Noir, Maria thought. *The Church of the Black Snake.*

The helicopter veered toward the palace instead, flying low over a stone wall manned by armed guards, an army barracks, and gardens and fountains, the grounds well lit by decorative lights that splashed multiple colors on the lawn statues. It descended onto asphalt with markings between the three wings of the palace. Maria felt her stomach tightening at the prospect of seeing Malvado, and she wondered if she could kill him with her bare hands.

As the rotor blades slowed to a stop, her favorite two soldiers guided her onto the tarmac, where she watched Russel help Catoute down. Maxime jumped out last. The six of them walked through the humid night to the center structure of the palace, where armed soldiers saluted Russel and Catoute and opened doors for the entire party.

Inside the palace, Maria looked up at the high ceilings. With their footsteps echoing and Catoute's cane tapping, she gazed at paintings that hung on the walls and antique chairs and pianos. Everywhere they turned, soldiers watched them.

At last they stopped at a set of double doors, which Russel opened. The soldiers guided Maria into an enormous office, and Russel and Catoute followed. Maria's gaze darted from a gigantic oak desk to a painting of Malvado over the mantel of a fireplace which had seen little, if any, use over the centuries. The flag of Pavot Island hung on a pole behind the desk. Four plush sofas surrounded a square table. Bookcases filled with leather volumes served as frames for several maps.

The center of power, Maria thought.

A side door opened, and an imposing figure, clad in a royal-blue uniform fringed in gold, strode into the room. Broad shoulders. A shaved head peppered with gray hair.

Beady eyes. A wide nose and full lips.

Malvado.

The soldiers saluted their leader, who marched past them and stared down at Maria.

Her limbs turned limp, and she felt saliva collecting at the back of her throat. Malvado was a giant, standing well over six feet tall. Even Maxime looked puny in comparison.

Malvado glanced at the bandage on his son's nose but said nothing. When he looked at Maria again, she felt like a child. It would never have occurred to her to abuse this man as she had Russel and Maxime.

"You are Maria Vasquez," Malvado said in English with a French Caribbean accent. His nostrils flared as if he was sniffing for the smell of her fear. "You look so small standing there, woman."

Maria said nothing.

Malvado moved behind his desk and sat in his chair. "Why did you come here to free Andre Santiago? Who is he to you?"

"I never heard of the man before I arrived," Maria said.

"You're lying. You didn't come here to enjoy our sunsets and beaches." Malvado gestured to Russel and Maxime. "What do you two have to say for yourselves? You didn't look like this two hours ago."

Maxime shifted his weight from one foot to the other. "Her appearance is deceiving."

"Miss Vasquez, you have cost me time, resources, and money. Worse, you've helped infect my country. The students and activists are out of control. I find myself admiring you, and under normal circumstances, I'd enjoy punishing you myself or allowing Maxime to do it. But Mambo Catoute has convinced me you will serve a greater purpose in her custody. William, kindly transport our guest to L'église du Serpent Noir, then return. You have much work to do in the morning."

Russel bowed. "As you wish."

Malvado approached Maria again and caressed her cheek. "Should you survive Mambo Catoute's plans for you, it will be my pleasure to see you again."

Maria shuddered.

"Take her to the Church of the Black Snake."

Janvier spread out a map across the table. At Jake's request, Jorge and Stephane joined the war council, and Jake had changed into his own clothing and given his uniform to Stephane. Louider and several delegates had already departed.

Andre tapped the map. "The key is to strike all of our targets simultaneously. The shock factor will even the odds."

Pharah reentered the room. "I just received word that Maria's been transported from the Ministry of Defense to the palace."

"Then I'll be leading the charge on the palace," Jake said.

Andre looked up from the map. "And I'll be joining you."

"Not a chance. We need someone to coordinate things from here."

"Father Alejandro is the perfect candidate for that."

"You're too important a symbol to risk losing in battle."

"I've been rotting in El Miedo for thirty years. I don't intend to sit by in a cave while my people fight a revolution for what I believe in."

"And I didn't spring you out because of some sense of international justice. I did it to save a friend in Miami. Your wife expects me to bring you home alive."

"My wife knows I'm a man of deeds. My home is here, not Miami."

"If you get killed, my friend is screwed. I've been through too much to allow that to happen."

"Then you have an excellent reason to watch my back and keep me alive. I'll be there to take that bastard Malvado down."

As Jake watched Andre exit the room, Jorge joined him.

"Le Père is a leader of the people," Jorge said. "He doesn't like to take orders."

"Neither do I."

Maria sat sandwiched between her guardian soldiers in the backseat of a Hummer that roared away from the palace. She felt as if she had just been sentenced to crucifixion by Pontius Pilate, only she didn't know the nature of her sentence. A flare went off in the sky above the rain forest.

"I guess Jake and Andre are still loose," she said.

Russel stared at her. "Not for long. A star as bright as Andre's can't remain hidden for long, and Helman will come looking for you. Why do you think we made such a public show of bringing you here?"

Shit, Maria thought. *They're using me as bait.* "Why do you care about Jake anyway? I did all the heavy lifting. All he did was lose his hand and get high."

"I don't disagree with you," Russel said. "Helman had me worried, but you turned out to be far more trouble than him."

All in a good day's work, Maria thought.

The Church of the Black Snake appeared at the end of the road. Unlike the palace, it didn't glow in the night; rather, it seemed to swallow the light around it and spit it out as darkness. They passed through a checkpoint with only two armed soldiers, and the Hummer stopped near a flight of stone steps.

The party climbed out of the vehicle, and Maria, stretching her spine, watched Mambo Catoute hobble up the steps.

Tough old broad, she thought. *All gristle.*

One of the soldiers prodded Maria with the barrel of his machine gun, and she followed Catoute up the steps and through wooden doors adorned with hand-carved snakes.

Inside, cool air raised gooseflesh on her arms. The soldiers' footsteps echoed around them, and Maria noticed Russel's visible unease in the church. They followed a balcony overlooking an enormous cathedral and descended wooden stairs to the lower level. A gigantic chandelier with burning candles hung from the ceiling.

Catoute led them to an archway recessed between rows of benches and opened a door, and they entered a stairway, which curved down to another level. At the bottom, they passed an office door, then a wider door, which Catoute opened. They filed into a round chamber equal to the cathedral in floor space. Along the curved stone wall, shelves rose from the floor, circling the entire chamber. Unlit candles covered the shelves.

Thousands of candles, Maria thought.

Catoute made her way past a podium and gestured at chains with manacles coiled on the floor. "Chain her up there."

The soldiers guided Maria into a circle, perhaps twelve feet in diameter, painted on the floor.

Maria squinted at the rust-colored circle. *That looks like blood.* "I love what you've done to the place," she said to Catoute, who ignored her.

The soldiers secured the manacles to her wrists, then removed the handcuffs.

Russel examined the candles with a grim expression, then rejoined Maxime and the soldiers. "Let's go," he said to Maxime. "I'd like to get some sleep before morning."

Maxime nodded and grunted.

"You two stay here," Russel said to the soldiers, who exchanged worried glances.

"Not inside this church, they don't," Catoute said.

"We're not leaving a prisoner of the state in here unattended."

"Then make them wait upstairs. They can't be in here while I make preparations for Kalfu."

Kalfu! Maria's heart tightened with fear.

"In that case," Russel said, "I'm assigning more men to watch the outside of this place. I respect your religion, but

I'm not losing my head over it."

After the four men departed the chamber, Maria turned to Catoute. "Now that they're gone, let's talk. Just us girls."

Catoute snickered. "What would you like to know?"

Maria looked at the circle around her. "Are you planning to sacrifice me to Kalfu?"

"Kalfu doesn't want you. Malvado does. Kalfu wants Jake Helman."

Maria swallowed. "What does he—it—want with Jake?"

"I have no idea, but I'm sure it will be extremely unpleasant and extremely painful." Catoute held her cane out before her. "You never should have come here."

Maria glanced around the chamber at the candles. "I need to go to the bathroom."

Catoute took a pot out of a cabinet, set it down outside the circle, and kicked it forward. A roll of moldy toilet tissue occupied the pot.

Gee, thanks, Maria thought.

Jake, Andre, and Stephane stood by the road in the jungle. Cicadas chirped around them, and flares flashed like lightning above them.

"I'm not letting you out of my sight," Jake said to Andre.

"That's fine by me."

Headlights appeared in the distance.

"Here they come," Stephane said, stepping into the middle of the road. "You two hide."

Jake and Andre sought cover in the jungle.

The canvas-covered truck stopped, and Stephane approached the window. Jake thought he saw the men inside wearing berets.

"Libération de l'île Pavot," the driver said.

"Libération de l'île Pavot," Stephane said.

The driver jerked his head toward the back of the truck.

Stephane ran along the truck to its rear and shone his flashlight inside it. Then he waved to Jake and Andre. "Come on!"

Jake and Andre joined Stephane, and the three of them climbed into the truck. Among a dozen or so crates stacked floor to ceiling sat six men, including Louider, all of them wearing camouflage uniforms. The crime lord smoked a cigar.

"Louider," Andre said as he sat on a crate.

"You didn't think I was going to let you have all the fun, did you?" Louider removed a stack of cigars from his pocket and offered them to the newcomers. "Cubans?"

All three men accepted, and as the truck pulled away, Louider helped light the cigars. Jake had never enjoyed smoking cigars, but when would he ever have the chance to smoke a Cuban again? The tips of the cigars glowed in the darkness despite the flashlight beams illuminating the truck's gloomy interior.

"Nine trucks just like this one are on their way to the agreed upon locations," Louider said. He gestured at Jake with the cigar. "You have an interesting method of choosing qualified marksmen. Andre, did they treat you well in prison?"

"It was prison. I have nothing to compare it to. The

guards were decent to me, or at least they were never cruel."

"I hope not. I paid them to look after you."

"I suspected as much. Thank you for the special meals on holidays."

"I wish I could have done more. Bribery is difficult when you're dealing with snake cultists."

"Ain't it the truth."

During the hour that followed, Jake thought of nothing but Maria. He had to believe she was alive, that they were holding her as bait to lure them, or why would they have sent her to the palace? The question was: Had Russel taken a machete to her as he had Jake?

I'll kill him if he did, Jake thought.

In the cab of the truck, one of the men banged on the wall.

"We're almost there." Louider raised his high-tech machine gun with its silencer. "Brace yourselves."

The truck stopped and they heard voices. Three flashlight beams materialized before them. Standing, Louider blasted his machine gun at the lights. The men holding the flashlights cried out before falling to the ground. Only Jake saw the flickering souls rise and fade. He heard more silenced shots coming from the front of the truck.

"Wait here," Louider said. He hopped over the truck's gate and disappeared.

Jake and Andre exchanged worried looks. A blast of suppressed machine gun fire rang out, then Louider climbed into the truck.

"Tell them to go," Louider said to one of his men, who banged on the back wall. The truck surged forward.

"Caught two of the fuckers hiding in the bathroom."

All human so far, Jake thought. As the truck followed the bumpy road, the checkpoint station receded from view, the road around it littered with corpses.

At least I didn't have to kill them.

A few minutes later, the truck stopped again. This time Louider jumped out before anyone appeared at the truck's rear. The suppressed gunfire of three weapons created a staccato rhythm. It stopped, then resumed.

"Oh, shit!" one of the men out front said.

Louider got into the truck. "I hate zonbies."

"I told you to shoot them in the head," Jake said.

The gangster shrugged. "We did. After we shot them in the chest."

"How many?"

"Eight. The same as the first checkpoint."

The truck growled its way forward.

Jake checked his watch. "It's 3:35. We've got a lot to do before 5:00 if dawn is at 6:00."

"Everything but this location and the palace are out of our hands," Andre said. "Have faith in the rest of our people."

The truck stopped, and Luider lowered the gate and hopped out. "Everybody out!"

Jake and Stephane obeyed, then helped Andre to the ground. The compound looked identical to the one Jake had spent the night in: six army barracks surrounded by work lights, plus what appeared to be a paddock for horses.

A pair of dead soldiers appeared, and Stephane raised his machine gun to his shoulder.

"The heads," Jake said. "Free their souls."

Stephane's laser scope sited one zonbie's forehead. He triggered the weapon, firing two suppressed semiautomatic rounds, and the zonbie's head danced on its shoulders. The corpse collapsed, and a shimmering soul rose into the sky and faded.

Jake looked around for some reaction, but no one else saw the pitiful creature's energy escape its body.

Stephane fired again, taking out the second zonbie soldier with a single shot.

Jake watched another soul flicker into the night air. He found the sight disturbing and comforting at the same time.

Stephane admired his new toy. "I *like* this gun."

"Oh, my Lord," Andre said behind them.

Jake and Stephane joined him at the rear of the truck, where the rest of Louider's men unloaded crates. On the horizon, hundreds of shapes worked in the poppy fields.

"My people," Andre said.

"Come on." Jake tapped Andre's arm. "You're sticking with me, remember?"

The three men rushed to the first building, Stephane and Andre carrying machine guns and Jake carrying a Glock. Inside the building, Jake flipped a light switch. Andre gasped at the stench of human waste and rot.

Jake blinked at the empty interior. "Poor bastards already turned."

They ran past the next three buildings. When they reached the fifth, Stephane nodded in the direction of the poppy fields. Four men on horseback galloped toward the truck.

"Overseers," Jake said.

"What kind of human beings treat others this way?" Andre said.

"Louider will handle them. We've got dirty business of our own."

They stormed inside the structure. A woman wearing African robes stood with her back to them, chanting over a naked male body on a table. Eleven more emaciated bodies occupied tables waiting for her. The Mambo jerked her head in their direction, alarm in her eyes. A soldier sitting in a chair nearby jumped to his feet and reached for his machine gun.

Stephane triggered a blast from his weapon. The rounds tearing the wall and soldier apart made more noise than the gunfire.

"Cover the door," Jake said to Stephane, then he led Andre past numerous tables supporting zonbies stripped of their clothing. "Take a good look."

Heads turned toward them.

"They've turned, but they haven't been embalmed. Unattended, these guys will rot away into nothing. That's where this fine woman comes into play." Jake pointed at the Y incision dividing the torso of the zonbie before the Mambo into three sections. "She swaps out the blood and the organs for sawdust and preservatives and makes it possible for each of those poor sons of bitches to be programmed like a machine."

Andre glared at the woman, who appeared to be thirty. Her eyes grew wider as if she recognized him.

"The humane thing is to put them out of their misery,

put them down, free their souls." Jake walked to the back of the building and stood at the foot of a medical table. A male zonbie looked at him. He aimed his Glock at the man's head and fired, splattering the wall with brain chunks. The zonbie's body jerked, his eyes closed, and his soul rose.

Jake moved on to a teenage girl who sat up, her breasts discolored blue. After he pulled the trigger, she fell back down. A middle-aged man with a potbelly, down for the count. A once attractive Hispanic woman with blonde hair matted with her own brains after Jake shot her. With methodical precision, he freed their souls one after another. The zonbies didn't panic or flee.

When Jake reached the zonbie the Mambo had been treating, the creature lunged at Andre, who blasted it in the chest. The firepower drove the zonbie onto the table again, where Jake executed the dead thing and freed its soul.

Andre stood over the unmoving zonbie, smoke rising from the barrel of his machine gun.

"That one was just about ready," Jake said. "It had been programmed with a survival instinct."

Andre stared at the Mambo. "How *could* you?"

"I'm only following orders," the woman said in a defiant tone.

A low growl rising from Andre's throat became a full roar as he swung his machine gun over his head and split the woman's skull open.

THIRTY-TWO

Lying on her back with the stone floor beneath her head, Maria drifted off into a half sleep. Several times, she opened her eyes at the sound of Catoute's chanting, only to close them again. She saw no point in engaging the withered creature in conversation; she wasn't seeking information, after all. If Jake really was still on Pavot Island and Malvado's people intended to use her as bait, there was nothing she could do but try to warn him if he showed up.

When he shows up.

Maria sensed movement somewhere in the darkness near her, and when she opened her eyes, she saw six pairs of feet approaching her. Blinking to make sure she wasn't dreaming, she looked at the people in the shadows.

Jorge and Pharah!

Jorge, wearing an African robe, held one finger to his

lips for Maria's benefit. Pharah wore a white pantsuit with her hair tied up in a matching ribbon. The others in the party—two men and two women Maria didn't recognize— wore robes similar to Jorge's. The six of them moved in a triangular formation, with Pharah on point.

Maria sat up just enough to glance at Catoute's back. The old woman was kneeling, and Maria heard a chicken cluck. As Maria turned to her rescue party, the chain attached to one of her manacled wrists clinked. The rescuers stopped, and Maria jerked her head toward Catoute, who stiffened.

The old woman clawed at her black cane, stood up, and turned with slow deliberation toward Pharah and the others. The chicken flapped its wings, its legs tied together with wire.

Catoute's eyebrows rose. "What brings you here, Daughter?"

Pharah stepped forward. "This is your day of reckoning."

Smiling, Catoute shook her head at the tall man standing by Pharah. "Issagha." He remained stoic, and Catoute wagged a crooked finger at him. "I guess you were more ambitious than I ever realized."

"The church is sealed," Issagha said with a touch of regret.

Catoute moved forward, her cane tapping the floor. "And who is this other rabble?"

Maria watched Jorge stiffen.

Pharah stared at Catoute. "Where's my daughter? Issagha says she's vanished."

"You're standing on her, dear."

With dread filling her eyes, Pharah looked down at the faded red circle at her feet.

Maria jumped to her feet, the chains pulling at her.

"You wicked, wicked woman," Pharah said. "You took Sivelia away from me when she was just a child, and now you've betrayed her."

Catoute brandished her cane. "She betrayed me! That's why I sacrificed her to almighty Kalfu."

"You'll pay for this, I swear. If not in this world, then in the next."

Catoute spat chocolate-brown phleghm on the floor. "We'll see who pays." Cocking her arm, she hurled her cane like a spear at Issagha.

The cane struck him in the throat, and he screamed as he collapsed, his body going into spasms.

Pharah's eyes widened. "Issagha!"

The cane writhed on the floor, then slithered toward Pharah, who jumped backwards.

Maria gasped in disbelief.

Pharah drew the white wrap from around her waist and threw it at the black snake. The wrap descended on the serpent like a shroud, ensnaring it.

Catoute hissed like a serpent herself.

The black snake entwined around the white wrap, which began to slither as well. Two long snakes, one black and one white, battled each other on the floor.

Oh, Jesus, Maria thought.

Jaws snapped at each other, fangs flashed, tongues darted in and out. The white snake seized the black snake behind its head and clamped down on it.

"No!" Catoute said, her face contorting as if she'd lost a child.

The white snake gnawed on the black snake, which snapped its body like a whip. The ebony body continued to writhe even after the white snake had separated its head.

Sinking to her knees with tears in her eyes, Catoute screamed.

The white snake slithered toward Pharah, who picked it up by its head and tail. The younger woman stretched out the white snake, then wrapped it around her waist. She crouched beside Issagha, who had stopped moving. Wincing, she rose. "Your magic is weak. Your time as a Mambo is at an end. Help us or stay out of the way."

Catoute looked at Pharah, one side of her upper lip twitching. "I'll see your blood on that floor next, bitch."

"Put a gun on her," Pharah said.

Throwing back his robe, Jorge revealed a machine gun, which he aimed at Catoute. "Get up."

Glaring at Jorge, Catoute managed to rise.

"Somebody get me out of these chains," Maria said.

Pharah glanced at Catoute. "Where's the key?"

"I don't know. I didn't think I'd need one."

Pharah faced Maria. "I'm sorry. We've got something more important to worry about right now. You'll just have to wait."

"This is some rescue," Maria said.

"Don't take this the wrong way, but we didn't come to rescue you."

Maria glanced at Jorge, who shrugged with a guilty look on his face. She turned back to Pharah. "Don't take this the wrong way, but that old bitch keeps talking about summoning a Loa named Kalfu, and as far as I can tell, I'm standing in the middle of the landing pad. Get me *out* of these."

Pharah nodded to Jorge. "Go ahead. Look. Everyone else—start lighting these candles."

Andre stood gasping over the corpse of the Mambo he had just slain, his face wet with her glistening blood. "Monsters."

Jake set one hand on the man's shoulder. "Jesus, you're no Mandela."

Andre wiped the blood on his face. "No, I'm not. After thirty years in El Miedo, I'm filled with rage."

"You're only human."

"Is there more to see?"

"I'm afraid so." Jake led Andre and Stephane to the last structure. With difficulty, he ejected the magazine from his Glock, slapped another one in its place, holstered the gun, and drew a flashlight, which he aimed at putrid black smoke billowing out of a ventilation shaft in the roof.

"What is it?" Andre said.

"When the zonbies are too far gone to be of any more use, they recycle themselves. One of the key ingredients of Black Magic is the self-cremated remains of the undead."

Andre turned pale. "It's like the Nazi concentration camps, only even more perverse."

"We're on a schedule," Jake said.

They returned to the truck. The four overseers lay dead on the ground, their horses tied to the truck. Louider and his men had unloaded all of the crates and were prying them open with crowbars.

"Uh-oh," Andre said, looking in the direction of the jungle opposite the poppy fields.

Jake turned around. "Ah, fuck."

Two dozen zonbies emerged from the trees two hundred yards away. All of them carried machine guns.

"Maria said the patrols carried machetes. I guess they stepped up their game."

"Louider!" Andre said.

Louider joined them and cursed. Then he called out to his men, who came running. "What do you propose, Helman?"

"We don't have any choice," Jake said. "But taking out that many"—he pointed in the direction of the poppy fields—"will bring many more."

"I'm beginning to see the downside of your plan," Andre said.

"Spread out," Louider said to his men, who moved into action. "Helman, you can't shoot a machine gun with one hand. Andre, you can't shoot at all. Both of you get into the back of the truck and lie down. Stephane, you'd better cover their asses."

Jake glanced at the zonbie patrol marching forward, rifles and machine guns clenched in their leathery hands. He looked the other way at the hundreds of zonbies who continued to work in the fields without the overseers' supervision.

"Make sure you wait until you see their white eyes," Jake said to Louider. "It will be easier to hit them in the head that way."

Louider waved in a dismissive gesture.

Jake climbed into the truck and helped Andre up. Stephane followed. They lay down in the truck and switched on their flashlights.

Then the shooting started.

Jorge grabbed the leather around Catoute's neck, and two dozen keys rattled on a ring. "Got it!"

He pulled the ring over the old woman's head and raced over to Maria, who stood watching as Pharah and the others in their party lit the candles one by one with kitchen matches.

"What are they doing?" Maria said as Jorge inserted different keys into the locks on the manacles.

"Each candle represents the soul of one zonbie. We need to light all of them."

"For what reason?"

Jorge looked her in the eye. "To enlist the zonbies in our cause."

Maria's mouth hung open for a moment. "This is Jake's crazy idea, isn't it?"

"Oui. You know him well."

"But there are *thousands* of them. At the rate they're going, it'll take all day."

Jorge continued to try different keys. The manacle on Maria's right wrist snapped open. The same key unlocked the other manacle.

"Where's Armand?" Maria said.

"Dead. He was killed outside El Miedo, along with eleven others."

Maria felt as if she'd been kicked. She had liked Armand, had felt a connection to him. "I'm sorry. Very, very sorry."

"Merci."

Moving forward, Maria gazed at the candles that had been lit so far. Maybe a hundred with four people working.

"It will never work," Catoute said, drawing out each word.

Jorge aimed his machine gun at her. "Thank you for showing such concern for our cause. We'll give it a shot anyway."

Rubbing her wrists, Maria stood behind Pharah as she lit the candlewicks. "How is this *supposed* to work?"

"Look closely at the base of each candle, and you'll see a single human hair wrapped around it," Pharah said without interrupting her task. "Each hair belongs to the zonbie whose soul the candle controls. My mother programs each zonbie with a simple list of commands when her priests and priestesses embalm them—work the poppy fields at night; return to your shelter at sunrise; obey all commands from your overseers—then modifies those orders as she wishes with these candles. Now are you going to stand there gawking, or are you going to give us a hand?"

"I have a better idea." Maria ran over to the cabinets against the curved wall. "Jorge, put Catoute in her own chains so you can help."

"No," Catoute said in a strangled voice.

Jorge prodded her forward with his gun.

Maria opened the cupboards and searched their contents. There were no magic herbs, human baby skeletons, or spell books inside, just cleaning chemicals, loose hardware, half-empty paint cans, and dirty rags. She pulled out box after box: a sander, a circular saw blade, a level, a mallet, dried-up paint rollers . . .

"I'll remember you for this," Catoute said.

"And I'll remember you," Jorge said.

Found it!

Maria stood up with a blowtorch and twisted the valve that controlled the gas. "Anybody got a light?"

Through the canvas covering the truck bed, Jake heard the suppressed gunfire of Louider and his gangsters. He also heard the unsuppressed gunfire of the zonbies, which tore through the canvas, whizzed overhead, and punched into the truck's side. A man screamed. The horses whinnied. Another man screamed. One wheel on the truck blew out, and the rear left side lowered. A third man screamed.

"They're taking a beating out there." Jake leapt to his feet, drew his Glock from its holster, and ran to the truck's gate.

Andre sat up. "Jake!"

A figure lumbered before the gate. Stephane pointed a flashlight at it, revealing milky white eyes and hardened gums. The zonbie aimed his machine gun at Jake, who shot it in the head. The corpse dropped from view, and Jake's personal light show began.

Jake hopped out of the truck and landed on both feet. Andre hopped out next, followed by Stephane.

"Under the truck," Jake said over the gunfire.

All three of them crawled under the truck. Stephane leveled his machine gun and opened fire, and Andre imitated him.

My Glock's useless down here, Jake thought as he watched zonbies shuffling in their direction.

"They're too close!" Andre said. "I can't even see their heads."

Stephane blasted his weapon, exploding half a dozen kneecaps. Immobilized zonbies fell over like chopped trees. "Mow them down! Either you'll stop them so they can't get to our men, or you'll force them to expose their heads."

The zonbies who had just collapsed rose on their hands and arms, as if doing push-ups, and crawled toward the truck, dragging their legs behind them. Glowing red dots appeared on two foreheads, which promptly disintegrated.

Afraid to wiggle out from beneath the truck backwards, Jake crouched low and duckwalked, then sprang up and threw his back against the truck's gate. Peering around the corner, he counted five different muzzle flashes around the front of the truck, accompanied by the sound of suppressed action.

Three men down, he thought. One for each scream he'd heard.

In the other direction, a dozen zonbies were dead on the ground, and another dozen marched forward, guns blazing.

Not a good sign.

Bullet holes appeared along the truck. A horse collapsed, leaving the remaining three kicking and whinnying.

Jake shouted under the truck, "Hold your fire!"

Looking at him as if he was crazy, Stephane stopped firing, then Andre.

Holstering his Glock, Jake sprinted over to one of the horses, planted one foot into a stirrup, and threw the other over the saddle. Using his only hand, he untied the reins and guided the horse to the road they had used to enter the compound. He had learned to ride horseback at camp one summer, and twenty years later wondered if he still remembered the basics. He circled the zonbie brigade and waited for Louider and his men to stop firing.

When they did, Jake wrapped the reins around his stump, drew his Glock, and took a slow ride in a straight line behind the zonbies. He dropped four of them before the rest even realized it and did his best to ignore the golden souls rising from the deactivated corpses.

The horse bucked, and Jake tried to get the animal under control while continuing to fire at the zonbies. The horse refused to cooperate, and the zonbies refused to die. Instead, two of them fired at the horse, which whinnied and fell back with a cry, its body riddled with bullet wounds.

Jake managed to roll free of the carcass, but the reins

tied him to it. Rising on one knee, he took out three more zonbies at close range, then ducked behind the dead horse as the remaining zonbies opened fire. The horse's carcass shook and spewed blood. Jake heard suppressed gunfire and knew his companions had come out from cover. Then silence.

Jake looked over the dead animal at Louider and his four surviving men as Stephane and Andre joined them. Jake approached the men, then froze when they all aimed their machine guns at him. Dropping facedown to the earth, he covered his head with his hand. Team Louider opened fire and stopped. Jake looked behind him. Another six zonbies littered the ground, their souls flickering and fading.

Almost fifty, he thought. Many more than he had hoped to put down. As his teammates approached him, Jake pointed past them in the opposite direction. With fearful expressions, the men turned around.

The hundreds of zonbies in the poppy fields had already covered more than half the distance separating them. Jake saw the men stiffen and felt his own heart pound. He had never seen so many zonbies in his life, their machetes reflecting moonlight.

THIRTY-THREE

"Everyone, get back to the truck!" Louider said.

"We'll never make it. Follow me!" Jake sprinted in the direction of the empty drug den. He didn't turn around to see who followed him but pumped his arms and legs as fast as he could.

Hurdling over the two steps leading to the building's entrance, he jerked the screen door open, flipped on the light, and seized the open inside metal door. Two of Louider's men ran inside, followed by Stephane and Andre.

Machine gun fire from three different weapons erupted in the night: long, continuous bursts that came to a sudden stop, replaced by screams.

Pressing his eye against the screen, Jake saw half a dozen machetes rising and falling. Then a hideous face with dripping flesh leaned forward, mashing its bulging eye against the screen where Jake stood. He snapped his head back, aimed his Glock at the thing's head, and fired. The zonbie fell, and Jake slammed and locked the door before he had a chance to see its soul rise.

"Louider?" Andre said.

Jake shook his head.

Outside, fists pounded on the metal door. They sounded soft and squishy, like rotten apples.

"That door should hold them," Jake said to the two remaining gangsters dressed as soldiers. "You two watch it just to be safe. *Only shoot at their heads.* We can't spare the ammo." He entered the empty drug parlor. "These walls are made out of cinder blocks. They aren't coming through them. That leaves only the windows, six of them."

"Too bad there are only five of us," Stephane said.

"And a good thing that all of you have these fancy ATAC machine guns." Jake flipped off the overhead light.

Light from the work lights shone through the windows, casting moving shadows on the ceiling.

At the door, one of the gangsters switched on his flashlight. "Cross your fingers that Pharah comes through for us."

Rotting fists continued to hammer at the door.

Maria ran from candle to candle, igniting their wicks with the blue flame from the blowtorch. Jorge, Pharah, the other man, and the two women used matches to light the candles on one half of the chamber while she worked the other half. When she had completed half of one row, she continued at the next highest row and reversed direction. In ten minutes, she doubled the efforts of the other five people.

This will take an hour, she thought.

Chained in the middle of her summoning circle, Catoute laughed. "You're like ants, scurrying around a dead dog!"

Ignoring her, Maria finished her second row and started on her third.

This is taking too long!

Keeping her hands steady, she aimed the blue flame at the wicks, ignoring the sweat the heat produced on her face. She hoped Jake was having an easier time.

A large rock crashed through one window and thudded on the floor.

"Stephane!" Jake called out. "Fire a grenade into them."

A ratcheting sound cracked the darkness, and a silhouette filled the window.

Stephane fired a grenade from his ATAC, and the window disappeared in a cloud of smoke.

Jake raced to the window in time to see an explosion that scattered, chopped, and incinerated half a dozen bodies.

Too much damage, he thought. They were defeating their reason for coming.

Footsteps thumped on the roof.

"They're climbing!" Andre said.

Machetes rained down on the corrugated roof.

Halfway finished lighting the candles on her side of the chamber, Maria cast a concerned look at her partners, who were only one-quarter finished between the five of them.

Just worry about yourself, she thought.

Catoute continued to cackle. "You're on a fool's mission, Daughter!"

At least the old witch isn't talking to me.

Jake shone his flashlight at the ceiling, silhouetting the feet of the zonbies standing up there. "Maybe a dozen."

"Thanks for busting me out of prison," Andre said.

"You're welcome."

The first machete blade ruptured the roof.

"Done!" Maria said.

Some 1,300 candles burned on one half of the chamber, their flames steady and yellow. She ran past Catoute, who sat cross-legged on the floor of her summoning circle, frowning.

"All of you move over to your right," Maria said. "Draw an imaginary line down the middle. You take half and I'll take half. We can *do* it!"

Six machetes broke through the roof, withdrew, and reappeared, the sound of their blades grinding against the plastic roofing almost unbearable.

Andre aimed his machine gun at the roof.

"Don't do it," Stephane said. "You'll do more damage than they are."

Andre held still.

"How're you guys doing?" Jake said to Louider's men at the door.

"Fine," one of the men said.

Then a loud crack echoed through the building, and the first zonbie dropped through the ceiling.

Jake shoved his flashlight in his belt, drew his Glock, pressed it against the zonbie's left temple, and fired. He heard the spewing of liquefied brain, then the zonbie collapsed and his soul rose.

Two more zonbies fell to the floor around him. Stephane's laser sight cut the room in half. Two muzzle flashes later, Jake stood alone again.

"Thanks," Jake said, spots flashing in his eye.

"Don't mention it," Stephane said.

The door crashed open, and Louider's men screamed in stereo.

Maria finished lighting her candles, then checked out what

remained to be done. Pharah, Jorge, and the others had completed lighting one-third of their remaining candles.

Sighing, she started at the top and worked her way down. The blowtorch ran out of gas. "Goddamn it!" She adjusted the valve, but her well had run dry.

Catoute's cackling echoed around her.

She's doing that on purpose to psych us out.

Looking around, Maria spotted a torch burning on the wall and snatched it. She had to stand back, and it took longer to light the wicks, but it was still faster than using matches.

"Everyone—grab a torch!"

Zonbies wielding machetes flooded through the doorway and jumped through the hole in the ceiling.

Jake, Stephane, and Andre ran to the rear of the building. Stephane opened fire, the intense muzzle flash of his ATAC illuminating the approaching zonbies. Heads exploded, sawdust billowed, and bodies toppled. Then darkness.

"I'm out of ammo!" Stephane said.

"Andre," Jake said, "shoot!"

The muzzle flash from Andre's machine gun revealed the number of zonbies inside the building had doubled.

"Shoot your grenade," Jake said.

"I don't know how!"

Stephane seized Andre's weapon. In the darkness, Jake heard a cocking sound. He smelled smoke, and the center of the building erupted with a flash of light. Jake felt the concussion, then chunks of flesh and bone pelted him, and burning bodies staggered around. He was about to suggest they flee out the closest window when half a dozen arms reached through it and clawed at him.

"We did it," Pharah said. "They're all lit!"

All six of them held flaming torches as they admired their handiwork: 2,500 candles filled the chamber with a golden glow.

"Now what?" Maria said.

"We deal with my mother."

They strode to the summoning circle, where Catoute sneered at them.

Pharah crossed her arms. "Well, will you help us in exchange for saving your own skin?"

"Go to hell," Catoute said.

Jorge retrieved his machine gun and aimed it at Catoute. "If we kill you, we stop Malvado's slaves in their tracks."

"That would free the zonbies' souls, but it wouldn't increase our troop levels. I'll just have to change their orders myself." Pharah turned to Jorge and Maria. "Gag her." Then she crossed the chamber and kneeled down on the floor, facing a section of candles.

"Use your hand while I get a rag," Maria said.

Wrapping one arm around Catoute's shoulders, Jorge placed his other hand over her mouth.

Maria returned to the cabinets and retrieved the longest rag she could find, an old bandana.

Catoute's eyes grew wild at the sight of the rag in Maria's hands.

Jorge winced and removed his hand. "Bite me again, and you'll lose what teeth you still have."

Catoute sputtered, but Maria silenced her with the rag, which she tied behind her head. "Let's hear you cackle now."

Pharah raised her arms and chanted.

Mother and daughter, Maria thought. *They have the same bloodline.* She leaned close to Jorge. "If this works, will we control the zonbies?"

Jorge shook his head. "Jake and Pharah agreed it was better to give them a choice."

"I sure hope he knows what the hell he's doing."

The zonbies slammed Jake against the wall below the window. They pulled at his hair and scratched his face with long fingernails. He felt cool metal graze his skin, then saw a machete pass before his eyes.

Stephane jumped beside him and triggered Andre's ATAC. Even with the silencer on, Jake winced at the suppressed gunfire as well as the muzzle flashes. The smell of gun smoke filled his nostrils, which he preferred to the smell of rotting flesh and human waste. The gun clicked, but the zonbies released him and he slid down the wall.

Holding the ATAC with its barrel pointed at the ceiling, Stephane reached down for Jake. "On your feet, soldier." Stephane's eyes bulged at the sight of the machete blade sticking out of the middle of his chest, and he dropped to his knees, which brought him face-to-face with Jake.

"Stephane!"

Stephane's eyes rolled up, and blood seeped out of his mouth. He slumped forward, and the ATAC struck the floor.

Jake drew his Glock and stood, allowing Stephane to slump over. He aimed the Glock at the forehead of the zonbie who had killed Stephane and squeezed the trigger.

The zonbie's scalp and skull fragmented, blowing brain fluid out the back of his head. When the zonbie's soul flickered out of his skull, Jake glimpsed Andre backing away from two zonbies in the opposite corner. Jake put a bullet in both zonbies' heads, dropping them.

"What happened to Stephane?" Andre said.

"He's gone and we're surrounded. By my count, I have one round left. Do you want it for yourself?"

Andre hesitated before answering. "No. You do it for me."

"When will we know if it's working?" Maria said.

Jorge stared at Pharah's back. "We won't know one way or the other until this is over."

Maria hated waiting.

Jake aimed his Glock at Andre's forehead. He had only one shot with which to spare the man an agonizing death. There would be no such easy way out for himself.

"Wait," Andre said. "They're leaving!"

Jake turned and saw the shadowy zonbies shuffling toward the door. He scooped up his fallen flashlight and pointed it at their backs. *What do you know?* "It worked!"

The zonbies filed out of the building, leaving Jake and Andre with the corpses of their three fallen comrades. Jake retrieved Stephane's ATAC, and Andre located the other one.

"Let's go," Jake said.

Stepping over unmoving zonbies, they made their way to the front of the building. Jake's clothes clung to his sweaty body. The work lights and moonlight provided ample illumination in the compound.

Jake stopped in the doorway, Andre beside him. Easily two hundred zonbies stood motionless in concentric circles radiating from the truck, all of them clinging to machetes. Jake moved between the zonbies, avoiding their blades. They didn't react to his presence. Lumpy bald heads. Long, stringy hair. Glazed-over eyes. Rotting teeth. Skeletal arms. Emaciated bellies. All of them dead. *Un*dead.

"Sweet Jesus," Andre said behind him.

"We must have killed a hundred of them," Jake said, scanning the bodies on the ground. He stopped at the corpses of Louider and his men, hacked to pieces, and collected their weapons. He handed a hand radio to Andre, who switched it on.

"This is Le Père," Andre said.

"Go ahead," Alejandro said over the speaker.

"Unit one has achieved its objective. We sustained significant casualties."

"Roger that. I'll notify unit two."

They walked through the motionless zonbies to the truck, where the two remaining horses whinnied. Jake reached into an open crate and passed clips and grenades to Andre, who reloaded the two ATAC weapons. Jake ejected the magazine from his Glock, slapped another one in, and stuffed his pockets with reloads.

"They're just . . . standing there," Andre said.

"They're waiting for instructions."

"All units report success," Alejandro said over Jorge's hand radio.

Pharah stopped chanting, a look of surprised satisfaction on her face.

Jorge spoke into his radio. "Copy that. We're commencing phase two."

"Roger that," Alejandro said.

Pharah moved closer to a section of candles and altered her chant.

"What's she doing now?" Maria said.

"She gave a general order to the zonbies to stand down. Now she needs to propose a specific attack plan to each division."

Unbelievable, Maria thought, glancing at Catoute, who squirmed in her summoning circle.

Fingers opened and closed. Heads turned on cracking necks. Bodies shifted.

"Jake?"

"I see them."

A handful of zonbies detached themselves from the crowd and moved closer to Jake and Andre.

"Should we get in the truck?" Andre said.

"No."

A male zonbie wearing a dirty suede vest, blue jeans, and motorcycle boots stood before them. Long, matted hair hung over broad shoulders and arms that must have been muscular before atrophying. He seemed to focus on Jake and Andre, and cracked lips separated as his jaw moved up and down.

"He's trying to talk," Andre said with wonder in his voice.

"They don't have any vocal cords left." Jake felt a powerful sense of sympathy for the creature. "But he's sentient." He glanced at the miserable faces around him. "They *all* are. Before they were like machines or cult members—brainwashed, with no will of their own, doing only as they were commanded."

"And now they're fully conscious," Andre said. "But trapped inside their dead bodies. Souls *do* exist. Malvado will burn in hell for what he's done to these people."

"*Your* people."

The zonbie pointed at Andre.

"He recognizes you," Jake said. The mass of corpses pressed in around them. "They all do."

The zonbie brought his hand to his forehead, forming a salute.

Blinking, Andre returned the salute and held it.

Almost in unison, two hundred leathery hands saluted as well.

THIRTY-FOUR

Pharah stopped chanting and stepped back from the last section of candles. She turned to Jorge and nodded.

Jorge raised the hand radio to his mouth. "What's the status on our draft choices?"

"All players are reporting to the field," Alejandro said.

Maria laughed. "It worked? Son of a bitch, it worked! What now?"

"All we've done is increase our ranks. We still have a war to fight."

Jake reached for the handle of the driver's side door.

"I'm pretty sure it will be easier for me to drive stick than you," Andre said.

"Good point." Jake rounded the truck and climbed in on the passenger side.

Andre started the engine and switched on the headlights. "Onward, Christian soldiers."

The truck surged forward. Andre twisted the steering wheel and turned into the poppy field, the bumpy terrain rocking them from side to side.

Andre glanced at his side mirror. "They're running."

Jake looked at his mirror and saw scores of zonbies with ATAC machine guns chasing the truck. "They'll keep up. They don't tire, they don't run out of breath, and they don't need to go to the bathroom."

"Just like machines," Andre said.

"With souls."

Poppy flowers surrounded them, bloodred in the moonlight. Half a mile later, Andre drove the truck uphill and stopped. As he and Jake climbed out, the zonbie army passed them without stopping or seeming to notice them. To Jake, it felt like watching the New York City marathon being run by dead people. They watched the army trample poppies and disappear over the hill's opposite crest.

Jake scrambled into the back of the truck and handed a gasoline container to Andre, who unscrewed its cap, pulled out its nozzle, and crossed the hill's surface with gasoline trailing him and soaking the poppies.

"Got a match?" Andre said.

"Nope."

Laughing, Andre tossed the gas container aside. They got into the truck and drove away.

Fifty yards later, Andre stopped again and they got out. Jake watched the man raise the ATAC to his shoulder and activate its laser scope.

Jake lifted the hand radio to his mouth. "Le Père to base."

"This is base. Go ahead."

"We're in position."

"Go for the gold."

"Copy that."

Andre squinted. "A little red, glowing dot. The wonders of modern technology."

"Wait until you discover Facebook," Jake said.

Andre squeezed the trigger, and the grenade rocketed forward, detonating the gas can and igniting the hillside. Orange flames shot twenty feet into the air, then blew sideways, consuming a hundred yards' worth of poppies before it even spread.

"We're roasting marshmallows here," Jake said into the hand radio, which he hitched onto his belt.

Far in the distance beyond the compound, thunderous explosions shook the night.

"You just fired the shot heard round the island," Jake said.

Malvado stood on the third-story balcony of his study with his arms folded behind his back. Dressed in a black silk robe, he had heard what sounded like thunder in the distance and had gone out to investigate. No signs of lightning, yet the thunderous percussions continued.

"Ernesto?"

He turned at the sound of his mistress's voice. Inmola was a model from the UK, tall and slender, with dark brown skin, like his. She wore an identical silk robe, though she left hers open, revealing the contours of her body.

"Is something wrong?"

Malvado returned his gaze to the jungle around the palace. "I don't know."

Inmola slid her arms around his waist. "Come back to bed."

"I have too much on my mind. There's something in the air, something electric. I can feel it."

"Let me take care of you. I promise I'll make you forget your worries."

He offered her a serious smile. "I don't want to forget them."

His cell phone rang. Detaching her arms from around his waist, he answered it.

"This is General Buteau. We have a crisis. Make that *crises*. You'll want to come to the command center right away."

Malvado switched the power off. "Help me get dressed."

Ten minutes after the truck had passed the zonbies again and after entering a strip of woods, the headlights shone on the surface of a narrow river.

Andre killed the engine but left the headlights on. They got out, and Jake heard distant explosions in all directions. Lowering the truck's gate, Jake climbed up and dropped the ramp, then led the two horses out one at a time. A large, heavy sack rested on each horse's back. Jake carried out four more sacks.

"Supposedly, this is where the river is shallowest," he said, "with the least current. It's almost stagnant."

"So? I'm told the water's stocked with piranhas."

"Not piranhas. Something else. Watch." Taking a knife, Jake slit one of the sacks open, and grainular white powder whispered out.

Andre furrowed one brow. "Sugar?"

"Salt." Jake hurled a fistful of salt at the water's surface.

The water rippled, then churned, foaming. A creature the size of an eel leapt out of the water, steam and smoke hissing from its smoldering body. The water seemed to explode in two or three places at once, blood and scaly chunks of flesh rising to the surface.

"What the hell?" Andre said.

"Biogens: biogenetically engineered weapons. My old boss Nicholas Tower financed their creation. Bill Russel was in the process of selling them to President Seguera to deal with rebels in the Philippines when I fouled up their plans. Since Russel brought Seguera here, I figured he sold a supply of Biogens to Malvado as well. If a man's willing to turn his own subjects into zonbies, why wouldn't he purchase some genetic hybrids capable of devouring a human being?"

"Incredible. But you stopped those"—he gestured at the water—"with salt?"

"Tower designed dozens of different Biogens, each with its own Achilles' heel as a control factor. For this breed it was salt to prevent them from escaping into the sea and causing damage to the ecosystem."

"But human beings have salt in their bodies. How can these creatures eat them?"

"Other minerals in our bodies neutralize the salt's effects on the Biogens, making us tasty morsels." Jake threw handfuls of salt at the water. "Come on. Help me out."

Biogens flapped around on the water's surface, shrieking and writhing in the moonlight, their red eyes filled with hatred. Seeing them again unsettled Jake; his past continued to chase him.

When he and Andre had emptied the entire sack, Jake opened another and started rubbing salt on his arms and legs. Then he and Andre rubbed salt on the legs of their horses. They each grabbed one end of another sack, swung it, and let it soar into the air, splashing into the river.

"Ready?" Jake said.

"No."

The sky above them lit up, and they heard helicopters. Climbing onto the saddles of their horses, they guided the animals to the water's edge.

"It should be only four or five feet deep. Keep that sack on your saddle, and you should be fine." Jake punctured each corner of his sack, then handed his knife to Andre, who did the same.

Jake guided his horse into the water and felt the animal resisting the current. The horse moved deeper into the water, which covered Jake's boots, then rose to his knees, then his thighs.

At least my balls are safe.

Around him, the water stirred, then foamed and writhed. Silvery Biogens, ruptured and bleeding, broke the surface.

His horse whinnied and tried to rear up.

"Easy, boy," Jake said.

The horse continued forward. The water rose to Jake's ass, then his waist.

So much for my balls.

The water continued to bleed around him.

Christ, how many of these things are there?

The water receded, slipping away from his thighs and then his shins, and his horse clopped onto the embankment. The animal didn't need Jake to spur it faster. Turning his beast to face the river, Jake saw Andre emerging from the river on his horse.

"That was a little too close," Andre said.

The zonbies appeared on the other side of the river and stopped on its bank.

"Are they afraid?" Andre said.

"No. They're not alive so the Biogens wouldn't eat them. But they were programmed never to cross the river, and now they have to disobey that order."

The zonbie with the long hair waded into the river, then another, then a dozen. Soon the entire foot brigade crossed with their machine guns held above their heads, the headlights from the truck illuminating them.

The roar of a helicopter grew louder. Trees shook and bowed, the river grew choppy, and the horses reared up. The helicopter descended, its spotlight targeting dozens of zonbies.

The creatures looked up at the aircraft with helpless expressions.

No sooner had Jake wrestled his horse under control than he heard a loud whining beside him, and it reared up, giving him a perfect view of the helicopter as its interior exploded.

A soldier fell out, screaming and burning, and crash-dived into the river, which carried him away. With smoke billowing out of its side, the helicopter went into a tailspin and disappeared behind the trees. Jake heard the sounds of metal groaning and twisting and glass shattering. Then the fuel tank ignited, and a fireball rose into the sky.

Glancing over his shoulder, he saw Andre loading another grenade onto his ATAC.

"I fight for *all* the people," Andre said.

This isn't possible, Russel thought as images of destruction filled the monitors in the command center. Burning buildings, overturned vehicles, civilians with machine guns running for cover.

He and Maxime huddled around Buteau, while uniformed aides crisscrossed the room from terminal to terminal and telephones rang.

"What the hell is going on?" Malvado said as he stormed into the room like a force of nature. He wore his complete uniform, including medals and a sheathed sword.

"We're under attack," Buteau said. "Armed forces have assaulted the airport and central military base. There are reports of explosions all across the island. Two of our helicopters have been shot down, two more are missing, and our fighter planes never made it off the runway."

Malvado's face trembled. "Santiago and Helman are behind this!"

"This is the work of more than two men," Buteau said. "As far as we can tell, a dozen different operations involving thousands of personnel are under way at the same time. Except for the Ministry of Defense, Pavot City has already fallen."

"Pavot City? *The capital?* Then what are you doing here, General?"

"Commanding the troops."

"Get out there and *lead* the troops! William and my son can monitor the situation here."

Buteau rose. "Yes, Mr. President. *Which* troops would you like me to lead?"

"How about the forces outside the palace? Make certain I'm safe!"

Buteau bowed and exited, and Russel slipped into his chair.

"I think you'd better see what's being broadcast on your TV network," Russel said. He tapped some keys, and a familiar face filled the screen and spoke in French.

"Hello. I'm Andre Santiago. I've spent the last thirty years incarcerated in El Miedo prison, while all of you watching this have lived under the crushing oppression of a dictator Ernesto Malvado. Tonight all of that changes. I'm free and soon you will be, too. A coalition consisting of the People for Pavot, Pavot for the People, the Church of St. Anthony's, and citizens across our nation have banded together to overthrow this illegal government. Spread the word. Arm yourselves. Take the fight to the streets. This will be your only chance to stand up to Le Monstre. Libération de I'île Pavot."

"This message was recorded earlier. He repeats it in English, then Spanish, in a continuous loop."

Malvado's beady eyes grew wide. "How?"

"They seized control of the network. Control the media and you control the message."

"Bomb the TV station!"

"With what? You have no air force." Russel glimpsed a flashing icon in one corner of the monitor. "Here's an incoming message from Solaine at the Ministry of Defense."

Solaine appeared sweaty and distraught in the webcam image.

"What's your situation, Colonel?" Malvado said.

"Grim," Solaine said. "They've broken through our defense perimeter on the ground floor, and we don't have any helicopters on the roof."

"You have *guns*, don't you? Shoot them!"

"I don't think that will do much good, Mr. President."

"Why not?"

"Because it's difficult to kill men who are already dead. We're being attacked by your zonbies, and they're armed."

Russel blinked at the screen. *Zonbies?* He looked over his shoulder at Maxime, then at Malvado, whose face turned several shades lighter, his mouth hanging open.

"Destroy their heads," Malvado said.

"Bondye, forgive us for what we've done," Solaine said. "But I think instead he's punishing us."

THIRTY-FIVE

"Are we just going to stand here until the war's over?" Maria said.

"We have to protect Pharah and these candles," Jorge said.

A burst of static came over his hand radio, followed by Alejandro's voice. "This is base, making a general announcement. The Ministry of Defense has fallen. Pavot City, including the television network, is ours. So is the airport. Malvado's plantations and businesses have fallen. Bienvenida City is in play. I fear this will be my last update."

Maria looked at Jorge, then at Pharah.

Over the hand radio, they heard shouting.

"Libération de l'île Pavot!" Alejandro said.

Machine gun fire erupted, then silence.

Maria felt numb. "Shit."

"Your plantations are all abandoned and on fire," Russel said. "There's no communication at your sugarcane fields or rum factory, but it's safe to believe they've fallen as well. Other than your personal fortune and the treasury, you've been wiped out."

Malvado stared at Russel. "How did this happen?"

Russel mulled over his response. It would do no good to remind Malvado he had warned him about Helman. "We failed to recognize that the different elements on the fringe of society could overcome their differences to unite against you. Now they've provided a backbone to the general population. We're outnumbered, but even with your air force shut down, we aren't outgunned. We can still come out of this in control."

"But we'll be broke," Malvado said.

"The country may be broke but you won't be. The men at the top always manage to prosper."

"We'll need to use the treasury's coffers to repair all this damage. If we kill the rebels and the zonbies, there will be no one left to replant my poppies. It will take years for things to return to normal."

Russel held back his laughter. *Normal, he says.*

Maxime set both hands down on the console. "Where can we go? Let's empty the treasury and run."

Malvado made a fist and struck Maxime in the face. "Don't speak to me of fleeing! We're not cowards; we're Malvados. We'll stay and fight for what's ours. I refuse to believe these peasants can overthrow my army. William, tell Buteau to order all troops to surround the palace. We have to hold our ground."

Russel reached for his phone. "You got it."

An explosion shook the palace.

Jake and Andre emerged from the forest on their horses and slowed the animals to a stop.

The rear of the palace appeared less than a mile ahead. A fireball rose from the wing on the left side. The sky flickered with light, then the third floor of the château's middle section exploded debris into the air. A third explosion occurred just short of the right-hand wing, the resulting fireball hurling military vehicles aside like toys.

Above the roof, a helicopter came into view, trailing smoke. With its nose pointed down, the helicopter descended at a forty-five-degree angle. Its blades struck the earth and pitched the machine sideways at the ground, creating yet another explosion.

Jake and Andre looked at each other. Then hundreds of zonbies ran past them.

Grabbing the reins of his horse, Jake kicked his steed forward. "Yah!"

Russel helped Malvado to his feet and Maxime shook his head while chalky dust swirled around them.

"Are you all right?" Russel said.

"It will take more than mortar fire to unnerve me," Malvado said.

The sounds of machine gun fire seemed to come from every direction at once.

A voice came over the radio. "This is General Buteau. Come in!"

Russel grabbed the microphone. "What's your status?"

"It's over. It's all over. There're too many of them, and they have firepower like I've never seen before. The palace is on fire. Evacuate. Evacuate!"

Dead silence.

"Father, look!" Maxime pointed at the TV.

Malvado raised his gaze to the monitor in time to see a statue of himself in a village square topple. Outside, an explosion roared.

"Only Mambo Catoute can protect us from these zonbies," Malvado said. "We have to get to the Church of the Black Snake."

Russel whipped out his cell phone and struck a button. "I need two armored cars out front to transport President Malvado to a safe location. I don't care if all hell is breaking loose!"

Jake rode his horse just behind the zonbies, careful not to trample any of them. Andre rode alongside him, raising his ATAC in one hand like a knight holding a lance.

The line of running zonbies stretched a quarter of a mile wide. Scores of soldiers wearing red berets came running around the corners on both sides of the palace.

They're terrified, Jake thought.

The zonbies didn't even slow as they fired their machine guns, mowing down the oncoming soldiers with little resistance.

The perfect fighting machines.

Jake's throat constricted as a wall of dark souls rose from the scattered bodies and faded. He had never seen so many souls at once.

Russel led Malvado down the palace corridor, with Maxime bringing up the rear. All three men held Glocks.

"What about your wives?" Russel said.

"To hell with them," Malvado said.

"And your mistress?"

Malvado considered the question with an expression of regret. "Perhaps another time . . ."

"They're all wearing black snake tattoos. There's a good chance they'll be executed."

Malvado shrugged. "Casualties of war. I'll just have to find younger wives and an even younger mistress."

A prince among men, Russel thought.

They heard machine gun fire inside the palace, followed by screams. As they neared the grand stairway, Russel raised his left hand, signaling Malvado and Maxime to stop.

Two shadows moved along the wall ahead, then two figures carrying high-tech machine guns. Filthy creatures with sunken eyes and tight, leathery flesh the color of a rotting fish.

Russel aimed his Glock with both hands and squeezed off two shots, dropping the corpses. Peering over the stairway, he reached forward and retrieved one of the machine guns, which he examined. Then he chuckled.

"What's so funny?" Maxime said.

Russel tossed the machine gun to Maxime, who studied it with admiration.

"This is a big part of your problem," Russel said to Malvado. "That's the ATAC 3000, the most sophisticated machine gun ever developed. The firm that created and manufactured it shut down a few months ago, making these very rare limited editions. One of them outputs as much firepower as ten conventional weapons. No wonder they were able to take down your choppers; the pilots had no idea they were in danger flying so low."

"But how did these rebels get their hands on them?"

"Good question. If I had to guess, I'd say Louider's Black Hand. In the end, everyone's turned against you, even your own slaves. Come on, Max. Let's you and me carve up some turkeys."

Jake and Andre galloped their horses along the side of the palace's left wing in the midst of the zonbie platoon. The flares in the sky had become more infrequent, and the explosions around the palace had been replaced with layers of deafening machine gun fire. Jake prayed Maria was safe. He had no idea where she was being kept.

A trio of soldiers broke their cover behind some bushes and fled across the side lawn.

An ATAC fired, cutting them in half and spilling their guts across the green grass.

Russel and Maxime unleashed their firepower as they ran down the stairway, blasting zonbies off their feet, then annihilating their skulls as they passed them. Malvado ran behind them. In the great hall, the three men rushed to the entrance.

Russel glimpsed two Humvees idling in the driveway below. "Let's go."

They ran outside and down the cement steps. Fires raged all around them in the palace, the gardens, and the trees.

A soldier jumped out of the first Humvee and opened the back door. Malvado slid across the seat, followed by Maxime.

"Take them to the Church of the Black Snake," Russel said to the waiting soldier.

"What about you, William?" Malvado said.

"I'll be right behind you in the second vehicle."

The soldier closed the door and returned to the front seat. The Humvee rolled forward, then gained speed.

Russel strode over to the driver of the second Humvee. "Follow them."

The second Humvee pulled away from the curb, and Russel crossed the lawn to the helicopter that had transported himself, Mambo Catoute, Maxime, and Maria from the Ministry of Defense earlier. Boarding the empty helicopter, he climbed into the cockpit and examined the flight controls.

Jake watched two Humvees speed away from the palace and Russel get into the helicopter. "You follow your man," he said to Andre. "I'll follow mine."

"Right." Andre faced the army of zonbies. "Anyone who wants a piece of Malvado, follow me!"

Jake kicked his horse forward and raced for the helicopter. As he galloped around the aircraft, he glimpsed half the zonbies running after Andre on his horse and half of them streaming into the palace. He felt sorry for anyone they found. Hopping off his horse, he drew his Glock and climbed into the open bay of the gunship.

Russel activated the helicopter's rotors. He had flown his share of whirlybirds in his life, and this one appeared no different than the others.

Clicking a series of toggle switches, he recoiled when a figure slumped into the copilot's seat. A Caucasian man with a bandaged stump for a left arm.

Helman.

Jake leveled his Glock at Russel. "Going somewhere?"

Russel raised his hands. "You could say that."

"Where are you off to?"

"Depends on how far the fuel will take me. Haiti. Jamaica. Hell, I'll settle for Cuba, if necessary."

Jake grunted. "Someplace will always take in a mercenary like you, right?"

"I have a wide skill set, and my business is built on relationships."

"And knowing when to check out."

"It goes with the territory. I should have seen the handwriting on the wall as soon as you showed up."

"You just exploit one third-rate country after another, don't you?"

"I go where I'm needed."

"Kill the engine."

Russel clicked the toggles back into place and powered down the engine. "I don't suppose I can convince you to come with me?"

Jake shook his head. "You're not going anywhere."

"My staying here doesn't serve any purpose. What are you going to do? Arrest me? Execute me? Come on. Those would both be empty gestures. I'm a facilitator, not a despot. You and I are both pragmatic men."

"You cut off my hand."

"I admit I got carried away. It happens when a man like you or me spends too much time with people like these."

Jake didn't like the turn the conversation had taken. "Where's Maria?"

A flicker of a smile flashed across Russel's lips. "Mambo Catoute's got her in the basement of the Church of the Black Snake. She's fine—or at least she was when I left her there."

"Did you touch her?"

"No." He pointed at the pressure pad over his eye. "But look at what she did to me. I bet she's wild in bed. Forget I said that."

"I'd love to sit and chat with you, but I'm in kind of a—"

Russel kicked the Glock out of Jake's hand and caught the weapon.

Using his stump, Jake slammed Russel's gun hand against the rear partition of the cockpit, and the Glock fired. Jake punched Russel's chin and heard the man's teeth shatter. Russel's face turned beet red.

Jake slammed Russel's gun hand against the partition again and jerked his own arm back, using his stump to force the Glock from Russel's hand. The gun clattered on the floor.

Confined in the cockpit, neither Jake nor Russel could engage in full body contact. Since he was certain Russel knew several martial arts, this came as a relief. But Jake also knew that with one hand missing, he had to take the man down fast or not at all.

He punched Russel in the nose and felt cartilage crunching beneath his knuckles.

Grimacing, Russel seized Jake's head in both of his

430

hands and jerked him forward, delivering a head butt that caused red spots to flash before Jake's eye and in his brain. Russel delivered a kick to Jake's solar plexus that sent him sprawling over his seat, groaning.

Russel reached for the fallen Glock, but Jake drove his heel into the man's hand. This time Russel cried out.

Jake jammed his left elbow into Russel's lower back, forcing the man to stand erect and arch his back, abandoning the Glock. Jake snaked his right arm behind Russel's back and over his shoulder. Cupping Russel's chin, he slammed the man's head against the controls again and again.

Russel groped at Jake's face, and Jake turned his head away. Russel clawed at Jake's left eye and gasped when it popped out of his skull. Jake caught the glass eye in his right hand, then shoved it through Russel's broken teeth. Russel opened his mouth wider to scream, and the glass eye rolled over his tongue and down the back of his throat like a ball in the side pocket of a pool table. Russel gulped the glass eye, his own visible eye bulging in its socket.

Jake forced his stump against Russel's throat. Gripping his left forearm with his right hand, he pressed his arm against Russel's Adam's apple, crushing it against the glass eye he felt but could not see. Russel's fingers danced in the air, and his body spasmed. Clenching his teeth, Jake put all his weight on his arm, crushing the man's windpipe. Russel's body shook, and his hands dropped at his sides. Jake finally released his grip when he realized he might break his own arm.

Black energy rose from Russel's corpse, and Jake scooped up the Glock from the floor.

THIRTY-SIX

In the middle seat of the Humvee, Malvado grimaced. A flare in the night sky silhouetted the Church of the Black Snake as they approached it. How had two Americans—one of them a *woman*—caused so much damage?

The Humvee ground to a halt, and the soldiers opened the doors and climbed out. Maxime examined his ATAC. The second Humvee pulled up, and eight soldiers poured out.

"I don't see Russel," Maxime said in a sarcastic tone.

"I saw him going for the helicopter," one of the soldiers from the second Humvee said.

Malvado glanced at the sky but saw no helicopter.

"It serves you right for allowing a foreigner in your inner circle," Maxime said.

Malvado slapped Maxime across the face. "You will not speak to me like that."

Maxime glared at his father. "Your empire is collapsing around you."

Malvado stepped closer to his son. "Pray it holds up, because you're nothing without it."

In the distance, silhouetted in the moonlight, an army of one hundred zonbies raced toward them.

The living soldiers looked to Malvado for orders.

"Sergeant, park these vehicles bumper to bumper, perpendicular to the church, so you can use them for cover."

The sergeant saluted and repeated Malvado's orders to two of his men, who rearranged Humvees.

With the Humvees parked according to Malvado's directions, the twelve soldiers took up positions behind them. The zonbies had cut the distance between them in half. A wall of machine gun fire assaulted the vehicles, with such power that the enormous trucks shook, but the armor plating and bulletproof glass held up.

"Shoot them in the heads!" Malvado said.

With a look of disgust, Maxime took up position between the Humvees and fired his ATAC.

Malvado watched with pride as the heads of half a dozen zonbies exploded and their falling bodies caused zonbies behind them to pile up.

Maxime fired a grenade at the pile, and body parts rained down.

"Someone's leading them on horseback," the sergeant said.

"Give me those." Malvado snatched the sergeant's night vision binoculars. On the left side, a white-haired man rode a horse among the zonbies. "Maxime, Santiago's out there!

Shoot! Shoot them all!"

Maxime raised his ATAC to his shoulder and scanned the advancing horde. "I don't see him."

Malvado looked through the binoculars again. Maxime was right: Andre had dismounted his horse. *Or he's been killed.* Malvado handed the binoculars back to the sergeant. "Finish them off."

Even as Malvado ran up the stairs and through the church entrance, one of the Humvees exploded behind him. The orange fireball threw the vehicle into the air and dismembered the nearest soldiers. He didn't look to see if his son had survived.

Andre dismounted his horse when he saw the machine gun fire cutting down the zonbies ahead of him. He recognized the muzzle flash and the sound of an ATAC machine gun.

A grenade exploded in the middle of the zonbie force, casting body parts and sawdust in all directions. Several more zonbies staggered around on fire.

Crouching behind a tree, Andre loaded a grenade onto his own weapon, raised the stock to his shoulder, and sited a familiar figure.

Maxime Malvado.

Lowering his scope, he fired the grenade under the Humvee. The resulting explosion flipped the Humvee over and decimated half the number of soldiers. The remaining zonbies charged forward, weapons firing. Smoke enveloped the other Humvee and machine guns fired. Silence followed.

The smoke cleared and Andre moved forward. Zonbies and soldiers lay motionless on the ground, arms and legs strewn about in a random pattern. Seeing no sign of Maxime, Andre concluded the upside-down Humvee had crushed him. A single zonbie rolled over onto its back. Its legs had been blown off, and sawdust poured out of its midsection.

Free its soul.

Meeting the creature's pitiful eyes, Andre aimed his ATAC at the zonbie's forehead and squeezed the trigger. Nothing happened. Discarding the weapon, he drew his Glock and finished the job. The zonbie turned still.

Andre ran into the church, which had not existed when he had been a free man. Running along a balcony that overlooked a cathedral, he spotted a large figure in a royal-blue uniform heading for a doorway below. "Malvado!"

The figure turned.

Andre gripped the Glock in both hands, aimed, and fired three times. None of the shots hit the mark, and Malvado disappeared in the doorway.

Andre ran to an opening in the balcony, down the wooden stairs, then across the floor. Reaching the doorway through which Malvado had escaped, he gazed down at stairs that curved beneath the floor he had just covered. As he stepped forward, he heard a whistling sound, then felt his chest turn numb. The gun fell from his hands and clattered down the stairs.

Malvado stepped out from behind the doorway,

gripping the hilt of the sword he had just buried in Andre's chest. He wrenched the blade free of Andre's shattered ribs, and blood gushed out of the long wound.

Andre swayed on his feet. "Malvado . . ."

Setting his left hand on Andre's right shoulder, Malvado drove his sword through Andre's belly.

Andre's body turned rigid and he shut his eyes. Unable to move, he sucked in his breath. When he opened his eyes, Malvado's sweaty face filled his view.

"Pavot is *mine*."

Then Malvado pulled the sword out and stepped back, and Andre felt himself tumbling forward.

Maria recoiled at the sound of machine gun fire.

"That's right outside," Pharah said. "It sounds farther away because we're underground."

"Somebody give me a gun."

Jorge pulled a .38 from his belt and passed it to Maria, who popped the cylinder open.

"Old school," she said, snapping the cylinder shut with a flick of her wrist. "You got any more ammo for this six-shooter?"

"Oui." Jorge took a box out of his pocket.

"I wish you'd brought a speed loader."

"I'll remember that next time I help overthrow a government."

An explosion roared in the distance, and everyone in

the chamber looked at the ceiling.

"I hope that was our explosion and not theirs," Pharah said.

Another explosion sounded, and the lights went off, leaving only the candlelight, which cast long shadows on the walls.

"It may not matter whose they are," Maria said. Hearing the chinking of keys on cement, she turned toward Catoute, who stomped on something. "What have you got there?"

Catoute shook her head in an innocent manner.

With her revolver aimed away, Maria crossed over the rim of the summoning circle, crouched low, and tapped the calf of Catoute's outstretched leg. "Step back."

Catoute removed her foot from a single key.

Shaking her head, Maria reached for the key. "And what did you think you were going to do if you unlocked these bracelets? Run up all those stairs without us catching you?"

"Look out!" Pharah said.

Catoute kicked the gun out of Maria's hand, and it flew out of the circle and spun across the floor. A hand sank into Maria's curls and snapped her head back, and she felt the sharp point of a dagger press deep into the left side of her throat.

Catoute pulled Maria up by her hair and rotated her knife hand, pressing the dagger. "I've cut more than a few throats in my time. Use any fancy police moves on me, and I'll shower in your blood."

Maria felt her lips drawing tight. *Son of a bitch!*

Catoute glanced around the chamber. "Drop your guns. I'm an old woman with nothing to lose."

Maria heard the sharp clatter of guns on the floor.

Oh, fuck.

Bloody sword in hand, Malvado ran down the stairs, avoiding the splotches of blood on them. Halfway down, he scooped up Andre's Glock and sheathed his sword. At last he had slain his sworn enemy.

I should have done it years ago.

At the bottom of the stairs, he stepped over Andre's bloody body without paying any attention to it and went to the wide door leading into Mambo Catoute's ceremonial chamber. The door refused to open. Recalling the heavy bolt that locked it, he rushed over to a bookcase leaning against one wall and pulled it forward, revealing a secret passage. He entered the narrow storage room, flipped a light switch, and then closed the bookcase behind him.

The sweet aromas of Catoute's herbs overwhelmed him. Crossing the room, Malvado stopped at another panel and listened. He heard Catoute's voice, which reassured him, and pushed the panel and entered the chamber, which was lit by Catoute's zonbie candles. Five people stood in a half circle with their backs to him. Catoute held a woman by her hair, pressing a dagger against her throat. Not just any woman: Maria Vasquez, the bitch who had caused so much of his trouble.

"We have company," Maria said in a strangled voice.

Jake stuck one foot in a stirrup and threw his other leg over his horse's saddle.

"I wish I could take you to New York with me."

Taking the reins in his hand, he kicked the horse into action and rode toward the Church of the Black Snake. After hearing an explosion and seeing a fireball rise into the sky ahead, he made his horse gallop faster. A second explosion outlined the church in orange light.

When he reached the stone structure, no living soul remained outside. The body parts of soldiers and zonbies were scattered around the road, driveway, and parking lot. He got off the horse, drew his Glock, and ran into the building. His footsteps echoed as he ran along the balcony overlooking a circular cathedral, where dozens of armed zonbies marched through a doorway below.

With his heart pounding, he raced down the cathedral stairs, illuminated by a massive chandelier. By the time he reached the bottom and ran across the dais, the last of the zonbies had disappeared through the doorway. He followed them, stopping only to take in the sight of the blood on the walls and the stairs below.

Zonbies don't bleed.

Squeezing the butt of his Glock, he hurried down the stairs. At the bottom, he saw the zonbies crowded in a circle. Pushing his way through them, the touch of their arms causing him to shudder, he gazed down at Andre, who lay clutching his stomach in a pool of his own blood. A nasty-looking gash crossed his chest.

With blood trickling from both corners of his mouth, Andre turned to him and spoke in a faint whisper. "Jake . . ."

Jake kneeled and cradled the man with his stump. "Go ahead."

"Tell . . . my . . . wife . . ." Andre convulsed and coughed up blood, and when his head fell back he had stopped moving.

Jake laid Andre's head down and pulled his stump free. He closed his eye for a moment. All of this had been for Edgar, but now Jake had to worry about Maria. Rising, he met the gazes of the dead things standing near him. "Libération de l'île Pavot."

Maria watched Malvado enter the chamber through a swinging panel. At first she had thought him a zonbie until she registered the gold trim decorating his royal-blue uniform. He held a Glock in one raised hand. Closing the panel with his other hand, he looked at Catoute and Maria. "Stop!"

Pharah, Jorge, and their companions jumped at the sound of Malvado's booming voice. Jorge stooped to retrieve his weapon.

But Malvado aimed his Glock at him. "Kick that over here."

Jorge kicked his machine gun across the floor, and Malvado slung it over one shoulder.

Malvado's words came out in staccato: "I hereby declare

this rebellion null and void. Andre Santiago is dead. I killed him myself. You have no leader. What's going on here?"

Maria felt Catoute nodding.

"You see those candles? I can stop your slaves from tearing us to pieces."

Malvado studied the candles. "Then you'd better hurry. They're all over the palace grounds." He narrowed his eyes. "Pharah?"

Pharah nodded and Malvado grunted.

"Unlock these shackles," Catoute said. "This woman has the key."

Malvado strode forward and looked down at the summoning circle. He stared at Maria and she saw his bloodlust. She dropped the key on the floor. Aiming his Glock at her, Malvado stetched one leg into the circle and used his foot to slide the key toward him. He picked it up and entered the circle, positioning himself to see Jorge and the clerics. "Miss Vasquez, you've been a thorn in my side all week. I will savor your flesh with my morning coffee."

The way he enunciated every syllable caused Maria to cringe as much as his words did.

"We need her alive for now," Catoute said.

Malvado's lower lip curled. "Don't forget who's in charge here."

"Yes, my lord."

Malvado unlocked the manacles, which fell to the floor.

Catoute did not move. A low moan rose from within her, a humming sound that became a chant. Maria thought she heard words rooted in Spanish and French, but most of them belonged to a language she didn't recognize.

As the incantation grew louder, Pharah stepped forward. "What are you—?"

Malvado aimed his gun at her, stopping her in her tracks.

A chill ran through Maria, as if icicles had reopened the scratches on her arms and legs. The candles flickered, and a shadow seemed to fall over the summoning circle. Malvado's startled expression told her she was not the only one to experience the sensation. Pharah gaped at the floor and Maria looked down. The head of a young black man emerged from the stone like someone rising from water. The man continued to rise, his eyes glowing bright red. Soon his entire naked body stood before her.

He's beautiful.

"Kalfu," Malvado said, walking out of the circle.

Maria's eyes hurt from widening so far. *Kalfu!*

The Loa approached with a smile. He stood under six feet tall, and if Maria had been standing straight, they might have seen eye to eye. Only because Catoute's dagger held her head back did the supernatural being look down at her.

Those eyes . . . so hypnotic.

Kalfu glanced at the other people in the chamber, then returned his attention to Maria. He leaned so close to her that she smelled a strange mixture of odors that his body gave off: oils, cologne . . . sulfur?

The red glow in his eyes grew more intense. *"Hel-man's wo-man."*

He knows Jake!

Kalfu's pink tongue slid out of his mouth and spilled

forward, impossibly long. She felt its slime-covered, sandpapery surface touch her right ankle, then travel up to her thighs, leaving a sticky, wet trail behind it. The tongue rubbed against her crotch, her panties offering little protection from it, then rose to her stomach. She stared at Kalfu's satisfied expression as his tongue retracted into his mouth. It touched her breasts, slimed her throat, and finally pushed against her lips, forcing its way against her clenched teeth. She twisted her face away, sharp pain telling her Catoute's dagger had pierced her flesh and drawn blood. Kalfu's tongue returned to his mouth, and he licked his lips.

An explosion blew the heavy door to pieces, and smoke billowed into the chamber. Maria couldn't help but recoil at the roar. She heard a multitude of footsteps before a dozen zonbies armed with machine guns stormed inside, most of them with bullet-riddled torsos.

"No!" Malvado's voice cracked with fear.

A figure entered behind the zonbies, waving a Glock in one hand—his only hand.

Jake.

THIRTY-SEVEN

Jake followed the zonbie brigade into the chamber. As the smoke cleared, he saw Maria standing in her panties and a dirty muscle shirt within a red circle on the floor. Mambo Catoute held a dagger to her throat, and a naked black man, no more than seventeen in appearance, stood before her.

A summoning circle, he thought.

Ernesto Malvado lurked just outside the circle, his features twisted with terror. Pharah, Jorge, and three of Pharah's followers stood near the circle. Another man lay dead on the floor.

The zonbies swarmed throughout the chamber, waving their guns.

Malvado aimed his Glock at one of the creatures and fired, missing his target.

In unison, the zonbies dropped their weapons on

the floor, causing Malvado to blink with confusion. The undead creatures drew their machetes from leather sheathes attached to their belts.

Malvado's entire face twitched. "No. No!"

The dead men and women advanced on the dictator, who fired at them in a random and desperate pattern.

"Kill my daughter," Catoute said.

Malvado glanced at the old woman.

"It's our only chance. Kill her!"

Malvado drew his sword, buried it in the head of the nearest zonbie, and darted past another one. The zonbie with the sword in its head collapsed and ceased moving.

Jake noticed the naked black man watching the soul rise and fade had glowing red eyes.

Kalfu!

Malvado closed in on Pharah.

Her eyes widened. "Father?"

Malvado pressed the barrel of his Glock against Pharah's forehead and squeezed the trigger. The gunshot roared through the chamber, and Pharah fell to the floor with half her face missing, her white outfit splattered with blood. Her glowing golden soul rose and faded.

The zonbies stopped advancing on Malvado and stood as still as statues.

Catoute shouted in a language Jake didn't recognize.

The zonbies reacted at the same time, moving in different directions, advancing on Jorge and the others.

Ah, shit! Jake thought. Pharah had been able to tap into Catoute's spell over the zonbies because they were from the same bloodline. With Pharah dead, Catoute regained control of her army. Jake's comrades had become his enemies again. Several zonbies surrounded the circle but didn't enter it.

At least Maria's safe from the zonbies in there, even if she's with Kalfu.

"Kill them! Kill them all!" Malvado said.

Seeming to mimic Malvado, Catoute barked orders in the foreign tongue.

A trio of zonbies advanced on Jake with raised machetes. The rotting faces that had seemed pitiful just moments ago now appeared horrific. He raised his Glock and fired at the long-haired male zonbie who had served as de facto spokesperson for the undead army.

A bullet hole appeared in the zonbie's forehead, opaque yellow liquid spraying out of the wound. The zonbie looked heavenward and collapsed in a heap of dead flesh, his soul rising and fading.

Jake aimed at the second zonbie, his elbow aching, and fired. The gunshot dropped the zonbie, and another glowing soul rose and faded.

A woman screamed, and Jake glanced at Pharah's bokors. The zonbies near the candles fell on the priest and priestesses there, raising their machetes and swinging them down in powerful arcs. Blood spattered the candles, and the screaming woman fell to the floor. Jake couldn't see what happened to the remaining man and woman, but he heard their screams. Another three zonbies backed Jorge against a section of candles, some of them toppling to the floor.

The third zombie, a woman with dark skin and braided hair, advanced on Jake, coming so close to him that he pressed the Glock against her forehead and blew it open, spilling brain juice. She hit the floor hard, and her soul rose and faded.

Jorge had picked up an ATAC. As the man decimated the head of one of his attackers, Jake advanced on the summoning circle. He knew of only one way to turn the tide. When Katrina's zombies had taken over the drug trade in New York, Laurel had told him the one sure way to stop them was to kill her. Standing at the edge of the circle, he aimed his Glock past Kalfu—who stood with an amused expression—at Catoute, who ducked her head behind Maria's.

Damn it.

Jake moved around the circle's outer perimeter, keeping his Glock trained on Catoute, who moved in direct relation to him, keeping Maria in his line of fire.

Maria's lower lip quivered, tears filling her eyes.

Two zonbies ran for Jake, whose hand trembled. Maria looked straight into Jake's eyes, then closed hers. Jake prayed she was giving him permission to take the shot. He heard the zonbies shuffling in his direction. Sweat stung his eye. He squeezed the trigger, erupting Catoute's skull into fragments as she flew back.

"Jesus!" Clapping her hands over her ears, Maria fell to her knees on the floor.

A gray, cancerous-looking soul rose from the old woman's motionless body. It reminded Jake of Old Nick's soul: rotten to the core after a lifetime of evil deeds.

All around the chamber, zombies staggered and collapsed, like marionettes with their strings cut at the same time. A dozen souls rose at once, and Jake knew that across Pavot Island, some two thousand more were doing the same thing.

"Maria, get out of there!"

Maria looked at him with questioning eyes, and Jake realized the gunshot had deafened her. But she leapt out of the circle anyway. Kalfu snatched her by the hair in midair and swung her back into the perimeter. Crying out, she landed on her knees, facing Jake, her face a mask of pain.

Jorge rose and faced Malvado, blood flowing from a machete wound in his neck. Malvado picked up Jorge's ATAC from the floor, aimed it at him, and squeezed the trigger. The gun clicked.

"*Hel-man*," Kalfu hissed.

Jorge picked up a new weapon: a .38 revolver.

Malvado aimed another ATAC at him and it clicked.

"Let her go," Jake said to the demon. "You can't interfere with a positive soul on this plane anyway."

Jorge aimed the handgun at Malvado, who aimed a third ATAC at him. The empty machine gun clicked.

Kalfu grinned at Jake. "But I'm not on your plane. This circle is a portal linking our dimensions. None of the rules you know apply. I can do whatever I want."

Shit, Jake thought.

Jorge stepped forward. "You killed Humphrey and my brother."

Malvado sputtered. "They were enemies of the state."

"If I killed you now I'd be hailed as a hero. But I have a better idea: it's your turn to serve as El Miedo's only prisoner."

"What do you want?" Jake said to Kalfu.

"I want *you*."

Jake's spirits sank. "I made a deal with Cain. The slate is wiped clean between me and the Dark Realm."

"Cain serves his functions in the Realm; I serve mine. You caused the demise of one of my brides."

Katrina, Jake thought.

"Don't do it, Jake," Maria said in a quivering voice. "Let him take me."

"I don't have a choice and he knows it. I'll take responsibility for my actions. You take care of Edgar." He glared at Kalfu. "I won't pledge my soul to you, but I will take Maria's place in that circle."

Kalfu guffawed. "I don't care what you pledge. Stand before me and I'll *take* what I want."

Maria shook her head.

"Let her go first," Jake said.

"I'm not the trusting type," Kalfu said. "Come to me and I'll let her go."

Jake toed the circle. "If I do as you ask, there's nothing to prevent you from taking us both. Under that scenario, she's already doomed."

"Remain stubborn and I'll enjoy her flesh for eternity. Perhaps I should anyway. You'll agonize over her fate for the rest of your life and into the afterlife."

"The same principle applies to you. Perhaps you will torture her spirit forever. But if I ascend to the Realm of

Light, you'll know for eternity that you had a chance to claim my soul and failed. You'll have her soul, and I *will* agonize over that. But in the end, I'll beat you. If there's one thing I've learned about you demons, you're sore losers."

"I'm not a demon," Kalfu said.

"You *are* a demon. That's why your energy resides in the Dark Realm. You're just too vain to admit it."

"I know all the best Loa!"

"You would say that. You always do. The legends say so. Your reputation is well known in vodou circles."

Kalfu's features twisted with anger. "What do *you* know of *me*?"

"Your other name is Carrefour, and you control the crossroads." He gestured at the circle. "Catoute believed she summoned you, but all she really did was ask you to open the crossroads to her. You could have said no if you wanted to."

Kalfu's fiery red eyes glowed brighter. "Because I wanted you. It will please my master if I present your head to him on a platter after you struck that deal with Cain."

"Your master? In many legends, you're confused with Satan."

"I am not Satan! I am not a demon! I am a renowned and respected Loa in all dimensions!"

"I don't respect you. I don't even fear you. I don't care what Loa you *claim* to know. In my book, you're just a thug who abuses women. Let her go and face me man to man. If you don't, everyone in this chamber will know you're nothing but a coward, and we'll spread the word. On *this* plane, your reputation will suffer."

Kalfu turned to Malvado. "Push him into the circle, and I'll teach you everything I taught Catoute. You won't need a bokor to work black magic for you anymore. I'll make certain Pavot remains your kingdom."

Malvado raised his eyebrows.

"Never trust a demon," Jake said. "They'll betray you every time."

The color of Kalfu's skin turned bright red. *I'm not a demon!*

Malvado took a tentative step toward Jake.

But Jorge, still holding the .38, shook his head. "Don't make me kill you after I just decided to spare your life."

Malvado stopped in his tracks.

"I will make you the most powerful man on earth!" Kalfu said.

Malvado spread his arms in a helpless gesture.

Clenching his free hand into a fist, Kalfu jerked Maria to her feet, and his tongue slithered into her ear.

Maria grimaced.

"I'll teach you pleasures undreamed of, all the while practicing unimaginable torture on your soul. We'll be linked for eternity, and you'll give birth to my spawn."

Maria squeezed her eyes shut.

Enough, Jake thought. "I'll give you one last chance, Kalfu: let her go. You have my word I'll stand in her place."

Kalfu smiled. "If you make a deal with a higher being and renege on your promise, your soul will wind up in the Dark Realm when you die no matter what. Cross me, and you'll only guarantee that *you'll* become my bride."

Lowering his hand, Jake dropped his Glock on the floor. "Let her go."

With an inhuman snarl, Kalfu shoved Maria forward, and she staggered out of the circle into Jake's arms.

"Don't do this," she said.

He caressed her face. "It's already done."

Tears streaked her cheeks. "Then stay here with me. At least we'll have some time together."

"This way is better. Trust me."

Maria threw her arms around his neck and kissed him, and he tasted her one more time. When he broke the embrace, she clung to him.

Jake eased her away with his hand. "Never give up hope."

Maria inched back from the circle, avoiding Malvado.

Jake faced the red-skinned demon before him.

"Come to me," Kalfu said.

Jake took a deep breath, exhaled, and swallowed.

"Don't do it," Jorge said.

Jake stepped into the circle.

Kalfu charged at him, his eyes blazing.

Jake stood still and rigid, awaiting his fate. *Please let this work.*

Kalfu flung his arms around Jake and opened his mouth wide, bearing sharklike teeth that had grown too long for the inside of his mouth. But his arms never closed around Jake. Instead, the impact of the collision threw him backwards and knocked Jake out of the circle. Kalfu landed on his ass, his penis slapping his right thigh. He shook his head with a dumbfounded expression.

Jake glanced at Maria, who wore a similar look of bewilderment. Then he stepped back into the circle.

Kalfu ran at Jake again, but this time Jake shoved him aside.

"What have you *done*?" Kalfu said in an enraged voice that echoed around the chamber.

Jake tore open his shirt, revealing the medallion he had taken from Russel. "Surprise."

Kalfu screamed. Sores appeared all over his body, and six-inch horns emerged from the sores, splitting his flesh apart. The horns protruded from his torso, limbs, and forehead, even between his legs. Blood seeped from the wounds and formed red steam.

"The Anting-Anting," Jake said. "Russel took it from Tower, and I took it from him. Tower's research files revealed the amulet only has power within a summoning circle. Old Nick's entire penthouse was a summoning circle, which is why he wore an Anting-Anting when he faced Cain. Too bad I don't have a magic sword to go with it."

Kalfu closed his hands into fists, the thorns that had formed on his inner fingers digging into his palms. His body trembled as he crouched in a fighting stance. "You tricked me!"

Jake smiled. "It happens. Get over yourself."

Kalfu turned to Malvado once more. "Give me the woman!"

Screaming, Malvado looked down at the white snake that had wrapped itself around his ankles.

Pharah! Jake thought.

Without hesitation, Maria charged Malvado. To Jake's

amazement, she leapt into the air and kicked his back with both legs. Malvado flew past Jake and crashed into Kalfu, impaling himself on several of the Loa's horns like a man in an iron maiden. Maria landed on one side and scrambled back to her feet. Malvado stared straight into Kalfu's glowing red orbs, his mouth opening but nothing coming out.

The white snake uncurled itself from around the dictator's ankles and slithered toward the circle's edge.

With Malvado's larger body still impaled on his horns, Kalfu ran after the snake and attempted to stomp on it, but the snake vanished and his foot struck the floor. Seeing the glint of the pommel protruding from Malvado's belt, Jake drew the sword free. Kalfu peeled the giant man from his bloodied horns and flung him to the floor. Blood gushed from Malvado's multiple wounds, and he didn't move.

Kalfu faced Jake, who braced his stump against the demon's chest for leverage, and drove the bloodstained blade into his sternum and out his back. Kalfu screamed, then pitched forward, bringing his monstrous features within inches of Jake's face. Malvado's dark soul flickered behind them.

"You lose," Jake said. "Now go away."

Kalfu continued to scream, red steam engulfing him. Then he dropped through the floor as if a trapdoor had opened. Malvado's sword clattered on the floor, and the demon's scream and the dissipitating steam lingered.

Jake left the circle and Maria ran into his arms.

"Did you kill him?" Jorge said.

"No," Jake said. "I only hurt his pride."

Maria examined the Anting-Anting on his chest: a warrior slaying a demon with a sword. "How did you know that would work?"

"I didn't. But it was the only chance I had."

She swallowed. "Then he really could have taken your soul?"

"The odds were in his favor."

Maria kissed him again, but this time it wasn't good-bye.

THIRTY-EIGHT

Emerging from the church, they surveyed the bodies littering the road. Great flames consumed the palace, with no fire trucks in sight. The horse Jake had ridden had disappeared. Maria still wore only her undergarments; she had refused to wear the clothing of any of the people killed below or the zonbies or anything in Catoute's church. Jake held her in his good arm.

"If anyone hears me," Jorge said into his hand radio, "come in."

A burst of static. "This is Renaud."

"What's your status?"

"Pavot is a free island, thanks to all of us. Those . . . things helped us, then stopped moving. They're all dead now."

"Andre is dead, too. So is Pharah. And Malvado, Maxime, and Catoute."

"A lot of good people and a lot of bad people. There's dancing in the streets. Come join us in Pavot City."

"I'm at the palace."

"We can see the flames from here."

"I'm with the *Americanos*."

"Bring them. They're national heroes."

Jorge looked at Jake and Maria, who shook their heads.

"They need medical treatment, nothing too serious. I'm going to take them to a safe location. I'm sure the celebrating will continue tomorrow."

"Copy that."

Jorge hitched the radio to his belt. "Now we need to find a vehicle."

Jorge pulled up to the resort in an open jeep. Music blasted from all over the grounds.

"Our old suite?" Maria said.

"It's only been a few days," Jake said. "Our reservation's still good. We just need a key to our room."

"I'll stop at the front desk," Jorge said.

"I wish I still had my clothes," Maria said.

Jorge climbed out of the jeep. "I'll stop by the Church of the White Snake in the morning. If I can, I'll bring your clothes. If not, we'll get you new ones tomorrow."

"Will you ask the front desk for some bandages? I'd like to change Jake's dressing."

"Oui."

They watched him enter the office.

"Thank God he made it," Maria said.

"Thank God all three of us did."

"Poor Edgar."

After Jorge left them in their suite, they showered together and scrubbed each other clean. The front desk didn't have any suitable dressing for Jake's arm, but Jorge promised to bring some in the morning.

Maria washed their clothes in the sink and hung them outside on the patio to dry in the warm night air, and then they crawled into bed nude and held on to each other. They didn't make love but slept face-to-face.

An hour later, Jake stirred when Maria sat up beside him. "What is it?"

Light flickered outside the window, and he thought he heard a distant rifle shot.

Maria got out of bed and walked over to the glass door, which she opened. "Come here."

He followed her onto the balcony. Fireworks exploded in the sky, casting dazzling colors onto Maria's naked body. He slid his hand around her smooth waist.

"Happy July Fourth," she said.

"Yeah. Happy Bastille Day."

This light show they watched together.

Jake and Maria pulled on their clothes when they heard a knock on the door. Morning sunlight streamed through the windows. Jake opened the door for Jorge. To his surprise, Ramona stood beside him.

"You remember my cousin?" Jorge said.

"Of course. I understand I owe you my life."

"I'm sorry I couldn't do more," Ramona said.

Maria joined them.

Jake gestured inside. "Come on in."

"Ramona's come to change your dressing," Jorge said. "We brought you an eye patch, too."

"Great." Jake sat on the cane-framed sofa, and Ramona sat beside him and unwrapped the dressing on his stump. Jake put on the black eye patch.

"We can't get through to the airport," Maria said.

"The telephone lines were down. They're working now. Try them again."

Jake watched the dressing come off his stump and examined his arm. Sutures held the pink folds of flesh together. It was his first time seeing the wound since Russel had cut off his hand. He glanced at Maria, who looked away.

"Let me see if I can get us a flight out of here," she said and left the room.

Ramona inspected the wound. "It looks clean. You should heal nicely." She applied some disinfectant, than wrapped the fresh dressing around the remainder of his forearm.

"What are the casualties?" Jake said.

Jorge sat in a chair. "It's too soon to tell. We suffered losses, of course. Malvado's forces suffered far worse."

"What happens now?"

"La Mère is returning in a few days. She has graciously accepted to serve as our interim president until elections can be held."

"She's a symbolic choice."

Jorge nodded. "Symbolism is important right now. Andre's story must have a triumphant ending."

Propaganda, Jake thought. "And Malvado's forces?"

"El Miedo is no longer empty. It's overcrowded. So are our municipal jails. Some of his soldiers will serve life sentences for war crimes. Some will serve shorter sentences. And others will be permitted to rejoin society. But all of them wear the black snake on their arms and will pay a price."

"What about you?"

"I'm a musician. I'll go back to playing music. At least now I can audition for the national orchestra. But first we must bury the dead and honor them."

Maria returned a few minutes later. "I got us onto a flight leaving at 2:00 p.m. Um, I need some clothes."

"We'll take you shopping," Jorge said.

"I need clothes just to go shopping."

Ramona reached into her bag. "I brought you shorts and a T-shirt."

"Thank you so much."

Jake stared at his stump. He could have sworn he still felt his missing hand. "What about our passports?"

"I have them," Jorge said.

On the drive to Pavot City in Ramona's white sedan, they saw people with exuberant expressions waving the Pavot flag from the side of the road. Jack and Maria sat in the backseat. Neither spoke.

The charred ruins of overturned cars filled the streets of Pavot City, but that didn't stop the crowds from celebrating. Streamers and confetti flew from the windows of apartment buildings, and musicians played in the street while men, women, and children danced upon the discarded billboards depicting Malvado. Smoke continued to billow from abandoned factories.

It's good we came, even if we let Edgar down, Jake thought.

They drove through a citizen's brigade outside the airport. Ramona and Jorge convinced the armed civilians that Jake and Maria were friendly to their cause.

At the curb outside the terminal, Jorge shook Jake's hand. "Thank you for everything."

Maria hugged Jorge. "Good-bye. I hope we see you again someday."

Jorge smiled. "I don't think you will. Neither of you will ever return to Pavot Island. But I'll think of you often."

"Libération de l'île Pavot," Jake said.

"Libération de l'île Pavot."

Jake and Maria boarded the airplane with a beleaguered-looking group of American businessmen. The plane was filled to capacity, unlike the trip over.

"They don't realize it, but this island is safer now than it's been the whole time they were here," Jake said.

"They're probably just upset they're going to have to pay the workers higher wages."

Jake rested his head against his seat and sighed. "It feels weird to be heading home."

"The vacation's over. Back to work."

Jake laughed and Maria squeezed his hand.

As soon as the plane touched down Jake felt at home again, even though Florida was as alien to him as any foreign country. They passed through the arrival gate in Miami International Airport, and Maria held on to his left arm. He assumed she was being considerate by leaving his remaining hand free. All he wanted to do was retrieve Edgar and return to New York City, where he hoped a new life awaited him.

Two well-groomed men in crisp black suits, one slim and the other heavyset, approached them.

Federales, Jake thought.

"Jake Helman and Maria Vasquez?" one of the men said.

Jake blew air out of his cheeks. "Yeah . . ."

The man flashed a State Department ID. "Adam Weissman with State. This is my partner, Bob Freeman."

"What can we do for you boys?"

"We need to question you about what just happened on Pavot Island."

"We don't know anything. We were tourists, and we're just glad to be home."

Weissman gestured at Jake's stump. "According to our records, you had two hands when you flew over there. Follow us, please."

Jake sat in one interview room with Weissman while Maria sat in another with Freeman. The room was much tighter and more claustrophobic than those he had occupied before.

Weissman opened a file folder on the metal table between them. "Five days ago, you and Miss Vasquez landed on Pavot Island. Three days ago, our satellites detected increased helicopter traffic over the island. Two days ago, we detected what we believe to have been napalm in the jungle. Yesterday a full-scale revolution overthrew Ernesto Malvado's government. And today you and Vasquez came home."

Jake studied Weissman. Clean-cut, professional, and slick. "We're a two-man mercenary team, only Maria's a woman. They call us Rambo and Shambo wherever we go."

"Please tell me what happened on that island."

Jake sighed. "My girlfriend and I"—the words sounded

strange to him—"took a cheap vacation on Pavot Island. We stayed at the Pleasant Mountain Resort, where we booked a suite for one week. On our second day there, we visited Pavot City, where we met an artist at a café. I asked him to draw Maria's portrait. He had just finished when soldiers arrived. A man and a woman sitting behind us drew guns and fired at the soldiers, who mowed them down. Our artist companion told us to run. The soldiers mowed him down, too.

"With the soldiers in pursuit, Maria and I split up. I was captured in an abandoned factory and taken to the Ministry of Defense. An ex-CIA spook named Bill Russel interrogated me. When I insisted I knew nothing about the people the soldiers had killed, he cut off my hand with a machete. I woke up in a clinic, where I was treated. Then I was relocated to a work farm. A group of—what shall we call them? freedom fighters?—rescued me and took me to a cave where Maria was waiting. We stayed there when the fighting broke out. And now here we are. I feel like a prisoner all over."

Weissman took notes. "How do you know Bill Russel was ex-CIA?"

"I crossed paths with him once before when I worked for Nicholas Tower."

"What did Mr. Russel have to do with Tower?"

"He designed the Tower's security systems."

"Where is he now?"

"Wherever spooks go when they get scared."

"We picked up several radio and TV transmissions that

mentioned you and Miss Vasquez by name. Did either one of you kill anyone while you were there?"

"No. I told you, we were on vacation."

"What happened to Malvado?"

"I heard they killed him."

"Why?"

Jake shrugged. "I guess it was the will of the people."

Weissman looked him in the eye. "Okay, let's start over. Slower this time and in greater detail."

THIRTY-NINE

"Look at that crowd," Maria said as she steered their rented Monte Carlo onto Miriam's street.

Sitting beside her, Jake counted three TV news vans and four police cars parked along the street. Eight police officers held back a crowd of almost a hundred people who waved their fists in the air to the beat of salsa music booming from an unseen sound system.

"Libération de l'île Pavot! Libération de l'île Pavot! Libération de l'île Pavot!"

Maria pulled over to the curb ahead of the farthest police car, and they got out and made their way through the crowd to a policewoman who stood before caution tape.

"Maria Vasquez. I'm on the job in New York City. Miriam Santiago is expecting me."

"Just a minute," the policewoman said, then spoke into her hand radio.

Scanning the crowd, Jake saw three cameras mounted on tripods and two handheld rigs.

"Go ahead," the policewoman said.

Maria and Jake ducked beneath the caution tape and crossed the lawn. The crowd's chanting grew louder. The front door opened before they reached it, and Fernando beckoned them inside. He clasped Jake's shoulder and nodded to Maria.

Inside the living room, a lanky policeman stood near the window with a bored look on his face.

Miriam emerged from a bedroom, followed by a female assistant. She wore a light blue silk dress, and her eyes lit up at the sight of her visitors. "Jake . . . Maria . . ." She kissed them each on the cheek, then inspected Jake's stump. "I'm so sorry."

"We're sorry about Andre," Maria said. "He was a good man. Brave."

"I was with him when he died," Jake said. "He told me to tell you he loved you."

Miriam's eyes filled with tears. "I'm sorry he died, but I'm glad he got to see Pavot Island liberated. It was always his dream."

"And now you'll be the interim president," Maria said.

"I shared Andre's dream. I'll see it through. Come into the bedroom with me. Let's speak in private."

Jake and Maria followed Miriam into a second bedroom. The first thing Jake saw was the empty birdcage on the plush chair in the far corner on his left. The second was the man lying on his back in the bed, sheets pulled up over his stomach.

"Edgar!" Maria ran to the bed.

Heart quickening, Jake moved beside her.

Edgar offered them a weak smile. His lips appeared dry, and shades of gray dotted his hair.

He looks ten years older, Jake thought. *Animals age faster than human beings.*

"Hey, partners," Edgar said in a croaking whisper.

"He's having trouble speaking," Miriam said. "He hasn't used those vocal cords for speech in a year."

Maria grasped Edgar's arm. "I don't believe it." Her face bunched up and tears flowed.

"Don't cry," Edgar said.

"When did you turn him back?" Jake whispered to Miriam.

"I started making preparations as soon as you left for Pavot Island. Two days later, I cast the reversion spell. It took a full day for him to return to normal. It was a long, painful process that left him in shock. He only started speaking yesterday. I'm leaving for Pavot Island in a few hours, but I'm keeping this house. Stay here as long as you like until he's able to travel. I'll leave you alone with him now." Miriam exited the room and closed the door behind her.

Jake moved closer to the bed.

Edgar stared at his scarred face. "You look awful."

"You got old." Jake's voice choked with emotion.

Edgar dropped his gaze to Jake's stump. "What the hell happened?"

"I always said I'd give my right arm for you."

"That's your left arm and you never said that."

Maria hugged Edgar. "I'm so glad you're back."

Edgar looked over her at Jake. "Where did I go?"

"That's a long story," Jake said.

"Katrina?"

"She's gone. You took care of her."

Edgar gazed at the ceiling and swallowed. "I dreamed . . ."

"What?"

"I don't know. What about those *things*?"

Maria straightened, her face wet with tears, which she wiped. "You mean the zonbies?"

Edgar cocked one eyebrow.

"I know all about them, big guy." Maria put an arm around Jake. "Jake finished off the ones in NYC."

Edgar narrowed his eyes. "Are you two an item now?"

Jake looked at Maria, allowing her to speak.

"It's complicated," she said.

"How long have I been out?"

"You've been out of commission for almost a year," Jake said.

Edgar's eyes widened. "What about Martin?"

Well, he joined a science fiction social-networking site run by a giant mutant octopus god, but I got him out of that. "He's fine. So is Joyce. We'll call them as soon as you feel up to it."

"Why the hell are we in Miami?"

"We'll get around to that."

"I'm going to talk to Miriam," Maria said. "You two catch up . . . in small doses." She kissed Edgar's forehead. "I'm so glad to see you." She hurried out of the room.

"She's not as tough as she acts," Edgar said.

"She's tougher."

Edgar swallowed. "Wherever I was, whatever happened to me . . . you came back for me, didn't you?"

Jake nodded. "But I couldn't have done it without Maria."

With effort showing on his face, Edgar raised his right hand. "Thank you."

Jake clasped his friend's hand. "You're welcome."

Outside, the celebratory music continued.

MEDALLION
P R E S S

Be in the know on the latest Medallion Press news by becoming a Medallion Press Insider!

<u>As an Insider you'll receive:</u>
· Our FREE expanded monthly newsletter, giving you more insight into Medallion Press
· Advanced press releases and breaking news
· Greater access to all your favorite Medallion authors

Joining is easy. Just visit our website at <u>www.medallionmediagroup.com</u> and click on *Super Cool E-blast* next to the social media buttons.

medallionmediagroup.com

MEDALLION

P   R   E   S   S

Want to know what's going on with your favorite author or
what new releases are coming from Medallion Press?

Now you can receive breaking news, updates, and more from
Medallion Press straight to your cell phone, e-mail, instant
messenger, or Facebook!

Sign up now at www.twitter.com/MedallionPress to stay on top of all
the happenings in and around Medallion Press.

For more information
about other great titles from
Medallion Press, visit

medallionmediagroup.com